An elf in exile . . .

Rhys allowed himself a moment's regret, then pushed it aside. He ought to have expected this. He was no longer a member of the Blessed Nation but its hated enemy. Outcast, eyeblight, traitor, kin-slayer. Killing Nath had not completed his fall from perfection, only increased it, renewed and redoubled it. The shame and the injury he had inflicted on the Gilt Leaf had not escaped the attention of the tribe's upper echelons, and like Gryffid they intended to avenge Nath and carry on Nath's work.

The scouts moved closer to Rhys's tree, and Rhys tensed the long muscles in his legs. All was not lost—yet.

. . . and a pilgrim seeking her destiny . . .

In Kinsbaile, Ashling had been forcibly hurled into the full presence of that great spirit, pushed into communion with a being most mortal creatures could not see or feel, let alone understand. After a decade of seeking, and only tantalizing glimpses and half-remembered intuition to show for it, Ashling beheld her patron spirit as it was. Even before she saw its shape, she understood its power. It was a wild and primal thing of speed and strength, unfettered by mortal limitations or concerns. It was the embodiment of the untamable desire for freedom itself, a living expression of the fierce joy freedom creates.

. . . have made enemies of an entire world.

Cory J. Herndon and Scott McGough continue the epic tale of the wilds lands of Lorwyn.

EXPERIENCE THE MAGIC

Lorwyn Cycle · Book II

Cory J. Herndon and Scott McGough

Lorwyn Cycle, Book II
MORNINGTIDE

©2008 Wizards of the Coast, Inc.

Published by Wizards of the Coast, Inc. MAGIC: THE GATHERING, WIZARDS OF THE COAST, and their respective logos are trademarks of Wizards of the Coast, Inc., in the U.S.A. and other countries.

Printed in the U.S.A.

U.S., CANADA,   EUROPEAN HEADQUARTERS
ASIA, PACIFIC, & LATIN AMERICA   Hasbro UK Ltd
Wizards of the Coast, Inc.   Caswell Way
P.O. Box 707   Newport, Gwent NP9 0YH
Renton, WA 98057-0707   GREAT BRITAIN
+1-800-324-6496   Save this address for your records.

MAGIC
The Gathering®

Lorwyn Cycle · Book II

Morningtide

Cory J. Herndon and Scott McGough

Wizards
OF THE COAST®

Lorwyn Cycle, Book II
MORNINGTIDE

©2008 Wizards of the Coast, Inc.

Cover art by Steve Prescott
First Printing: January 2008

9 8 7 6 5 4 3 2 1

ISBN: 978-0-7869-4790-4
620-21633740-001-EN

U.S., CANADA,   EUROPEAN HEADQUARTERS
ASIA, PACIFIC, & LATIN AMERICA   Hasbro UK Ltd
Wizards of the Coast, Inc.   Caswell Way
P.O. Box 707   Newport, Gwent NP9 0YH
Renton, WA 98057-0707   GREAT BRITAIN
+1-800-324-6496   Save this address for your records.

Visit our web site at www.wizards.com

Dedication

The authors dedicate this book to
the next generation, once removed:

Spencer Saavedra, Brayden Saavedra,
Logan Herndon, Adam McGough, Krysten McGough,
Kaitlyn Watson, and Owen Watson.

Acknowledgments

The authors wish to thank Phil Athans and Susan Morris for their hard work, keen eyes, and steady hands on the till.

For inspiration, the authors would also like to thank Bullock & Starr, Pullo & Vorenus, Jake & Elwood, Chick & Wilbur, Felix & Oscar, Nobby & Fred, Lone Wolf & Cub, Fry & Bender, Shaun & Ed, Bo & Luke, Stan & Kyle, Lenny & Carl.

A lone rider emerged from the bright, blinding mist at the edge of the Gilt Leaf Wood. The long-limbed elf rode tall and proud on a flawless golden cervin, their backs straight and eyes forward. The rider knew how glorious the two of them would have seemed to an onlooker, how regal and excellent, how *perfect* . . . if it hadn't been for the two broken and jagged stumps upon his brow, the shattered remains of once-regal horns.

The rider's stoic mouth crinkled into a wry smile. The wisest path for a notorious, disfigured Gilt Leaf outcast would be one that avoided the great tribe's territory entirely. It was doubly unwise to travel undisguised, as the rider did now, but it was the absolute height of suicidal foolishness to ride brazenly into the largest Gilt Leaf encampment in the region. The slightest glimpse of the rider would rouse the Gilt Leaf's elite Hemlock hunters to full-throated, baying pursuit.

At the very least, some sort of substantial hat was in order.

For now, only familiar and unalarmed camp sounds came from up ahead, so he coaxed the cervin to a gentle stop. The rider had volunteered for this duty, insisted on it despite considerable risk. No, it was not very wise at all for the ragged and harried prey to stop, turn, and draw the hunters' attention . . . yet that was exactly what this prey was intending to do. If all went as planned, the kithkin of Kinsbaile would be singing about this escapade for the next twenty years.

The rider inhaled deeply and gently prodded the cervin's flexible ribs with long, cloven hooves. The lean steed strode forward through the underbrush and broke into a wide clearing that was lit by bright yellow pillars of diffuse sunlight.

The small glade was bright and breezy, alive with both color and sound. Six Gilt Leaf hunters stood clustered at the far edge, each bearing the insignia of the Hemlock Pack. None were mounted, but the rider made ready to turn and bolt at a moment's notice. He noted two of the Hemlock carried polished longbows. And while perhaps foolhardy, the cervin's master didn't relish the task of outrunning their deadly, likely envenomed arrows.

A tug of the reins and a squeeze of the knees made the cervin rear, thrashing the air with her forelegs. When the steed settled back into the sod, the elf called out.

"Hail, noble elves of the Hemlock Pack." The rider's sonorous voice rolled across the clearing and echoed off the trees. "Go now and tell your leaders that Rhys has come to reclaim his rightful command. Stand down, or face me . . . if you dare."

The Hemlock archers were even better than their reputation. The last echoes of the rider's words had scarcely died among the brambles and moss when two bowstrings twanged, releasing two razor-sharp stalks of arrowgrass directly at the interloper.

The blighted elf was prepared, of course, though the bolts whizzed past far too close for comfort. The strong, nimble cervin was not as graceful or as quick as it should have been, and its long legs seemed to falter. Together, steed and rider barely managed to hop out of danger.

"If 'barely' is the difference between life and death," the elf muttered, "I'll take it."

The Hemlock elves charged. They shouted out to their comrades and drew their swords as they ran. More elves appeared from the thick woods to the north and west of the clearing.

Now for the fun part. The rider swung the cervin around to expose her rump to the infuriated Hemlock hunters. He dug his hooves into the cervin's side, urging the steed into a powerful leap over a gentle rise and on into the deep woods. The rider crouched low, nose almost touching the animal's sleek, tawny fur, and smiled again. Things were off to a fine start so long as no one managed a wildly lucky or unlikely shot.

The rider's heart pounded as arrows and hunting cries whipped past, and the smile became an exhilarated, happy laugh. They would sing of this in Kinsbaile, oh yes. In fact, just to make sure the ballad started off right, it would only be proper to provide the first verse . . . and maybe the chorus.

Humming as the golden steed galloped through the trees, the rider composed the first lines of a rousing and heroic epic. The cervin's hooves beat the time.

* * * * *

Iliona, eldest faerie in the Vendilion clique, watched the last of the elf hunters disappear into the emerald wood. The elves had, as predicted, pursued their quarry with an overwhelming pack of rangers and archers. "I count fifty Gilt Leaf hunters," Iliona said, quickly calculating the number of elves bounding nimbly through the brush and low branches. Yes, at least a half-hundred seasoned soldiers from the largest and most powerful tribe in the world. "Looks like it's working."

"I don't like this," came the reply. "These are Hemlock. Fifty spotted means at least twice that number got by you unseen."

The woods grew still as the shadows and foliage swallowed up the last of the elf hunters. "That's the last of them," Iliona said, a bit miffed. "Half of the last of them, if you will." She kept her eyes forward, watching the woods for signs of motion. "They've taken the bait." Iliona stretched her long, translucent

3

wings and buzzed up into the evening air.

"I still don't like it."

"You've made that clear," Maralen said. "But you have to admit it's working so far." The buzz of Iliona's wings took on an angry edge. The eldest Vendilion hated how the strange elf maiden's voice fouled her delicate ears. Iliona hated that she was obliged to hang on every word as if it had come from the blessed lips of Queen Oona herself.

Iliona slowed her wings, and the irate noise receded. Maralen was tall for an elf and haughty even for her kind. She wore clothing cut in the style and fashion of the far northern Mornsong tribe, elves rightfully famed for their hauntingly beautiful voices rather than their skills on the forest trails—but an elf was an elf. Though not of this place, Maralen moved as swiftly and confidently on Gilt Leaf soil as she would on her own home ground. She swept through the brambles without rustling a single leaf.

Unaware of Iliona's simmering ire (or, more likely, unconcerned by it), Maralen spoke again. "It won't be long now. As soon as we get confirmation the elves are not looking back, we go in." She turned and smiled quizzically, cocking her head to one side. "Then your part of the plan kicks in and you get to be in charge again. Maybe that will loosen those clenched teeth."

Iliona sensed her siblings' approach a moment before Maralen, and the eldest Vendilion smiled.

When Maralen finally did hear the buzz of tiny wings, she said, "See? Confirmation already."

Iliona zipped forward to greet her siblings before Maralen did. The twins Veesa and Endry descended from the dark forest canopy in a cloud of glittering smoke and dust, spiraling in mad circles as they came. Their hard, chitinous skin reflected a mosaic of vivid colors as their dragonfly wings struck icy blue sparks from the smoke and dust surrounding them.

"We're back!" the twins trilled. Iliona clapped her hands happily, and moments later all three faeries were chasing each other through the upper edges of the forest.

"Pay attention, my dears."

The faerie trio stopped short. Endry even winced. Far below, Maralen waited silently with her arms crossed. The wretched elf woman did not speak again, but Maralen did cock her head to one side and raise a threatening eyebrow. The Vendilion clique exchanged a guilty, sullen glance, and as one they shrugged. Hands joined, the trio spun gently down to Maralen.

The dark-haired elf stared hard into six smooth, featureless eyes. Iliona felt Maralen's thoughts worming around inside her mind, their edges hard and sharp with curiosity. Without a single spoken word, Iliona knew what the twins knew, what Endry and Veesa had seen—and Maralen knew it too.

"Damn that kithkin," Maralen said.

"Trouble?" Ashling's listless voice stole through six feet of brambles from the opposite side of the hedge. The flamekin pilgrim kept her broad-brimmed metal hat pulled low over her eyes so that only her chin was visible, and the cold yellow fire that naturally licked up from Ashling's collarbone and elbows was dim and muted. The pilgrim cleared her throat. "Iliona?"

Maralen frowned, and Iliona knew why. Earlier, Rhys declared his unwavering confidence in Ashling, but Maralen had not been so sure. She had respectfully opined that the flamekin's listlessness was a serious concern. Rhys had brushed that concern aside, leaving Maralen to simmer in her own quiet anxiety. Iliona savored every moment of it.

"There's good news and bad news," Iliona told the pilgrim. In addition to being the biggest faerie in the clique, Iliona was the oldest, which made her the most responsible—which, as the saying went, was a bit like saying Iliona was the driest stone at the bottom of the Wanderwine.

"Actually," Veesa said, her wings a solid blur as she hovered over Ashling, "there's good news and bad news and worse news."

Endry chimed in. "And yet," he said cheerfully, "it's still funny to me."

Ashling's flames brightened a little. "Tell me what happened."

"The good news is, the elves are chasing the cervin but haven't caught up."

"And the bad news is, the elves are chasing the cervin but haven't caught up."

"Answer her question," Maralen said with forceful calm, "quickly and plainly."

Iliona sulked for a moment. Then she said, "It's going wrong,"

"The Hemlock elves are doing what we wanted," Veesa added.

"But our side is *completely* messing it up."

Ashling craned her head back and gazed up at the glittering creatures from beneath the brim of her hat. "How, exactly? What is the problem?"

"Singing," all three faeries said in unison. Iliona had not seen this for herself, so she was the most eager to explain. "She's singing about how this will make her even more famous. About how clever she is." The biggest faerie's eyes sparkled. "And it's starting to show."

Silent as a shadow, a lean, familiar figure materialized along-side Ashling. The pilgrim's clenched jaw relaxed somewhat as she spotted the newcomer, and she bobbed the brim of her hat respectfully. "What do you think?"

"We'll just have to hurry," Rhys said. He stepped forward and turned so he could face both Ashling and Maralen. "We won't get another chance like this. We got what we needed—a clear path into the camp. I say it's enough. We go forward."

"But what then?" Ashling said.

"She's right," Maralen said. "The whole rescue hinged on most of the Gilt Leaf's leaving camp to chase you through the woods. When they realize she's not you they'll be back, and they'll be very, very angry. We might get in, but we're hardly at our best." She glanced pointedly at Ashling. "If that happens we can't fight our way out through the entire pack."

"Not on our own," Rhys said. "But two very angry giants on our side might tip things in our favor."

Maralen cocked her head. "So the new plan is the first half of the old plan?" she said. "We sneak in, but instead of sneaking out we have another running battle for our lives." She crossed her arms. "Now *I* don't like this."

"Too bad," Rhys said. "This is my part of the plan, remember?"

"Let's go," Ashling muttered. She tilted her hat back, and pale orange flames bloomed from her eyes. "We're wasting time."

Maralen scowled but finally relented with a sigh. Iliona knew what the wretched elf was thinking even without oaths and mind magic. Their original plan was less than perfect to begin with, and now it was unraveling. Over half their party was dazed, obsessed, or otherwise unreliable, but they were going forward anyway. Iliona smiled at Maralen's sour expression, and she felt her siblings smile along with her. The exhilarating contact ended when Rhys suddenly thrust an index finger at the fluttering trio.

"You two." Rhys pointed at Iliona and Veesa. "Go on ahead of us into the camp. Brush aside any elves between here and the vinebred pens."

"What about me?" Endry said.

"You catch up to our decoy and help if you have to. Just make sure you're all back to the river in time—we won't be able to wait for you."

"I don't think you understand," Endry said, "The Vendilion

clique works together. As a team." He folded his arms as he hovered.

"That's not what we need right now," Rhys said.

"Well, I still want to go with my sisters."

Rhys lashed out with one hand and grabbed the sputtering, indignant Endry by his clawed feet. "Endry," the elf said, "what do you know about yew poison?"

Endry rotated his body so that he was peering at Rhys through the corner of one eye. "Not much," he admitted.

"Want to know more?" Rhys released his angrily buzzing prisoner. The elf then produced a small clay bottle from his pack and pulled the cork. A sour, oily herbal smell rose from the bottle. All three faerie sniffed the air excitedly.

Endry zipped toward the mouth of the bottle but Rhys recorked it and drew back his hand. "What I'm asking of you is important, and I don't ask it lightly. It's worth a reward, in my opinion. A significant reward. But only if it's done exactly when and exactly how I want it."

Endry's eyes darted between Rhys and the bottle. "Deal," he said.

"Me too! Me too!" Iliona and Veesa chimed in as one. For a moment the eldest Vendilion forgot she was indentured to a malformed elf hag and lost herself in the joy of finding something new.

Rhys removed the cork and extended his hand. He waved Iliona and Veesa back as Endry floated closer. The male twin drew a tiny, pinlike blade. He turned his face away from the sour waft emanating from the open bottle and gingerly dipped his pin's sharp tip down into the neck. When he withdrew the pin, Endry brought the glistening spike close to his face.

"It's like liquid gold," he whispered, "that can *kill* you." He giggled and rose high above his sisters to trill, "Let's get started!"

Iliona and Veesa quickly visited Rhys's bottle in turn, wetting their own tiny blades in the yew poison. A moment later all three faeries were racing around each other in a flurry of incandescent smoke and scintillating noise.

"Hang on to your cloudgoats, smelly giants!" Iliona crowed. "Faeries to the rescue!"

* * * * *

"Oh, Rhys went back to the Hemlock Pack,
With a wink and a nod and a jaunty air.
He sang, "Can't catch me," then he showed them his back.
"You can't catch a fox if you're chasing a hare."

Not bad, Brigid Baeli thought. Needed work though. Too much Rhys, for one thing.

The kithkin archer guided her steed over a fallen tree, hugging it tight as they arced through the air. Springjacks were fast, and from a standing start they could jump higher than any cervin, but they were nowhere near as light on their feet. The glamer that made the elves think they were chasing Rhys on a cervin included masking the springjack's heavy tread and its wide, distinct tracks, but it couldn't prevent the shock of each leap and landing from rattling up Brigid's spine.

This was a grand adventure, and she relished the look on the elves' faces when they realized their prey was half as tall and twice as wide as they expected—and further that he was a she, riding not on a golden, stilt-limbed deer but on a stump-legged, coal black farm animal. She clenched her hands tighter around the springjack's thick, sturdy horns, knowing that to her pursuers it appeared Rhys was hauling up on the cervin's slender guide chain.

Brigid spurred the springjack on, and the sturdy beast rumbled forward, feet pounding the forest floor. She had been thinking of this escapade as another verse in the popular, ever-evolving ballad "The Hero of Kinsbaile," but as the chase went on Brigid became more certain it would demand a song of its very own. The longer the Gilt Leaf hunters chased her, the longer the others had to raid the camp. Also, the longer she kept the Hemlock Pack after the hare when they wanted the fox, the funnier her song would be.

Of course she had volunteered for this: practically speaking, springjacks were the only mounts readily available, and her extensive skills as a rider made her the obvious choice. Brigid also had something to prove beyond her practical value. Initially, she had gone along with Rhys and the others only to serve as a spy, an agent acting in a scheme that she hadn't bothered to explore or understand, which had led her to actions she now viewed with shame and self-reproach. She had lied to her friends—for these people had been friends to her—had attacked them, abducted them, and delivered them to those who meant them harm. Though she repented her actions in the end and threw in with the ones she'd betrayed, that too felt less like nobility and more like . . . another betrayal.

In short, Brigid had not lived up to the Hero of Kinsbaile's reputation, the living legend she herself had created and defined with her own exploits. The Hero of Kinsbaile craved neither rank nor glory, but glory found the noble archer all the same—that was the whole point. When the people of Kinsbaile needed a bold figure to protect them, they called upon their hero. There had always been a Hero of Kinsbaile.

For the first time she could remember Brigid wasn't completely sure she was that hero.

The only way she saw to remove the tarnish from that cherished self-image was to rebalance the scales. Only after she had returned to her allies more than she had taken and restored the genuine camaraderie her ill-considered actions had destroyed, only then could Brigid Baeli reclaim the hero's mantle.

A sturdy silverwood arrow hissed past, impressing upon her once more the very real danger she courted. Silverwood, not a simple arrowgrass shaft—the Gilt Leaf wanted Rhys dead for certain. Brigid ducked down and pressed her chin between the springjack's shoulders. The soft, curly wool tickled the inside of her nose, but she stayed low. They might want Rhys dead, but he certainly wasn't the one the archers were currently targeting with their deadly volleys.

The nearest elf was on foot and more than a hundred yards behind her through a thick curtain of trees. An archer herself, Brigid knew how difficult that last shot had been, how strong the arm that bent the bow, and how close it had come despite the challenging target she presented. She must not take the Gilt Leaf hunters lightly or she'd die. That would never fit the whimsical tone of her new song.

More arrows whizzed by, and she prodded another burst of speed from the springjack. The elves were closing in fast, now well within range of a random arrow's scoring a direct hit. A wide smile stretched across Brigid's features. So much the better, she thought. It had to be real danger or it wouldn't be as exciting in the retelling. In the grip of the moment, she heard herself switch from humming to boldly singing—singing, naturally, "The Hero of Kinsbaile."

> She rides a fiery springjack.
> Her courage never fails.
> Fight on, now, Brigid Baeli,
> The Hero of Kinsbaile!

That was more like it! Pride swelled in her chest, her courage bolstered itself, and her self-assurance returned. The kithkin rider launched into the second verse that detailed the time

Brigid single-handedly defeated the entire Dundoolin team in the annual archery contest. It was at the beginning of the third verse, the ever-popular "wolf-slayer" segment of the ballad, that Brigid noticed something was wrong.

The springjack bounded high, brushing the back of Brigid's head against low-hanging leaves. She felt papery flakes and grit flutter under her collar. It trickled down the back of her tunic and itched. The wind in her face stiffened, and the irritating dust grew thicker against her face and shoulders. She wondered if somehow that last branch had left her with an old, dried-out bee's nest lodged in her hair so that the husk was now disintegrating all over her as she rode.

The springjack hit a soft spot in the dirt and lost a step. Brigid lurched to the right as the beast recovered its rhythm. She felt her knuckles straining and quickly loosened her grip on the springjack's horns before they cracked. Her eyes widened and darted back and forth from horn to stubby horn to ensure she had done no damage.

The kithkin raised her head. She saw Rhys's shoulders above her, thin and translucent as a ghost's—a ghost whose center was also occupied by her own very real body. She shouldn't even have been able to see it at all, and if it was fading already the glamer had very little time left. Brigid twisted back over her shoulder. Then she swore.

She was leaving a stream of tiny, glittering flakes of glamer in her wake. It was not the dried-up remains of a hive that was disintegrating but her outward appearance as a noble elf. A growing icy numbness squeezed her stomach as the narrow, pointed shape of a cervin's head gave way to the squat, rounded skull of a purebred Kinsbaile springjack.

"Spectacular glamer there, Maralen," she spat, speaking through the springjack's wooly curls. "Very effective. I wove stronger magic skipping rope when I was a kithling." Perhaps kithkin thoughtweft wasn't always as visually convincing as illusions that came from glamer, but it was at least durable enough to survive a chase through the woods.

She would browbeat Maralen in person later. The plan had been to be seen—in sight but tantalizingly out of reach—in order to prolong pursuit as long as possible. The elf archers were still firing blind, but if they closed the gap any further their sharp eyes were sure to find her. They would draw back their bows, lead their target, take careful aim . . . and realize they were shooting at a decoy half-wreathed in the tattered remains of a magical disguise.

Brigid heard a sharp elf voice in the distance shout, "There he is!" just as her mount cleared the top of a jagged crest of rock. She was no longer thinking about her song, or the grand adventure, or of taking Maralen to task for shoddy spellwork. Instead, Brigid was thinking about her own bow and the quiver stuffed fat with arrows slung tight and low across her back.

The springjack was panting hard. She had maybe another five minutes of full sprint left. Brigid could stay ahead of the elves for four of those minutes. Then she would dismount, send the springjack out of harm's way with a hearty slap to the haunches, nock an arrow, and wait for the elves to catch up.

Her finger absently traced along the quiver's leather strap. One way or another, Brigid Baeli would shoulder her share of the burden. She would keep the elves occupied here, as many as she could, far from the others back at the camp. Honor, pride, and duty demanded it. The Hero of Kinsbaile could do nothing less.

Softly but firmly, Brigid resumed humming.

Ashling followed Rhys and Maralen on the approach to the Gilt Leaf hunters' camp. The color and intensity of Ashling's fire had changed—had *been* changed—in the past few days, shifting away from its former vibrant red toward a paler, more muted yellowish orange. The flames that now rose from Ashling's shoulders and collarbone surrounded and engulfed her skull behind a stoic face of dark, malleable stone. Something about the flamekin's new coloration combined with her persistent somber mood prompted the Vendilion faeries to speak of Ashling as "that two-legged torch in a death mask."

The light from Ashling's flame all but disappeared in the perpetual afternoon daylight, but she knew that wouldn't hold once she entered the deep shadows among the trees. She concentrated and dampened her fire as low as she dared without actually dousing it entirely and losing consciousness. Yellow flames were thinner than the red, but they required more concentration to control.

Pulling her flame into herself and out of public view was less strenuous than it ever had been before, but Ashling took little pride from the fact. Her inner fire had become weak and diffuse, so it was hardly a triumph to dim it further. The others had noticed, of course, and everyone from Rhys to the Vendilion faeries had commented upon it. So far none of her comrades had voiced the obvious, that the differences in Ashling's appearance and demeanor only manifested after they rescued her from Kinsbaile. Even if no one else said it and Ashling herself could not, the timing and the truth were obvious, undeniable.

Ashling had dedicated her life to the flamekin pilgrim's path, taking it wherever it led in search of the ancient, elemental spirit that had chosen her at birth. The pilgrim's quest was meant to be a long one, consuming the better part of a lifetime, if not its entirety. Ashling had vigorously sought her own elemental for over a decade, eager, even impatient for her journey's conclusion every step of the way.

In Kinsbaile, Ashling had been forcibly hurled into the full presence of that great spirit, pushed into communion with a being most mortal creatures could not see or feel, let alone understand. After a decade of seeking and only tantalizing glimpses and half-remembered intuition to show for it, Ashling beheld her patron spirit as it was. Even before she saw its shape, she understood its power. It was a wild and primal thing of speed and strength, unfettered by mortal limitations or concerns. It was the embodiment of the untamable desire for freedom itself, a living expression of the fierce joy freedom creates.

The elemental appeared to Ashling as a majestic white steed with hooves and mane of fire. Huge and towering, the horse spirit's presence was one of effortless grace, indomitable spirit, and inexhaustible stamina. It was rampant action, frenzied motion, the sheer joy of wild abandon manifest as equine muscle and mystic power.

Inexplicably, it had felt terror at the sight of her. True, the terror subsided quickly once their two flames joined into one, but if Ashling lived to be ten centuries old she would never feel anything as truly frightening as the raw primal fear of this divine elemental. In her nightmares, in her fugue states, the horse's terror was monumental, overwhelming . . . infinite.

Entering the presence of her elemental was the culmination of her life's work, and it had nearly destroyed her. Ashling had touched the spirit directly, tasted its awesome power for herself far sooner than even her most impatient expectations. Now, the ambitious pilgrim saw she had not been ready, not been worthy. She had communed with her elemental too early, too soon, and that forced communion came at a price she could not pay.

Her former confidence and impatience shamed her. How wrong she'd been. The pilgrim she had hoped to become would have taken the elemental's fear away, would have found a way to help the great spirit instead of standing awed and overwhelmed.

Worst of all, contact between Ashling and the elemental was now irrevocably established. Even if she could shut out the painful memories of fire and the shameful truth of her own failure, even if she could blot out Kinsbaile and resume her path as a wiser, less-hurried pilgrim, it would not matter. She was not free. The elemental knew her, had merged with her and perhaps even accepted her on profound levels. It had her scent and it could find her whenever it wished. As a pilgrim Ashling had pursued the spirit, but now she knew with dire certainty that the spirit was pursuing her. And when it caught up to her, she did not know if she could survive its glorious fire.

Harried by both the Gilt Leaf elves and that vast, primal entity, Ashling's sleep was shallow and fitful. But at least it was dreamless. Her waking hours were not so blessed. At least once a day, every day, Ashling would become overwhelmed by visions of fire and the sound of thundering hooves. They stopped her in place no matter what she was doing, rendered her frozen and insensate, and left her weeping. Illusory flames surrounded her on all sides, engulfed her, vaporized her body, and filled her mind with smoke and blinding ecstasy. Twice now Rhys had been forced to stand face-to-face with Ashling and bark out her name until her faculties returned. Iliona had also caught Ashling in this state. The faerie's abrasive mockery brought Ashling back even more quickly.

Now Rhys held up a clenched fist, and Maralen stopped beside him. Ashling also went still, but it was the rising echo of distant hooves as much as Rhys's signal that silenced her. The pilgrim squeezed her lips together and clenched her eyes shut against the phantom sounds. She had a job to do, a role to play, and she would not give Rhys cause to regret his faith in her.

Ashling crept up and stood on Rhys's left side opposite Maralen. The elves intently studied the thick line of trees twenty feet ahead, and Ashling followed their line of sight until her eyes came upon the bodies of two Gilt Leaf archers slumped among the dead leaves.

"Careful and quick to the tree line," Rhys said, "on my mark."

Rhys waited a few heartbeats and sprinted toward the trees. Maralen gave him a two-stride head start, then followed. Ashling fell in behind Maralen, and together the women reached the motionless sentries just as Rhys finished inspecting their unconscious bodies. Ashling saw the sentries were breathing, but the Gilt Leaf elves were otherwise slack as dead things.

Rhys looked up from the unconscious sentry. "We're clear," he said. He gestured and slipped through the trees into the Gilt Leaf camp.

Maralen paused to glance back at Ashling. The elf maiden stared until the pilgrim nodded angrily.

"Don't wait for me," Ashling said. Maralen cocked her head quizzically, smiled, and followed Rhys through the trees.

Ashling moved in once Maralen was gone from sight. The pilgrim had never seen the inside of a hunting-pack's camp before, but she also knew this was not a typical pack or a typical situation.

There were rows upon rows of small, single-occupant lean-tos, each constructed of a single branch and a single gigantic leaf. There were three larger tents scattered across the shallow basin that stretched across the camp's interior, cervin pens, and cuffhound kennels, but all were either empty or attended by comatose elves. Their decoy had drawn away almost all of the rangers, archers, and officers, and the Vendilion sisters had done their work so well there wasn't a single active elf in the entire camp besides Rhys and Maralen.

Rhys raised his fist again and waved it, signaling Ashling and Maralen to come close. When they were all huddled together behind a thick rowan, Iliona and Veesa fluttered down from the canopy. For once the faeries were quiet, and there was a moment of perfect silence before Rhys finally spoke.

"We're here," he said. "The vinebred pens are right over there. My thanks, ladies. You did well."

Iliona smiled and batted her eyes. Veesa hooked a sharp finger between her lips and coyly turned away as she hovered.

"Yew poison is fun." Iliona's voice rang like a tiny chime.

"How do you want to go in?" Ashling said.

"Same way we got this far," Rhys said. "The faeries will scout ahead. I'll go in after them, then Maralen, then you." He lifted his head and craned his neck so that his right ear pointed skyward. "I don't hear anything coming our way, and that's good. The spells we have to cast will take some time." He leveled his eyes at Ashling. "Are you ready?"

"I am."

Rhys nodded. "Good. Now then." He glanced upward at the faerie sisters, then at Maralen. The dark-haired elf nodded, and Rhys said, "Off you go."

Iliona and Veesa stifled a merry titter and streaked toward the nearby walled enclosure. Rhys counted softly to himself until the glittering trail of dust and smoke in the faeries' wake disappeared from sight.

"If they had bumped into anyone unexpected," he said,

"we would have heard something by now." Rhys bounded forward, covering the stretch of ground between the rowan and the wooden gate in three long strides. Ashling was quietly impressed: Horns or no horns, Rhys was an accomplished ranger, swift, sure, and silent. She realized Maralen was staring, and Ashling said, "What?"

"I just want to know if you can do this."

"I said I was fine."

"That is not what I asked," the elf woman said. Her eyes were clear and concerned. "Can you do this? It's going to take all three of us, and I still don't really understand how your fire magic is going to help do the job."

"It's more than fire—" Ashling began, but before she could finish a tall, broad figure separated from the shadow of a tree and knocked Rhys off his feet with a powerful swipe of his fist. Rhys seemed more surprised than hurt by the blow.

"Looks like the faeries missed one." Maralen rushed forward without reply, hissing curses as she went.

Rhys regained his feet. The former Hemlock leader and the Gilt Leaf sentry eyed each other warily. Ashling hesitated. All the other Gilt Leaf had been dispatched without a struggle. Why did the sight of this last sentry cause Rhys and Maralen such concern?

Maintaining her position at the rear, Ashling moved up to flank their enemy. They had gotten around the bulk of the Hemlock Pack. How much trouble could one more elf be?

* * * * *

Brigid Baeli stood in the sunlight and shadows near the center of a shallow dell. Her springjack had ambled off amiably after a less-than-amiable swat on the backside, so Brigid faced the sounds of approaching elves alone. The Gilt Leaf hunters sounded less numerous than they had, and their smaller number

19

were also less frenzied and more deliberate in their approach. They had even stopped blind-firing arrows at her.

She could guess the reason: Her glamer was gone, long gone, and without that magic masking her trail the elves would have quickly realized they'd been fooled. This was bad for the others, of course, but in truth it was good for her. With the ruse exposed, it was pointless to continue gallivanting across the forest. Brigid could do more if she doubled back. She could make herself far more useful, maybe even participate in the main rescue itself. First, she'd have to deal with those few remaining elves still chasing her, but in Brigid's estimation there were no more than twelve of them. Not an easy task, to be sure, but it was far more encouraging being outnumbered a dozen to one than a hundred to one.

Brigid checked her surroundings one last time. It was a good place to make a stand. She had ample space and room to move. There were also trees within dashing distance if she had to retreat and take cover. She had not had time to prepare the ground as extensively as she would have liked, but she was confident she could make do with what she had. Her eyes followed the rough lines she had scratched into the dirt with the tip of an arrow. She was surrounded by a crude square with small kithkin fetishes and totems at each corner.

The elves were possessed of strong woodland magic, but the kithkin were industrious creatures of hearth and home—they took raw, wild Nature and made it habitable, even welcoming. Kithkin magic could make any place a haven, a place where Brigid's people could rest and recuperate—and, if necessary, defend themselves.

The edges of Brigid's dell suddenly fell silent, and she smiled. With a theatrical shrug, Brigid tossed her bow from her shoulder and stepped back to catch the polished weapon in her outstretched hand.

"Let me save you the trouble," she called. She drew an arrow from her quiver and nocked it onto the bowstring, but she did not draw. "You have me surrounded."

Brigid heard a short, sharp bird call. Ten Gilt Leaf hunters appeared simultaneously around the perimeter of the dell. Five held longbows with arrows drawn and ready. Four more stood with drawn swords. The last elf was empty-handed but bore a complicated insignia of rank on his leafy, leather breastplate.

Brigid kept smiling. So far, so good. Only ten? Only five archers? Perhaps she had prepared too much.

Still, Brigid had to admit they were an impressive-looking bunch. The Gilt Leaf hunters were all tall and keen-eyed, serious, stern things that struck her as dangerous and elegant at the same time. Males and females alike wore their hair long and braided around their thick, curving horns.

The elf with the insignia stared coldly at Brigid, disgust twisting his fine features. "A kithkin on a springjack," he said. He shook his head. "Disappointing. Wretched kithkin, you have trifled with the Gilt Leaf. You should have been content to remain beneath our notice."

"I hadn't finished preparing for guests," Brigid called back. "But if this is how you plan to behave I must insist you show a bit more respect for your host."

"This is elf territory," the officer snarled. "You are the guest here, you ugly little beer barrel, and an unwelcome one at that."

Brigid glanced casually down at her feet, then looked back up. "Feels like home to me." How long would they wait? The elf facing her considered what she'd said, balanced her strangely calm demeanor against the urgency of their shared situation. He pondered a full second longer than Brigid expected, but then the officer turned his back on her. Her muscles tensed as the elf called out to his archers. "End this."

Five elf bowstrings twanged in unison. Brigid abandoned her

casual air. Ignoring the incoming missiles, the kithkin planted her feet and fought back, firing five arrows at five elf archers in rapid succession. Gilt Leaf archers were undisputed masters of their craft, but Brigid had a lifetime of training and practice that made her the equal of any archer alive, elf or otherwise. If her magic was as solid as her eyes and her arm . . .

Brigid's first two arrows passed directly under the elf bolts streaking toward her, while her third hit an incoming missile head-on, shattering both into a cloud of splinters. Her fourth and fifth bolts came as a complete surprise to the Gilt Leaf archers, who clearly expected her to be skewered before she ever had a chance to aim.

Cries of pain and surprise echoed from four of the elf archers. The officer turned to face Brigid once more with an angry oath on his lips, but his voice died in his throat when he saw what the others saw.

Five stalks of arrowgrass hung motionless in the air around Brigid, several feet away from their target. A sixth elf bolt joined the others as the last archer standing fired again, but that too stopped dead as soon as it reached the outline of Brigid's totem-studded square.

Brigid did not pause. She let fly at the officer, then twice at each of the sword-bearing rangers. She hit each of the elves at least once, though as she did the remaining Gilt Leaf archer lodged three more arrowgrass bolts in the walls of her makeshift homestead.

Undaunted, the last archer changed tactics. He darted to the left and fired again from the deep shadows. Then he sprang back past his original position and let fly once more. Brigid stood balanced on the balls of her feet, her head still but her eyes darting after the elusive elf. She felt a stinging breeze on her cheek as his last arrow stopped two feet from her face, and Brigid pinned the archer to a tree at the northeast edge of the dell.

The kithkin stifled a self-satisfied chuckle. She turned back to face the rangers, but a lean, powerful body tackled her in midturn. The impact knocked the air from her lungs, and Brigid grunted, but she held on to her bow. Never let go of your weapon, that's what she'd been taught. She felt the elf officer's weight bear her to the ground, and if she'd had any breath left she would have grunted again.

Brigid stared into the furious elf's features for a moment as they struggled, and she slammed her broad forehead into the officer's finely chiseled nose. She heard a crunch and felt warm blood splash across her face as she wriggled out from under him. Kithkin were expert grapplers—their muscles were concentrated in a dense but flexible package, and they were tenacious fighters. The officer may have been twice her height, but he was neither twice as strong nor twice as skilled. He may have established a firm grip on Brigid, but he could not hold her long.

Sure enough, Brigid easily pulled free and broke clear of the officer. She rolled to her feet just as another elf ranger rushed in with his sword. She spun her sturdy bow up to deflect the falling blade to one side, into the dirt. Brigid smoothly grabbed the elf's wrist, dropped onto her back, and kicked out with both short, stubby legs. The elf ranger's right knee shattered under her heels, and the Gilt Leaf hunter toppled, his face a silent mask of agony.

Brigid crawled away and bounced to her feet. She quickly accounted for all of the elves in the dell—nine down, or at least, nine wounded to the point where they no longer threatened her. Only the officer remained.

She planted her feet and faced him squarely. She had her sword, but so did he. Exchanging arrows and brawling were one thing, but she could never match a Gilt Leaf officer's swordplay. If he drew his long blade he would surely cut her to pieces.

The officer clearly had similar thoughts. He glared at Brigid, and his hand fell to the hilt of his blade. She could think of only one way to keep him from using the weapon, so Brigid lowered her head and charged, butting the tall elf in the stomach. The officer's long body folded around Brigid's head as she bore him backward. Her thick, powerful fingers clawed and hammered at the sword until it fell from his hand.

To her surprise, the elf chose not to lunge after the blade. Instead, he brought his knee up sharply into Brigid's chin, straightening her body out and dropping her flat onto her feet. For a split second Brigid and her opponent locked eyes. Through the ringing in her ears, the kithkin grinned again. Beating *this* elf would, at least, be worthy of a new line, if not an entire verse, of her favorite ballad. The officer lashed out with his long leg, trying to drive his hoof into the kithkin's throat, but Brigid twisted and took the blow on her left shoulder. Pain half-blinded her, and she swore explosively, but it was better than a crushed windpipe.

Her left arm hung limp. She circled around the officer and forced him to turn his back on his fallen weapon. She drew an arrow from her quiver and held the point out toward her foe.

"Ten against one." Brigid spoke through ragged, rasping breaths. "No matter how this ends, I still got the best of the Gilt Leaf."

The officer's lip curled. Disdaining the sword behind him, he stepped forward and kicked Brigid in the face. The blow came so quickly the kithkin didn't realize what had happened until she was staggering backward.

The arrow fell from her hand. Brigid regained her balance and shook her head clear. She smiled through the blood and the fog of pain. "Nice," she said. "You're learning. But your lesson isn't over yet."

"It will be." The elf returned her smile, though on his face it was far crueler. "Soon, beer barrel. Very soon."

She flinched as the officer took a step toward her. He strode on, unhurried, resolute, and Brigid backpedaled to stay clear of those flashing hooves. Things could have been worse—but they could have been a damned sight better too. For the first time Brigid wondered if this fight would end well enough to actually become a verse in her ongoing epic—and if she'd be around to hear it.

* * * * *

Rhys crossed swords with the last Gilt Leaf sentry. Ashling approached cautiously. Now that she saw the enemy up close, she had a better idea of why Rhys and Maralen were so disturbed. He was tall, even taller than Rhys, and broadly built. He was also covered from horns to hooves in form-fitting wooden armor that seemed to be loosely woven from tough, braided vines.

Ashling chided herself. Of course the vinebred pens would have a vinebred sentry. The vinebred were the Gilt Leaf's most powerful living weapons, creatures enchanted with living coils and tendrils that improved their strength, speed, and ferocity. The most famed of elf sages and seedguides tended the symbiotic nettlevines and trained them to grow into and around their hosts until there was no distinction between the two. To someone like Ashling it appeared to be a fate far worse than total submersion in the Wanderwine.

"Hey," Iliona's light, airy voice said. "We already downed that one."

"He's not playing fair," Veesa said. "Let's kill him again."

Rhys and the vinebred silently jockeyed for an opening. Maralen's eyes remained locked on the duel as she said, "A capital idea, ladies. Please do."

Veesa struck first, shooting past the vinebred's defenses and slashing him with her yew-smeared blade. The enchanted Gilt Leaf barely winced, and he continued to stalk Rhys without any evidence of being poisoned.

"Stay back," Rhys said. "The stuff I gave you won't kill, so this one won't even notice it."

"Won't kill?" Iliona was appalled. "What's the fun in that?"

"You mean all those elves we killed aren't dead?" Veesa pouted. "That's not fair! We were having a contest!"

Ashling decided it was time to show Rhys and the others why there had never been a vinebred flamekin. She pushed back the brim of her hat to unleash a sudden flare of bright red fire. Her lethargy burned away, and she felt stronger and more vibrant than she had in days.

"Rhys!" she said. "Stand clear!"

"Now that's a capital idea," Rhys said. Ashling drew back her open hand and cast it forward as if skipping a stone across a pond. A thin sheaf of flames flew from her fingers to the vinebred's broad back and ignited the vines there. The fire wouldn't burn long, as the vines were far too green, but it would be enough if Ashling could keep the pressure on.

The sentry's roar was more anger than pain, but it still set Ashling's teeth on edge. She prepared a much hotter and more substantial blast of fire, determined to kill the vinebred outright rather than let him make that sound again, but she had already given Rhys all the opening he needed.

The Gilt Leaf outcast pounced while the vinebred twisted and thrashed beneath his smoldering green carapace. Rhys drove his blade into the vinebred's chest, and the point erupted out the other side in a spray of greenish black liquid. Ashling's triumphant cry withered in her throat as Rhys continued his attack. He released his two-handed grip on the sword and stabbed his short dagger sideways through the vinebred's neck.

The enchanted creature staggered back, both of Rhys's blades still in his body. Rhys dropped low and seized a fist-sized rock. He swung his arm in a wide arc as he stood and smashed the stone into the vinebred's face, crushing rock, wood, and bones alike.

"More," Rhys shouted. He dropped the broken rock and picked up another. "Don't just stand there. Help me put him down!"

Maralen responded, leaping forward with a small, previously unseen dagger in one hand. She ducked under the vinebred's flailing arm and drove the knife into his rib cage, once, twice, three times as Rhys continued to hammer the sentry's head with the second stone. Iliona and Veesa circled the melee, striking repeatedly through the gaps in the sentry's woven wooden armor, further peppering their foe with abuse and invective.

Ashling scooped up a fallen elf's sword and rushed forward to contribute to its owner's defeat, but the vinebred crumpled to his knees before she got close. Ichor pumped from his wounds, and the ground, already slick with the vile stuff, became saturated.

The vinebred's hands dropped to the soil, and his shoulders slumped. His head remained high and his neck straight as he fixed his fluttering eyes on Rhys standing over him.

"Eyeblight," the creature hissed. His voice was deep and muffled, an echo from the depths of a wooded ravine. "We will find you."

Rhys turned to Ashling and gestured for her to hand him the sword. Numbly, the pilgrim passed the blade to Rhys and stood back. The outcast elf raised the weapon high and dug his hooves into the sod. With a single, swift stroke, Rhys struck the vinebred's head from his shoulders.

The borrowed blade and the head hit the ground simultaneously. "Move," Rhys said. Without waiting for them to follow, the blighted elf marched through the outer edge of the vinebred enclosure. Ashling was the first to follow, and a moment later she, Maralen, and the faeries all joined Rhys inside the confines of the pen.

The vinebred enclosure was silent and still, eerily lit by Gilt Leaf lanterns that cast the pen's interior in a sickly green pall. Rhys, Maralen, and the faeries continued across the clearing without glancing at the unsettling shapes that all but covered the ground, but Ashling was not so focused. She had to pause to take in the details of her surroundings, no matter how chilling and horrifying they were.

Dozens of creatures lay prone and motionless on the ground. They came in various shapes and sizes, but each was at least partially covered by vines. Most of the vinebred here were elves, but Ashling recognized smaller shapes that could have been kithkin or boggarts. There were also animals, cuffhounds and cervin and other four-legged beasts. She could see and hear them all breathing. The vines moved, grew, expanded, and contracted around the assembled bodies, but otherwise the vinebred here were somnolent, drained, and dead to the world.

"Ashling," Rhys whispered sharply. "Over here."

Ashling gingerly stepped through the garish green scene to reach the far side of the enclosure, where Rhys and the others waited. What she had first thought was a solid deadfall of trees and brush was in fact a huge mound of nettlevines. Two mounds, in fact, representing two vinebred creatures so large that they didn't fit inside the pen so much as serve as its western wall.

"We found them," Rhys said. "Now all we have to do is wake them up."

"And escape," Maralen said. She was staring out to the east, where Brigid had led the bulk of the Gilt Leaf pack.

Rhys followed her gaze and nodded. "That will be the easy part. Now let's begin," he said. "We don't have much time."

Confused, Ashling looked east and listened hard. Her ears were not as sharp as an elf's, but it wasn't long before she heard what Rhys and Maralen heard. The hunters were coming back. They had either caught and killed Brigid or had abandoned the chase entirely.

Rhys beckoned. "More light, please."

"I'm not a lantern, you know," Ashling scowled. "All right,

all right," Ashling removed her hat. Living flames flared bright orange and yellow, their rejuvenated vigor overpowering the pale green glow of the lanterns.

"Thank you." Rhys and Maralen joined hands and began speaking in a language Ashling didn't understand. Iliona and Veesa hovered overhead, mercifully silent in their fascination.

Under the light of Ashling's flame and the influence of elf magic, the two great mounds of vines writhed and rustled. Finally, and with great reluctance, the nettlevines covering the western wall began to recede.

The officer's hoof glanced off Brigid's left temple, and she staggered down onto one knee. She was doing her best to defend herself, but her best was currently getting her face kicked in.

Brigid spat blood through split and swollen lips. It was hard to prepare for blows she couldn't see or hear coming. She forced herself to stand, eyes locked on her tormentor as he taunted her with the promise of another kick that could come at any time. He had her more or less at his mercy, yet his face showed no signs of triumph. His sharp, elegant features were creased in mild disdain, but his eyes were terrifyingly calm. He would not be rushed through the important chore of reducing Brigid's skull to mush.

Though unhurried, the Gilt Leaf officer was relentless. His blows came in a steady, measured stream, and whether they landed or not each one forced her to keep moving. He stalked her calmly, deliberately, never allowing her to relax but neither pressing in for the kill once he had slipped another blow past her defenses.

He was maneuvering her steadily toward the thick tree line at the edge of the dell, where there would be no room to move and no place to dodge or stagger between kicks. The hunter would crush her against a wall of bark and wood.

This was no way for the Hero of Kinsbaile to die.

The elf came forward into a column of sunlight that lent a glorious golden sheen to his face and horns.

The kithkin archer drew herself up. "I am Brigid Baeli," she said. "B-A-E-L-I, for the record. The Hero of Kinsbaile."

The elf's stoic expression soured. Brigid braced for the lethal kick she knew was coming. She wondered if he would even waste a whispered curse on her before the final blow fell.

The hunter said nothing, however. His hooves remained firmly on the ground and he stood rigid, still wreathed in sunlight like a statue of some divine hero.

"Meh," the officer said. He pitched forward and thudded to the ground, stiff and straight as a log. A glittering, winged figure spiraled up from the shadows behind the stricken elf.

"Did you see that?" Endry said. His eyes shone, and he waved a tiny metal spike at Brigid. "Come on, kithkin. We're supposed to meet everybody at the river, and if my sisters beat us there I'll never hear the end of it."

Brigid had never been so glad to hear the tinkling voice of a faerie—or anyone's voice, for that matter. Even the ringing in ears couldn't drown out the male Vendilion. She was saved.

Brigid exhaled one long, steady breath and slid seat-first to the ground. "Endry, my boy," she said, "I need a moment."

Endry rose over Brigid and turned toward the river. "Come on, come on. It's time to go."

"I haven't finished my moment."

"Get up, or I'll carry you."

Brigid slumped flat on her back. "That actually sounds appealing."

Endry darted over Brigid and flew in circles above her. "Then think again, kithkin. If I have to carry you, I get to stab you first."

"Stab me? Why?"

"For the fun." Endry produced the tiny sliver of sharp metal and waved it around once more. "Yew juice. Rhys gave it to me. It's my new favorite thing."

"Rhys gave you juice on a pin?"

"No, stupid, he gave me *yew* juice for the pin. I stuck half the creatures I saw on my way here and each one instantly keeled over like a badly packed sack of potatoes." Endry counted off the tips of his fingers. "I got a bird, two squirrels, a stoat-looking thing, and a big, fat springjack. It's been a good day." The tiny faerie blinked. "I must be running low. Your playmate there took a long time to fall."

"He was determined," Brigid said. She frowned. "Wait. You stuck my springjack?"

"Tubby, black wool, stubby horns? I sure did." Endry waggled his blade. "It made a very satisfying thud when it fell."

Brigid sat up quickly, forcing Endry to spiral out of the way.

"It might just be asleep," Endry said.

"All right, stop talking," the kithkin said, biting back a curse. There was no time for verbal wordplay with the one of the Fae. "I'm ready now."

"You don't want to be carried?"

"I want to be carried. I don't want to be stuck."

Endry considered this. "How about stuck but not carried?"

Brigid rolled her eyes. She stood up, staggered a bit, and marched toward the river.

"All right, all right." The faerie zipped up and faced Brigid, keeping perfect pace as he flew backward. He spread his arms and waved his hands in a wide, swooping circle. Bright blue dust swirled from his hands and encircled Brigid. The kithkin archer's feet floated off the ground. Endry giggled to himself and darted off toward the river.

Brigid drifted after Endry, towed along by the faerie's magic. She moved slowly at first but ever faster, until passing leaves slapped her face hard enough to sting. She covered her face with her hands to prevent new injury and curled into a tight ball to protect her existing ones. At least Endry did not drag her through any solid obstacles, though she was certain that was only because he didn't want to actually delay their progress. Should have let him poison me, she thought.

"Come on!" Endry shouted. "Everyone's heading for the river! We don't want to miss the boat!"

"Perish the thought," Brigid muttered. She concentrated on restoring herself to fighting form. The straightforward healing magic she knew was reliable but slow. It would take time to feel the full effects, but thanks to Endry she had the time and the opportunity. Once her recovery was well underway, Brigid could turn her thoughts to more important matters—such as translating all her elf-inflicted injuries into short, punchy rhyming couplets that would joyfully compel kithkin festival-goers into spontaneous sing-alongs.

She looked forward to teaching everyone the words.

* * * * *

The Gilt Leaf elves' return was nowhere near as measured or silent as their departure. Ashling heard distant birdcalls and the muted growls of deep-chested dogs. The Hemlock hunters would be on them soon, their thirst for Rhys's blood palpable after the double insult of his presence, both real and illusory.

The faerie sisters floated at opposite ends of the double-mound of prone giants and vegetation. Ashling edged closer to Rhys and Maralen while they worked their magic. Both elves stood fixed and rigid, unblinking eyes rolled back in their sockets. Rhys had one hand half-extended toward the nettlevine mound, and Maralen's arms were crossed, her hands clasped upon her own shoulders. A soft, lilting song rose from the back of the elf maiden's throat.

The wall of vines wriggled and seethed like a bed of snakes, though the giants Brion and Kiel remained motionless. Ashling peered into the writhing mass. The braided wooden veneer was far from complete, as the vinebred sentry's had been, but the growth was thickest around the giants' heads and shoulders. Ashling followed the stoutest, sturdiest tendrils coiling around the brothers' throats, then back up into their broad, fleshy ears. Tended properly, nettlevines grew into and around their host until they covered it like a second skin. The vines merged with the host's body until it was no longer two separate entities but an entirely new individual: a vinebred.

The giant brothers were in this predicament because of Rhys . . . and Maralen, and Brigid, and Ashling herself. Their enemies in the Hemlock Pack had caught up with them outside Kinsbaile, but Brion and Kiel had been in the way. This chance encounter quickly escalated from misunderstanding to full-fledged combat. It took all of Rhys's former comrades to subdue Brion and Kiel, and, once it became clear that the Gilt Leaf would prevail, Rhys and the others had chosen to escape.

It had been a practical decision, one made under duress, but even so it was a shameful memory for all of them. Especially Rhys. When he had presented his plan for rescuing Brion and Kiel to the others, he had said that abandoning the brothers wasn't the last difficult choice he'd make, or the most traumatic, but it was the easiest to remedy. He also said that the brothers had access to an oracle of some sort, one that might help them better understand the mysteries and threats that surrounded them.

Maralen's song reached a crescendo, and the elf woman staggered back. She steadied her head between her hands, closed her eyes, and breathed deeply.

"I'm done," she said. Her wide black eyes snapped open. "Rhys, can you hold it there?"

"I can." Rhys nodded his head, and the jagged shadows of his broken horns danced across his face. "Ashling."

"Ready."

Enchanting the nettlevines onto a creature was a precise and exacting discipline, but disenchanting them off one was even more difficult. Rhys and Maralen could perform the complicated and sustained rituals to wake the brothers, but they could not complete the removal in the short time they had. The best they could do was ease the nettlevines' grip. It would be up to the pilgrim's magic to pull Brion and Kiel out of their forced hibernation completely.

The flamekin stepped forward and adjusted her hat across her upper back like an undersized turtle shell. This was where they all found out whether she deserved Rhys's confidence, herself included.

She drew her focus inward. Her flames followed, dwindling down into her joints, where they flickered like dying candles.

Rhys understood this much: Flamekin spells did not simply burn, and pilgrims sought far more than to simply ignite bigger and brighter fire. Flames were her magic's primary form, but it was not heat that now flickered up from Ashling's eyes and joints. It was initiative, inspiration, the itch of curiosity, and the impulse toward action. A flamekin's fire was joyous, creative, and urgent—in short, the perfect antidote to nettlevine-induced stupor.

Ashling felt the color of her flames shifting, dull yellow giving way to misty silver-white. White flames were the most potent she could produce, their fire suffused with her spirit and emotions as well as her intellect and discipline. It was cool fire that soothed Ashling's troubled mind, but her comfort soured when she heard the distant echo of equine hooves.

Ashling's throat tightened. She squeezed her eyes shut. Slowly, deliberately, Ashling extended her white fire toward the vine-encrusted giants. She could feel them, ponderous and immobile as mountains. They were asleep, empty. They had no initiative and no urgent impulses of their own. Ashling could feel this absence in them, and, with a carefully focused push, she felt her magic flowing into that hollow void, slowly but inexorably filling it.

The pilgrim's mind sizzled. She saw how the nettlevines worked now, understood the connection between vine and host. Rhys and Maralen were fortunate the giants were so large—with so much creature to cover, the nettlevines had not had time enough to worm their way into the brothers' deeper recesses.

The pilgrim smiled behind closed eyes. She was likewise fortunate that the brothers were giants. They were creatures of appetite, and it did not require much to stir those appetites. Ashling felt Brion's frustration and physical hunger. His stomach had hardly begun to accept the fact that it would never be filled again, that all its nourishment would come through the nettlevines. Kiel was likewise chafing under his shroud of inactivity, but the larger giant yearned not for food or drink but for stories, for tales to absorb and digest and store away.

Ashling reeled. She had never sustained white flames on this scale before, never achieved this kind of intensity. She was taxing herself harder than she ever had before, yet she was not losing power but gaining it, becoming more alert and energized with every passing moment. She reveled in the sensation for a moment until the sound of hooves rose in her ears alongside the actual noise of the approaching Gilt Leaf elves.

"Now," Maralen's voice said. "Ashling, it has to be now."

Ashling opened her eyes. She flared, bathing the vinebred enclosure in smoky white glow. Malleable streams of pale fire curled toward the brothers and twisted around the tendrils that held them. The seething wall of nettlevines hardened and went rigid under this blazing caress, though the flames did not consume so much as a single leaf.

Brion and Kiel responded. Ashling smelled the delicious waft of roast ox. She heard a woman's name clearly through the buzzing, crackling sounds of the brother's waking minds: *Rosheen*.

"On. Your. Feet." Ashling's growl rasped painfully through her throat and stung her own ears. Her arms and legs shot out straight. White flames danced along the edges of her spread-eagle form. The flamekin's eyes released twin jets of cold white fire, and Ashling shouted. "On your feet! Let's go! Rosheen is waiting!"

The smaller, rounder, more uniform mound of vines shifted. The woody mass rolled forward, stretching and snapping the nettlevines that anchored it to the ground. Rhys and Maralen had to spring back to avoid being crushed.

Ashling pulled her white flames back into her body. Her feet settled onto the ground. Panting, she watched a huge, thick hand push through the shroud of vines from below. The giant's arm bent at the elbow, and thick, calloused fingers scratched at a newly exposed patch of bald pate.

"You don't have to shout." Brion's voice boomed through the mass of vines still covering his face. "I heard you." He sat up higher, and more of the nettlevine covering pulled away from his body. Now half of Brion's face and one of his shoulders were completely exposed. Through unfocused eyes, Brion peered down at the tangle of nettlevines beside him. He curled his hand into a fist, raised it overhead, and brought it down on top of the other mound with a tree-rattling thud.

"Get up, Kiel." Brion still sounded sleepy, petulant as a child. "You can't yell at me to wake up if you're still sleeping."

The second leafy mass crunched under Brion's fist. Before the ham hand could rebound from the blow, Kiel's long arm ripped up through the vines, and his gnarled fingers latched around Brion's throat.

"Didn't yell." Kiel's voice was deeper, slower, and more

gravelly than his brother's. "And don't hit."

Brion struggled, but Kiel's grip was firm. Brion heaved and thrashed until he'd hauled his brother loose from the vine thicket. Both giants toppled back so that Kiel landed half-atop his brother, motionless but still clamped on tight to Brion's throat. Without their huge bodies to support the nettlevines, the entire thicket behind the giants slowly collapsed into itself. The vines' wriggling slowed, and the tendrils withdrew.

Brion coughed and spat foam. "All right, all right. You didn't yell, and I don't hit."

Kiel's fingers relaxed. He drew his arm back, planted two flat palms on the forest floor, and levered his long torso up off the ground. Kiel drew his short legs beneath him and rocked back onto his feet. He gathered ankle-length chin whiskers in one hand as he stared intently at Ashling.

"Hello, flamekin," he said to her. "You burned up. I don't think you liked it much."

Brion cleared his throat and looked over at Ashling. His gaze traveled on until it settled on Rhys and Maralen. "Hey, Boss," he said amiably.

A score of Hemlock archers and a half-dozen cuffhounds broke through the trees. The dogs circled wide to flank their prey, and a score of arrowgrass bolts arced high over the giants. Brion chuckled as the elves' arrows clattered against his skin. One or two briefly lodged in his thick hide but shook loose when Brion stretched and yawned into the back of his hand.

"Aren't those the elves that tied us up?" Brion's sleepy eyes sharpened and a joyful malevolence crept into his voice. "I hate those elves."

The first cuffhounds reached the giants and swarmed around the brothers' feet, snapping and snarling. Brion glanced down, momentarily confused, and bared his clenched teeth. "Bad dogs," he said.

Brion dropped down and swung his meaty arm in a broad, sweeping arc. He turned a half circle with his arm extended like a scythe, his thick, braided beard spinning wildly around his face. As he turned, Brion scooped up all six cuffhounds in the crook of his elbow. The dogs yelped and howled, but they were helplessly crushed against the giant's brawny arm.

Brion straightened his legs as he completed his turn and cast his arm up. The dogs shot high into the sky and disappeared over the far side of the forest.

Ashling fought off the sound of hoof beats and spoke through a cold, sour sting in the back of her throat. "Come on, Kiel," she said. "Please. It's time to go. Rosheen is waiting."

Brion pushed past his brother with a joyful whoop and thundered toward the oncoming elves. Gilt Leaf archers screamed under an avalanche of giant and broken vines. Brion plowed on, and more elf cries rose from the woods. Ashling felt the impact of two huge hands clapping together, and the trees around Brion all bent away from the concussion.

Ashling called out, "Kiel! Please."

Kiel nodded. He tilted his face down at Ashling, then crouched and lowered his shoulder. He extended his arm like a ramp, up which Ashling obligingly ran. The flamekin planted her feet in Kiel's thick-muscled shoulder, dug one hand into his fleshy earlobe, and hung on tight.

"You understand?" she said. Kiel nodded. To the others she shouted, "He understands! Get on, and let's get out of here."

Rhys hesitated, then grabbed Maralen's hand and dashed toward Kiel. The elves quickly joined Ashling on the giant's shoulder. Ashling waited until Rhys and Maralen were secure, then said, "Kiel, take us to the river."

"Brion," Kiel said.

Rhys shouted. "He's right. We can't just leave him."

"We won't." Kiel strode toward the sounds of his brother's battle until Ashling saw Brion stomping and clapping his ham hands among several dozen Gilt Leaf hunters. Though he was clearly having his way (and having a great deal of fun in the bargain), Brion was slowly being surrounded. The elves had defeated him before, but this time they did not seem inclined to take him alive.

"Brion." Kiel stomped up behind his brother and latched on to the back of Brion's belt and collar. "Time to go."

"Hey," Brion began, but Kiel threw himself backward and jerked his brother into the air over his head before Brion could finish his objection. Ashling, Maralen, and Rhys all shouted together as they were almost shaken loose.

Brion was too heavy to hold for long, even for Kiel, so the larger giant let his brother drop without relaxing his grip. Kiel spun Brion down so that his brother's braids brushed the ground, and Kiel swung Brion back up. The Gilt Leaf hunters nearby fell back, well clear of Kiel's windmilling arms.

Kiel spun through several more revolutions, building up speed and momentum until Ashling was nauseated and Brion was a circular, howling blur. With a grunt, Kiel released Brion and sent his brother hurtling toward the far side of the enclosure, a massive, thick-skulled, tough-skinned missile that flattened everything in its path.

"Time to go," Kiel said. "So we're going."

Brion was fully enraged now, at Kiel as well as the elves. He leveled whole copses and tore up huge chunks of sod on his way back to his feet.

"It's a start," Rhys said. "But we can't toss Brion all the way from here to the river."

Ashling struggled for a response, but it was Maralen who spoke. "Leave Brion to us," she said. The elf maiden's head was cocked, and she was smiling. Iliona and Veesa swept down, circled Kiel's head, and zipped off toward Brion in a stream of sparkling dust.

"Brion," Maralen said. Her voice was smooth and lilting. "Behind you."

Confusion clouded Brion's features, and he stopped short. He turned around, and Ashling followed his eyes across the enclosure. A single elf stood there, haughty, shimmering like a smoky ghost. Ashling recognized Gryffid, the elf who now commanded the Hemlock Pack, the one who had sworn vengeance against Rhys and the others . . . and who had led the capture of Brion and Kiel in the first place. Gryffid, who now stood three times bigger than a normal elf and was partially transparent.

It was a good glamer, Ashling thought. An illusion big enough to catch the attention of an angry giant.

"You there. Fat man," the false Gryffid said, and its voice was that of the Vendilion sisters. "Catch me if you can. I don't need you anymore anyway. Not when I can have Rosheen."

Kiel stiffened at this, and Brion bellowed so loudly the leaves blew off the trees. "I'll scrape you off the sole of my boot with a stick, little elf turd."

The absurdly large figure of Gryffid turned and sprinted off into the woods, heading west toward the Wanderwine. Brion was right behind him, crashing through the trees and hollering all the way.

"Go, Kiel, go!" Ashling lowered her head as Kiel surged forward, trampling all trees still standing in Brion's wake. Without the giants to contend with, the main force of Gilt Leaf elves poured into the enclosure, but they were too late and too small. Each of the giant's long strides was worth fifty of his pursuers'.

The ground shook as Kiel bounded along. Rhys clung tight. "If your first decoy doesn't succeed . . . ," he said. He shook his head in astonishment. "Excellent work, Maralen."

The dark-haired elf smiled proudly. "We make a good team."

"Yes. Excellent work all round." Rhys turned to Ashling and shouted, "Now if Sygg holds up his end, we're home free."

Maralen shouted back, "Only if Brigid makes it in time. Which she will, because I told Endry to make sure she did."

Ashling respected Maralen's confidence. Faeries were fickle at best, but when Maralen gave the Vendilion clique an order, they carried it out. Even now the combination of Fae magic and giant muscle was putting good distance between the elf hunters and their prey. Before long, the sounds of the rushing river were louder than the hunting cries of the elves and the baying of their cuffhounds.

Kiel crested a steep hill, and Ashling saw Brion's back thundering straight for the river. He was entirely consumed in his headlong rush, and Ashling once again credited Maralen. The elf woman had a sharp tongue, but no one could bait and lure the temperamental like a faerie.

Kiel jumped, and for a moment they were all weightless. They soared silently for a dreamy moment. Then the giant came down hard, driving his stubby legs into the soft ground. Kiel's first bounding leap closed the gap between themselves and Brion, and his second brought them within arm's length.

The braided giant's quarry had vanished, and now Brion stood momentarily flummoxed at the edge of the riverbank. He flinched when Kiel slammed into the ground beside him, but only a little.

"Where'd that elf go?" Brion said.

"In the water," Rhys shouted. "Get in the water!"

Kiel draped one long arm across his brother's shoulders and force-marched Brion into the river. The Wanderwine flowed free and strong here, and any creature less massive than a giant would have been swept away. Brion and Kiel moved steadily forward, however, wading out to the center of the river until the water was up to their thighs.

"Where's the merrow?" Maralen said. "Where's Sygg?"

Rhys swung out over Kiel's shoulder, hanging onto the giant's dangling earlobe with one hand. "There," he said, pointing.

Ashling looked. A long serpentine shape loomed just below the surface of the river. Its body undulated, and its long, flat tail thrashed. A sharp-finned head broke the surface of the water, and Captain Sygg's wide, smiling face rose from the waves.

"I've got an empty ferry that needs filling," Sygg said. He craned his eyes up and down the giant brothers, and he whistled. "My, my. I take that back. We've got a full payload today, haven't we?"

"We can't leave yet," Maralen said. "Endry and Brigid—"

"We're here! We're here! Nobody has to wait." Endry emerged from the woods on the opposite bank with Brigid in tow. "We're on time. Nobody can ever say different."

"You're here," Iliona gloated, "but you're last."

"Just like you've been last since the day we were born."

"All right," Sygg said gruffly. "Everyone get into the water. This is going to take some effort, and I need to get started."

Endry came forward and dropped Brigid onto Kiel's back. Sygg slid beneath the current, and Ashling followed the merrow captain's course as he circled the Wanderwine's newest and most temporary island.

"If there's no big, glittery elf here to stomp on," Brion said, "I'm going back for the normal kind."

"You won't have to go far," Rhys said. "They're right behind us."

Indeed, the Hemlock hunters were now streaming down the hillside toward the riverbank. Brion and Kiel's skin was thick enough to scorn arrowgrass, but Ashling and the rest were not so fortunate. If Sygg didn't conjure an escape for them, this whole endeavor might yet end in tears.

But Sygg was circling them so rapidly it seemed the current

didn't exist. As Ashling watched, the Wanderwine's course actually changed, bending around them. A wall of water swelled up behind them, rising almost to Kiel's shoulders, while in front the surging waters dwindled to a trickle.

Arrowgrass shattered on Brion's bald head. Kiel raised his arms to shelter his passengers from this lethal rain. The spinning current at last pulled the giant's feet from the riverbed, but instead of swirling with it, the giants floated calmly in the center of the strange vortex.

The riverbed before them was empty, dry but for some broad, shallow puddles and an oozing layer of mud. Brion and Kiel rocked back into the huge half shell of shapewater Sygg had created. Ashling and the others had traveled via the ferry captain's water magic before, so they knew that there was no real danger of being drowned. Nonetheless, they all scrambled up onto Kiel's broad chest to avoid the rising water, the pilgrim faster than any of them. She didn't relish even the slimmest chance of immersion. Not again.

Captain Sygg shot up from the edge of the whirlpool, rising until his entire body was clear of the waves. "Away we go!" he shouted.

The surge of water behind them broke. It drove the huge shapewater craft forward, the conveyance as wide as the river itself and moving so quickly that Ashling had to wrest each breath from the air as she rushed through it.

The Vendilion clique trilled triumphantly. Ashling turned back and saw elves pouring into the empty riverbed behind them. If Sygg's latest shapewater ferry was large enough to carry giants, it was also large enough to commandeer all of the Wanderwine's water for a time. Ashling didn't know how long it would take for the river to reestablish its full strength, but for now every last ounce was under Sygg's control. Behind them, there wasn't enough river left to float a kithling's paper boat. Even if the Hemlock hunters had the tools to continue their pursuit, they no longer had the means. If they were lucky, the hunters would remain in the empty riverbed until the waters came rushing back, drowning them all.

Ashling exhaled. Even if the remainder of the Hemlock Pack survived the rushing currents, they had done it. The giants were free. They were as safe as one could get when the most powerful tribe in the world wanted them dead.

"Say, Boss?" Brion spoke thoughtfully, and from the intense look upon his face he was not used to bending his brain in thoughtful directions. "What's next?"

Ashling waited for the reply, and she noticed the others doing the same. Even the faeries stopped cackling.

"We finish escaping," Rhys said. "After that . . ." He raised his head and leveled his eyes at Ashling. "I don't know. Believe it or not, this was the easy part." He tightened his grip on Kiel's loose, leathery skin. "Let's just get where we're going and sort out 'next' once we catch our breath."

That seemed to satisfy Brion. Ashling was not surprised to find it satisfied her too. For now, she was content to hang on, suffer through the wet wind and river spray, and enjoy the blessed absence of hooves thundering through her skull. The Wanderwine had almost killed her not long ago, but it seemed her elemental was not welcome between its banks.

CHAPTER 4

Daen Gryffid of the Hemlock Pack strode past the downcast faces of his assembled hunters. Second Officer Culloch stepped out, turned crisply on his hooves, and saluted.

"Orders, Taer?"

Gryffid marched by his lieutenant without slowing or returning the salute. His horns quivered angrily with each step. Halfway between the line of hunters standing at attention and his command tent, Gryffid called back over his shoulder, "Find Uaine and bring him to me."

"Yes, Taer! Right away, Taer!" Culloch's hooves beat a rapid tattoo across the matted grass, a spring in his step growing with each stride he took away from the angry daen.

Gryffid lowered his horns and pushed past the tent flap. The Hemlock's failure today was disgraceful, catastrophic—and entirely his responsibility. He rightly despised Rhys as an eyeblight and outlaw, but he could not ignore what he knew: that his former comrade was also a formidable opponent who could not be taken lightly. So far Gryffid had managed to get it all entirely backward, dismissive of Rhys when he ought to be vigilant, overly cautious when he ought to be bold. The eyeblight made fools of Gryffid's hunters, but only because they followed his standing orders so precisely. If spotted, Rhys was to be taken alive. Nothing else mattered.

So Gryffid had no cause to follow his first instinct, which was to decimate the pack. And besides, to order such a culling was beyond his current station. He was only the acting commander of these assembled packs, and the Blessed Nation's true warrior elite would never accept a large-scale punitive bloodletting that they didn't order themselves.

Marching hooves approached the tent flap, and Culloch said, "Taer! Second Officer Culloch and First Officer Uaine reporting."

"Wait outside." Gryffid straightened his armor and slid his sword from its sheath. He inspected the blade, nodded, and sheathed it again. He could not kill a large number of his own pack to atone for their shared failure, or even to reestablish true Blessed discipline. But he could make an example of one or two.

Gryffid swept through the tent flap and squinted in the harsh daylight glare. Culloch stood beside Uaine, supporting the taller elf with both arms. Uaine had led the pursuit of the false Rhys after the ruse was discovered. They found him beaten bloody and unconscious, with half his hunters wounded or worse. Now Uaine stood groggy, his eyes unfocused and his skin pallid. Gryffid strode over and paced around the pair, silently appraising them.

"You've been poisoned," Gryffid said to Uaine. He continued to stalk in slow circles around his subordinates. "What was it, moonglove? Hemlock? Boggart piss?"

Uaine groaned. "No, Taer. It was . . . unfamiliar. Not sharp or searing like moonglove. Not bitter like hemlock. More like . . . smothering. Succumbing to a great weight."

"Yew magic." Gryffid spat. "The outlaw's special weapon. You're lucky to be alive, Officer."

"Yes, Taer."

"And it was yew poison that incapacitated the sentries you left behind." Gryffid stepped around in front of his officers. He leaned forward, jutting his face into theirs. "Elf glamer, kithkin guile, and treefolk poison. Is this all it takes to embarrass the Hemlock of Gilt Leaf?"

"But the giants, Taer—" Culloch began.

"Speak up, Second Officer Culloch."

Culloch let Uaine sag and saluted Gryffid. "Taer, the giants were loose."

"And you didn't adjust your tactics?"

"There wasn't time. Those big buggers hadn't moved an inch in days, and suddenly one of them dropped out of the sky on us."

"I see." Gryffid drew his silver sword. "But ultimately, Second Officer, the means and the method of your disgrace do not matter. It is the disgrace itself that must be redressed."

Uaine stared at the gleaming blade through half-lidded eyes. The stricken elf shrugged off Culloch's arm, saluted, and leaned forward with his neck stretched long.

"I accept your judgment, Taer." Uaine twisted his face up and met Gryffid's eye. "If it pleases the daen, I ask that he spare my horns."

Culloch stiffened. His face darted from Gryffid's upraised sword to Uaine's exposed neck. The second officer saluted and bent at the waist alongside Uaine.

Gryffid raised his sword higher. "You will both be buried as Gilt Leaf hunters." He would honor these two in death, but first he had to kill them, to make them his example. When news of this execution spread across the packs under his command, the story would not be one of failure and punishment, but of the strength of Gryffid's resolve and the ironbound surety of his pack's discipline.

"Hold, Daen Gryffid." The voice was sharp, clear, and precise. Gryffid had not started his downswing but held the blade high as he turned his gaze on the newcomer. The elf was clearly Gilt Leaf nobility, dressed in shimmering silver fabric and broad, hardened leaf armor. He wore no weapons and carried only a livewood staff with a thick curl of live leaves at its upper end. The noble elf's head was long and angular, his crisp, squarish features arranged tightly around the center of his elegant face.

"And just why should I do that?" Gryffid asked. "Identify yourself, if you please."

"I am Taercenn Eidren, Perfect of the Gilt Leaf, here on my own authority as well as that of the Sublime Council. I have business in this region, *acting* Daen Gryffid, and I'm afraid my business takes precedence over yours." Eidren threw back his proud horns. "Lower your sword now, my friend, and come sit with me. I would speak with you privately."

There was truth in the newcomer's words. The daen could smell it. And he had heard the name, of course. There wasn't a Gilt Leaf alive who hadn't heard the name Eidren. Grudgingly Gryffid complied but asked tersely, "You are relieving me of command then?"

"Certainly not." Eidren smiled, showing his dazzling white teeth. "At least, not yet. I am here to evaluate your command, not assume it. I am not a hunter, Daen, but an artist, a livewood sculptor." The Perfect smiled. "A first for the Hemlock Pack, to be sure. I am mindful of minimizing any . . . confusion about who is in charge here. Pack discipline must be maintained. So for now, rest easy, Daen. You are still tasked with the capture of the eyeblight traitor Rhys and with administering the appropriate punishment. We of the Sublime Council are all in clear agreement on that. But you are also hereby charged with pursuing my quarry, which is of even greater importance to our Blessed Nation. Our goals overlap, yours and mine, so I have decided we shall achieve them together."

"You have decided?" Gryffid challenged.

"Please, relax, Gryffid. I am here in an advisory capacity only.

All that is required of you is to be advised."

"Taercenn." Gryffid sheathed his sword and attempted to calm himself as Eidren had bid him. Relaxation quickly proved impossible, but with effort he at least removed the scowl from his features. "I don't understand. What other quarry could be more important than the eyeblight that slew your predecessor?"

"Yes, the traitor Rhys," Eidren mused. "But tell me, does he not travel in the company of a dark-haired elf maiden from the Mornsong tribe?"

Gryffid nodded.

Eidren's smile did not change. "En route to marrying me," he said, "Peradala of the Mornsong and her entourage were slaughtered at the edge of the Gilt Leaf Wood. This maiden, Maralen, was the only survivor. I would like very much to speak with her—especially considering she was my intended's personal servant." Eidren tilted his horns toward Gryffid's nearby tent. "Now. The rest of what I have to say is for a daen's ears only. Let us retire together."

Eidren strode past the assembled Hemlock hunters and disappeared inside Gryffid's tent. The daen glanced at Culloch and Uaine, both still bent and waiting for the blow that would never come.

"Culloch," Gryffid said. "Is the river flowing yet?"

Culloch straightened. "Almost back to normal, Taer. It was a close call there. It returned more swiftly than expected, but we lost no more hunters." His eyes flicked to the newcomer, and he added rigidly, "my Daen."

"Take two squads of ten. Follow the Wanderwine's banks for ten miles or until you pick up their trail. Report back to me."

"Taer!" Once more the officer was off and running.

Gryffid turned to Uaine. "As for you . . ."

Eidren's head emerged from the tent. "I'm waiting, Daen," he said. "We have much to discuss."

The Perfect slipped back out of sight, and Gryffid clenched his teeth. "Stand down," he told Uaine. "Don't go anywhere. We are not finished."

Dreading the influence of an artist on his hunting pack, a livewood sculptor no less, Gryffid strode across the grounds and entered his tent.

* * * * *

Rhys crouched atop a half-buried boulder and shaded his eyes with his hand. He looked out over the thick forest to the east. Gryffid and the Hemlock Pack were somewhere in those woods by now, and they would move far more quickly than Rhys's party had. The Gilt Leaf hunters would also come straight to them, as there was simply no way to move two giants through the woods without leaving a trail that the Hemlock could follow. Rhys hadn't even bothered to cover their tracks until now, concentrating instead on moving the cumbersome group along as quickly as possible.

His party's progress had been disappointing. The giants' growing hunger slowed them all, distracting "the boys" and diminishing their fabled stamina. Well-fed giants could wander for weeks without interruption, but the brothers' bellies were empty. After only a few hours on the trail, both were gasping for breath through red, strained expressions. Rhys had had to order them to stop and rest twice so far, and each delay brought the Gilt Leaf hunters closer.

Things had improved when Iliona reported a small herd of hill pigs in the valley ahead. The promise of fresh meat spurred the giants on, and once Brion and Kiel smelled the distant herd for themselves their fatigue vanished entirely. The brothers' strong finish all but made up for their slow start, and now, when they would have had to stop and gather their strength anyway, they could also gorge themselves on solid food while they rested.

Rhys rotated his head so that one of his sharp ears was aimed down into the valley behind him. The brothers' pig hunt had lasted all of three seconds, which was about two seconds of panicked squealing more than Rhys cared to endure. Now the primary sounds echoing up from the grassy basin were teeth crunching against bone and lip smacking against lip.

He unfurled a broad brown leaf that bore a rough map of the countryside. Even with the giants fully fed and back to their robust selves, they could not stay ahead of the Hemlock hunters for more than a day or so. He had to act, and before he could do that he needed to know what his options and assets were. It was time to talk with Sygg.

Rhys hiked through the tall grass leading down to the river-bank. He had spent more time on the Wanderwine in the past month than in the previous ten years, and so far the river had been very good to him. His destinations were not always his to choose, and he often did not like what he found there, but what the kithkin liked to call "Big River" always carried him quickly, directly, and without complaint.

A colorful fin broke the river's surface. Rhys smiled wryly. The river never demanded answers or payment, but Captain Sygg was another matter.

The merrow's broad face rose above the Wanderwine, river water running in rivulets down his open eyes and smiling mouth. He accelerated as he approached Rhys on the banks, broadening his wake and rising waist-high above the surface.

Rhys strode out from the grass onto damp clay. "Captain Sygg. Timely as always."

"Taer." Sygg slowed as he neared the bank, sending a fat swell over the edge and across the front of Rhys's hooves. "Oops. Pardon me."

"Not at all. I was just about to gather the others and bring them here."

Sygg's smile widened so that the sharp tips of his teeth showed. "Striking out on the next leg of your journey already?"

"Yes." Rhys nodded. "Once we determine its direction, of course."

"By my recollection," the merrow said, "I signed on for a giant rescue." He rose higher on the water until he was peering over Rhys's head, then dropped back down to eye level. "I see a pair of rescued giants. My work is done." He bobbed on the water, bowing respectfully. "Unless you care to make further arrangements?"

"Perhaps I shall," Rhys said. "And if I do, I have the highest confidence I'll get my money's worth from Sygg and the Wanderwine."

The merrow beamed proudly. "What did you have in mind?"

"I'm thinking we should head upriver," Rhys said, "into the mountains."

"Giant country." Sygg rubbed his chin. "Risky."

"We'll have giants with us," Rhys said. "Blood relatives of the locals. That should ensure a friendly reception."

"Ha! So you get along with all your relatives, do you?" Sygg beamed. "Besides, my experience says giants don't like visitors. Bringing two wayward boys back home might just guarantee an all-out brawl between them and their kin. I don't relish being accidentally squashed by forty-foot lumps of angry muscle. I was right the first time: This is risky."

"But worth the risk," Rhys said. "I can't speak for Ashling or the sapling or Maralen, but I think they'd all agree with me. We need answers."

"Not me, I'm afraid." Sygg sent a wide sheet of water splashing backward and rose high above the river so that only his tail still thrashed the water. "Sorry, Daen, but I've no interest in going upriver. Especially not into giant country."

"I see. And you're sure about that?"

"Quite sure. If it's not giants, it'll be flamekin. Aside from our pilgrim friend with the hat, in my experience the flamekin carry little love for me or my kind." Sygg clenched his fist and poked his upraised thumb toward the sky. "Come on, Taer, you don't need my transport when you've got faeries and giants."

"I'm not carrying those giants." Veesa said.

"Separately or as a pair," Endry added. Both faeries descended, then chased each other away, off through the moss-covered branches.

Rhys watched them go. "I may have faeries," he said, "but I still need *reliable* transport."

Sygg shrugged and showed Rhys a sad smile. "Sorry, Taer. I have to be about my own business."

Rhys nodded. "Very well. Then our bargain is done. You've held up more than your end. Farewell, Captain. I hope we will meet again."

Sygg bowed at the waist. "Until we bargain again," he said. The merrow rose up, bent his sinuous body, and slid beneath the Wanderwine with barely a splash.

Rhys had expected the captain to depart, but that didn't mean he was happy about it. The river wouldn't have taken them all the way into giant country in any case, but it would have gotten them more than halfway there. Traveling with Sygg would have also provided Rhys with more time to ponder the long series of important decisions he would soon be forced to make.

In some ways, Rhys regretted the giants' quick and successful rescue. His current comrades were far less precise and more improvisational than he ever would have allowed in a Gilt Leaf pack under his command, and their execution of his plan left a great deal to be desired. But when the final result was success with no losses, Rhys was prepared to be flexible.

Still, he was plagued by a constant, lingering, low-grade dread. He had led or participated in a hundred strategy meetings, high-level discussions among peers with a common interest. In this company, that common interest was far from clear.

A single definite thing connected them: the actions of Rhys's mentor, Colfenor. The great yew sage had intrigued and connived to arrange them all according to his grand and maddeningly impenetrable designs. Through Gaddock Teeg—the late mayor of Kinsbaile—Colfenor had sent Ashling to find Rhys, and Brigid to abduct Ashling. The great red yew used the pilgrim to power a terrifying ritual, fanning her innate elemental flames into a sacrificial inferno that the treefolk sage then threw himself upon. As he burned, Colfenor spoke of a profound change, a catastrophic upheaval that soon would shake Lorwyn to its roots.

Rhys and the others had heard Colfenor's last words, but they could not understand them. Mere players in the sage's elaborate game, they had no real understanding of its purpose, would never have it until they pooled what they knew and acted in concert to learn more. The various party members all had essential pieces to the puzzle, but only one of them could assemble the pieces into a coherent whole.

Just as Rhys's thoughts turned once more to the sapling, she appeared among the trees in front of him. As always, Lorwyn's newest yew seemed rooted where she stood as if she had always been there, yet not two seconds ago the space she occupied had been empty.

The sapling did not so much resemble Colfenor as evoke what the old log might have been as a newborn female. The resemblance was only slight, but it was enough to unsettle Ashling and unnerve Rhys. The nameless treefolk was well over nine feet tall, her bark ruddy and fresh. Her trunk was lean, no wider than an elf, and crowned by a simple array of four main boughs. Two long, branchlike arms hung from half-way up her trunk. Her wide facial features stretched between her arms, sharp ridges of bark carving out brows and cheeks around a bent, protruding nose. Her huge, asymmetrical eyes were a rich, reddish gold that filled each socket to the brim, her irises ragged circles of green and black.

The sapling had no name—or rather, she had not yet told them her name. Trees usually had years, even decades to decide on a name before becoming fully mobile and self-aware treefolk, but thanks to Colfenor, the sapling had become sentient from the beginning. Since a treefolk's life cycle was long, slow, and deliberate, and since the sapling was only a few weeks into hers, it would be months or even years before she determined her own name. And possibly longer before she saw fit to articulate it. So for now, she was just "the sapling."

Her expression was open and calm. Rhys heard roots probing into wet soil, but the sapling was motionless except for a slight breeze through her needles.

"I was just about to come looking for you," Rhys said. The sapling creaked slightly in the breeze. Her features shifted with the sound of squeaking bark, and she pursed her wide, crooked lips.

"Thank you, brother." Her voice was light but strong. "We have much to talk about." Rhys stared as the sapling twisted at the center and turned her tall face toward the sun. "The words will come to me soon."

"But not yet."

The sapling turned back to Rhys and twisted her face from side to side. "Soon though. I know it will be soon."

Rhys's jaw tightened. "Very well."

"With your permission, brother, I will excuse myself." The sapling rustled off, sliding through the soil and vanishing into the trees behind Rhys. He resisted the urge to whirl about to catch her in motion. No matter how fast he turned, he knew he would only see her standing still and placid in one spot as if she had grown there.

The sapling's inability to tell him what he needed to know was maddening, but he could not fault her for it. Through Colfenor, she was the inheritor of every last scrap of yew knowledge and lore from the very beginning of history. He couldn't expect her to produce the specific details of her sire's last, great act when she couldn't even tell him her name.

She was also still connecting to the soil of Lorwyn, taking her first steps outside the Murmuring Bosk where she was planted. Each step she took introduced her to new ground, new sensations, and new sources of nourishment that came in strange, exotic flavors. Until she learned the language of Lorwyn itself, the sapling simply could not articulate the answers to the questions they had—assuming she even had those answers. Until then, they would have to trust and confide in each other in order to wrestle with their shared mysteries.

On that score Rhys was not hopeful. Maralen, Brigid, and Ashling were all steeped in secrets: the kithkin's unpredictable loyalties and dedication, the strange elf woman's origins and relationship to the Vendilion clique, the traumatized pilgrim's dour mood and as-yet-mystifying role in Colfenor's ritual. Rhys had come to rely on each of his new companions to varying degrees, and they had each satisfied and disappointed him in turn. He knew all three had come to rely on him also, and he imagined he had likewise satisfied and disappointed them.

Rhys tossed his head, frowning at the uneven shadow of his broken horns on the ground before him. He also had his secrets, though at least his greatest and most humbling was now openly displayed. If for no other reason, Rhys would continue to travel with this group because none of them had ever expressed reservations about his disfigurement and complete lack of status.

If they could bear the presence of an eyeblight, even follow him as their leader, he could certainly endure their quirks and foibles, no matter how troubling.

He brushed his thoughts aside when he heard voices approaching. They were not raised voices, but to his keen ears they rang like bells.

"How can that possibly be my fault?" Brigid was saying. "I'm not the one who cast a glamer that was about as robust as a soap bubble."

"No," Maralen replied, "you're just the one who raked up the soil while the crop was still maturing."

"Enough with the gardening talk," Brigid said. "What does that even mean?"

The two emerged from the woods side by side, facing each other as they walked. The Vendilion clique hovered over Maralen and Brigid.

"What do I mean," Maralen mused. They had not yet noticed Rhys in their path. "Let's see, how can I make this clear enough for a kithkin to understand?" She raised a finger and gasped as if struck by a great revelation. "I know. Iliona? Veesa? Endry? How does that song go?"

The Vendilion faeries spread out and began to hum. Combined, their voices were almost painfully sweet and ethereal, one mellifluous sound rising until it filled the air. Their shared note peaked, and as its last echo died a new song began, a jaunty tune delivered in flawless three-part harmony.

"Da-da-da, da-da-da, da-da-da, da-dale,

"Da-da-da, da-da-da, Hero of Kinsbaile."

"Yes, yes, splendid." Maralen smiled through closed lips and narrow eyes. "That's the one. A facile, childish melody buried in gibberish."

"So what?" Brigid shrugged her broad shoulders. "You don't like lively songs?"

Maralen's face grew colder, though her smile did not change.

"I don't like songs that undermine my magic. Not when we've got important work to do."

Brigid turned and made a point of noticing Rhys. "Oh, good. A reasonable person." The archer faced Maralen and said, "All this sounds like a problem with your preparations, not my performance." Brigid turned back to Rhys, her hand absently plucking the bow on her shoulder, and she said, "You're not with her, are you? You think I got the job done, don't you?"

Rhys crouched down on one knee so as not to be looking down on Brigid. "You got the job done, kithkin. Though I would have preferred if you'd lasted a bit longer, one has to admire a decoy who survives the hunt."

The Vendilion clique giggled. Brigid scowled.

"Great," she said. "Just great. Here I am, trying to do right by you ingrates and all I get is grief. This one," she pointed at Maralen, "questions my competence, you damn me with faint praise, and Ashling won't even speak to me."

"Ashling barely speaks at all anymore," Maralen said. "She's been sulking over the giants since we got here. I don't think she's said more than three words to any of us."

"But she avoids me."

The elf maiden smiled sweetly. "She avoids the sapling too. I can't imagine why she'd single you two out for special treatment— Oh wait. Yes I can. Between the two of you she was almost turned to a cold cinder."

Brigid fumed. "Why don't you all come right out and say it? You're still mad at me."

"If that were true," Rhys said, "you wouldn't be here at all. I'd have left you facedown in the mud by the docks of Kinsbaile with my dagger in your neck."

"Thank you!" Brigid said. "At last, some honesty."

He ignored the sarcastic kithkin and turned to Maralen. "How goes the giant feast?"

"Mercifully, they're almost done." Maralen shook her head and shuddered. "That is, they're almost out of pigs. I thought an all-out giant gorging would be something to see. Now I'm afraid I'll never see anything else." She tilted her head back and closed her eyes. "Yes, there it is again," she said. Maralen opened her eyes and smiled. "The stuff of nightmares."

"So they don't require supervision?"

"Ashling was with them," Maralen said. "And they won't be hard to handle. Brion was already falling asleep when I left them, and Kiel was starting to nod."

Rhys nodded. "Sygg is gone," he said.

"Gone? Where?" Maralen frowned. "He just left us here?"

"I gave him leave to go."

Brigid's expression only grew more troubled. "I didn't even get to say good-bye or anything. I owe him a— Well, let's just say I had hoped to make amends to him especially."

"I'm sure we'll see him again," Rhys said. "He's too useful. Sooner or later we'll need his help. I believe we can count on him when that time comes, so long as we can contact him and cover his expenses. None of us are exactly made of gold thread at the moment."

Maralen shrugged. "I guess we'll just have to muddle through on our own in the meantime." She smiled at Rhys. "Say, what is our next move, anyway?"

Rhys glanced to the east and said, "I've something to take care of in the woods first."

"Why do you feel the need to announce it?" Veesa asked with an arched eyebrow.

"Not *that*," Rhys said, stone-faced. "Now listen. You all should get ready to move while I'm gone. We can't stay here."

"How long will you be?"

"Not long, I hope. And I'll find you if I have to."

"All right then. You do whatever it is you have to do, and we'll break camp." Maralen bowed. She started toward the river with the Vendilion clique hovering over her head. Her long-legged stride quickly closed the gap between her and Brigid, and the two resumed arguing once more.

"Childish melody?" Brigid muttered. "Gibberish? You Mornsong snobs wouldn't know a good sing-along if it ran up and bit you on the rump."

Maralen coughed lightly, and the trio hummed "The Hero of Kinsbaile."

"See? That's exactly what I mean. That's a real song you're humming there, you wretched little gadflies." Brigid's voice grew faint as she and Maralen disappeared over a rise. "I'd teach you the words if I thought you were smart enough to remember them. But right now, I really need to get away from you chattering things and restore my sanity."

The faeries mocked and hooted. Brigid's footsteps separated from Maralen's and moved off toward the river alone. Rhys was glad to hear them all go, and not just because they took their bickering jibes with them.

He turned his face to the east and inhaled deeply through his nose. He couldn't actually smell anything out of the ordinary, but something was out there. Whatever it was, it was making Rhys anxious.

Rhys stared over the forest behind them. He reached down and scooped up two fingers' worth of mud and smeared a dark stripe down one side of his face.

Before he and his party took the next step on their journey, Rhys had to make sure they wouldn't be pounced upon the moment they took it.

* * * * *

Ashling sat between the sleeping giants with her arms straight and her palms on her knees. Nestled in the base of their shallow valley, Brion snored to her right while Kiel muttered and belched on her left. She had only met a few giants during her pilgrim's journey, and every last one had been aloof, distant, or downright unfriendly. She never expected to be inspired by them.

The flamekin pilgrim closed her eyes and took a deep breath. She marshaled her thoughts and focused on her inner fire. With careful, precise exertion, Ashling shifted her almost-transparent yellow flames to gleaming, solid white. She had not progressed far enough on the Path of Flame to conjure white flames as potent as these, not now and not earlier when she helped free the giants from the nettlevines. She should not be able to sustain them at this intensity or with such ease.

In fact, she should not have been able to change the color of her flames at all until after she completed a large-scale communal ritual with her flamekin peers. By rite and tradition, a pilgrim's progress on the Path was not recognized until it had been shared with and confirmed by the rest of the tribe. Yet here she sat, her undeniably white fire casting diffuse shadows against the brothers' sleeping bodies and glinting against Kiel's chin whiskers and Brion's bald pate.

Now Ashling pushed these distracting thoughts aside and allowed the soothing balm of her inner fire to comfort her. Underneath the confusion, pain, and trauma Ashling carried, she felt once more the familiar thrill of anticipating where her path would go from here. It felt comforting to remember she was, after all, just a pilgrim.

Rhys intended to make for giant country to find Rosheen Meanderer, older sister to Brion and Kiel. The giantess was said to be gifted with strong oracular abilities and a wealth of hidden knowledge—if any one creature in Lorwyn could help them discover the truth behind Colfenor's actions in

Kinsbaile, it was Rosheen. Until now, Ashling had been torn: Brion and Kiel would certainly agree to go with Rhys, so if she went as well she could explore the strange bond that seemed to have formed between her and the brothers. She didn't relish spending more time with Colfenor's cursed sapling, however, or enduring the new treefolk's vacant, half-inquiring stare. If only there was some way to make the journey to Rosheen with Rhys and the giants but without the sapling.

Ashling was so intent on her own thoughts and the transformed color and texture of her magic that she almost didn't notice the sound of galloping hooves. They started off low and distant but quickly grew louder, stronger, and faster.

For the first time, the sound did not paralyze Ashling with crippling dread. Her white flames and the ghostly glow they produced fortified her, protected her, calmed her, and gave her courage. The pilgrim opened her eyes and stood. Brion and Kiel continued to sleep in the bright white glow emanating from the flamekin's body, unaware of its brilliance or the increasingly thunderous sound of hoof beats.

"Come on then," Ashling said, and her words sounded so defiant and strong that they emboldened her further. "If you want this fire back you're going to have to take it." Cold white flames flared from her shoulders, elbows, wrists, and knees. She felt her magic flowing from her, seeping into the soil below her feet, spreading outward. She pulled the power back into herself and held it behind clenched jaws and sealed lips. The approaching thunder shook the ground. Ashling's vision went white as the valley and the sleeping giants all disappeared behind a rising veil of fire.

Ashling smelled the horse as clearly as she heard it, rich, smoky, and sweet. She closed her eyes and saw fractured glimpses of the great spirit: a flash of fiery orange mane, black hooves striking sparks from sharp red rock, blurs of muscle and bone wrapped in gleaming white. She felt the fear again, the terror that she and the spirit both felt. Perhaps they inspired it in each other. Perhaps they were feeling the same fear.

But she did not falter, and for her part she overcame the fear by balancing it with righteous indignation at Colfenor, for what he'd done to her, and the elemental, for allowing it. Suffused and surrounded by profound white fire, Ashling saw for the first time that the appearance of the elemental spirit did not mark the end of her pilgrim's journey, but the beginning of its final and most profound phase. The next steps she'd take would be the most difficult and dangerous by far, and now she knew it was never intended for her to take them alone.

From this point on she would have no companions, no partners, no mentors—but she would have a steed.

Ashling threw back her head and laughed. She was a flame-kin, a pilgrim and a walker of the Path of Flame. No longer would she run from her future, nor simply stand and wait for it to find her while she wrung her hands and cowered. She would not be driven before the great horse spirit, nor borne along behind in its wake. Ashling was a pilgrim, and she would defiantly rush forward to greet what awaited her on the path ahead. This was her journey and she was its principal, the one who chose its course and set its pace. Her path stood before her, as it always had. Together, she and her elemental would ride from here to her journey's end.

The fiery white horse reared up before her, towering over the tallest trees. It snorted black smoke from its nostrils and slashed the air with its front hooves.

Ashling sprang toward the spirit, rushing up to embrace it. Thunder rumbled and flames roared, but even these sounds were dwarfed by Ashling's mad, ecstatic howl. The strange chase was on.

The white flames on the valley floor went out, leaving a circle of soot and black ash to smoke and smolder between two oblivious, still-sleeping giants.

Brigid Baeli intended to speak with Ashling to lay the ground-work for her atonement, so she hiked down into the valley where Brion and Kiel were sleeping. Ashling was there, sitting between the giant brothers, and though Brigid raised a hand and readied a jolly shout, the greeting died on her lips.

The flamekin had not yet seen Brigid. She was clearly distracted, waving at a fluttering insect Brigid could not see. The kithkin archer assumed one of the faeries had settled in for a little verbal sparring. This quickly proved not to be the case, for even at this distance Brigid would have been able to make out the sparkling wings of the diminutive creatures. No, it was more like Ashling was batting at an errant thought or irritating sound.

The waving stopped, and the pilgrim dropped to one knee in a sprinter's crouch. Ashling slapped her hand against one side of her stony forehead in pain, but it was pain she resisted. Her eyes flared white-hot.

The pain finally snapped Brigid out of her shock, and she ran toward Ashling. Nothing was more important to a kithkin than the community, and currently this little group was all the community she had.

Besides, what sort of hero doesn't dash to the side of an ally in need?

She'd covered perhaps thirty yards before Ashling vaulted from her crouch and broke into a dead run straight toward Brigid. It was close to the last thing Brigid expected, and it threw her off stride. She tripped on a root, fell to her knees, and threw her arms over her head to prevent Ashling from trampling her.

Brigid's eyes widened between her own forearms as a huge gout of fire consumed the pilgrim in midleap. One moment Ashling was bounding forward, the next she was suspended in midair, then she was gone in a blazing flash of gold and white. Then nothing.

Nothing, that is, but a fierce wave of heat that physically pushed Brigid backward. The backs of her hands blistered, and she smelled her long hair burning. Above and beyond the lingering roar in her ears, Brigid heard the beating of hooves. Was it her imagination? And if not . . . whose hooves were they, and where were they headed?

"Nowhere," Brigid said. "That's where." She carefully peeked out from behind her raised arms. Ashling was gone, and all that was left behind was a smoking hole in the grass. The giants hadn't even flinched.

Pushing herself to her feet, Brigid reconsidered which of the paths before her would be the wisest to take. She had been raised in Kinsbaile on the banks of the Wanderwine, and talk of travel naturally turned her thoughts to the Big River. "I suppose if I can't make peace with the one I killed," she muttered, "I can with the one I shot. I did shoot him a lot."

"Moving on, eh? Good idea."

Brigid whirled on the sound of the faerie Endry hovering just out of reach overhead. "Get out of my hair, faerie."

"You know, you never offered to apologize to us," Endry said. "A lot of good faeries— All right, they were kind of stupid, and no one really liked them, and it's not like there aren't plenty more dumb faeries who aren't Vendilion where those came from. . . ."

Endry shook his head. "Let me start over. You know, a lot of mediocre faeries burned up because of you."

"Really?"

"Yes," Endry said indignantly. "Not that you care."

"Well," Brigid said, "I suppose I'm sorry."

"You don't really mean that," he said. "I can tell."

"I'm doing the best I can," Brigid replied.

"Apology not accepted," Endry said. "Why don't you go practice on someone your own size and come back when you can bring yourself to apologize properly."

"I'm already going," the archer said, "but not because you want me to."

"That's what they all say," the faerie replied.

"I mean it," Brigid said, batting a hand at him as she set off down the path.

"They say that too," Endry said. "Now get going, will you? I'm a busy faerie, and getting rid of you is just one of many, many things I've got to do."

"What's that supposed to mean?" Brigid asked. "No, never mind. I don't want to know. If you see Rhys, or Maralen I suppose, let them know I haven't betrayed any of their secrets. I just need to find someone, somewhere, who will let me be the Hero of— Are you listening?"

The faerie had already buzzed away.

"Don't know why I even bothered," she muttered to herself. But it wasn't long before her steady footsteps made her start humming a familiar, jaunty tune. The Hero of Kinsbaile was on the road again.

* * * * *

It had been far too long since Sygg had traveled alone up the Wanderwine, unfettered by fragile landwalkers and the responsibilities of a ferryman. He rode with abandon upon the imposing currents two-legged creatures rightly feared, expertly playing the interwoven tracks of moving water against each other for speed his richest customers could never afford and would never see.

Sygg spun lazily to the surface with a bubbling cackle. He surveyed the bright sky with its blue, pinks, greens, and golds. He was in a bit of a hurry, but he allowed his tail to push him lazily against the current as he took a moment to rest and enjoy the view. Merrows did not sleep like landwalkers, but they did rest for extended periods in a state that could approach a conscious trance. Accomplished swimmers could do this with little effort and without losing touch with the waking world, and Sygg was among the most accomplished swimmers the merrows had ever seen.

This rest was more conscious than most. He was nearing a special place that he'd been heading toward in his roundabout way since departing from the others. He pushed himself faster and faster against the current and felt a tiny bow wave break against his head crest. If he was going to do it, the time was now. But was he going to do it?

Yes, he was. He'd hoped this day would never come, but now it was here. When he had warned his friends from the Paperfin school—as much as members of that haughty enclave could be friendly—he had told them all they needed to be prepared for anything. For his own sake as well as theirs, he hoped the merrows from his crannog had taken him seriously.

Sygg held his tail rigid against a stable current and dropped to the riverbed, sinking like a log head-down, maintaining his position easily with ventral and dorsal fins that waved like faerie wings. He had to be cautious not to stir up too much of the muck before he could pinpoint the exact spot he needed to find. When he did find it amid the mud and cloudy silt, he paused for the merrow equivalent of a deep breath, and he started to dig.

The ferryman burrowed deep into the brackish mud at the bottom of the Wanderwine, tearing away at half-rotted plants and scattering the collected silt of the rainy season swells into the clear running water. A cloud of muddy brown enveloped the merrow ferryman's body.

Just when Sygg was starting to think he'd gotten the surface and subsurface landmarks wrong after all, the ferryman struck gold. Well, gold plating on bronze, but one would never have been able to tell without close inspection, and never when confronted with the slime and muck at the bottom of the greatest of all the Lanes. As the faeries had their Great Mother Oona and the boggarts their Aunties, a grand cultural parent of sorts ruled the merrows.

The Father-Lane was what the river's inhabitants had called it long ago, before they ever encountered kithkin or elves, and they still used the name among themselves today. "The Father-Lane provides." "The Father-Lane sends strong currents to lift his children." "The Father-Lane protects our secrets as we protect his." That last saying was a popular one and was used to justify a great many things.

Merrows were not gestated and birthed like landwalker children, and merrow parents would look after their new brood as closely and carefully as an average landwalker couple, but every merrow knew their true father, mother, and creator was the river.

Without too much effort, Sygg took hold of the golden handles atop the kithkin-sized chest and heaved, kicking up a new cyclone of muck with his powerful tail. After a few seconds of thrashing that cleared away more mud he pulled it free.

"Thank you, Father-Lane," Sygg murmured and flexed his gills to draw breath from the deep, cold water. He swam up to the river's edge and rested the chest upon a large, flat rock. The sturdy wooden box had not seen the light of day for a very long time. He rocked back on his tail and reached down to flip the latch. Had he been a moment faster, he would not have felt the sound of a footstep in the water—the sound of the latch would have obscured it.

Someone was following him. An unfamiliar landwalker, but one fully aware that merrow made up for their relatively poor surface-level hearing with sensitivity to even the slightest vibration in the water, up to a mile away. Sygg had "heard" the splash of a foot—a small foot, and only once. Whoever or whatever it was had realized the error and frozen in place.

An elf? Without looking he could not be certain. That there was only one was a blessing, though it was entirely possible an entire pack was moving swiftly through the forest canopy that grew right up to the river's edge.

The merrow captain did not panic—that was fishy behavior. Merrow were not fish, and those who behaved as if they were little more than river trout did not deserve to be called merrow in the first place.

The merrow considered the chest, still latched. He had to open it soon and had thought this the perfect time, but this stealthy pursuer gave him pause. The cloud of silt was already dispersing into the currents, and Sygg would be visible to any landwalker who made the effort to look. He quickly flipped open the chest and removed a small, unassuming piece of flat, carved bone and tucked it into a pouch on his waist. Then Sygg buried his chest once more—a bit haphazardly, but the object he had already taken was the most important thing within it. If he lost the chest now, it wouldn't really matter.

Another splash. Well, well, he'd been just in time. The stalker had grown impatient, or uncertain.

The chest safely concealed, the merrow swam a few dozen yards downstream and broke the surface with a wriggling silverfin clutched in his razor-sharp teeth. He caught a slight movement maybe a hundred yards upstream, as if a landwalker had shifted balance in surprise. Not much surprise, from the feel of it. Without turning in the direction of his stalker, he lustily tore out the savory contents of the fish. He consumed the entire thing, bones and all, in a matter of seconds. Only a few inevitable scraps floated down the river, but they would be enough.

Sygg launched into a jolly river song as he set off down the Wanderwine, a tune as old as the merrows themselves but one that every singer worth the name had personalized when they were but a wee fry. Sygg swam, dipping his face into the water now and again as if he hadn't a care in the world.

The landwalker followed. Sygg's pursuer was clever, moving with an uneven and unpredictable pace that proved he knew full well how much the ferryman could hear.

What the landwalker couldn't know, and couldn't feel or hear, was the sound of hundreds of powerful, tiny fins driving hard and fast against the current. Sygg continued to swim directly for the sound while edging gradually toward the southwest riverbank. When he was completely surrounded by the silverfin shoals, he stopped moving his own fins and let himself sink lazily beneath the surface. The song continued to bubble to the surface for a few seconds before the currents carried it away.

* * * * *

Brigid nearly roared a boggart curse when Sygg disappeared into the Wanderwine, taking his cheerful, footstep-concealing song with him. He appeared to be feeding, or, from the silty cloud that enveloped the merrow captain, perhaps wrestling an arbomander. The kithkin archer had still not decided on the best way to approach the merrow, and so for now she simply stayed close. The moment would present itself. The Hero of Kinsbaile would hail her ally, and her ally would see the hero was not a traitor after all but the victim of sorcery and betrayal. Someone who might be worthy of . . . well, if not worthy of forgiveness then simply worthy. If true heroics like those she'd displayed helping Rhys rescue the giants didn't change everyone's opinion, she'd change their opinions one at a time, starting with those she'd aggrieved most. Ashling had perhaps suffered worst as a result of Brigid's arrogance and weakness, but Ashling was out of reach. Brigid had also punctured Sygg quite a bit, so the merrow ferry captain became her new priority. It was only what a proper hero would do, the archer told herself.

Unfortunately, the aggrieved in question wasn't going along with her admittedly slapdash plan. After several minutes, Sygg had still not surfaced, so Brigid risked leaving the water to tread quickly along the bank. She kept to the reedy shallows, stepping carefully from stone to stone so as not to blunder face-first into the muck, until she reached the spot where the merrow had disappeared.

In for a thread, in for a spool, Brigid said to herself. She slowly took her first step from solid ground to the almost nonexistent current among the cattails. The water here came up to her knee but slowly rose another few inches as her boot settled into the mud. Sygg had been down for a long time. Perhaps he was gone. She hoped not.

An almost-comical sucking sound accompanied another hard-won step away from the riverbank that brought the water over Brigid's waist. She hummed a few bars of "The Hero of Kinsbaile" but couldn't get her heart into it. The water was cold, and she was beginning to wonder if she'd given herself a fool's errand.

Brigid's next step didn't happen exactly as the kithkin intended. Oh, her foot lifted, her knee bent and rose, and her body's unconscious sense of balance readied to shift her weight to the moving limb. The problem was, only the foot was moving:

Her boot remained firmly ensconced in the muck. Brigid barely had a moment to grab half a breath before the current pulled her free of the other boot and away from the shore.

When Brigid was but a kithling, the youngest of seven children known collectively (and only semiaccurately) as the "Baeli Bastards," she'd been fond of proclaiming the many great feats she planned on accomplishing in adulthood. One of the boldest such proclamations had been her announcement that she, Brigid Baeli, would one day be known as the Hero of Kinsbaile. Another, and one that had won her the derision not just of her six siblings and most of the other kithlings her age, was that she, Brigid Baeli, would become the first Kinsbaile kithkin in the entire known history of Lorwyn to learn how to swim.

As that last half gasp slipped from Brigid's lungs into the swiftly accelerating current, she wished, and not for the first time in the last few weeks, that she'd gotten around to actually accomplishing the second boast.

* * * * *

The sapling found the hardest part of interacting with the creatures of flesh, fire, and bone was remembering the names. The newborn yew did not even have one, would not feel the need for one for some time. She did not, could not, answer to "Colfenor." Colfenor was a different tree entirely. The gender-specific pronoun she found herself stuck with was a result of the others' assumptions, not realizing that neither she nor her predecessor Colfenor was male or female, as they understood it. Yet "she" seemed to make the flesh-folk more comfortable than the rather more appropriate "it."

The sapling knew Lorwyn like the back of a leaf, from the Gilt Leaf Wood to Mount Tanufel to both ends of the Wanderwine. She could tell anyone who asked (not that anyone did) the exact birth order of each of the Vendilion faeries. That Iliona budded first was obvious to any observer that knew anything at all about the Fae, but the sapling knew that Veesa was older than Endry. Males were rare and always the last to detach from the Great Mother. She could describe the bitter heat of the flamekin highlands, the stones that withered the roots and made a tree despair. The sapling could name the last twelve mayors of Kinsbaile in order of succession, age, hair color, or a thousand other variables. The sapling could see what caused Rhys to trigger the death wave that had annihilated his comrades and shattered his own horns. She knew what Captain Sygg kept concealed in a golden chest beneath the muck and murk of Lorwyn's great river.

The sapling also knew what was coming, understood why and how, though she doubted she could ever put it into terms an elf or a kithkin might understand.

But all of that knowledge derived from Colfenor's experiences and were suffused with the old yew's perceptions and prejudices. The sapling had never seen these places herself, never felt the magic in their soil or the touch of their sky. She had never met Rhys until now, yet she knew the elf so very well. She had been created in Kinsbaile, yet the world she knew stretched back into time hundreds of years.

Colfenor's legacy to her was knowledge, perhaps even wisdom. What Colfenor had not given her was an identity, a sense of place in the world. And knowing Colfenor as she did—she'd already begun to think of the old yew as a separate entity living within her—the sapling believed that was part of Colfenor's design.

"Hello, Saprolingaling," a faerie said, fluttering into the sapling's branches. It was Endry, to her surprise, and alone at that.

"You may call me 'Sapling,' " the sapling replied. "Or 'the sapling.' Please don't address me as—"

"Colfenor, I know, I know," Endry buzzed. "Or Colfenette, or Colfenora. You mentioned it. And I didn't. I called you—Never mind." The faerie took a perch on a branch brow and added, "Was just saying 'Hello.' No need to bite a faerie's head off."

"I assure you I have no intention of biting anything at all off of you," the sapling said. "The rays of the sun and the embrace of the elements—sun, soil, water, winds—that is what sustains me, tiny creature. Feeding upon your kind would be both pointless and, frankly, impossible. I suppose I could chew you up, after a fashion."

"Now that I'm talking to you," Endry said with a sly grin, "I can't imagine why the others are so opposed to the notion."

"I have spoken with Rhys," the sapling said. "My purpose is tied to him. I do not require the kinship of any others." The sapling's visage darkened. "Yet he does not seem to care. He has not even asked after Colfenor's instructions. He knows not what must be done. My birth was only the beginning."

"Is that so?" Endry asked, his grin sliding into a frown of feigned concern. "They don't trust you, you know. Especially the matchstick. And now that she's gone, they're looking at you with suspicion."

"A flamekin follows her path," the sapling replied, somewhat surprised the faerie didn't seem to realize what was so obvious. Had Endry not heard the thunder of hooves, the beating of otherworldly wings as she had? What else could explain what had happened?

She continued. "The kithkin has slipped away as well. Probably in pursuit, I would think. It is peculiar, what is unseen by others. The kithkin is doing what Rhys and I should be doing. Our path is the same as hers. They will converge. They must. It is all happening too soon, too soon."

"See? Now that is interesting, and we should talk about that. When you don't share little tidbits of important information, it makes people distrust you. Even your favorite elf."

"You mean Rhys," the sapling said.

"Yes," Endry sighed with real exasperation. "Rhys. Was Colfenor this dense? No, he couldn't have been. No one is this dense." He hovered in front of the sapling's wide, crooked features. "I'm saying Rhys is just as suspicious of you as the rest of them. He's off following his own path. If you want him to follow yours, you're going to need to take a more active hand in things . . . or a more active branch, or however you'd say it. "

"But I am the vessel of Colfenor's knowledge," the sapling said. "I need Colfenor's most able student to properly employ it. The flamekin, the elemental, these were means to an end. The knowledge must not be lost. The work is not finished."

"And I'm telling you," Endry said, "he isn't interested in that. He's gone. He's playing with his giant friends. Now tell me, what seedguide plays with giants, yewling? The mortal enemies of your kind?"

"He will return to me," the sapling said. "Together we will see Colfenor's great purpose achieved. No matter what you believe, that is what he is destined to do. This I know. I cannot leave his side."

"Suit yourself," the faerie said with a faerie shrug, "though I wouldn't say you're at his side now."

"He will return," the sapling replied confidently. "There is much for us to speak of. Much for us to do. I've told him this. We must find Ashling."

"He doesn't seem to think there's much at all for you to do, and I wouldn't be so sure you'll find the flamekin. Vanished in a flash, as I saw. No, if Rhys meant for the two of you to fulfill some spectacular destiny, wouldn't he have invited you along on whatever mysterious elf errand he's running?"

No, that was not right, the sapling told herself. There was only one priority, and it was Colfenor's plan. There could be no delay or her seedfather's dream would never come to fruition. Days, months, seasons, centuries would pass, and, over time, the sapling's inheritance would slip away.

"Too soon."

"You said that already," the faerie said. "What's too soon?"

"Everything," the sapling said. "If not, there would be no need for beings like myself . . . or Rhys . . . or her."

"You could do something about it," Endry whispered from the sapling's branches. "You could find the flamekin and maybe the kithkin too. You've got all that history in your trunk, don't you? You know where the flamekin's gone. You know what took her there. Who is in control of your destiny, yewling? A dead tree, burned away to ashes?"

"Yes," the sapling said quietly. "He is." The yew gazed back at what remained of their little band and saw only a quiet elf maiden, a guttering campfire, and a lingering sense that her intended purpose was no longer so clear.

"Rhys might not come back until too late," the faerie replied, "and the flamekin will be forever lost. And then what of that destiny?" Endry fluttered back down to hover before the yew's face. "And just because I can see you need me, I'll go with you. My sisters have everything here well in hand, and you could use some help. You can see I'm the only friend you've got here, right?"

"How do you know these things?" the sapling said, feeling raw suspicion for the first time in her short life. "You are little more than an insect. Your kind does not live long enough to accumulate such wisdom."

Endry laughed quietly. "I know these things because she knows these things, and if you don't understand that, well, I think that's something else you'll need to learn. Just trust me—the only way you're going to get what you want is if you bring that flamekin back to Rhys. He's not going to follow anyone's orders, least of all yours. You have to make it happen. Trust me."

"Trust you," the sapling said. The faerie . . . the faerie was right. It felt good to reach that conclusion, any conclusion, even if it conflicted with the knowledge that was Colfenor's gift.

"Are you coming or aren't you?" Endry said, disengaging from the yew and setting off in a direction that, the sapling knew, led directly to the pilgrim's only possible destination.

And Rhys was still gone. Ultimately, that was what made the decision for her. That, and Endry's assertion that she had to take an active hand in fulfilling her own purpose. It may have been simple goading, but it had at its heart an essential truth—Rhys had, since her birth, almost completely ignored the sapling's presence in every way.

The sapling slipped away from the small campfire and followed the faerie down the narrow, overgrown path without another word. It was, she decided, what Colfenor would have done.

* * * * *

Brigid was more surprised than relieved when the current released her. She'd been perhaps half a minute from completely shutting down, having already hacked up two lungs' worth of brackish river water. Now she gulped cold, clammy air, and though it was thin and damp, it was air.

As her blurry vision returned, the kithkin archer saw she hadn't been released by the river's currents so much as removed from them. Brigid sat heavily on the floor of the shapewater bubble and threw a weak but defiant wave to Captain Sygg hovering in midstream on the other side of her new—and, she hoped, temporary—prison.

The merrow did not wave back but swam steadily forward

and poked his upper half through the shapewater wall opposite Brigid.

"Why do you follow me, kithkin?" the ferryman demanded with an angry flap of his gills. Brigid's eyes moved to the merrow's sharp-clawed fingers and reckoned she would never get her blade clear of its sheath in time if Sygg wished to tear out her throat. Not that the kithkin intended to give him any reason to do so.

"I wronged you," she began.

"You're damned right you wronged me," the captain said. "You wronged all of us, and the others forgave you. I went along with their plan provided I didn't have to deal with you any further. You knew this. Therefore I must assume you're hunting me. The others might believe you were under the influence of thoughtweft—personally, I don't think they're that stupid, I think they're allowing you to help because they frankly need your help, even if you can't be trusted."

"I can be trusted," Brigid protested. "And the others told me—"

"What they needed to in order to gain your help. You think any one of them expected you to survive, riding out there as a decoy?" The merrow showed teeth. "They expected you to die. And as far as I'm concerned, you should have."

"So why pull me out of the river? Why not just let me drown?" Brigid said. She was suddenly weary, tired of Sygg's refusal to listen to her apology, tired of her guilt and the distrust she saw in their eyes.

"I didn't want you to die without hearing me tell you to go fletch yourself, archer," Sygg replied. "And now, if you'll excuse me, I am going home. I'm going to try to ready my people for blood, because in all my years I haven't seen so many landwalkers so ready to slaughter each other, and it's only a matter of time before they turn their eyes to the crannogs. You won't stop me."

"Stop you?" the kithkin said. "I want to help you! I know what I did, Sygg, I know you don't trust me. I want to earn that trust back, starting with you, the one I wronged most of all."

"You want to apologize to someone, find the pilgrim and apologize to her."

"She's gone. Disappeared in a flash. I can't atone to her. But if you can forgive me anyone can."

"I don't forgive you."

"But that doesn't keep me from trying to earn your forgiveness." Brigid found herself having to crouch a little within the confines of the bubble. It helped clear her head, or perhaps that was the righteous pride creeping back. For the once and future Hero of Kinsbaile, pride was never too far beneath the surface.

"Captain Sygg, perhaps you'll never forgive me, but I cannot live with what I did. I was influenced, and manipulated, but yes, I did it. And if you won't forgive me, I'll balance the scales despite you. I'll get you to your home safe, and I'll help you protect your people. What can you do against dangers from above the waters? You can barely stand to be on solid ground for more than a few minutes. You need me."

"I do, do I?" Sygg said.

"You can do whatever you feel you must to keep yourself safe from me," Brigid continued. "I'll do whatever I feel I must to atone for my deeds. Take me with you, Captain. I'll follow your orders and together we'll help your people prepare for this . . . this thing that's coming, whatever it turns out to be. Take me with you, or return me to the river to die."

"You're persuasive for a kithkin," Sygg said, his familiar grin returning. "Give me your sword, and your bow, and you have a deal."

"My sword?" Brigid objected. "Without a sword—"

"Without a sword, I'll be able to turn my back on you. You'll get it back when you earn it." The merrow took the kithkin weapon and slipped it onto his eelskin belt. The bow he tossed into the river.

"Are you out of your mind? I—" Brigid began.

"That's some apology."

"Fine," Brigid said. "Now will you return me to the shore so we can proceed?"

"No," Sygg replied. "I don't have time for you to keep up with me on foot. You might want to brace yourself."

Maralen withdrew from the others once Rhys went about his errand in the deep woods. It was easy enough to find solitude—Rhys was busy, Sygg was gone, and Brigid had wandered off. Ashling and the giants were all three rooted in the valley below, and the Vendilion faeries were only too happy to leave Maralen to her own devices. The sapling, as far as Maralen was concerned, was barely there in the first place.

Maralen fought the urge to fidget. The constant annoying buzz at the back of her skull had grown louder lately, more forceful. She been able to block out the drone as one would a chronic toothache, but now it resonated down her spine and across her shoulders, and she felt cold fingers of nausea flexing deep in her stomach. She could not account for this sickening unease, but she understood it was not to be ignored. Something was wrong and she dared not stay here.

The Mornsong elf trusted Rhys had something important and significant to do before they pressed on. He must be especially frustrated by the challenges of shepherding this unruly gang of strangers and misfits. She knew he did not need to hear her nebulous concerns—even if he cared to address them, he was already eager to move on, and nothing she said would hasten him along any faster. And the longer she stayed in this place, the more she needed to hurry him.

The buzzing sickness had grown steadily worse since they rescued the giants. At first Maralen assumed these sensations came from the Vendilion's increasingly sullen resistance to her authority, but now as the sick feelings reached their peak she realized the opposite was true. Her sudden weakness and discomfort had emboldened the faeries' disobedience, not the other way around.

Maralen staggered as she walked, and she stopped until she regained her balance. For a moment she did not recognize where she was, and that sent a small jolt of panic through her. Groping like a sleepwalker, Maralen forced herself to move on, away from the valley and the river, away from the others. They must not see her like this.

She forced herself to walk for as long as she could, barely aware of her surroundings. She leaned heavily against a medium-sized oak. The bark was rough but cool against her forehead. The waves of nausea and piercing sound were now overwhelming, crashing noise from a sea of angry, beating wings.

The cold fingers in her gut tightened, and Maralen cried out. A vague chorus of breathy voices filtered through her foggy mind, but the words of its song were distant and diffuse. Grimacing, Maralen strained to understand.

Return, the grand but distant chorus sang. *All you have borrowed, all that you are.*

Maralen dropped to her knees, her stomach heaving. If she had eaten breakfast, it would now be splattered across the grass. Her voice rasped through clenched teeth. "Leave. Me. Alone."

Return to me. All of it.

Maralen coughed, her eyes watering. She dug her fingers into the soil and concentrated on the only reply she had: *I'm not through with it yet.*

A fiery white explosion rocked the valley where Ashling and the giants rested. Maralen felt the nauseous presence withdraw.

The distant chorus dissolved into hisses of outrage and murmurs of ire.

The buzzing in Maralen's head eased, and the icy fingers relaxed their hold on her innards. Maralen stayed on all fours for a moment to gather her strength and appreciate the luxury of breathing and thinking normally. When her vision cleared, she spotted a new mound of dirt to her immediate right, one with a small circle of fresh white toadstools around its summit.

The dark-haired elf's mind raced. Now there could be no doubt Maralen's uncertain dread had a name: Oona. The Queen Mother of the Fae had bestowed upon Maralen great influence over the Vendilion clique. It was meant to be a gift, a remarkably generous gift, though only a fool accepted a faerie's present at face value. Maralen was no fool. She expected Mother Oona to demand this particular gift back, but not so soon or so forcefully.

Maralen spat her mouth clear, wiped her lips with the back of her hand, and struggled to her feet. Her first instinct was to call on the Vendilion, but she feared that would only make things worse. They were Oona's children, and if it came down to a struggle between Maralen and the Fae Queen, there was no doubt with whom the faeries would side.

The white fireball in the valley was troubling, to say the least, and it carried a whiff of the elemental fire that had consumed Colfenor. If something had happened to Ashling or the giants, they all might be stuck here for hours. Maralen could not afford to wait.

She squared her shoulders. What she must now do was not wise, but it was her best and perhaps only option. Children, she thought. Vendilion. Attend me.

For five agonizing seconds there was no reply. Then Veesa's bored, impatient voice said, "What is it now? And we aren't your children. Ew."

"Quiet, and listen to me." Maralen spoke so low her words were barely audible. "What just happened in the valley?"

"Oh, that? The flamekin blew up. Or at least, that's what it looked like. There was a big ball of fire and she was gone."

"I see. And the giants?"

"They're fine. Still there, still intact, still making a lot of disgusting digestive sounds. And smells."

"Never mind that. Are the giants still asleep?"

"They are."

"Good," Maralen said. "I want you to bring them a special dream. Nothing fancy—and let me stress this in particular: nothing flashy. Be subtle. Subtle, do you understand? Under no circumstances let them notice you. The notion has to appear as if it came from within."

"What notion?"

"More of a memory, actually. I want them to wake up yearning for their sister. Make them dream of Rosheen, the warmest and best times they ever had together. Make them believe their sister is calling to them, that they want to go to her, and that it's urgent. I want them to hear, taste, and smell how badly she needs them close by." Maralen nodded to herself. "That's all. Do this well and their own natures will take care of the rest."

"All right. If you insist."

"Oh, I do." Maralen was about to dismiss Veesa, but then she said, "Where are Iliona and Endry? They should have answered me too."

"They're still busy carrying out the earlier pile of *work*," Veesa said, spitting out the last word with uncharacteristic bile. "You should ease up, taskmaster. There are only three of us, after all, and we're very small."

"In appearance, perhaps, but we both know what you three are capable of. Keep that in mind. Now get on with it. I want you all back here as soon as you're done. No dawdling."

"As you wish." Veesa's thoughts drifted away, and Maralen allowed herself a thin smile. She was still nominally in control, still barely able to protect herself. She would have to take steps to improve that situation and to make the improvement permanent. The Mornsong elf had grown quite tired of feeling—of being—*temporary*.

Maralen dusted the soil from her hands and knees, straightened her clothes, and headed to the edge of the woods to wait for Rhys.

* * * * *

Rhys moved swiftly through the deep woods. He was well camouflaged by mud and a makeshift ghillie suit he had assembled out of the tall grasses back at the hillside. He quietly bounded from one limb to another, disappearing against the foliage every time he stopped. Silent, invisible, he sniffed and tasted and felt the world around him.

There were three Gilt Leaf scouts along the forest floor, a mere thirty yards from Rhys's tree. They were lightly armed with only daggers and were clad in thin leather armor. Their sleeveless tunics had high collars, each bearing a vivid white and purple emblem that marked the elves as hunters from the Nightshade pack.

The presence of the Gilt Leaf's premiere scouts confirmed Rhys's worst fears. If Gryffid had deployed the Nightshade in this region, he already had an inkling that Rhys had doubled back. The least-experienced elf tracker would have found them in less than a day, and the Nightshade were far better than that.

Worse, Rhys knew that as a mere daen, Gryffid did not have the authority to order the Nightshade scouts this far outside their own territory. Taercenn Nath had gathered the Nightshade, Hemlock, and Deathcap packs under his authority, but Nath was dead, and the Nightshade had daens of their own. Someone with a much higher rank than Gryffid must have come to replace Nath, an Exquisite or better, and it was this unknown quantity who had dedicated these elite trackers to Rhys's destruction.

Rhys allowed himself a moment's regret, then pushed it aside. He ought to have expected this. He was no longer a member of the Blessed Nation but its hated enemy. Outcast, eyeblight, traitor, kin-slayer. Killing Nath had not completed his fall from perfection, only increased it, renewed and redoubled it. The shame and the injury he had inflicted on the Gilt Leaf had not escaped the attention of the tribe's upper echelons, and like Gryffid they intended to avenge Nath and carry on Nath's work.

The scouts moved closer to Rhys's tree, and Rhys tensed the long muscles in his legs. All was not lost—yet. The longer it took for these scouts to report back, the more of a head start his party would have. If Rhys could delay these scouts' return, or prevent it entirely, it might make the difference between escape and capture.

Rhys clutched the hilt of his dagger. He waited until the lead elf was almost directly below him and stepped out into space. Rhys curled his feet beneath him as wind whistled past his ears and along the jagged edges of his horns. He stared down between his hooves at the increasingly large image of the lead scout's horned head.

In the moment before he made contact, Rhys heard one of the other two scouts say, "Taer—"

The lead scout ducked forward just as Rhys's hooves brushed the top of his head. Rhys stomped down hard on the elf's back as he crushed the scout to the ground. He felt the muffled shock of impact through the other's torso, and he heard the wet crunch of breaking ribs.

Rhys flexed his legs and bounced back up, rising several yards over the broken elf. He barked out the sharp syllables of a yew spell and hurled his dagger at the Nightshade farthest from him. The other scout threw himself into the dagger's path with his arms stretched out, but his aim was off and Rhys's throw was too strong. The envenomed dagger punched through the brave scout's hand and sent the elf spinning clumsily to the soil. Rhys's intended target ran into deep woods.

Rhys snarled. This was not cowardice, nor even a practical retreat in the face of a better-armed foe on unfamiliar terrain. Nightshade scouts were trained to avoid open combat in favor of returning with the information they'd gathered. The surviving scout fled not out of fear but because he knew Rhys would only win if the news of his arrival never reached the Gilt Leaf headquarters.

Rhys dashed after the fleeing scout, now cursing the shaggy ghillie suit. The loose-fitting shawl of vines and grass was perfect camouflage, but it caught the wind like a sail and hampered his headlong sprint. He twisted and shrugged free of the suit as he ran up a brambled hillside. Rhys stopped at the top of the rise and drew his sword. His heart thumped in his chest, and he struggled to listen over the deafening pound of blood in his ears.

Isolating the soft sounds of one Nightshade scout would have been a considerable challenge, but Rhys found the job far easier—and therefore far more troubling—than he expected. He didn't hear one Nightshade scout but several. A half dozen or more, in fact.

Rhys let the tip of his sword sink to the ground. He stood and stared into the deep woods, listening. A series of soft, infinitesimal sounds drained the last of his initiative.

The woods were thick with Nightshade scouts, all of whom were now withdrawing. Rhys had stopped one, perhaps two, but there were far more. This battle was effectively over, and he had lost.

Behind him, from the bottom of the rise, the scout who had

taken Rhys's dagger in the hand groaned. Rhys sheathed his sword and bounded down the rise. He found the dagger where the elf had fallen, its angled blade smeared with blood and yew poison. He found the scout several paces away from that, face-down and dragging himself through the dirt.

Rhys circled around in front of the scout. "Name and station, Hunter."

The scout groaned again. He lay flat for a moment, and then forced himself over onto his back with a grunt.

"I do not hear your words," he rasped. His face was pale and drawn. There was foam at the corners of his mouth. "Traitor. Eyeblight."

"Who sent you?"

The elf turned his face away.

"Gryffid commands the Hemlock," Rhys said. "Does Nightshade's elite now answer to a mere daen?"

The scout said nothing. Rhys watched quietly as numbness settled over the other elf's chest. The scout panted, his breaths coming quick and shallow, until at last his muscles relaxed and his chest ceased to rise.

Rhys stared at the corpse as it cooled. He was kin-slayer once more, but he envied as well as mourned these latest victims of his folly. They had served the Nation and died with honor in its name. Now their work was done. They had no mysteries to unravel, no strange and secretive comrades to manage. They had stayed true to their place in the world, accepted the righteous and rigorous discipline perfection demanded, and now that place and their glory were secure for all time. They would be remembered as loyal, disciplined hunters of the Gilt Leaf.

Rhys stooped down and lifted the dead Nightshade scout in his arms. He carried the body over near the other dead scout. With a simple prayer of respect, Rhys arranged their bodies next to each other and crossed their arms over their chests.

He had chosen this, and, though he no longer had any status in the Nation, Rhys was yet an elf, and he would not waver. He feared he would never get used to killing his own kind. Then he feared he would. He was a villain to his former comrades, a monster. Gryffid and whoever was backing him were right to thirst for Rhys's blood.

Rhys bowed his head one last time, bade farewell to his enemies, and headed back to the valley where the giants had dined on raw, wild pig. Before he was through, he intended to earn a great deal more of Gilt Leaf ire.

* * * * *

Ashling hurtled headlong, though she had no idea how fast or in what direction. She was definitely moving, however, and had been for some time. She was not certain when the pursuit had ceased to be a pursuit, but she felt like a merrow who had been chasing the Wanderwine only to be swept up in the current.

Standing up to meet the elemental's challenge might not have been the wisest decision, but she was sure it was the correct one. At the very least it was better than shaking in fear and drifting without purpose. Now that she had a hold of her prize, it took even more of her strength and resolve to hang on.

She clutched to the elemental's body, clinging and clawing madly with hands and feet, doing everything in her power to maintain a physical grip upon a thing that wasn't entirely physical. Old doubts arose again, the gnawing sense she was not meant to be with this creature, not yet, if indeed she ever was. They were supposed to remain separate. Connected but apart. There was no way to surrender to these doubts in her current situation, or even acknowledge them, and so she continued to ride her steed through a hazy realm of fire.

Not a steed. A guide.

The elemental's hooves forged a blazing road through the sky, and the entity snorted, forcing a queasy grin from Ashling. A pilgrim was only a traveler, after all, and oh, how they were traveling now. Lorwyn appeared far below the elemental's hooves. The landscape rolled by like a hand-drawn kithkin map unfurling. Ashling saw mountain, river, field, and fen through sheets of flame that flowed like water. The entire world appeared behind and below the fire, but it neither burned nor withered. Instead, the flames supported the world like solid ground and carried everyone on it along like the waters of the Wanderwine.

Shapes grew clearer outside the enveloping flames; shapes that flashed by so quickly Ashling finally had a true physical sense of their velocity. Yet there was something off about the shapes—repetitiveness, a pattern. As if she was seeing the same journey over and over.

Yes. You see the repeating cycle of what has been, what is, what will be. Soon it will begin again. It has always been this way.

The elemental's voice sounded much like her own but older, more seasoned. She turned over its words in her mind. "Will my journey ever end then?" she said. "Or will I simply return to the beginning and start again?"

The flamekin didn't really expect an answer and was proven prescient when the fiery being resumed its silence.

No, there was a difference between ignoring her and not answering. Ashling relaxed the parts of her mind that ordered things in terms of language, distance, and time. She felt her hands and knees relax their grip on the elemental, but she did not slip. The flamekin took every bit of her *self* and her *identity,* everything that made Ashling *Ashling,* and willed it to the back of her mind, where, with any luck, it would safely remain for when she needed it. Then, Ashling embraced the fiery creature wholly and completely, without her body, and at last she felt what the elemental *meant*.

Nameless, formless, and free, the union of pilgrim and elemental flared bright and hot, merging with the sky of fire that enshrouded the world above and below them. Everything melted, everyone consumed in the great conflagration that marked the end of the world. Ashling's manic glee returned, and she shouted aloud once more. She was herself, she was the horse, she was all flamekin everywhere. United with her tribe and her elemental, Ashling knew that the world's end was theirs, the final reward for all pilgrims and the ultimate fate of all flamekin. They would enter the all-consuming inferno together. It was theirs. They created it, they owned it, and they would experience its ultimate devastation firsthand.

The flames around her grew hot, and Ashling felt herself slipping away, all that she had been and would ever be converted into just one more flame in a raging inferno. To her dismay and delight, Ashling found the combination of steed and rider and tribe not only welcoming the chance to join this great fire but yearning for it—until all thought and sensation came to a sharp, sudden stop.

"Ashling has not been destroyed," the sapling said. "It may have appeared that way, but that is impossible. She was either taken or left of her own accord."

"How do you know?" Endry said. "Did you even see it happen? I saw it happen. The kithkin archer too, not that I care what she thinks. That flamekin just jumped into the air, there was a big flash, and she was gone. You have to at least admit it's possible. Come on, admit it."

"No," the sapling replied. "I won't admit it because it isn't true. Colfenor chose Ashling for a reason, for her unique connection to her elemental and her . . . unorthodox interpretation of the Path of Flame. I know firsthand what that connection feels like, and I tell you the soil beneath my roots says she is here but not here. She is of Lorwyn but not within Lorwyn. She is in the realm of the elemental fire. No flamekin can survive that for long, and there's only one way out—Mount Tanufel."

"So you say," Endry said. "But your roots could be wrong."

"That's doubtful," the sapling said. "The ground has no reason to lie, and despite a few kithkin epic poems to the contrary, flamekin do not just disappear in a flash for no reason. But when in communion with the higher elemental powers—"

"Now you're just making up words."

"I'm relating some of the knowledge my seedfather passed

on to me," the sapling said. "You needn't believe me. Or follow me, for that matter."

"I'm following you because you've told me you want to go somewhere that doesn't exist. I've met people other than you—thickheaded kithkin, mostly—who think there's a big, magical flamekin city on Mount Tanufel."

"There is a flamekin city on Mount Tanufel. And it only makes sense that Ashling would go there when she achieved the white fire."

Endry sighed. "You stink at banter."

"My intent was not bantering. I thought we were conversing."

"And you're not nearly as much fun as I'd hoped," Endry said. "Say, do you ever look down?"

"Rarely," the sapling admitted. "My root-feet can find the path."

"And if there's no path?"

"No path? What—"

The rest of the sapling's question was smothered as she found herself skidding facedown along a steep, muddy slope. Tiny green branches at the tips of her boughs twisted and bent but did not snap—yet.

The sapling's slide ended abruptly, though a small avalanche of wet rocks and green leaves continued on down to the edge of the Wanderwine, which she now clearly saw with one independently rolling eye.

"Yes, funny thing about those paths," Endry said. "Not a lot of them cross the river. Which brings me to my next question—can yewlings swim?"

"I had not—" The sapling pushed herself onto her root-feet, bending one leg sharply at her knotted knee to stand like a billy goat on the side of a mountain. "I had not considered that."

"You did know it was here, right?"

"Of course. I was merely focused on my goal."

"You're as single-minded as a— well, as a tree."

"Yes, I am."

Endry fluttered impatiently before the sapling. "If Ashling needs you like you say," he said. "You'll just have to float across. I sure can't lift you. I mean, I can lift a lot, don't get me wrong. Especially if my sisters are helping." He cocked his tiny head toward the sky. "Hey, I wonder what they're up to? Maybe I should—"

"Your suggestion is a good one," the sapling admitted. "But I fear that will not work either."

"Come on, yewling, everyone knows wood floats on water."

"Not all wood," the young yew replied. "I am alive—I believe the kithkin term is 'green.' I won't float. No, I'll just have to walk."

"Wait, are you crazy? You can't walk across the bottom of the Wanderwine! Let's find some ferryman somewhere. It won't take us that far out of our way. Or better yet, get back in touch with your elements. Water. It's elemental. You can— Hey, look at that! A fuzzy silverbee!"

"There really is no need to keep following me."

"Bah! I'm not following you. I'm enjoying my freedom!" Endry replied. "Come on, yewling, isn't all this exciting? The freedom? The freedom from the people who want to push us around all the time? People who are always saying things like 'Shut up, Endry,' and 'Wait your turn, Endry,' and 'Eat that weird berry, Endry.' " He laughed and let out a tiny faerie whoop of delight, turning a backflip in midair. "But not anymore, yewling! You and me, we're going to take in the sights!"

"That won't help us reach the flamekin," the sapling said and began a slow, careful descent of the bank.

Endry orbited the yew excitedly. "She's not going anywhere! Well, not going anywhere where we don't know where she's going, isn't she? No, wait— Did I just say—"

"Unless faeries have learned how to swim since my seedfather passed, you should not follow me too closely," the sapling said and stepped into the swift current. She splayed the many toes of her root-feet, allowing herself to stay upon the surface of the muck without sinking too deeply. As long as she kept moving, she should be able to reach the other side without risking much more than a case of waterlogging.

"Hey, shouldn't you take a breath before you do that?" The faerie spoke just as the sapling's face slipped beneath the surface. The currents dragged through her needled boughs—she'd be lucky to have any growth left at all after this—and she had to extend her root-feet deeper into the river bottom to keep from being swept away. It slowed her progress considerably but did not cause undue concern.

The sapling knew her lack of experience in what flesh creatures called "the real world" was an impediment to fulfilling her seedfather's wishes. Still, she could hardly have been expected to anticipate a merrow towing a kithkin down the Wanderwine at an amazingly high speed, and so the sapling did not blame herself when Sygg and Brigid tore past. Nor did she watch them as they shot down the river, instead taking that moment to direct sap away from the branch the merrow had (unintentionally, she assumed) broken off. The merrow and the kithkin had been of no concern to Colfenor, so they were of no concern to the sapling.

The broken branch began to heal over while the sapling trudged on through the middle of the river. An hour or so later, she emerged on the south bank.

Endry was waiting for her when she stepped onto the gray, wet sand. "See anything interesting?" the faerie asked.

With complete honesty, the yew replied in the negative.

* * * * *

Brigid awoke from the second fitful catnap of her seemingly interminable voyage down the currents of the Wanderwine. Her small, sturdy shapewater bubble was still filled with surprisingly fresh, clean—albeit decidedly clammy—air. The landscape blurred weirdly overhead—the bubble was of course transparent, and the dim light was enough to make out shapes above the surface—and every once in a while a silvery thing (or a great many silvery things) whizzed past. Once or twice she'd made out the shape of an arbomander lazily floating downstream. The huge amphibians tended to block out any light from the surface. What Brigid had not known was that arbomanders looked completely different from beneath. When seen from the riverbank, they resembled floating sand bars encrusted with fungi, but their undersides were a pale sandy color that more or less matched the hazy brightness of the sky from this underwater vantage point. Brigid also saw thick, paddle-shaped tails almost twice as long as the bulky trunk. The arbomanders' hind legs were more like long flippers than walking limbs, and their forelegs were splayed, webbed, and tipped with claws half as tall as Brigid herself. And all of them sported feathery tendrils of varying length and shapes growing from their gills—but the patterns of each arbomander's frill were completely unique.

The archer also learned arbomanders were but the largest and most visible, to kithkin at least, of a myriad of river-dwelling amphibians. A pair of these creatures, possibly siblings or mates, followed them for a mile or two, keeping pace easily while hovering directly above Brigid's bubble. Each was a different shade of vivid blue, and the kithkin found she missed them when they left off and returned to whatever previously unseen amphibians got up to at the bottom of the Wanderwine.

And there were other things few, if any, kithkin had ever seen at all from any angle: twisted, ancient logs that had merged with the mud; bottom-feeding catfish that rivaled arbomanders in size but which never left the muck and gravel; and what she thought might have been a merrow cemetery.

It was surprising so much light reached this far down. Brigid guessed she was moving along about twenty feet beneath the surface. Yet neither she nor Sygg—his undulating tail waving at her up from up ahead—had kicked up so much as a wisp of silt on the entire journey. It must be some potent shapewater magic, Brigid reasoned. Their passage left no tracks upon the currents. If Sygg chose to drown her, Brigid imagined she wouldn't be much more than catfish food.

She tried to stretch and was again reminded of perhaps the most unpleasant aspect of Sygg's magic. Even someone of Brigid's size could not unfold her arms without great effort. She had plenty of air, but it didn't feel as if there was plenty of air. She'd fought off an impending attack of claustrophobia for hours now with deep, steady breaths.

Brigid's heart nearly stopped when her forward motion did. Inertia did its level best to crumple her against the forward end of the shapewater coffin, and the bare sole of her right foot slipped against the shimmering surface. Her ankle twisted painfully—it didn't snap, thankfully, but it was not an injury she could ignore if she planned to walk any time in the near future.

The archer assessed all this before her heart started beating again, finishing just in time for a partially eaten merrow corpse to collide against the shapewater bubble's surface with a sound like a leg of springjack striking a kettle. Brigid screamed in terror for perhaps the first time since she was a kithling.

The dead merrow rested there, causing the inner part of her cramped confines to bow uncomfortably inward. The corpse was in shadow, but this close to her face it didn't matter. Brigid had an intimate view of the dead merrow's left eye socket, where a writhing, wormy creature appeared to have consumed the previous occupant. The dead merrow's right eye was white and cloudy, its jaw was half gone, and the hanging mandible flapped against the bubble with a ping, ping, ping. Then it moved, disappearing to her left with a jerk, leaving behind a momentary cloud of fleshy debris and brownish green silt that sparkled in the current.

"Kithkin." A slithery voice whispered in Brigid's left ear. This time she didn't scream, but it wasn't for lack of effort. Sygg had reached through the shapewater and clamped a wet, scaly palm over her mouth, and firmly shook his head. "Water carries sound, you know," the merrow scolded.

"What—"

"Something is wrong." Sygg's perpetual level of reproach toward the archer melted into an anxious scowl. "There are dead merrow in the current. This shouldn't be."

"They're not, you know, kicking around still, are they?"

"What are you talking about?" Sygg said. "They are dead."

"Right. I knew that," the kithkin said, marshaling what was left of her composure. "So, we're staying down here because there's, what, boggarts up topside?"

"Perhaps," the ferryman replied. "I have spotted fourteen of my kind so far. I must return them to the riversoil without delay. The Wanderwine has had enough of them, I think."

The kithkin could hardly believe her ears. "Shouldn't we try to find out what killed them first?" she asked as calmly as she could. "Perhaps by splitting up? One of us in the water, the other, you know, dry. Drier."

"You don't understand," Sygg said. "If they are left in the water, the Wanderwine will never release their souls. The Father-Lane is a jealous parent and doesn't care to give his children over to the Mother-Bed. Yet he must. So you see why we can't—"

"If it killed them it can kill you, and then I drown."

Sygg eyed Brigid with sudden suspicion. "Perhaps Kinsbaile's archers have been 'gigging frogs in a bucket' as the kithkin saying goes. Killing merrow in a crannog."

"That doesn't even make sense!" Brigid snapped. "Why would Kinsbaile—any kithkin—want to kill merrow? Without the river, we'd all starve, and merrows are the keepers of the river."

"How should I know?" Sygg snarled. "Maybe you've figured out some way to travel the Lanes without our help. Some kind of cunning kithkin contraption like your wingbows and dirigibles and your . . . your gardens."

"That's mad," the kithkin said. "Just listen to what you're saying."

"But the natives of Kinsbaile get up to some mad things, don't they? Remarkably strange little ceremonies—like the whole town turning out to burn Colfenor."

"I didn't—" Brigid began but caught herself. This petty arguing wasn't getting her out of her bubble. "You make a good point. But Captain, if I have to remain in this bubble for much longer, I'm going to lose my mind. I give you my word: I will not act against you in any way."

"Even if you find a phalanx of kithkin archers waiting?" Sygg said, still suspicious. "Or maybe you're just supposed to kill me once you're ashore? Finish off the last merrow of Crannog Aughn?"

"Sygg," Brigid said. "I didn't even know your crannog was Crannog Aughn until just now."

"Very well," the merrow said. "I will place you on the south side of the river—opposite from your village."

"I know on which side of the Wanderwine Kinsbaile sits."

"Then you understand why I might wish to avoid a kithkin attack if this is some sort of trick," the ferryman said. "I will be following just under the surface, close to shore. I hear no activity in the crannog, but my hearing is not to be trusted if landwalkers are waiting in ambush." Sygg flashed a few dozen teeth. "When we are within a hundred yards, wait on the shore while I inspect the locks and sublevels."

"Shouldn't I be inspecting the 'landwalker' part of the place? You just said—"

"You just watch for landwalkers approaching over the piers or planks. And I would think an archer of your renown could hit a moving kithkin—or what have you—at a hundred yards without flapping a gill," Sygg said. "That's why I went and dug your bow out of the muck."

"Yes, thank you for that," Brigid said, not bothering to mention that the immersion had done the bowstring no favors.

"I will let you know when the coast is clear below," Sygg added.

"How?"

"In a minute," the merrow snapped. "When the coast is clear below, I'll begin to move up through the inner structure. You meet me on the south pier. Then we can circle around to the north side."

"You sound," Brigid said, "like a man who thinks he knows what he's going to find."

"I don't know what we'll find," Sygg admitted. "I hope it is not more dead— Well. Just because they are not making noise does not mean they are not there. It doesn't mean they're all dead." Brigid sensed he wasn't just talking about the crannog's population as a whole now but of people close to him. Did the surly captain have a family, some merrow clutch?

"One of those bodies—someone you knew?"

"Aye," Sygg said. "A few someones." He flexed his gills and snapped his teeth in a merrow expression of determination. "And there may be more if we don't get going. I'd say hold on, but there's not really much point. Take this." He reached out of the bubble for a moment, and when his hand broke the shapewater again it held what looked like a small glass ball. The kithkin extended her open hand and took the sphere, which felt cold and familiar—it was shapewater, and if there was one thing she knew by know it was the feel of shapewater pressing against her skin.

"What do I do with it?" Brigid asked.

"Hold onto it," the merrow said. "And that took me an hour to shape, so don't lose it. That's how we're going to keep in touch. Listen for my voice." With that, Sygg slipped back through the shapewater bubble's surface with nary a pop. The next moment Brigid was moving again. Moving very fast.

She broke the surface of the water where the river was only a few feet deep and cattails grew thick and tall. Brigid struck them headfirst and landed with a wet smack facedown at the edge of a small turtle's nest, close enough that the nest's owner skipped past pulling its head inside its shell and instead snapped at the kithkin's nearby nose.

The pain caused Brigid to jerk back but not in time to keep the little brute from drawing blood. "Fantastic," she said as she pushed herself to her feet. With effort she managed to put most of her weight onto her good ankle and keep from falling back into the mud.

Satisfied her point was made, the turtle receded into the center of her nest, leaving the strange invader to limp to somewhat drier ground. It wasn't hard to find a fallen log upon which she could perch somewhat comfortably for her inspection of Crannog Aughn.

The inspection, as it happened, lasted all of five minutes, if that. Brigid hadn't known what she expected—boggarts, or elves, maybe even kithkin (though she doubted that in her heart)—but she certainly hadn't expected to see a trio of skulking, hunchbacked merrow emerge from the upper tier of Crannog Aughn, sidewinding along on their tails across the south pier and into the shallows near the shore. They were headed— They were in fact headed toward Brigid.

"Kithkin ambush, eh?" the archer murmured and almost jumped when Sygg seemed to respond.

"Archer," said Sygg's voice from the shapewater ball through a veil of bubbling distortion. "What do you see above? I haven't found a bloody thing in the—"

Brigid never learned where Sygg hadn't found a bloody thing. The shapewater ball in her hand simply lost all surface tension and became normal water again. Brigid stared in shock at her wet, open palm for a split-second, but it was enough to keep her from spotting the jagged bone harpoon before the missile knocked her trusty helmet off her head.

* * * * *

Sygg pulled a bone spear from the quiver on his back and held it firmly in one hand, using the other to steer as his powerful tail drove him forward at top speed.

No, that's not the way, he told himself. The cautious approach is the smart approach. Even if he burned to see his fry and his remaining mates, he had to survive to reach the crannog. He stopped swimming and let the current carry him soundlessly toward home, only slicing the water with his tail to avoid the odd corpse now and again. He recognized some of them but so far had seen no more family.

The ferryman had nearly let the kithkin drown when he'd spotted Creiddylan's body. She'd been his favorite mate by far, a friend as well as the mother of more than two dozen of his offspring. Creiddy had been the one who ensured Sygg kept in touch with all of his fry, and their mothers too. She had been the reason Sygg even felt he had a family. Many was the ferryman who never met a single one of his merlings, but the captain had been amazed at how good it made him feel to see them grow into strong, young merrow. He owed that to Creiddylan, and now her body would probably never find a home within the riversoil. Her soul would never become one with the Wanderwine but would instead drift along its currents for all eternity. And hers wasn't the only kin he'd seen dead in the water.

A tangled pair of merrow tumbled past Sygg. If it hadn't been for the flash of the hook as he floated past them, he never would have supposed these were anything more than unfortunates the current had knocked in a grisly embrace. The hook told a different story. Even now one of the corpses clutched its weapon in a death grip, while the business end was jammed into the gills of his companion. The companion had obviously suffocated on her own blood, but there was no sign of what killed the hook wielder until Sygg floated past them and looked back.

The female had torn open the male's left abdomen with, it appeared, her bare claws. Chunks of white flesh and gray skin were still evident at the end of her fingers. Four deep gashes showed Sygg that the merrow with the hook had a completely bisected heart.

Still wary of moving too quickly but no longer able to simply float along the river's currents, he settled for a lazy tail-paddle that brought him to the outer locks within minutes. The crannog beneath the surface was much larger than the portion above, but the underwater levels were for merrow only. He was relieved when he saw no air bubbles within the locks themselves. If land-walkers were down here, they were holding their breath. So far, so good.

A shadow moved past out of the corner of his eye. He whirled in midcurrent but only saw a stream of white bubbles where the movement had been. The current instantly swirled the bubbles away, but by then Sygg could not see whatever had caused them.

The shadow had been the rough size of a merrow, he supposed, though he couldn't fathom why any merrow still here wouldn't have welcomed him.

He glanced again at the two dead merrow in their murderous

final embrace. Perhaps this merrow had no reason to welcome him. He gripped the bone spear a little more tightly.

After a few minutes of exploring the crannog's interior and finding no sign of any merrow or landwalker, living or dead, Sygg partially relaxed. The shape he'd seen was probably just a catfish, or perhaps even a young arbomander. He was too relieved by the lack of corpses inside Crannog Aughn to let it worry him too much.

No, the more urgent worry was keeping an eye on that kithkin archer. He still didn't trust her, but now he needed her help. With only a little effort, he formed a shapewater sphere in the palm of his hand—it only took an hour to make a sphere for a land-walker like Brigid to use—where it reflected his dimly lit face as he willed it to connect with its twin. The kithkin better not have lost hers.

The ferryman had only just made contact with the kithkin when he saw a second lantern-eyed face appear in the reflection on the shapewater's skin. He recognized the face as Gulhee, Sygg's own second cousin who carried cargo to and from kithkin villages. Before Sygg could shout a single word of alarm, his kinsman slammed him in the face with a large, flat rock.

After what felt like an eternity blazing her way through a universe of pure flame, dropping onto the stone of Mount Tanufel was like a bucket of cold river water in the face. Ashling must have been moving at some speed, for the end of her elemental ride left a twenty-foot, smoldering furrow in the ground.

Though her steed—or guide, depending on one's point of view, she supposed—was no longer carrying her through the realm of fire, Ashling thought she could still feel its presence. She spat burning bile as she pushed herself to her feet and scanned the skies. The elemental seemed to appear and disappear from the visual spectrum at will, but, yes, it was still here. If she concentrated on their tenuous connection . . .

There. She spotted the blazing creature against the bright golden sky, looking as if it had just emerged from the sun itself. It wheeled in the sky, circling the mountain itself for a few minutes, and finally descended to settle upon Lorwyn's tallest peak. It stood there, a tiny equine shape surrounded by fiery wings clearly visible even at this distance. Once again she felt the buzz of contact with the elemental, and she knew it saw her as clearly as she saw it.

Not a steed. A guide.

"I have just about had it with your pronouncements," Ashling said and realized it was true. All her life had been devoted to finding and communing with this creature, and here it was toying with her. She knew the Path of Flame was not a casual stroll one took to pass the time, but ever since she'd made contact with this creature it seemed bent on tormenting her. No more.

"You want to play follow the leader?" She asked. "Well, I'm through playing. This isn't a game anymore. It's a hunt."

The elemental, if it heard or understood her words, did not respond, so she continued venomously, giving in to the simmering anger and resentment she felt toward this creature, and Colfenor, and the kithkin—all of those who had put her through that burning nightmare in Kinsbaile. Perhaps in the end this was the true meaning of the Path of Flame: burning away illusions and child-like dreams of communion and understanding. "I'm going to find you, and we're going to come to terms. And if anyone gets in my way, they're going to burn."

The elemental on the mountaintop flared white against the sky, and its wings unfurled until the horse disappeared, leaving only a blazing, upturned crescent.

You do not understand.

With a final flash and a sound like thunder, the elemental vanished. Try as she might, Ashling could no longer see it. Just a wisp that might have been steam escaping from a volcanic vent.

The elemental was gone, their connection broken. After a dazed moment the rest of her surroundings pulled into sharper focus. Nothing else mattered for those first few seconds but the void in her soul the being had left behind, and that absence felt even worse than the sudden violation of power she'd experienced in Kinsbaile.

There was ground—stone—beneath her back, and her body had weight against it. Ashling felt unusually cold after the heat of pursuit and her angry declaration. Her flames had subsided nearly to the point of going out entirely. Ashling hadn't felt so dim since just before the elemental had forcefully reanimated her, the first time she had made terrible contact. The elemental fire had been so raw and pure she had not even tried to contain it.

Still, the anger and sense of betrayal burned within her, alongside more than a little guilt. The guilt was involuntary, but it was there, joined with the shame of being used and her determination not to be used like that ever again.

As her mind reasserted control in the elemental's absence, Ashling's flames burned brighter once more, flickering chaotically up and down her body. She had a new purpose, a new take on the Path of Flame, but she was still a pilgrim. A pilgrim remained calm in adversity—and also in pain, suffering, fear, guilt, and, most of all, fury.

New and unexpected sounds intruded on her introspection as the rest of her senses returned to full burn. Ashling did not even recognize the sounds as voices at first, so long had it been since she'd heard the speech of her mountain home. No other creature in all of Lorwyn could mimic the true flamekin tongue, with its whispered scrapes and hollow exhalations of brimstone. She was once more among her kind. How many she couldn't immediately say. Ashling could only hear two individual voices, but there could be others here, silent and waiting.

The elemental had carried the pilgrim home but only just, and now it waited atop the peak that had given her life. The warm surface of Mount Tanufel was unmistakable once she let licks of her flame touch the subsurface rock. The rock was but the tip of an entire mountain of living stone stretching thousands of feet below the surface of Lorwyn, yet the contact, once made, was impossible to withdraw. It was utterly different from the touch of the elemental or the realm of fire, but still it reminded her that she was not the flamekin she'd been when she set out on her wanderings.

Ashling was a bit further up the summit than she'd initially realized. The furrow cut into the stone by her arrival ended at a boulder sitting atop a finger of deep gray rock halfway up the mountain. Ashling knew this place now that she made an effort to focus on something other than the elemental. Only a few feet away on either side of her was a drop that wouldn't end for several thousand feet, a fall that would return even the strongest, stoniest flamekin to the stone whence she came. The voices came from the direction of the mountaintop, which rose another few thousand feet before her, before ending in the flat top of Tanufel Crater, the elemental's distant perch. Mount Tanufel was rife with outcrops and spiky protrusions of metallic stone, and she could have been resting on any one of them. But judging from the appearance of her two visitors she was upon the one that served as a lookout in times of war, spires forgotten and unused for generations.

The two speakers halted their conversation when Ashling abruptly sat up, ramrod straight. She knew them both, or rather knew their ironwood cloaks. "Monks of the Ember Fell," she hailed. "Greetings. I am Ashling, a pilgrim. I ask you to allow me to pass unhindered." She let the statement linger in the air without adding much threat to it. She would not be cowed or halted now, but the Ember Fell were not enemies she wanted to make. It would only add more difficulty to a hunt that she knew was going to be very difficult indeed.

Monks of the Ember Fellowship of the Mountain were flamekin holy warriors, the spiritual descendants of the last warrior flamekin to fight the elf tribes for dominance long ago. Or so they claimed. Ashling had known a few of them before she departed on her path and found most of them did not spend as much time on the art of war as they claimed.

Each of the Fell was covered from neck to feet in plates of rare ironwood bark woven together with steel cords. Their heads and arms were bare and ablaze. To her surprise, their carefully sewn vestments—Ashling had heard the monk's uniforms took more than ten years to complete, with nine of them spent collecting naturally shed ironwood bark—made not a sound as they advanced toward her in unison. She noted neither of them moved into the fore. If these two monks had a leader, he wasn't present. If she chose, they would not be difficult to deal with. If she had to, she could call down her elemental power and turn their ironwood to ash.

Neither of the monks replied immediately. Instead they turned toward her as one and strode forward.

"I apologize for this intrusion," Ashling continued. "If you just allow me passage through the monastery gates, I will be honored to leave an offering for your continued—"

The strangers' blazing fists struck in unison, one in the center of her abdomen and the other hard against her jaw. Each of them followed the first blow with even stronger punches that sent Ashling reeling. The mountain peak spun like a kithkin toy, and Ashling staggered back a step, two steps, and an involuntary third step found only open space. The merciless stares of the Ember Fell met her angry cry without a trace of emotion, moving only to follow her rapidly increasing descent.

* * * * *

"What did you call them?" the sapling asked her faerie . . . companion. Yes, "companion" was the only word for him, though the word seemed unappealing for reasons she couldn't place. In the last day the young yew had experienced this sensation in varying degrees and flavors with increasing frequency.

"I called them 'groundling rats.' Dirt-eating mockeries of the Fae. Stinking grubworms who should all go crawl into the Wanderwine and drown."

"You realize they are all right here?" the sapling asked. "And they can hear you?"

"You think I care what they think?" Endry sneered. "They're no kin of mine, no matter what they say."

"They are your kin," the sapling said, somewhat baffled at the diminutive creature's inability to grasp this utterly obvious fact. There were perhaps twenty of the "rats," each one virtually identical (from the yew's point of view) to Endry but for the lack of silvery wings, and each one was devoted to busily pointing silver stakes through the sapling's root-feet. Each one, that is, who wasn't devoted to snagging her branches with tiny grappling lines and pulling mightily in an apparent effort to topple her onto her back. Why, she could not say. Therefore, Endry would have to do so before she was further deterred from her goal.

It wasn't the first time in her short life she had been logically correct and absolutely wrong, and this alarmed the sapling nearly as much as her increasingly frequent bouts of emotions that didn't seem to be quite hers.

"I am not talking to them," Endry reiterated. "They should have had the good sense to go die when they lost their wings."

"Some of us were budded wingless," one of the walking faeries replied unbidden. She took hold of a grappling line and joined the efforts of the others, which forced the sapling to strain every fiber of her narrow green trunk to keep from bending under the strain. Wingless or no, these faeries were as strong as Endry and his sisters.

"I don't care, I— Shut up! I'm not talking to you, ground rat!"

"That's really hurting my feelings," said another, one of several males. "You're the ones who invaded our exile. Like we want to talk to you, Flutterbunch."

"Flutterbunch?" Endry raged. "Come up here and say that!"

"Endry," the sapling said, struggling to keep calm in her voice. "I can't remain standing for much longer. If I fall, I'm not going to be able to get up again until these faeries release me. I don't think they plan to do so, but I'm sure they won't if you keep antagonizing them."

"No, definitely not," the male groundling with the hurt feelings agreed. "You two destroyed our village."

"I did nothing of the sort," the sapling objected. "I was not aware your—"

"Your stinky dirt village had it coming!" Endry cried, even more agitated than before.

"This tree stepped on our village," the female charged. "Now we need new homes. Your friend here is going to become those homes, once we get to carving her out, Buzz-fly."

"She'll live," the male added, "but I'll bet she goes crazy. Flutterbunch."

"You're crazy if you think— Wait, what am I saying? I don't care what you do with this yewling."

"You do not?" the sapling asked.

"You don't?" the female groundling repeated.

"I'm on a mission to find the flamekin pilgrim!" Endry said proudly. "And the pilgrim doesn't like this walking stick all that much. Gives her bad memories. Who needs her?"

The sapling was definitely feeling fear now, and she was almost certain this feeling was not an inherited echo of her seedfather's soul. It was far too instinctive, too sharp. The spike drivers had completed their work and scuttled to their grappling ropes, and the closest thing the sapling had to an ally was doing his level best to encourage the creatures that meant to carve her apart.

"You don't— You don't care?" the male asked. "But you were traveling with her and talking to her like she was just your best friend in the whole world."

"Yeah, don't give us that," a third groundling piped in. "This is really going to make you feel low. Low like a groundling!"

"Like us!"

"Make him feel what it's like to be one of us!"

"Figuratively speaking!"

"Yeah, figuratively!"

"Emotionally too!"

"Figuratively and emotionally speaking," Endry said, turning in midair to show the groundlings his hind quarters, "you worms can get used to this, because I'm leaving. You just have your fun. I won't be here to watch."

"Nora, you told us we'd be striking a blow for the wingless! That he'd let the Great Mother know of our plight!"

"If he doesn't care, why are we trying to pull down a tree? A tree, by the Mother! We're faeries! If Oona were to hear . . ."

The argument continued, but bit by bit the tortuous strain against the sapling's trunk eased as the tiny creatures released their grapple lines, joining in the chattering debate. Others wrenched the spikes from her feet with disgust, and she allowed sap to move to the injured areas. They would heal quickly; root wounds always did.

"If I may," the sapling said, "I would like to take a moment to make up for my carelessness."

"Yeah?" the talkative male groundling said. "And how will you do that?"

"Magic, of course," the sapling replied. "Please, take me to your village."

"So you can step on it again, right?" Endry asked, hopeful. "Right?"

"Why do even more damage?" Nora said and turned to her fellow groundlings. "Maybe we should spike her again."

"That isn't necessary. Please, Nora, is it? Let me help."

"All right then," the groundling replied. "Follow me, but keep your distance."

It took less than a minute to retrace the path and find the shattered groundling village, which the sapling had not realized was a "village" at all. It consisted of a large, rotten log along the rough, overgrown path the yew and the faerie had been following to Mount Tanufel. Unable to get around it, the sapling had instead gone through it.

"Some village," Endry spat. "Why even bother? You— You people are living like kithkin. Like *kithkin*." His wings buzzed angrily on the last word. "Yewling, just start stomping. You know it's the right thing to do."

"Endry," the yew said, "I think you should scout ahead."

"Not a chance," the faerie said. "I know you're just trying to shut me up. It's not going to work."

The sapling didn't choose to engage. Instead she stooped to take a closer look, bending her limber green trunk and legs in a fashion that would have snapped an elf's skeleton in four places. The log had been about three feet in diameter, dead and rotting yet still teeming with plant and animal life. Amid the ruined nests and huts that had made up the majority of the groundlings' homes were insects and creatures even tinier than insects, filling every nook and cranny of the smashed wood and moss. She was relieved to see no groundling corpses among the wreckage.

"Plenty of moss," the sapling said. "Colfenor knows . . ."

"Colfenor knows what?" Endry asked.

"What's a Colfenor?" Nora asked.

"Shows what you know," Endry said. "Colfenor was a great sage of the treefolk."

The sapling tuned out what was no doubt a wildly inaccurate biography of her seedfather and splayed her stem-fingers wide. She gently lowered them into place over the ruined portion of the log, bridging the yard-wide gap that marked her treefolk footprint. She began to whisper. The sound was like wind whistling through the branches of a lonely forest, and it allowed the sapling to touch the weblike maze of magical power that interlaced every square inch of the ground and wood.

The moss responded, whispering back in a faint collective voice that crackled like duff underfoot. It extended sharp fibers so small only a faerie could see them, and the fibers pierced the wounds in the yew's feet to feed on an infinitesimal part of it.

She'd been fortunate to find this particular breed of moss. It was a scavenger that fed on dead wood like the log, and this gave her a way to easily manipulate its growth. As the moss consumed the sapling's lifeblood, it transformed the sap from the stuff of life into the stuff of death—raw, concentrated yew poison. She had thought this might be painful to some extent, but exerting her will and Colfenor's gifts was instead only exhilarating, It was the natural process of life feeding itself, serving as a tool to create more life. The poison was not her goal, but the means by which she would rebuild the groundling's hivelike town.

The moss, though filled with deadly magic, grew along her splayed fingers like grapevines winding along a frame in a kithkin vineyard. The moss fed on what parts of the sap weren't used in creating the poison. With subtle shoves and nuanced coaxing the yew encouraged a facsimile of the groundlings' home to take shape beneath her hands, replacing every hut, mound, and cell with as much precision as root-memory allowed. The sapling felt the entire village still in the soil after the fact, and with her guidance the moss rebuilt everything in minutes. With creaks and an involuntary groan of relief she straightened and stood, taking in her handiwork. A touch here, a touch there—more or less as good as new. Except for the moss.

The moss would still grow. That was what the poison was for.

She found she'd timed this particular poison to work almost perfectly. No sooner had she declared the new log village complete than the sapling saw the moss begin to turn black and wiry. As it died, the moss solidified into a rough imitation of wood—every last bit of it. Now the village would not become overgrown by itself within hours but would probably last longer than it would have had she not stepped on it in the first place.

It was then that she realized no one else had yet witnessed her handiwork. The groundlings appeared to have made some kind of peace with Endry, who was hovering overhead and clearly enjoying himself.

"And that's how Colfenor slew Maralen, the Seven-Armed Giant She-Beast of Mornsong Valley, who also smells like a kithkin compost heap."

"I thought you said Maralen was a stupid elf who Colfenor ate during the Night of the Elf-Eating Treefolk," Nora said.

"And wasn't Maralen also the name of the cow?" her male companion asked. "The one whose magic dung turned the rest of Colfenor's stand against him?"

"It definitely was the cow," another confirmed.

"I'm just telling you the stories I know, my little ground rats," Endry said with what appeared, for him, to be great affection. "Judge for yourselves."

"Endry, it's done," the sapling said. "Groundlings, wingless, your home has been remade. The moss will return in time, but for now it should be exactly as you left it. Again, I'm sorry for the trouble I caused you."

"How did you— Oh, my," Nora said. The rest of her walk through the renewed log village was made in silence, echoed by the rest of the groundlings as they saw how complete the renewal was.

To the surprise of no one, it was Endry who broke that reverent silence. "Yes, well, Nora, other ground rats, one and all, we really must be going," he said in a tone the sapling found comically bizarre—it sounded as if he was trying to lower his voice by a full register and failing by half.

"Come, Endry," the sapling said.

"Wait," Nora said from atop a three-story moss-wood tower.

She ran up a broken twig that served as a bridge to the outside of the log and waved at the faerie. "Endry of Glen Elendra."

"What did you call me?" Endry said. "No one's ever called me anything like that."

"Was it improper?" Nora asked.

"No, I just— No. Thank you. I mean, no it wasn't. And thank you."

"I think I get it," Nora said. "Endry, will you do something for us? Will you tell Oona we are here? That we exist?"

"If I know it, she'll know it," Endry said, and this time the sapling heard no false note in his voice at all. It was, in the yew's short experience with the faerie, a first.

The groundlings' ruined village was a half mile behind them before Endry caught up with the yew, announcing his presence with a cheer. "Ha! I figured that one out myself. Bite a fungus, Veesa!"

"Figured what out? That I could help them remake their home?"

"What? No, that was stupid and not my idea, thank you very much. I mean the plan," Endry said. "I made them think I wouldn't care if they chopped you up. It flummoxed them good, didn't it?"

"So you do care?" the sapling asked, confused.

"No," Endry said. "And then I got them all to think I liked telling them stories. Ha! That was the second brilliant part!"

"You didn't?"

"Of course I did!" the faerie laughed. "How am I going to become a big, famous faerie hero—even more famous, I mean— if I don't practice my epic-storytelling technique?"

"Now you sound like the kithkin archer," the sapling said.

"You take that back." Endry said but not entirely convincingly. "And then there was that bit at the end. As if I'm going to tell Oona anything about those sods."

"But it was true, wasn't it?" the sapling asked. "Oona knows everything you know?"

"Oh," Endry said. "Well, maybe, yes, but . . . Oh. Rats."

"Why is your carapace pink?" the sapling asked.

"It isn't."

"Yes, it is."

"I'm not hovering around here to be insulted," Endry said.

"Hover where you like," the sapling said. "But you are pink, my friend. Perhaps you should have one of your sisters take a look at that."

* * * * *

It took Ashling three full seconds after her feet last touched solid rock to react with anything other than a shout of surprise. Then, with the ground below headed toward her at a dizzying speed and the rush of wind buffeting her tumbling body, the need to stay alight overwhelmed her, and she involuntary flared. Then her voluntary control took over, and Ashling pumped out as much flame as she could muster to keep the furious wind at bay.

But she was still falling. The sensation was nothing like the dreamlike ride she'd taken through the elemental's realm. This trip would end in death, even for her.

The memory of the elemental was still there. Focus on it. Call to it. Bring the elemental here. Surely she could do that. She'd done it without even trying twice already.

It refused to come to her aid, but her effort was enough to open a momentary flash of contact. The elemental could sense her animosity and anger, but its fear of her had justifiably returned. That much she felt in the connection she willed into being. But whether the elemental wished it or not, for a split-second Ashling was in direct contact with the elemental, and she felt no qualms about consciously taking the power that had once been forced upon her.

The explosion incinerated the tops of several trees that had the misfortune to be directly beneath her. Within the conflagration's center, the flamekin struggled to rein in the surge of energies, which refused to be bridled. Perhaps she could guide it and herself downward. Ashling was a bit alarmed at how easy it was when she put her mind to it. The borrowed flame turned into a wedge of directed heat and energy that consumed the trunks of the dying mountain evergreens to their roots and kept going, mushrooming against the rocky ground.

And still the borrowed elemental power raged through her. Ashling meant to take as much as she could get, to consume the elemental entirely if she had to, but she had badly underestimated how much power there was for the taking.

I should be dead, Ashling told herself as she felt her fall, already slowing, come to a stop some six feet above the flame-enveloped mountainside. And then she began to rise on a column of steam and black smoke. The more she shunted the power toward the ground, the faster she went. Soon she had the rocky spire from which she'd fallen in view, and with less effort than before. Perhaps the monks who had knocked her over the side might still be taken by surprise.

A swift kick to the head as she crested the edge of the outlook quickly disavowed Ashling of that notion. Ashling's head struck the side of the mountain next but bounced back without too much harm to anything but the pilgrim's pride. The uncharacteristically aggressive flamekin had clearly tracked her descent, her unlikely nadir, and her slowly accelerating rise. They hadn't been fooled for a moment.

She nearly used the rebound to counterattack wildly and without mercy, but something made her pause and take a good look at what she was fighting. Two of them. The same two. They were not as identical as she'd first supposed. The similarity of their garb and their strangeness had kept her from noticing differences in hue, build, and size. They had also adjusted their positions and were no longer side by side—the one with the slightly bluer flame stood to the fore by a few feet, while the more golden, slighter monk stood perpendicular to the other's shoulder, giving them reasonably safe 360-degree coverage. She didn't know what they were expecting other than her, but Ashling felt a bit slighted. She was channeling the power of an elemental, and they looked as if they were about to teach a simple lesson to an errant student.

Ashling had observed long enough. If these two wanted a fight, they'd get the business end of her elemental fire and then some. Her eyes flickered, and she sent the living flame slamming into the mountain, driving her toward her foes like a blazing arrow. Or she would have, had her connection to the elemental not been pulled from her grasp—the elemental's doing, she knew immediately. And she was falling again.

This plunge was neither as far nor nearly as dangerous. She skidded down the mountainside a few feet to land ingloriously upon her hindquarters with a thud. A small cascade of gravel showered down upon her shoulders and head, sizzling and popping as her fire raged furiously.

Another brief gravel avalanche scattered grit across her bent legs, and she followed the cascade back to its source. The blue monk stood at the inner edge of the outcrop, hands on his hips. He did not smile or even appear particularly friendly, but his eyes had lost the killing spark only another flamekin could recognize. He did, however, wave the golden monk forward and made a gesture toward the subordinate's belt. The gold monk uncoiled a length of woven steel and tossed the end to Ashling, then braced his foot against a sturdy rock.

"You impressed him," the golden monk said. "Can I interest you in a cup of kerosin tea?"

Iliona watched Rhys closely as he strode into the center of the burned-out circle at the base of the valley. He stared down at the smoking circle that marked the last place any of them had seen Ashling. The elf hunter sniffed the air, scowled, and looked up at Maralen. "Spread out," he said. "Find her."

Maralen stood at the edge of the clearing. "I don't think she's here anymore."

Iliona didn't feel Maralen's presence intruding on her mind, which meant the loathsome creature was too preoccupied by the other bent and twisted thoughts that rattled around in her dark-haired head. Good. Maybe she wouldn't notice Endry was missing, or how long the male twin had been gone.

"Don't think," Rhys snapped. "Just— Please, just send the faeries to scout the immediate area. Look for signs of Ashling or of the direction she went."

Rhys folded his arms while he waited.

Maralen nodded. "You heard him," she called. "Take a good look around and tell us if you see anything."

"Right away." Iliona beckoned for Veesa to follow her and shot high into the upper reaches of the trees. From his demeanor, Rhys obviously didn't expect the faeries to find anything useful. Being the pragmatic, paternal creature he was, the elf had to make sure.

Iliona broke through the canopy into the bright morning

sun, joined seconds later by Veesa. The Vendilion sisters joined hands and pressed their foreheads together as they talked.

"Waste of time," Veesa said. "The flamekin is long gone."

"And it's busywork," Iliona added. "Where is Endry?"

"I haven't seen him," Veesa said. "He muttered something about all the fun things there are to investigate around here. I imagine sniffing around for the nonexistent trail of a misplaced pilgrim doesn't quite measure up."

"I know it," Iliona replied. "That's why I stopped you here. I have a radical proposal."

"Ooh," Veesa said, feigning great interest. "Tell, tell."

"I got the idea when only you answered her call to give the giants their special dream. Maralen gave us orders. I say if those orders are carried out to her satisfaction, it doesn't matter which or how many of us got the job done."

"Disobey?" Veesa's eyes gleamed.

"Not directly. More like . . . loosely interpret."

"But Mother Oona made us promise to be good."

"Endry's already broken that promise. Otherwise he'd be here now, wouldn't he?"

"But we can't be bad just because Endry was." Veesa may have intended her words to be cautionary, but her delighted expression completely betrayed her true feelings.

"Oh, we'll be good. Maralen will get what she asks for. So why shouldn't we get what we want?"

"I want lots of things," Veesa said.

"But one thing in particular: to do as we please again."

"What do you have in mind?" Veesa said.

"You go look for the flamekin," Iliona said. "And you won't find her because she's not here anymore. So you do that, we both cover for Endry, and I'll hang back to watch Maralen and Rhys. I want to see know how closely she's paying attention to us, how much we can get away with."

"So you want me to search for the flamekin."

"Right."

"Even though I won't find her."

"Exactly. Maralen doesn't even really care about finding the matchstick, she just wants to put on a show. She hasn't even missed Endry, as far as I can tell."

Veesa grinned. "So I get to do nothing? I like plans that require me to do nothing."

"Then we're agreed?" Veesa nodded, her expression sharp and cold. Iliona released her sibling's hands and floated away. "Carry on then," she said. With a shared giggle, the Vendilion sisters split up.

Iliona slowly floated down into the canopy, careful not to betray herself by sound, sight, or thought. It took concentration and effort, two things the Fae were not fabled for, but she was able to maintain the slightest touch of contact with her sister without drawing Maralen's attention. Iliona hoped to find Endry soon. The sooner they mastered talking behind their overseer's back, the sooner they could exploit it.

Iliona lit on a thick branch and crouched among the shadows.

"So this is all down to flamekin magic," Maralen said, "Ashling's quest for her elemental."

"It seems that way," Rhys said.

"It is that way," Maralen said. "What else could it be?" Rhys held his tongue, but she saw the answer in his eyes. "You don't think Brigid has turned on us and taken Ashling away? Again?"

"She has done it before," Rhys said. "But no, I don't think that. I just want to rule it out." He started. "Where is the kithkin?"

"Haven't seen her lately." Maralen glanced around.

Rhys sighed. "Can you tell the Vendilion to look for her too?"

"Of course," Maralen said.

Iliona quailed. If Maralen called out to her at this range the game would be over before it began. The eldest Vendilion made herself as inconspicuous as possible, hardly daring to think a coherent thought.

Below, Maralen concentrated. A ripple of annoyance flashed across her features. To Iliona's relief, she heard Veesa's irritated assent.

"Yes, yes, we'll look for the archer too. I thought you were going to ease up on the chores you assigned us?"

Maralen smiled at Rhys. "It's done."

Iliona exhaled, but she did not relax. There was almost no way Maralen could have missed her lurking overhead, not unless her hold on the Vendilion was weaker than they thought. And that was definitely worth exploring.

Rhys peered at Maralen. "Anything wrong?"

"No, it's just . . ." The elf maiden tossed her head casually. "They're willful little bugs, is all. Keeping track of them is like counting blades of grass in a field."

Thorns on a rosebush, Iliona corrected. We're much more like thorns on a rosebush, because blades of grass don't cut you when you're careless.

* * * * *

Rhys stared coldly at Maralen. He didn't want her to feel like the bad news she had was her fault, but he had no other honest reaction to give.

"They're all gone," Maralen said again. "Ashling, Brigid, Sygg—even the sapling. There's no sign of them anywhere." She waited for Rhys to answer, and when he did not she said, "What do you want to do?"

"I want to find them." Rhys said. "But we have no time. The Hemlock are too close." He hated the plaintive tone in his voice, and when he heard it he wished he had not spoken at all. "I don't know how we can track everyone down and get out of here. We can't be in two places at once."

"Of course we can, Rhys. We've got faeries." She cocked her head and smiled. "You and I can take the giants to Rosheen. Endry already went after the sapling."

"He did?" Iliona blurted, then added, "That is, he *did!*"

"Yes, he did," Maralen confirmed with a peculiar expression. "He's hard to reach, but I did finally get his attention. She's having a bit of a wander, from what Endry tells me. She's not moving fast or in any one direction for long, so it should be a simple matter to stay with her."

Rhys turned and faced Maralen. "Good. I've been calling out to the sapling, but I don't think she hears me. I definitely don't hear her. It seems the close bond Colfenor and I shared isn't hereditary."

"We shouldn't need to worry about her anymore. And Endry says the sapling is looking for Ashling. He might wind up finding them both for us. And if not, I'll send one of the other faeries to find Ashling—or even Brigid, if you want. We can at least determine where they are and whether they need help."

"If the faeries can find them," Rhys said.

"They'll find them. Won't you, my friends?" Maralen coaxed obedient nods from the Vendilion sisters. "See, Daen? No worries there. They know Ashling and the sapling well enough to pick them out in a crowd, so to speak. It'll take some time to find them, but we can use that time to reach Rosheen and see what she has to tell us."

Rhys let this notion sink in. It might work. He shifted slightly so that he could see both the eastern horizon and Maralen in his peripheral vision. The dark-haired Mornsong continued to perplex and impress him. She had no longstanding personal connection to any of them, or to Colfenor's ritual. She played no role in it, bore no responsibility for it, and indeed had neither gained nor suffered from it. Yet the two people most intimately affected by the ritual, Ashling and the sapling, were gone, and Maralen was still actively seeking to unravel its mysteries.

Rhys knew Maralen was motivated by more than sheer kindness, but she was steadfast and eager to contribute. She also commanded the Vendilion clique, and while Rhys had a whole separate list of questions regarding that little arrangement, he was grateful to have them as an asset. It was true that there was very little a faerie could not find, so if Ashling and the sapling were still alive and in Lorwyn, they were within reach.

Before Rhys could answer Maralen, however, his keen ears heard something massive moving toward them from the west. Two massive things, in fact.

The uppermost branches of the tree line parted and Brion thrust his big, round head into the clearing. The giant's gnarled features twisted into a crooked-toothed smile. He seemed alert and energetic after his nap, mostly if not completely recovered from the brothers' recent ordeal.

He lumbered into the clearing amid a cloud of broken branches, planted his huge fists on his hips, and said, "Hello, Boss."

"Brion. Feeling better?"

"You bet, Boss."

Kiel emerged behind Brion, wiping out the tall branches his brother's entrance had missed. Kiel's eyes were half-closed, and he dragged his knuckles on the ground as he walked, as was his habit.

"We want to go see Rosheen," Brion said. "Kiel can't wait anymore."

"What?"

"Rosheen. There's something important we need to tell her . . . or hear from her. Not too clear on the details." Brion shrugged. "We just know it's time to go. That's how Rosheen works."

Kiel leaned forward and shoved his brother's shoulder with his knuckles. "Rosheen," the long-bearded giant said. "Tales."

"I know," Brion growled.

Kiel thumped him again. "Rosheen waits."

Brion bared his teeth. "All right, all right." He glanced down at Rhys. "Can we go now, Boss?"

"We can," Rhys said. He nodded grimly. "And I think we'd better."

Maralen exhaled, apparently relieved at how easy it had been to convince the giants. "So," she said cheerfully, "you boys do know where Rosheen is, I hope. It's easy to reach giant country, but finding any one giant in particular—"

"Rosheen's easy to find," Brion said. "You just have to know where to look and follow the sound of her talking."

"Fine." Rhys struggled to keep his shoulders from slumping. "That's it then," he said. "There's nothing keeping us here. If everyone's ready to travel, we should go."

Iliona and Veesa descended from the canopy. They flew in a figure eight around both giants' heads.

"Here we are! Hello, giants!" Iliona said. She called out to Rhys and Maralen, "Are we going to Rosheen's party now?"

"We are," Maralen said.

"In a moment," Rhys said. "First, I have to impose upon you once more. I have another job for the Vendilion."

"Of course." Maralen called out, "Iliona—"

"I'm right here." Iliona buzzed up from a patch of grass near the edge of the slope.

Maralen frowned. "Where is your sister?"

"Here." Veesa rose up from the same patch of grass. She darted over to Iliona and hovered there.

"I only need one," Rhys said. "The other should be sent after Ashling." He bounded down from the boulder and landed lightly next to Maralen. "If I may?"

"By all means."

Rhys beckoned the faerie sisters closer and unfurled his broadleaf map. "See this? This is where we are. And here is where we're going."

"You drew this?" Iliona said. "It's a good job."

"Thank you."

"You should have been a cartographer," Veesa said. "Or a calligrapher. You have beautiful handwriting."

"I was a Gilt Leaf daen," Rhys said brusquely. "I have memorized maps of the entire Blessed Nation and all its surroundings."

Both faeries flitted up beside Rhys, each looking at the map from over one of his shoulders.

"Such detail," Iliona said. She nodded to Veesa. "See? He even made little squiggles for the trees and little pointy shapes for the mountains."

"I see."

"Pay attention, please."

"Look! There's a little worm!"

"Enough!" Rhys snapped. "Please. This is a simple request. You see this spot here? Where the Porringer Valley abuts the foothills?"

"We see."

"There's a ravine there called Dauba. I haven't been through this territory in years, but it used to have a livewood bridge spanning it. I need you to confirm that bridge is still there."

"Why?"

Veesa yawned. "Faeries don't use bridges."

"Does that mean you don't know what one looks like?"

"No."

"Then it doesn't matter if you use it or why I want to you to find it. I remember a bridge spanning the Dauba Ravine. Find out if there is one. It's that simple."

"Iliona," Maralen said, "you go. I want Veesa here with me."

Rhys nodded. "Head straight for the ravine on the west edge of Porringer. Go now." Iliona bobbed her head to Rhys and zipped up into the trees.

Rhys turned back to Maralen. "If you're ready," he said, "we can go now."

"Quite ready." Maralen smiled and cocked her head. "Eager, in fact."

* * * * *

Gryffid marched across the Gilt Leaf camp to the cluster of command tents at its center. Taercenn Eidren had set up in Gryffid's headquarters, and the Perfect's presence had thoroughly undermined the acting commander's authority. The daens and officers of the Hemlock, Nightshade, and Deathcap still obeyed Gryffid's orders, but not before glancing at the taercenn for confirmation. So far Eidren had magnanimously backed Gryffid to the smallest detail, but it was clear that the hunters Gryffid led in the wake of Nath's fall were no longer solely his to command.

The daen slowed as he neared his own headquarters. Losing control of the Hemlock and other assembled packs was a terrible dishonor, but it was nothing compared to what losing the pack itself would have cost him.

A cluster of finely dressed courtiers huddled on one side of the tent flap, and on the other stood a squadron of fearsome, stoic vine-bred elves. Eidren traveled in exalted company, with the best and brightest elf nobles and the fiercest, most formidable elf warriors. These careless additions had changed the character of Gryffid's pack to the point where he himself almost didn't recognize it.

Gryffid was still a Gilt Leaf elf, however. He had sworn a terrible oath of retribution against Rhys, but even that did not erase his larger duty to the Nation. He was bound by the will of his superiors, and if he could not achieve his vengeance under Eidren's direction, he knew he would not achieve it at all.

That did not mean he had to sit back and let the taercenn define his duty for him. He stared for a moment more at the courtiers and vinebred, all of whom studiously ignored him. Gryffid straightened his back. He was leader of the Hemlock Pack, and he knew the quarry better than anyone else alive. His experience could cut this hunt short and bring about Rhys's much-deserved death, not just for his own sense of honor but also for the good of the entire tribe. Eidren did not have to accept Gryffid's opinions, but he did have to listen.

Gryffid strode past the assemblies on either side of the flap and entered the command tent. Eidren's influence was even more obvious here than it was outside. The new taercenn clearly went for a higher level of luxury than traditional field commanders. Under Gryffid, the headquarters was a typically sparse and severe affair: a chair for the commander, a table on which to spread maps, and a trio of green Gilt Leaf lanterns. Less than a day under Eidren saw the inside of the tent wreathed in shimmering bolts of fine cloth, rich green vines with magnificent red flowers trailing along the support posts, and the smell of hyacinth in the air. Eidren himself sat in the only chair, relaxed and comfortable despite his perfect posture.

"Ah, Daen," he said. He rose and waited for Gryffid to salute, firing it back as soon as it came. "Is there news?"

"Not yet, Taer."

"Not that you know of, you mean. Come." He stepped around the table and beckoned Gryffid closer. "If you're not here to report on your primary mission, you must have something equally important to declare."

"My only interest is in the traitor, Taer."

"Of course. Taercenn Nath spoke very highly of your dedication, you know."

"I admired Nath a great deal," Gryffid said stiffly. "He was an excellent general, an excellent elf. I was honored to serve him."

"I would expect nothing less," Eidren said. "But you and Nath were even closer than taercenn and daen, weren't you?"

"I . . . don't understand, Taer."

"Come, come now. We know Nath came here to assert control over the Hemlock, to guide it back to the Nation and back onto the path to perfection. In aid of this, he promoted you and took you under his wing, didn't he?"

"Yes, Taer."

"He combined three full packs, plus auxiliaries, and gave you command over one full third of his forces."

"Yes, Taer."

"He brought real discipline back. He recognized your potential and promoted you so that you might realize it."

"Yes, Taer."

"He honored you. He taught you what it truly means to serve the Nation. And to continue doing so even after certain . . . unfortunate circumstances . . . made service seem impossible."

"Yes . . . Taer."

"So let me ask you then." Eidren leaned forward so that his sharp, precise features were inches from Gryffid's face. "When the traitor Rhys disfigured you and killed all those elves outside Porringer Valley . . . did Nath teach you the use of glamer, or did you know it already?"

Gryffid's spine went cold.

"I know you saw Nath's body," Eidren said. "So you know what he looked like without his magical façade. My question is: Did he show you his secret before he died? Did he speak of duty and sacrifice, of the demands that perfection places on us all? Did he show you how to hide from the Nation even as you worked to advance it?"

"I— Taer, I . . ."

Eidren leaned back against the table. "Answer truly, eyeblight. Humor me and pretend your life depends on it."

Gryffid swallowed hard. "Nath revealed himself to me in the wake of the kin-slayer's foul yew magic. He told me that the Nation still had uses for the disgraced and the disfigured. He saw the injuries I had, and he saved me anyway. He offered me a choice of sorts: Conceal my imperfections and continue to serve, or die at his hand and be counted among the dozens killed by Rhys's poison spell."

"And you made the correct choice."

"There was no choice at all, Taer. I awoke impaled on the branches of a ruined tree, and since then I have had only two goals: to kill Rhys, then to die myself. I would give all that I have and all that I am to see the traitor dead. If I may be of use to the Nation after that, so much the better, but in truth I would be just as satisfied if this sacred duty were my last. The Nation must endure, and it will endure, but I see no role for me in it other than this."

"Service to the Nation is a hard and arduous path, Daen. Very few of us are able to do it for the long term, no matter how exalted or successful. I cannot measure your contribution in years, or even months. But I can promise you this: Rhys will be made to atone for what he has done. And you will be there to see it."

"I understand."

"I don't think you do. Nath explained he was but one of many of us, those who act in the best interest of the Nation in the shadow of the Sublime Council. Foreign influences—treefolk and the like—must not have undue sway with the king and queen. Nath toiled not for a single ruler but for the Nation itself, and he brought you into the fold—informally, to be sure, but not without due consideration."

Gryffid stood at attention with his back arrow-straight. "The taercenn did these things. He spoke of something like a secret society of noble elves, vinebred, and eyeblights who maintained the pretense of physical perfection and beauty when the reality would not suit their positions. They endured this lie rather than withdraw from the Nation and deprive it of their talents. He did not say much beyond that in the way of details."

"Then allow me," Eidren said. "The secret society Nath spoke of? It exists. I myself am a member of it, though I have not had to rely on glamer to project the face of perfection. My sacrifice is of a different nature."

"You? But Taer, I—" Gryffid let his sentence die unfinished. How far did this conspiracy's roots penetrate into the Gilt Leaf hierarchy? How many elves were only outwardly loyal to the Sublime Council? How many others like Nath, Eidren, and Gryffid were there?

"We are many," Eidren said, reading Gryffid's thoughts on his face, "yet all too few. The loss of Nath was a great setback to our cause. He was the most vigorous pursuer of our ends. He is not easily replaced.

"Are you aware of the situation that underlies your quest for Rhys's head? The lowland boggarts have run wild and are in near revolt. Roving packs of them prey on the countryside like bandits. The Sublime Council is hopelessly mired in the advice of treefolk and their seedguide lackeys. Traveling Perfects are drained of life and cast to die at the side of the road. The oldest living yew sage stages his own very public suicide by elemental fire in the streets of Kinsbaile. The stalwart daen of the Hemlock Pack wipes out scores of his own hunters, then brutally murders his taercenn in full view of the assembled packs.

"Taken together, these things all create a disturbing trend. Things are not as they should be. This is precisely the kind of situation our society originally banded together to combat. You want to kill Rhys and die, Daen? You do not have that luxury. The

Nation's continued future demands far more of you and requires a far greater sacrifice than you have so far made."

Gryffid snarled slightly, but he managed to turn his annoyance into words before Eidren could chastise his insubordination. "May I ask your permission to speak without regard to rank, Taer?"

Eidren smiled patiently. "You have it."

"You speak of luxury and sacrifice," Gryffid said, "yet you sit here filthy with the former and bereft of the latter." He reached out and took up a handful of shining silver cloth. "This place is more a dandy's sitting room than a taercenn's headquarters. Nath was a great hunter, and this is a hunter's business. Why have you, an artist, come here?"

"My response to your . . . remarkably eloquent and, had I not granted permission, *suicidal* outburst is twofold." Eidren reached over the desk and pulled out a wide roll of parchment. "First, it will please you to know that, while I am not quite the hunter Nath was, I have achieved results that will make our ongoing pursuit successful. I paid a visit to the Nightshade camp before I ever set foot in your tent." Eidren undid the ribbon and unrolled a detailed map of western Lorwyn on the table. "At my suggestion, the Nightshade daen flooded the region between Kinsbaile and the Murmuring Bosk with his long-range scouts. They spotted Rhys here just hours ago. By all accounts, he and his ragged little band are heading north toward the foothills. Why is anyone's guess, though I have my own suspicions, and I immodestly suggest they are right. They have been thus far." Eidren pointed at the map until he was sure Gryffid was looking, and the taercenn stood up straight. "Once you and I agree on the proper course of action, we can move out in force."

Gryffid's eyes widened. "Excellent news, Taer."

"I agree. Now, you really must speak far more carefully to me on the subject of sacrifice." Eidren stepped forward and Gryffid braced himself for a blow. The new taercenn did not lash out, however, but instead took hold of his high-collared robe with both hands and wrenched it open, exposing his chest.

Gryffid stared, unable to speak. Below his robe, Eidren's chest was almost completely covered by a complicated network of nettlevines.

"Nath is not easily replaced," Eidren said. "I was not up to the task—no single elf was. I was instructed to accept the embrace of the nettlevines, and I have done so willingly, eagerly, for the good of the Nation. With my strength and speed and focus thus improved, and with your able assistance in leading the pack, the loss of Nath will not be so keenly felt.

"I am in the prime of my life. In other circumstances, I would have served the Nation for another decade or more before I required glamer to hide my advancing age. Now I have but a year to do my duty, perhaps less. I am stronger, swifter, sharper, but I will be dead in a matter of months . . . or perhaps a bit longer, given my expertise with cultivation." Eidren drew his robe closed and turned away from Gryffid. "So speak not to me of sacrifice, Daen Gryffid. You hardly know the meaning of the word."

"Forgive me, Taer," Gryffid sputtered. "I did not know—"

"Nor did you need to, not until now. Listen well, and understand: The choices Nath gave you have not changed. You will be one of us, you will act according to our dictates but of your own free will . . . or we will destroy you long before you ever achieve your bitter goal. Glamers are child's play. We will make a vinebred of you too, that you may finally achieve some measure of true worth for the Blessed Nation. This is your pack, Daen, but it is my mission that takes precedence. You will not know victory, or defeat, or even death until I am through with you. Is that clear?"

"Yes, Taer. Perfectly clear."

"Very good. You're an excellent soldier, Gryffid, and a competent leader. Your prey is within your grasp. Go now, and lead your hunters to him."

Gryffid hesitated. "An all-out pursuit?"

"Spare no effort. I will always be right behind you, supporting you, guiding you. When you finally run Rhys to ground, I intend to be there to witness his comeuppance."

"Yes, Taer."

Eidren straightened his clothes and turned his back to Gryffid. "Dismissed, Daen."

"Thank you, Taer."

Gryffid quit the tent as quickly as he could. Outside, he strode past the courtiers and vinebred and signaled two of the Hemlock officers standing nearby.

"We're moving out," Gryffid said. "Muster everyone and everything. I want to be south of Kinsbaile by morning."

"Have we found him, Taer?"

"Yes, we have." Gryffid nodded at his subordinate. "And this time we won't rest until we have his head on a pike."

CHAPTER 10

"Your friend's awake, Rudder." The merrow's raspy, thickly accented voice was even more guttural than Sygg's. "Seen better days, I think. Where did you pick up one of their ilk?"

The speaker was hidden in darkness. Brigid could only see the shape of a merrow half again as large as the captain, casting her friend—ally, at least—in shadow. The fish-man floated in midair above Sygg, blocking the strangely filtered sunlight and casting the kithkin and the captain in murky darkness. Sygg was clearly visible, however, a shadow surrounded by chaotic orange rays that filtered through gaps in the crannog's inner wall. His gills pulsed weakly, and he did not waste his breath on a reply to the merrow who had laid him low.

No, Brigid corrected, the big merrow wasn't floating in midair. It was midwater. Moving water. Midstream. The crannog wall she saw was the interior of the structure's foundation, and the archer herself rested against another piece of it. She was no longer dry and protected in Sygg's shapewater air bubble but floating freely in the depths. Her lungs insisted on gasping for air that was at least twenty feet over her head. She knew she should be drowning, dying, but somehow she continued to breathe.

The breath she drew was sweet and pure and tasted faintly of— Best not the think of what it tasted faintly of. It was breathing—breathing river water, but breathing. Brigid wondered whether she could talk.

"As a matter of fact, I have seen better days," she said, gratified to hear her own voice, even muffled by water. "And I've seen prettier faces. What exactly is going on here, ah . . ." Think, Brigid. Some native merrow term of respect. "Schoolmaster?"

The hulking merrow lashed his tail and was upon Brigid in seconds. She silently swore to think harder next time. The archer pushed herself back but was understandably unfamiliar with the mechanics of swimming underwater, and so she didn't get far.

The strange brute didn't move to strike or harm her. He merely hovered where he'd stopped, suspended inches away from her wide-eyed face. The big merrow's long, grim visage appeared from within Sygg's shadow. The stranger resembled the enormous catfish she'd seen earlier except for the long, sharp, interlocking teeth that protruded haphazardly from its mouth even when closed, as it was now.

"Do you mock me, landwalker?" the merrow burbled.

"Forgive me, my merrow's rusty," Brigid said. "Would you believe I couldn't even breathe underwater until a few minutes ago? I won't be fluent in your preferred honorifics for at least another five or six."

"Breathing is a privilege that can be taken away," the merrow said. His teeth scratched and squeaked against themselves as he talked. "But I won't unless you make it necessary." His bulbous, milky-gray eyes glanced toward her hands and feet, which Brigid instinctively tried to move. Though there was nothing around her wrists or ankles, they now seemed firmly fastened to the slimy foundation boulder. The invisible bonds felt smooth and pliable but also extremely tough and resilient. They were certainly tight enough.

"Shapewater shackles?" Brigid said. "Better and better. So, Handsome, could I prevail upon you to tell me why you are here?

Because I do appreciate that gift of breathing. I really, really do, and I don't want to jeopardize that. But I'd really like to know. And I'd like to know why Captain Sygg is just . . . floating there. Is he all right?"

"Sygg suffered injuries, but I believe I've gotten to them in time. He is to go on a journey."

"That's wonderful," Brigid said. "Truly. I don't think he's traveled nearly enough lately. He and I, we journey together, you understand? So maybe we should just be moving on. Don't want to—"

"Do you ever shut your mouth, landwalker?" the merrow said.

"Just tell me what's going on. If you're just trying to, what, hold me hostage? So you can get Sygg to do something? Let me ask him! We're comrades, allies. I'm known in some parts of this world as the Hero of kmphblf. Funnummabiff!" Something soft settled over Brigid's mouth, and while it did not interfere with her breathing, it reduced her words to so much gibberish.

"That's better," the merrow snarled. Brigid's muffled sounds grew louder and more intense as her anxiety mounted.

"Almost," the merrow said. "See here, landwalker. Now that you are gagged, you have no hope of being understood. So please, just be silent. The malignants who injured Sygg may still be around."

"Whuffamuwifmeh?"

"Malignants. Merrow you do not want to meet, landwalker. Wait here. Quietly." With that, the merrow drifted up to resume his vigil over Sygg while Brigid was left to stew against a rock at the bottom of the river.

Stew she did. For the first half hour she attempted to speak, shout, yell, and scream through the shapewater mask, but she made no coherent sounds and received no response from the stranger. When she finally gave up on shouting, she decided it might be time to get a better idea of what had gone on here.

The light filtering in through the crannog foundation wall was the most obvious place to start. The gaps in the once-watertight timbers bore marks of violence, though they appeared to have withstood the blows without knocking the whole thing down.

All right, so she wouldn't be crushed by a collapsing crannog. She still she couldn't bring herself to just sit here bound and gagged.

There. The open lock. The upper half appeared to break the river's surface. Even if the big merrow took away her breathing rights, Brigid could probably reach that lock before drowning—if not for the bonds around her wrists.

After a half hour of bouncing her gaze from the unguarded lock to the floating, motionless merrow above, the Wanderwine's deep currents rocked Brigid gently back into unlikely and inconvenient sleep.

* * * * *

"This?" the sapling asked. "This is your shortcut?"

"You're awfully spry, for a tree," Endry remarked. "What, are you afraid?"

"Fear has nothing to do with it," the sapling said, "I'm simply being practical. There is no point in my setting out to cross that."

That was one of the most alarming things the sapling had yet seen in her short life. Even with all of her inherited knowledge, she could not ascertain how a being made entirely of wood and leaves might traverse an open river of slow-moving but quite molten lava.

The sapling had not expected this at all. She'd chosen this route as a safe and direct path to the base of Mount Tanufel, which loomed with what the faerie insisted was "ominous portent" over this deadly river of burning rock.

"I'm willing to try—"

"No, that's impossible," the yew interrupted. "Even if you had the strength to lift me, the strain of putting all my weight on a single branch—"

"So you lose a branch. I've seen you lose those already."

"You are not carrying me across the river of lava."

"You're the one who's in such a hurry to find a woman made of rock and fire," Endry said. "I was just offering to help."

"We can go around," the sapling said, "but I don't know if we will be in time."

"In time? Wait, in time for what?" Endry asked.

"I did not see it at first," the sapling said, waving a leafy hand at the molten rock, "but this proves the time is near. The mountain isn't ready."

"What?" Endry said. "Talk sense."

"We will need to reach Ashling soon or she will no longer be Ashling."

"All right then. If you say so. But how soon is soon?"

"Soon," the sapling replied. "That is all I know. Even Colfenor did not know the exact hour. But he saw the signs, recognized their import. As do I."

"Signs of what? I thought the idea was just to get everyone back together." He hovered before the sapling's face and stabbed a tiny finger at her eye. "Isn't it?"

"That remains to be seen," the sapling said. "Colfenor's knowledge, when it comes to the future, is less than perfect. Trust me, faerie. Things are changing."

"Sure," Endry said. "Things are changing all the time. That's what I always say. I say, 'Things, they sure do change.' Now can we get going?"

"You misunderstand," the sapling said. "I was not specific. All things will be changing."

"Oh. But not me," the faerie said. "I'll never change."

"No," the sapling said to the faerie with complete honesty, "you won't."

"Good," Endry said. "Now, come on, you're not really going to walk around this, are you?"

"Yes, I am," the sapling said. "I have no other choice. You may feel free to meet me on the other side."

"Not why I asked," the faerie said. "I just thought you should know I took a look around from a few hundred feet up while you were gazing into the distance and thinking your deep yewling thoughts. If you go the way you're heading, you've got a hundred-mile walk. But if you follow me we can take the bridge. It's only a hundred yards up-lava from here."

"A bridge?" the sapling said, perplexed. "This formation is new. How could someone have had time to build—"

"A natural stone bridge," Endry said impatiently. "Made of stone. It was just a big stone, but the hot rock melted right through it and left the top part of it standing. So it's a bridge, and there's enough solid stone left for you to walk across safely. If you're lucky. And careful."

"Let us take the bridge," the sapling agreed. "Lead the way."

* * * * *

A heavy thud jolted Brigid from her slumber, reminding the kithkin archer how very much she wanted to awaken on dry land again. The thud came again, this time accompanied by an ominous crack.

"Heeeeyh!" she shouted at her quietly burbling merrow captor. "Heeeyphooooo!"

"The spell has almost run its course," the merrow hiss-bubbled. "Be quiet, damn you."

Be quiet. Another thud, again no reaction from either merrow, and now the current moving around Brigid grew noticeably stronger. A low creak remained after the heavier sound, and the kithkin was fairly certain that when the creak ended the whole crannog was coming down on top of her head.

Brigid tried to shout through the mask as a fourth—and as it happened, final—thud became a crash, and the crash revealed the cause of the sound.

It was an arbomander, the biggest one Brigid or any air-breather had ever seen. She'd heard stories of them at the docks, of course. Every merrow ferryman had to outdo his competitors with tales of the wondrous giants of the deep that could change the course of rivers. And as if to prove those tales correct, the monster opened its mouth, and the kithkin felt the current shift toward its enormous jaws.

The pull was so strong Brigid's body pulled her shapewater bonds tight between herself and the stone wall behind her. She risked a look upward and cried out in alarm and anger when she saw that both merrow had disappeared. That low-down fish-man had absconded with Sygg and, what was worse, left her here to be crushed, drowned, or eaten, if not all three in rapid succession.

The arbomander knocked away almost half the foundation wall—the portion beneath the surface, at least—but its thick, muscular neck and tough hide served to keep the crannog standing for now. The rushing water pulled away her still unused bow, which had somehow remained on her back, though her arrows were long gone—and the arbomander swallowed it whole. Brigid cursed through her mask—and the oath became a scream when her shapewater bonds dissipated without warning. The rushing water sent her tumbling after her lost weapon. More importantly, without shapewater, she couldn't breathe.

Considering where she was headed, Brigid decided not breathing was probably a less urgent problem than it seemed. Trying to keep what air remained in her lungs, Brigid flailed wildly toward the surface. She was already growing dizzy, and soon she'd have to exhale, and then—

"Got you!" Sygg said, knocking the air from her lungs with a high-speed merrow tackle. Brigid's eyes widened in terror, which only increased, even when she felt they were moving up toward the precious surface. The terror vanished when she broke through and took long, humid gulps of air. Sygg held her aloft, letting her cough out what water had managed to infiltrate her lungs.

"Sygg," Brigid said after she could speak again, "you're alive. Again."

"I'm very hard to kill," Sygg agreed, "as you know, Brigid."

"Hey, you called me 'Brigid,' " The archer grinned weakly. "Not 'kithkin.' "

"You should breathe more," the merrow said, "and talk less."

"You've forgiven me."

"Not a chance. I just didn't want a dead kithkin in my crannog."

"Of course. Say . . . why are we in the crannog again?"

"If you two are finished," the strange merrow said, and Brigid noticed for the first time that the brute had surfaced on the far side of the crannog's interior, "the landwalker is right. We should leave." As if to emphasize the point, the arbomander's nose broke the surface, sending another shudder through the crannog walls. Within seconds, they were cracking and swaying in the current.

"How?" Brigid said. "I don't think I can climb up. . . . Someone tied me to a rock, and I had to swim, and in case you hadn't noticed I'm not quite built for it. I just don't have the strength." It hurt to admit it, but it was true.

"Complain later," Sygg said. "This thing is coming down on our heads." As if to prove the ferryman's point a chunk of the crannog's upper wall snapped off under the strain of unaccustomed weight and plummeted toward them.

"Let's go, Flyrne." Sygg unceremoniously tucked the kithkin under one arm. With the other he called forth a column of shape-water directly beneath them. The water carried them out of the falling wreckage's path and kept going until they emerged into the dazzling light of midday. Below, the crannog collapsed in on itself but not before a familiar hulking merrow emerged upon his own column of water.

Long, waterlogged timbers from the wreckage of Crannog Aughn rose to the surface, and a tide of blood bubbled up. From the center of this churning cauldron, a long black tail flailed weakly. The arbomander, it appeared, had not survived its destructive visit to the crannog.

"Sygg," Brigid said at last, "you were just, well, dead, or unconscious, or whatever you get. Shouldn't we go back down?"

"Yes," Flyrne said. "Sygg, you need to get back to the river. You're still not well. The malignancy—"

"Look at that water," Sygg said, his voice straining, as Brigid had feared it might. "That arbomander— No one was controlling it. That was the malignancy, Flyrne. And if it wasn't already, now the river's going to be thick with it."

"Then we move upriver," Brigid said, "away from the blood. Before Sygg passes out, I think."

Sygg only nodded. He grunted with the effort it took to lower his charge to the surface, even with Flyrne's help. The ferryman released her almost immediately, and it was all he could do to tread water against the current. Slowly the two of them started to drift back toward the bloody wreckage.

Fortunately, Sygg was not proud. "Flyrne, would you mind helping Brigid onto the bank?"

The brutish stranger took Brigid into a gentle shapewater sling that smoothly guided the kithkin archer to the shore. She wasn't sure this would have put any undue strain on Sygg, so she asked with more than a little rancor, "So, Flyrne? What was with the shackles? You tried to drown me, and now we're friends?"

"I don't apologize for my actions," Flyrne said.

"He thought I wouldn't understand what's happened," Sygg said. "Or worse, that it had already gotten to me, this . . . malignancy."

"Next time, you might try talking, Flyrne," Brigid said. "Asking, maybe."

"One doesn't talk to a malignant," the big merrow said. "Not twice. I had to be sure."

* * * * *

"I think what I like," Endry said.

"Yet you take orders from your Godflower," the sapling said.

"Oona," the faerie corrected. "Her name is Oona."

"Yes," the sapling said. "That is one of her names."

"You're stalling, yewling," the faerie said. "The bridge isn't going to get any more solid the longer you look at it. In fact, I'd say there's a bit less of it than before. I'd pick up the pace if I were you."

The sapling felt a momentary flash of embarrassment, for the faerie was exactly right—she was stalling, and from simple fear.

"There are things moving down there," the sapling said.

"That's the lava," Endry said. "It does that, I think."

"No, in the lava," the sapling said. "Aren't there?"

"I think that's your imagination," the faerie said as he buzzed out to the middle of the bridge. "No, it all looks fine to me. Now let's take that first step. I'll be right here in case you slip."

"If I slip you'll be able to pull off a branch to remember me by," the sapling said. "But I appreciate the concern."

One step. Simple. She'd taken a great many steps since breaking the soil and becoming aware of the greater world around her and the heritage she carried. One more, plus another twenty or so, and this fiery nightmare would be behind her. Surely no more than thirty.

"That stone has to be pretty thick," the sapling said. "It has to support my weight."

"You'll be like a feather landing on a springjack's fur."

"What?"

"As the kithkin say."

"No they don't."

"How do you know? You were just sprouted. Now get moving," Endry ordered. "That thing is definitely getting thinner—and smaller. Come on, yewling, onward and overward!"

"The heat. I can barely stand it here." The sapling felt as if she would burst into flames at any moment. "There has to be another— Endry?"

"Great Mother, it's a flamekin army at full blaze! We're all going to be burned alive!"

It wasn't Endry's words themselves that sent her bounding onto the bridge so much as their volume, proximity, and the effect both had upon the sapling's tightly wound nerves. The first contact she made with the incredibly hot stone was painful, but it was nothing she couldn't handle if she kept moving. If she stopped on the bridge, the superheated stone beneath her root-feet would surely ignite. Even at a lumbering sprint the yew could hear her bark crackling with each step.

Her tenth step overwhelmed the pain barriers she'd erected. The eleventh was pure agony.

"You're halfway home," Endry shouted as he passed over her boughs to hover before her. "Now I don't want to alarm you, but when I say jump, you're going to want to jump."

Twelve steps. Unendurable pain.

"What? Why do I—"

"Jump!"

Thirteen.

The stone beneath her feet cracked and popped as the heat took its inevitable toll on the bridge.

Fourteen.

The sapling looked down as a chunk of the bridge as wide as she was tall dropped into the molten river below.

Fifteen.

Something in the lava looked up at her, locked its gaze with hers.

Sixteen.

The something disappeared into the molten river.

Seven—

"Ow!" the sapling yelped when she reached the far side. The impact fractured the already battered rock, and the yew had to lunge forward and scrabble at the stone to keep from falling.

"Pull!" Endry cried from overhead. The sapling felt the faerie's clawed feet and long fingers take hold of a shoulder-branch, and the effect on the yew's efforts was immediate. The extra lift let her get a grip in the cracking rock. She bit back a scream as leaves and bark sizzled in the heat. These parts of her body would heal and grow back. Her entire body would not.

She reached the far side of the river in three more long, if unbalanced, strides.

"Twenty on the nose," she said. But she added twenty to that before she slowed her pace long enough to see to her injuries.

"Slow down, you're not the only one who's hurting. My wings were in terrible danger!"

"Endry," she rasped. Every bit of moisture she could pull from the air or uninjured parts of herself was going toward healing her still-smoldering extremities. "Did you see something in the lava?"

"Yes," the faerie said. "Fire. It's hot."

"Of course," the sapling said, choosing to keep what she'd seen to herself for now. "Tell me, are you all right?"

"Am I— Why, thank you for asking. My wings are a little dry, and this whole place stinks. Really stinks, like sulfur."

"That's the lava," the sapling said. "I'd like to get away from it too. Just give me a moment."

The sapling supposed she should grow used to such injuries. Nothing could replace the lost leaves except time, but her burns were already growing over with hardened sap and green, new bark.

From then on, their pace slowed. The mountain grew steeper, and although her roots had little trouble taking a firm hold even on the densest rock of Mount Tanufel, the going was slow and soon nearly vertical.

"I'm beginning to think," Endry said after the sapling pulled herself up over another ledge with agonizing slowness, "that we might need to find another route."

"Nonsense," the sapling said, her leaves visibly flexing with the effort the climb was taking. "This is the most direct path. You can fly, and I . . ." Her leaves went limp. "I can climb."

"You're almost dead," the faerie said. "You snap like kindling every time you move, and we're not even a quarter of the way up. Best to wait here and let me find a better route. Unless you want to turn back."

"Neither. The time is—"

" 'The time is growing short.' 'The time is near.' Yet you are wasting time by trying to climb a sheer cliff face," Endry said. "But I spotted another way up, I think." He laughed. "In fact, we might not have to backtrack at all."

"What is this new shortcut?" the sapling asked, examining the cliff face in question and grudgingly, but silently, agreeing with the faerie.

"A cave. About twenty feet up and thirty yards to our left."

"How do you know it leads where we need to go?"

"Because I feel lucky."

The cave entrance was dry and hot, far too reminiscent of the bridge for the sapling's taste, but it did lead them where they wanted to go—upward. She tucked her boughs close to her trunk and ducked inside.

"It's a bit dark," the sapling said.

"Right!" Endry said. "I suppose trees couldn't possibly expect to be gifted with faerie eyesight." He buzzed near the sapling's face. "And we can't just set you on fire, I suppose. Let's try this."

The faerie struck his hands together like flint striking stone, and a cold, tiny wisp of bright blue light appeared above his head. Immediately, the next forty yards of steep tunnel floor, wall, and ceiling appeared. Occupying at least thirty of them was a camp of some twenty-odd boggarts who did not look at all pleased to be suddenly awakened by a stomping tree, a chattering faerie, and his bright blue wisp.

"I don't feel lucky," the sapling said.

Gryffid marched to the edge of the valley slope, where a three-elf unit of Nightshade scouts was waiting by a large, mossy rock. "Report," he said.

"They were here, Taer. Less than a day ago. The outcast and the elf maiden both. There are also giant tracks leading down into the valley." The scout wrinkled his nose. "We held per your orders, Taer, but let me tell you, it smells like a slaughterhouse down there."

"Well done. Stand by for now. We will move in short order." Judging from the slight commotion rising from the woods behind him, Gryffid guessed Eidren and his honor guard were approaching. He moved away from the Nightshade scouts and waited.

The taercenn soon emerged from the forest, flanked on each side by three of his elite vinebred. Eidren was not smiling, but he had a bright, casual demeanor more appropriate to a gathering of worthies than a blood hunt.

"Progress, Daen?"

"Considerable, Taer. The scouts estimate we're not far behind. We should catch up in the next few hours."

Eidren scanned the sky. "If I may make a suggestion . . ."

"By all means."

"Proceed as planned. There's no reason not to close the gap between our prey and us until we're in striking distance. But delay that strike. He knows we're coming. He'll know when we're close. Let's give the outcast one more day of looking over his shoulder, wear him down a bit more before we take him."

Gryffid cleared his throat. "That's quite sensible, Taer, but I respectfully disagree. We found two more elf corpses in the woods, victims of the kin-slayer."

"Their names will be added to the curse we invoke over his broken body."

"Very good. But I don't think we can ask our forces to hold back once they find him. The entire pack is hungry for the traitor's blood."

"The pack, or just you?"

"As pack leader, I speak for the pack," Gryffid said. "Rhys and his cohorts will be tired enough after a hard slog. Asking the hunters to restrain themselves when their prey is right in front of them may prove difficult."

"That sounds like a simple question of discipline," Eidren said, "which I expect you to maintain. Be guided by me in this matter, Daen Gryffid, for the good of the Nation, not by thoughts of your popularity with the pack."

"I did not— Yes, Taer."

Eidren glanced down into the valley. "Carry on then," he said.

"Very good, Taer." Gryffid turned and surveyed the path to the valley below. The grass was tall and dry, and it covered every inch of ground they had to cover. In the sunlight, the sea of waving blades took on a golden yellow sheen. Rhys himself would hardly be foolish enough to hide under that tall golden carpet, but he had surely left signs of his presence here, perhaps even clues to his direction and eventual destination.

Gryffid decided to keep the order of battle Eidren requested— the cuffhounds and scouts to inspect the valley floor and learn what they could, followed by archers, rangers, and vinebred. He signaled the houndmasters and pointed down into the valley.

A score of cuffhounds and their handlers charged to the edge of the slope and stood in a line. Gryffid next signaled the Nightshade scouts nearby. Those three were quickly joined by a half-dozen more that seemed to appear out of empty air. The elite trackers advanced, arranging themselves among the cuffhounds, and stood with their heads high and proud over their stiff collars, their eyes sharp and clear as they waited for the signal to advance.

"Forward," Gryffid said, and his hounds and scouts instantly responded. The Nightshade elves dispersed and all but vanished from sight as the dogs cut a single, wide swathe through the thigh-high grass.

Gryffid turned away and signaled the host of archers and lesser vinebred. He held them at the ready while he followed the cuffhounds' progress through the tall grass, watching as the dogs reached the bottom of the slope and ventured out onto the valley floor.

Gryffid never gave his second wave the signal to advance. An anguished cry floated up from the valley at the very moment the cuffhounds set foot on level ground. A single mournful howl began, then quickly died away as if the throat that uttered it was being squeezed shut.

"Back! Back!" One of the houndmasters' voices echoed up the hill. "Bring them all back!"

Gryffid addressed his second officer, who was standing nearby. "Culloch. With me." He drew his sword and sprinted down the hill. Culloch lost only a few steps before following. As he ran, Gryffid noticed several of the Nightshade scouts stand upright in the tall grass. Breaking cover was unheard of for these trackers, but before Gryffid could even wonder why, all the standing scouts stumbled, teetered, and fell out of view.

Gryffid and Culloch reached the edge of the valley floor,

where all of the cuffhounds and their handlers were waiting. A half-dozen dogs and two houndmasters were lying prone as the others huddled round. Gryffid saw that none of the stricken hounds or elves was dead, but each was certainly useless—either stupefied or unconscious.

"What is going on here?"

The lead houndmaster was short and stocky for an elf. He bowed his broad, horned head and said, "Poison, Taer. It's not lethal, but the grass down here is all coated with it. Yew poison."

"And you didn't notice? The finest noses in the entire Nation couldn't tell they were walking into a trap?"

"It's not their fault, Taer." An officer of the Nightshade stood up from the grass beside Culloch and bowed down beside the huntmaster. "Our scouts didn't recognize the danger either, not until it was too late. There's more than yew extract at work here. Someone cast a powerful spell on this valley."

"The dogs don't smell magic, Taer." The houndmaster's head remained low. "Not on plants, anyway, when they're tracking live meat."

"Be silent. You're lucky to be alive. Every word you say encourages me to negate your good fortune." It was well within Rhys's power to bathe the entire valley in his toxic, foreign tree-folk spells and to cast them with such potency that they killed rather than incapacitated. He had shown no hesitation to murder his fellow hunters before. Why was he sparing them now?

Gryffid stared out at the seemingly innocent field of grass. The awful beauty of Rhys's maneuver slowly became clear. This was a delaying tactic, and a brilliant one. It would take hours to burn a path through the poisoned valley, and any elves who fell in the process would become a burden to those that remained. Dead, they could be left behind. Unconscious, they would have to be cared for or carried.

"Daen?" Eidren's calm voice came from directly behind Gryffid. "What goes on here?"

"The traitor has blocked our path, Taer." Gryffid waved his hand out over the valley floor. "We must go around this valley or force our way through, step by ponderous step. Either method costs us valuable time, time that he can use to escape or leave more surprises for us along the way."

"Hmm," Eidren said. "Troubling, to be sure. I can see why you hold such hatred for our quarry, Daen. A worthy opponent who is unworthy of respect."

"Well said, Taer," Gryffid mumbled.

"But if I may make another suggestion . . ."

"Please."

"Pull back your hounds and scouts for now. Clear the valley of Gilt Leaf, look to the wounded, and stand back. I will address our situation."

"Very good, Taer." Gryffid stepped back and with Culloch's help ordered the cuffhounds and Nightshade back onto the slope. A quick survey confirmed six dogs and five elves among the fallen. Not a crippling loss but a definite burden for the rest of the pack. Gryffid turned and watched Eidren to see what an artist could do that a hunter could not.

The glorious Perfect threw his capelike robe back, exposing his pale arms and shoulders. He stretched his livewood staff forward and tested the ground in front of him, inching out onto the valley floor. He was whispering to himself, his words melodic and lilting even though Gryffid did not understand a single one.

"There." Eidren stopped moving six feet into the valley floor. He raised his staff and spiked the lower end into the ground. Greenish smoke gathered around the knot of wood at the top of his staff. The taercenn opened his hands and placed them on either side of the upright stick. Slowly, Eidren turned his palms flat to the ground and stretched his arms out straight until his elbows popped.

The tall grass directly in front of Eidren began to wither and curl. The blades crumbled to greenish black powder until Eidren was standing at the center of a wide semicircle of flat, hard-packed soil devoid of vegetation. The dead zone spread horizontally until it was large enough for twenty elves to stand in side by side. Eidren drew his staff from the soil and stepped forward into the clear, dead space he had created.

The grass below and around Eidren's feet was gone, but the blades at the edge of his dead zone swelled fat and healthy. Just outside the reach of Eidren's spell, the blades shifted from dry yellow to lush green. Then they grew taller. These longer, thicker stalks braided around themselves, doubled back toward the soil, then slithered upward once more. Moments after this new growth began, Eidren's cleared space stood flanked by two solid walls of green.

When the walls were both taller than the tallest elf, Eidren nodded. He planted his staff in the ground and stretched his arms out beside it once more. The dead zone surged forward so that the poisoned grass between him and the far side of the valley fell, one row at a time, as if scythed by a team of invisible reapers.

Gryffid watched, joy and amazement competing with shame and suspicion. He had been wrong about Eidren. The new taer-cenn was no warrior, no proper elf hunter, but he had powerful magic as well as position. His work here was not only practical and efficient, it was . . . beautiful. It was art.

The walls of Eidren's path continued to grow and curl against each other even after they were fully formed. Colorful buds sprouted, flowers that should not and could not grow from simple grass. To Gryffid's frank amazement, recognizable symbols and shapes appeared in the strange new hedge, guided and inscribed by their master's hand until a delicate series of friezes adorned every inch of its surface. Gryffid recognized the symbols of the Sublime Council, of the Perfect king and queen, of the traditional Gilt Leaf coat of arms. For as long as this magic lasted, it would mark the path the Blessed Nation had taken through this valley and remind all who followed of the Gilt Leaf's dominance and prowess.

Quietly, Gryffid stole up alongside Eidren. "Magnificent, my Taercenn," he said.

Eidren kept his eyes on the advancing lane, but he smiled. "I told you I was an artist, Daen. I have sculpted living things this way all my life. This talent earned my current rank and station, as well as a betrothal to the highest-ranking Mornsong Perfect." Eidren lowered his hands, but the grass continued to fall as the lane extended across the valley. He turned to Gryffid and said, "If you were to go now, the way would be entirely clear by the time you reached the far end of the valley."

"Very good, Taer." Gryffid saluted and jogged back to the cuffhounds and scouts on the slope. "Get them ready," he told Culloch. "Those who can still track should proceed immediately into the trail the taercenn has blazed."

Culloch saluted. "Taer!"

* * * * *

Several hours after his cuffhounds crossed the poisoned valley, Gryffid discovered yew magic was not the only tool Rhys had employed to delay his pursuers. The Gilt Leaf had followed the outlaw's trail over half the distance between the forest's edge and Porringer Valley, gaining ground on their quarry with every step. Now, from where Gryffid stood atop a rocky hill, the sky was clear and bright, and the coastal mountains to the west were in plain view.

Gryffid followed the mountains with his eye, dazzled by the

breathtaking view. From his vantage point on the ridge, he could see for miles to the west, south, and east. Everywhere but north, the direction their quarry had taken and they must follow.

Two-thirds of the horizon was clear, but that final all-important third was hidden from view. An impenetrable fog had settled over the marshy depression that lay between two hills ahead, a fog that should not exist at this time of year. It was a far simpler obstacle than the poisoned grass, but it was also more effective. With almost no visibility, the Gilt Leaf hunters would have to work far harder to track him through the sodden scrubland and colorful swamps. The fog would also prevent Gryffid's archers from taking proper aim.

Gryffid turned to where Eidren was puzzling over the fog bank. The taercenn's talents did not extend beyond plants, it seemed, so in this case he was as stymied as the rest of the pack.

"This is good," Eidren said. "Excellent, in fact."

"Taer?"

"He's desperate, don't you see? Elf children can create a fog bank. If we weren't pressing him, he would have set up something more elaborate, more effective."

"It's very effective against our archers, Taer."

"I don't think you're taking my point," Eidren said. "Why would he set out to frustrate archers if we weren't within bow range? I think we're closer than any of us expected. For all we know, he's huddled in the middle of that fog, praying that we won't risk marching in after him for fear of another passive poison trap."

"If that's so," Gryffid said, "he has got a point. There could be any number of surprises waiting for us in there."

Eidren sighed sadly. "You really must start looking at the big picture if you intend to continue leading an entire pack," he said. "The fog doesn't conceal his weapons. It *is* his weapon. He made sure we saw what he could do with yew magic in the valley, and now the threat of poison is even more powerful than the poison itself. He wants us to waste time wondering, to slow us down by forcing us to tread carefully, and all the while he can devote more resources to setting up his next gambit. He's trying to force us to do what he wants us to do. Classic, time-tested military thinking, Daen. I'm surprised you didn't see that yourself."

"I see it, Taer. But it's classic and time-tested for a reason: It's effective."

"It's also predictable," Eidren said. "Which we may now exploit."

Gryffid nodded. "You have another suggestion, I take it."

"I do. Mount up and take a half dozen of your best cervin riders with you. I will send a dozen of my vinebred along as support. Go with all possible speed through the fog until you break out of the bank on the other side."

"And if we ride through another patch of poisoned grass?"

"Then I will be quite surprised. But you will not be in serious danger if he holds to his pattern. You might lose a cervin or two for the duration of this hunt, or become sick yourself, but I daresay my vinebred won't even notice a nonlethal dose of yew magic."

"It'll be slow going," Gryffid said. "His trail will be harder to spot."

"Then do not follow his trail. I say again, make haste. Traverse this obstacle and pick up his trail beyond it. By the time he realizes the fog hasn't worked, you will be upon him, or close to it, with the full weight of the Hemlock Pack close behind."

"But if he's hiding in the fog, as you said—"

"Then we will find him when we move through the fog in force. But I am certain he is not there. He's not the type to hole up and wait for better weather. He's headed somewhere, somewhere specific, and I strongly doubt this cheerful little bog is it.

"So you must hurry. Choose your squad and go. The rest of us can proceed with caution, with diligence. No matter if he's in the fog or beyond it, we will find him, and faster than he anticipates."

Gryffid glanced into the fog. "And if I find him before you and the others catch up?"

"Then you must deal with him accordingly. I insist that you spare his life until I have a chance to question him, however, and his companion Maralen. Beyond that, you may do as you see fit."

"Thank you, Taer."

"Not at all. Hurry now. Have you a reliable cervin to ride?"

"He is a serviceable steed, Taercenn," Gryffid said, "but he is nothing compared to the marvels in your stable."

"Then you shall have one of mine." Eidren beckoned one of his courtiers to him. "Go to my quartermaster and tell him I want his best cervin. Whisper, if he's available, or perhaps Zephyr. The choice is up to him, but in either case, bring the steed here immediately." The courtier bowed and slid away into the throng of elves.

Eidren said to Gryffid, "I suggest you collect your hunters, Daen, and wait for me by the edge of the fog. I will meet you there once I have assembled my vinebred."

Eidren crisply returned Gryffid's salute and departed. Gryffid sent Culloch to gather six riders, leaving the Hemlock daen alone on the hilltop. The new taercenn was perplexing to him. Granted, Eidren had been correct so far, and his assistance had been invaluable, but Gryffid was still uneasy. Perhaps he was just too accustomed to elf leaders who barked orders instead of making suggestions.

Soon six cervin-mounted Hemlock elves rode up beside Gryffid's hill. He stepped down and crooked a finger for them to follow. Culloch had not told them of their mission, and they were experienced enough to wait for Gryffid to deliver their orders in his own time. He led the six along a winding path through the scrub trees and stopped them near the edge of the fog.

Gryffid peered in. The smoky gray mist wasn't thick, but it still managed to baffle the eye. He crouched down, picked up a small pebble, and tossed it in. Though he followed its path closely, it disappeared from view less than a foot from the edge of the fog bank.

"Daen Gryffid." Eidren's smooth voice drew the attention of every Hemlock elf. "Allow me to present Whisper."

Gryffid fought back a gasp. Several of his riders were not so stoic. He felt no ire and made no plans to discipline them, however, for the taercenn's cervin was truly awe-inspiring. The animal stood almost to Eidren's shoulders, and its face was alert, proud, and vigorous. The huge steed's fur was moonlight silver with patches of black, and its eyes were piercing ice blue.

Gently, gingerly, Gryffid stepped up to Whisper. He extended his hand, and the cervin sniffed it. Gryffid laid a hand on the beast's long neck and slid himself up onto its back.

"You honor me, Taercenn."

"So glad." Eidren bowed. As he straightened, he added, "Here also are select members of my honor guard."

Eidren stepped aside to reveal a phalanx of vinebred warriors three across and four deep. Their faces were hidden beneath braided masks of wood and leaves. Among Gryffid's riders, the vinebred elves' arrival eclipsed that of Whisper, though this time there were no exclamations of astonishment at their beauty.

The vinebred marched past Eidren and fell in behind the Hemlock riders. Once positioned, the taercenn's honor guard stood as statues. They were, in their way, even more magnificent that the silver cervin, but theirs was a stern and terrible beauty.

Eidren turned away. "I'll leave you to it."

"Wait! Taer, I . . ." Gryffid struggled for words even after Eidren turned and patiently crossed his arms. "Will they follow my orders, Taer?"

"Of course, Daen Gryffid. But there's no need to worry about that. I've given them their instructions: Cross the fog and wait for me on the other side. Between here and there, they will serve as faithfully as members of your own pack."

"But they're not mounted. Can they keep up?"

"Hah! My boy, I expect you'll have trouble staying ahead of them. Off you go, now."

"You heard the taercenn," Gryffid said. He spun around on Whisper, eager to put Eidren and his vinebred behind him and plunge into the fog. "Ride fast and keep your eyes open. We're looking to take captives, not corpses, so if you spy anything living in that damnable mist, don't kill it."

One of his riders spoke up. "What should we do, Taer?"

Gryffid leveled his eyes at the hunter. "Break it," he said. "And call for me. Then stand on its neck until I arrive."

A soft, vicious chuckle bubbled up among the Hemlock riders, but the sound only echoed off the wooden shells of the vinebred.

"Now," Gryffid said, "ride!" He prodded Whisper, and the cervin lunged forward. They picked up speed quickly, and, though Gryffid heard the regular tattoo of Whisper's hooves on the soil, the ride was smoother than standing still.

Far more exhilarating too. The fog was stale in his nostrils but cool against his skin. Once in motion, Whisper required no further prompting. Gryffid didn't even have to steer, as the steed correctly anticipated his intentions before he could convey them through the slender guide chain and bit. Gryffid could not see more than a few feet past the cervin's head, but Whisper seemed to smell the path ahead and avoided all obstacles.

Gryffid heard the other riders behind him, and behind them the formidable sound of twelve elite vinebred keeping pace. The Hemlock cervins were fine animals, but they would not have been able to maintain this pace without Whisper leading the way. Cervins like this were reserved for the highest castes in elf society, and now Gryffid knew why. He had never traveled this fast before, not even on the rapids of the Wanderwine.

Such speed came at a price, however: In a matter of minutes they were climbing a slight upgrade, rising out of the sodden marshland Rhys had seeded with fog. Gryffid broke through the clinging mist and breathed clean, sweet air. He did not restrain Whisper, and so the steed maintained their breakneck pace. Together they pounded halfway up the incline. Then Gryffid brought Whisper to a rearing halt.

The Hemlock riders emerged from the fog in tight formation, followed immediately by the phalanx of vinebred.

"Spread out," Gryffid said. "Look for signs of elves or giants. Go!" He did not expect it to take long for the Hemlock's finest to pick up a giant's trail, and he was not disappointed.

"Taer!" One of his riders waved from between two trees fifty yards down the bank. Gryffid whistled the others to him and galloped toward the one who signaled. His heart pounded as he drew close. There was no mistaking the signs: Two giants had lumbered up this hillside just a few hours ago.

"Up!" Gryffid said. He tapped Whisper's ribs, and the silver cervin shot up the incline. Gryffid brought Whisper up once more and raised his hand to halt the others before they passed him.

More marshland stretched out before them, but this bog was not so wet and was totally without fog. Gryffid was able to see clear across the flats and on to the Dauba Ravine three hundred yards beyond.

A single, huge oak tree bridged the Dauba. For decades Gilt Leaf seedguides had painstakingly tended and trained the oak to span the gap. The thick, mossy bridge was black with the bright afternoon sun behind it. Two figures stood at its center, and though they appeared no larger than his clenched fist Gryffid saw they were elves: one male, one female. He had found Rhys at last.

"There they are," Gryffid said quietly. The figures on the bridge darted away and disappeared on the far side. Gryffid spun Whisper around. "They're here! Vinebred, with me. The rest of you wait for the taercenn before you follow."

Gryffid's riders did not have a chance to reply. All twelve of Eidren's vinebred broke ranks and stepped away from the other elves. This sudden coordinated action startled many of the cervin steeds, and as their riders regained control Gryffid's entire formation dissolved into disarray.

"Hold," he said, but the taercenn's honor guard had already reformed their phalanx beside the confusion. Whisper stood perfectly still as the vinebred charged past Gryffid toward the ravine. Gryffid wheeled his mount around in time to see the honor guard break into a full-fledged sprint. Eidren had not been exaggerating their speed—as Gryffid drove his heels into Whisper's flanks he knew that he would not catch them before they reached the ravine. Even atop a cervin as excellent as Whisper, the best Gryffid could hope for was keep the vinebred in sight as he trailed behind.

Whisper was as quick and as graceful as ever, but there was no joy in this ride. Gryffid stayed as low as he could, his body all but molded to the cervin's back. He watched the backs of the vinebred phalanx as he followed up the incline that led to the Dauba's edge. The hindmost was twenty paces ahead of him, and, no matter how hard Whisper ran or how urgently Gryffid prodded, the daen and his mount gained no ground.

The terrain leveled out. From atop his cervin Gryffid could see both the Dauba Ravine and the great oak bridge that spanned it. The first row of vinebred elves approached the edge of the bridge. The clatter of hooves against livewood echoed back to Gryffid and he felt a withering surge of dread.

"Stop," he called, but the vinebred ignored him once more.

The first two rows charged out onto the bridge and spread out to cover the entire span from side to side as they crossed. Three paces later all six of these vinebred warriors suddenly dropped through the surface of the bridge and disappeared without uttering the slightest sound. They were upright and in hot pursuit one moment, inexplicably gone the next.

"Halt!" Gryffid roared, and this time the taercenn's honor guard complied—though the daen was certain it was not his voice that finally gave them pause but the fate of their fellows.

"Withdraw," Gryffid said sternly. "Toward me. Slowly."

The remaining vinebred exchanged a glance. Grudgingly, they inched back from the invisible edge that had swallowed their comrades. When they once more stood on solid rock beside Gryffid, the daen dismounted. He glared at the vinebred, but the enchanted warriors refused to meet his eyes. Rhys, curse his name, had done it again, and once more the Gilt Leaf's failure was Gryffid's and Gryffid's alone. He should have known, should have seen the pattern Rhys's little gambits had taken. First, an innocent-seeming valley that crippled the unwary. Then an ominous-looking fog that concealed no threats whatsoever. Now, a seemingly intact bridge that actually led nowhere.

His hands trembling with rage, Gryffid pulled a small clay bottle from his belt pack. He cupped the bottle in his palm, drew his arm back, and gently bowled the bottle across the surface of the bridge. Though irregularly shaped, Gryffid's throw was perfect, and the bottle rolled smoothly, straight down the center of the pathway. When it reached the spot where the vinebred elves had vanished, it too dropped out of sight and vanished without a sound.

Gryffid's hot, rising rage cooled. The fury hardened into something sharp and brittle in the back of his mind. He stared hard at the place where the bottle had disappeared, and his lips curled into a feral sneer. He could see it now: The bridge was gone, but the illusory glamer laid down in its place told the unwary eye it was still there.

Gryffid drew his sword. With an angry incantation, he drove the tip of his weapon deep into the livewood oak bridge. A rolling wave of distortion rolled out from the blade and rippled along the surface of the tree. Gryffid rose and watched the ripples rebound and reflect until the entire bridge shimmered.

The solid span of live oak faded to reveal the latest of Rhys's horrific blasphemies against the Blessed Nation and its works. The bridge was shattered less than fifteen paces from the southern end. Gryffid could only imagine the brute force it must have taken to sunder the bridge so completely, but there was no mystery how Rhys had brought that force to bear. The marks of giant feet and fists were plainly evident on what little remained of the dying span. Rhys had not only ordered some of the lowest, most inferior beings in all Lorwyn to destroy a proud Gilt Leaf landmark, he had done so to spare himself the elf justice he so richly deserved.

Rhys had also earned the cursed name of kin-slayer once more. Destroying the bridge alone would have been sufficient to delay his Gilt Leaf pursuers, but he had gone on to conceal his crime so that more of his former comrades would fall to their deaths. He clearly expected to claim scores of elf lives when the entire hunting party marched across the bridge in full force.

Movement on the north cliff caught Gryffid's attention. He peered through the haze and saw two huge figures lumbering toward the edge of the ravine. He recognized the two as his former captives, the giant brothers that had been half-vinebred before the traitor Rhys helped them escape. The taller one with the long, scraggly beard only stared at Gryffid balefully across the expanse of the Dauba, but the smaller giant with the dark, braided beard leaped up and down, gesticulating wildly.

Gryffid simply stared as the smaller giant playfully pushed

and punched his brother. That smaller figure then turned, fiddled with something at his waist, and dropped his pants. The taller giant covered his face with his hands and shook with laughter as the other waggled his bare backside at the Hemlock hunters of the Blessed Nation.

The daen felt the insult in his stomach like an immovable lump of stone, but it was Rhys and not the giant's childish display that fogged his mind with black rage. If it took a year to cross the Dauba Ravine on foot, or ten years to grow a new bridge, Gryffid would endure it all.

After that, he would cut the eyeblight Rhys to death by inches, no matter what the taercenn said.

CHAPTER 12

Ashling drank deeply from a polished steel cup. Kerosin tea was poisonous to a creature of flesh and bone, but it was exactly what the pilgrim needed. She flared with an almost immediate sense of renewed warmth and vigor. She didn't burn hotter, just healthier. It was something only another flamekin might notice, and the monk in gold immediately did.

"Your strength has returned," the young monk said, a polite statement of fact, not encouragement or comfort. Ashling wondered if the flamekin youth would have remained so emotionless in the absence of his master. For those were clearly the roles these two lone occupants of the monastery filled.

The pilgrim also found it hard to believe these two were really the only monks in this venerated place. This was not the Ember Fellowship's true monastery, they'd told her, but a shrine and a fortress of sorts. The structure was built on geometries and sensibilities that would have been impossible to imagine for any architects but those made of living stone and flame. Curved, polished obsidian arches asymmetrically supported a convex roof lined with ironwood tiles that resembled the monk's attire more than anything else, but those that adorned the wall were cut into more regular shapes. The roof supported a spire that in turn resembled a rough-hewn stalagmite. It appeared to be a smaller sibling to the monastery proper, still some ways up the mountainside.

"The tea is good," Ashling said. "Thank you." Ashling set the drink down before her crossed legs and drew her upper body straight. "But I can't sit and sip any more until you tell me why you two tried to kill me."

"Be at ease, Ashling of Tanufel." The monk raised his hand palm outward. Ashling did feel a calming influence flow from the older flamekin. She instinctively flared, just a small flash, but it was enough to break the monk's spell.

"I'll be whatever I want," Ashling said. "But you're not catching me off guard again, and you're not going to manipulate me."

"I do not seek to manipulate you," the older monk said, "but to prepare you for the challenge ahead."

"All I really want to know is why you sent me over a cliff," Ashling said.

"You must enter the Ember Fell. None of our kind may attain the summit without doing so."

"I don't care what the rules are," Ashling said, jerking a thumb over her shoulder at the monastery. "You're talking to someone who just flew up the side of a mountain. Give me time and I'll make contact again, whether that high and mighty elemental likes it or not. Are you doing its bidding, keeping me here?"

"The power was not taken, but given—a gift best not kept too long, lest it consume you," the monk replied, "and its return is not yours to call at your whim. The white flame has come to you too soon, far too soon. We felt your torment, pilgrim, even from these lofty heights. We know what you have suffered. Yet this does not change the fact of the white flame. There is a reason the flamekin have not burned out over the centuries in wars and conflicts. It is the Path of Flame that keeps us in peace with our kin, and when one of our kind becomes possessed of such power—"

"Oh, it possessed me all right," Ashling said. "I know there are usually rituals. I missed them, Brother Monk. But what's done is certainly done, and I'm not going to go through a complicated dance with you to get what I want."

"You must gain Ember Fell under your own power. The Path of Flame demands it. You have touched the white flame, and it has touched you. The dimmest novice can see that. You must keep to your path, pilgrim."

"You've never even met me, so don't presume to tell me where I must go. The path demands nothing of me anymore. Yes, I'm a pilgrim. My entire purpose was to follow the path to my elemental, and I did," Ashling said. "It lured me and used me only to save itself. Maybe I respected the rituals, the beliefs, but that thing didn't."

"You mean you didn't do so willingly? Isn't the great spirit worth the sacrifice of a single flamekin pilgrim?"

"No." Perhaps it was the tea, or the opportunity to finally share her torment with two beings who could at least begin to understand it, but Ashling could contain her anger no longer. "In fact, I don't see how it was worth saving at all. These . . . things, these divine beings of fire and air—they're supposed to be better than that. Better than us. Better than any of us. Yet I looked that divine being in the eye, and I saw terror. Cowardice. It would have let me be completely consumed in its place."

"Such is our fate, the fate of all flamekin. To gutter out is the only true sin, pilgrim."

"Don't throw platitudes and proverbs at me," Ashling warned. "I do not plan to gutter, nor return to the living rock any time soon. I will flare when I die, and so brightly the elementals themselves—every one of them—will shield their faces." She pushed herself away from the table and stood, her flames tightly controlled but blazing hot.

"You sound like an assassin," the blue monk said. "But can you slay a god? Do you imagine we will allow you to destroy that which is most pure, the thing to which we all aspire, just because you feel abandoned? You're mad, you know. You easily attained a kind of perfection that most of the Ember Fellowship never approach, and now you seek to exploit and abuse it."

"Perfection? We hold to the creed of the elves now?"

"What would you call a creature that lives in a state without flaw? Whose every act is by definition proper and correct?"

"An illusion," Ashling said. "And any who worship such a being? Asses." Ashling clenched her fists, and her flames surged. "I'm going to the top of this mountain, Brother Monk, and I'm going to tame your perfect being. The white flame is mine to command. Is it yours?"

"Your threats are pointless, pilgrim," the blue monk said. "You've been judged worthy of scaling the summit by virtue of the white flame, and the path up the side of this peak is not up for debate. You will find no other way up. You will pass through the monastery or you will not reach your destination. I judged you worthy to enter this shrine, but only those greater than I can decide who reaches the mountaintop. I see now that you will most assuredly fail." Without another word he rose, bowed slightly to his student, and strode purposefully from the chamber. It struck Ashling as a remarkably petulant movement for one so outwardly steeped in wisdom.

"Charming fellow, your master," she told the monk in gold, who still sat at the table holding his cup of tea. "I'm not playing these games. If he tries to stop me . . . if you try to stop me, I'll—"

"We will meet you at the wall," the young monk said. "You are welcome to enjoy another cup of tea if you wish, but please understand, this is the only way to what you seek. Both figuratively and literally. The rocks to the west are impassable. To the east, nothing but crevasses and wind devils." He stood, nodded curtly, and followed his master from the chamber.

"Wait, what wall?" Ashling said.

"Follow," came the reply from down the darkened passageway.

* * * * *

When they arrived at the wall, Ashling began to get an inkling of just how tricky the task ahead of her was going to be.

"Why would the path simply end here?" The flamekin asked the gold monk. She didn't feel like talking to the younger monk's master, especially if he was going to refuse to make eye contact.

"You are wrong," the blue monk said before his student could. "This is where your path begins anew."

"That's really unhelpful," Ashling said. "But I don't suppose you're going to explain what you mean, are you?"

The blue monk shook his head.

"All right then, reveal the secret passageway, make the illusion disappear, do whatever it is you're going to do."

"You will reveal the way up," the blue monk said. "You will choose it."

"How?" Ashling asked. "Because if it's up to me, I'd like a simple door with the top of the mountain on the other side."

"Examine this wall, pilgrim," the blue monk said. "Look for patterns, shapes in the stone. The way will be revealed to you, but you will choose it from the patterns you see. You are of this mountain, Ashling. You were the last born of her stone, and you will not be the first to destroy her heart. Look to the wall. What do you see?"

Ashling took a few steps back. From this vantage point it was easier to see lines and fissures upon the surface of the stone. The longer she stared at the wall, the easier it was to see what the monk meant. The seemingly random lines soon started to form random shapes in the cliff face. Nothing she recognized, until . . .

"There," Ashling said. "A figure. Two legs, two arms, a head. That must be my guide. One of you, I'm guessing?"

"You are mistaken," the blue monk said and nodded toward his student. The gold monk stepped to the wall and pressed his blazing hand against the stone.

The wall came to life. The shape Ashling had seen glowed with golden light, light that burned hotter still until it was purest white, white tinged—but only just—with blue. She took another involuntary step back when the stone within those lines began to move. The shape she'd defined pulled itself out of the cliff face like a sculpture popping out of the mold, except this sculpture was a walking chunk of the mountainside fifty feet tall. It took a single step with a succession of pops and cracks that shook the ground and sent gravel skittering down the unmoving parts of the wall. Without ceremony, the monks also backed away from the creature, but it did not even acknowledge their presence. Its second step nearly flattened her, and a surprisingly quick swipe of its mittlike hand almost knocked her off the mountain. By the time Ashling had time to look up, the monks were gone.

"I'm going to kill them," Ashling swore. "When I come back down this mountain, I'm going to kill them."

The flamekin bolted for cover just as the huge, toeless stone foot—easily twice the size of Brion's—crashed into and obliterated the end of the path. With jerking, staggering movements, the gigantic rock-creature pulled itself completely free of its stony prison and took a second step so heavy that it opened a new fissure in the base of the mountain.

The pilgrim picked herself up and scrambled toward the nearest boulder, dimming her flame as she went. If she could avoid the rock giant's gaze for a few seconds she might be able to figure out a way to—topple him? Ashling figured it was better than standing around waiting to get squashed.

The pilgrim slipped into a cluster of boulders that marked the rain-washed remains of an old avalanche. Safely hidden for the moment, Ashling examined her enemy more closely.

The flamekin pilgrim realized this might not be a creature at all, or even an enchanted guardian, but instead one of those rarest of the rare, a true stone elemental. They were known to dwell in the mountains, and there was no mountain greater than Mount Tanufel in all of Lorwyn. Why the monks allowed this thing to slumber so close to their monastery was anyone's guess. Ashling had never expected to see its like, certainly not here. She'd been expecting to fight the monks again, not the mountain itself.

The stone elemental's form was roughly simian—long arms and squat, bent legs supporting a thick stone trunk—though its head resembled nothing so much as six feet of stone column with a face. As this thought crossed her mind, a rock fist the size of a kithkin house nearly smashed that mind and every thought in it. As Ashling tumbled away from the point of impact she spotted the second fist, this one drawn back to turn even Ashling's durable body to dust.

She hadn't the fiery elemental's power any longer, but Ashling did have her own reserves. Recalling her trip up the mountainside, Ashling marshaled enough magic for a steady jet of fire that pushed her just far enough out of the way to avoid the stone giant's blow. Its fist drove into the cliff face instead, leaving an impact crater ringed with cracks.

The time it took for the behemoth to extract its fist was enough time for Ashling to roll back onto her feet and start running. Any further thoughts of studying this marvelous and deadly thing fled. Ashling resigned herself to the only thing she could do. She ran.

Ashling headed to the west, not for any specific reason other than the fact the giant wasn't there. Despite running at top speed, the stone foot just missed her—the thing could cover half its height in a single stride, so running wasn't much of an option either.

Gathering her rejuvenated energies, Ashling readied something she wasn't sure would work without wresting more power from the elemental—and that power was achingly just out of reach. But she had to try. Bringing her flames to a full burn, Ashling focused them all downward into the mountain itself. As she had hoped, the blast launched her directly toward the giant's stone column of a head.

Its eyes glowed silvery white and did not blink at her improbable approach. Instead, it opened a wide, rectangular mouth and prepared to swallow the blazing flamekin whole. Ashling did not alter her course but did borrow a little of the fire that kept her aloft to ignite her fists. They lit the cavernous maw from within as her fists collided with the roof of the giant's mouth amid a crunch of shattering stone.

The monster's agonized roar sent Ashling flying backward the way she had come, utterly out of control. She tumbled through open space and tried to focus her flames or right herself, but that initial blast had cost her too much.

"What is happening to me?" she whispered moments before colliding with the forever-marred side of Mount Tanufel. Ashling was able to form a cushion of heat to absorb most of the impact, but what came through was enough to stun and disorient her for a moment. She maneuvered her heat downward again in an effort to stay aloft, but too late.

Fortunately, the stone giant's emergence had left more than a few handholds and ledges within the cliff, and the flamekin was able to push herself into a rough landing upon a ledge that had once fit perfectly against the monster's left elbow.

The giant's scream slowly died as it shifted its bulk around to face Ashling once more. It appeared to have no trouble pinpointing her on the shadowy ledge and was upon her in a single step. It drew back an obsidian fist and roared, still venting red plasma from the wounds she'd made in its open mouth.

"I hurt you," Ashling said. "How about that?"

The next stone blow came barreling toward her. She launched herself forward, not at the giant's fist but just above it. She kept her hands white-hot and scrambled up to the stone creature's shoulder. After a prodigious leap, she stood atop its head.

The next ledge—in the rough shape of the monster's left fist—was perhaps twelve feet above her and ten away. It was a dangerous leap, but if she missed, she was fairly confident she could cushion the blow and try again, even if it meant serious injuries in the short term. If she made it, she could be atop the cliff face and well away from the giant. If she didn't try the risky maneuver at all, the stone monster would flatten her with its craggy fists. Already the monster was raising those fists to reach her new position.

She summoned all the energy she had left—changed or not, her reserves were far from infinite—and took a flying leap off the top of the murderous guardian. The column-headed thing twisted to follow her, and that movement widened the gap between Ashling and the landing spot she'd chosen. Instead of a ten-foot gap, she now had to cover thirty.

Despite pouring everything she had into the effort, the flame-kin simply could not cover the distance in time—momentum and gravity fought just a bit harder. It was enough to throw her off balance again, and she landed next to the first crater the monstrous stone creature had created upon its emergence from the mountainside.

Ashling willed fire into her legs and lower torso, but it crackled and sputtered furiously. Without a substantial infusion of borrowed elemental power, she'd never be able to fly that far; she would have to climb.

"So be it," she said. At her words she thought she saw a

shimmer on the mountaintop, a flicker of wings. And there, a sliver of power, a fraction of what she'd taken but given freely. Then the elemental cut off contact again. Was the creature taunting her, or did it simply not understand Ashling's intent?

It was a question for another time. Fighting this creature was getting her nowhere fast. Ashling eyed the towering giant, fifty feet of stone that resembled something carved by a mad sculptor . . . and suddenly saw it in a new light. If she could avoid its fists, this creature could be her way up to the rest of the mountain. "The beginning of the path" indeed. The stone giant was the path, if she chose to use it.

While the monster struggled to track her movements underfoot, Ashling hooked her fingers into a crack on its left leg. She clambered up, hopped over to the right leg, and caught a new handhold. She repeated this movement three more times until she reached the behemoth's waist. Climbing it became far easier from that point on.

The stone giant finally spotted her when she launched herself from its shoulder toward the upper cliff face, willing her flames to keep her aloft just long enough to catch the lip of the overhang. Ashling immediately saw she was going to fall several feet short, however, unless she brought the overhang to her.

With a shout of defiance, Ashling poured fire from her hands and blasted away the two or three feet of rock above her. The stone overhang disintegrated into a rain of hot, molten pellets that peppered the giant's face and earned Ashling another enraged, cavernous roar. Ignoring it, she caught the glowing edge of the crumbling cliffside and scrambled up the rest of the way.

The mountain rocked and shook as the frustrated monster pounded the cliff wall into rubble, very nearly sending her tumbling back down the side. Ashling was able to hold on by driving her fingers into the fractured, cooling stone. She reached a safe, sturdy stretch of the tremor-shaken path just as the rest of the cliffside gave way, burying her enraged pursuer in an avalanche of stone, earth, and mud.

* * * * *

"Who ever heard of cave boggarts?" Endry derided the snarling mob of angry cave boggarts.

"They don't look like they want to talk," the sapling said. "Please, do not aggravate them further."

"On the bright side, I can get rid of this wisp," Endry said, "there's plenty of light from those torches. Get it? 'Bright side?' "

The sapling's wooden finger slipped between Endry's hands before he could clap.

"No, keep that. We may need it," she said.

"I don't think you're going anywhere, yewling," the faerie said. "And I don't need it, so—"

"We'll be leaving soon," the sapling said. "I'm just trying to figure out a way through this tunnel that doesn't kill all of them."

"Why?" Endry said as he buzzed in an agitated loop, "They're boggarts. Use your yew poison or go ahead and plant roots, I'd say. Assuming they don't burn you down before you find purchase."

The boggarts looked as if they would be more than happy to do just that. The yew stood on a ledge some ten feet above the boggarts. Their camp—more a stinking nest, really—was in disarray, and at least half of them carried torches or burning brands they'd ignited with foul-sounding incantations when the sapling and Endry had interrupted their slumber. The biggest boggarts in the little band, a scarred and tough-looking half dozen or so, were carrying spiky homespun weapons that looked more than capable of dismembering whatever the torches didn't burn. Though the sapling didn't understand the guards' growling curses and hissed threats, she got the message that they meant to do just that, and they weren't planning to wait for the fire to go out before they did it. Behind them were the smaller boggarts that looked just as threatening, and behind those, huddling in the firelight, were many young boglings. Every now and then one of them added a porcine squeal to the general hubbub.

The faerie was right about the light—the yew could see all the way up the sloping tunnel now, all the way to a rough wall that reflected dim sunlight that struck the stone with a different hue than the dirty orange glow of the boggart's fires. It wasn't the actual exit, but it was close to the exit.

Endry was also, morally speaking, not entirely wrong. These boggarts had been hunting travelers, the evidence was everywhere, from the decidedly ill-fitting kithkin clothing many of them wore to the chunks of worked metal that adorned their otherwise wood and bone weaponry. To say nothing of—

"Are those skulls?" Endry gasped. "Kithkin skulls?"

"I believe they are," the sapling said. "And they look fresh."

"All right, don't kill them," Endry buzzed. "These are my kind of boggarts."

"Perhaps just the leaders," the sapling said. Already she was sending the volatile ingredients of the poison flowing into her fingertips and the needles lining the backs of her wide hands, but something was holding her back. The problem was the dosage. Given time, she could easily produce a coma-inducing nonlethal variety of yew poison, but it would take hours just to pollinate. The poison immediately and literally at her fingertips would kill in even a minute dose. Yet they were cornered. Several of the boggarts, unable to gain purchase on the rock wall below the ledge, had hit upon the idea of forming a stack of boggarts, one at a time, until they could reach her. Already the stack was three high, another few boggarts and they'd be able to place fire to her roots. This might not have been lethal in most circumstances, but with no water in this blisteringly hot cave, it could do severe damage before it was done—assuming the boggarts didn't pull her limb from limb long before that happened.

"I'm sorry, boglings," the sapling said sadly and raised her hands, splaying her fingers wide. "Endry, leave. I will catch up. You don't want to be here when the air fills with poison."

"On my way," Endry said, "Good—"

The faerie's farewell ended in a thundering crash as something tremendously heavy shook the entire tunnel from outside. The sapling had to slap her hands against the wall behind her and thrust panicked root-filaments into the ledge below to maintain her footing. The boggarts began wailing and chattering in terror, dropping their torches and brands as they scooped up children and infants to bolt back down the way Endry and the sapling had come. The second crash, much louder than the first, sent a rain of faerie-sized stones clattering to the tunnel floor, and a few that were much bigger than that. The boggarts covered their young, and two of the bigger ones, having dropped their weapons at Ashling's feet, pushed mightily against a flat boulder until it rolled aside to reveal another, much narrower tunnel down which the sad little tribe of boggart brigands scampered. After a third thunderous, earth-shaking crash, the last boggart disappeared down the hole without bothering to roll the door into place behind him.

"Well. Solved that problem pretty handily," Endry said. "So how did you make the earth quake?"

"That was not—" Another crash, this one right overhead, caused a crack above to become a fissure, and the ledge beneath the sapling's feet crumbled away beneath her weight. The stone she'd gripped so tightly with fibrous filaments became nothing but dead weight, and she was thrown onto her back against the steep tunnel floor. The next crash was less powerful than the last but was enough to jostle the sapling's tenuous grip on the floor, and she began to slide down the incline feetfirst. Flailing with one hand, she caught the edge of the boggart's escape tunnel and held on tightly as the small avalanche of sharp stone tumbled down after her.

When the hail of rocks had passed, her bark was chipped and oozing sap from dozens of places. She'd lost an entire bough on her left shoulder but was otherwise more or less intact.

Another crash, moving up the mountain, further away still.

"So if you didn't do that," Endry said from whatever cleft had sheltered him during the sapling's tumble down the slope, "what did?"

As if in reply, the dim sunlight at the end of the tunnel flared with white firelight. It only appeared for a moment, but the sapling was uniquely attuned to the air around her—she breathed through the millions of tiny needles covering her body and limbs—and the lingering tang in the air was unmistakable to the yew.

"Ashling," the sapling said. "She's very close."

"Can you sense her?" Endry asked.

"No," the sapling replied. "I can smell her."

"How is she making the ground shake like—" Another crash, but one that barely knocked loose a few pieces of gravel. "She's not doing that, is she?" Endry amended.

"I don't think so. I think something's chasing her. Something with very, very heavy feet."

* * * * *

Endry and the sapling emerged onto a wide ledge well above the Ember Fell shrine in time to see Ashling's blazing form scrambling up the side of the mountain at a breakneck pace. They were far too distant to do anything but watch as the stone elemental did all it could to bring the mountain down upon itself. The stone giant roared, having no other way to vent the frustration that possessed every fiber of its simplistic mind. It lashed out at the wall that it had until recently been a part of, and the wall crumbled. But simplistic or not, the stone giant had been given instinct by the powers that created it. That instinct kept it from being completely buried, and within moments it was noisily pulling itself free.

"That was Ashling, wasn't it?" Endry asked.

The sapling did not immediately respond but instead laboriously hauled herself up to the foot of the rubble pile, now stamped with rectangular footprints. Only when her roots were once again on relatively stable and level ground did she speak.

"It was her," the sapling agreed.

"Looked different," the faerie said.

"Yes."

"So, are we going to try to stop that thing?"

"Yes," the sapling repeated. "But she must also be warned the creature still pursues her. She must survive. The time is—"

"The time is short," Endry said. "The flamekin must survive, everything's going crazy. I get it, yewling. Please, say no more."

"You will be able to reach her much more quickly than I."

"You've got that right," the faerie replied. He swooped down before the yew's face and zigzagged with excitement in the air. "Good luck, yewling. Remember, stone can smash wood. And if that thing steps on you, no one's going to be able to rebuild you out of moss. Don't get yourself turned to splinters now."

"I will do my best," the sapling said. "Go. Help her. I will catch up."

As Endry buzzed merrily up the mountainside, the sapling felt the rock beneath her root-feet shake with every step. Their progress had been remarkably good. They'd been fortunate to catch up to Ashling when they did, since most of the potential threats of Mount Tanufel—including those flamekin warrior monks—were focused exclusively on her. Apart from Endry, no one had any idea the sapling was here or what she was capable of—not the monks, not the rock elemental, not the things that waited even further up the slope.

Ashling needed no warning that her reprieve from pursuit was temporary. That didn't prevent Endry from warning her anyway.

"Ashling!" the faerie called. As it pulled its heavy stone body up the steep and treacherous mountainside behind her, the stone giant's every step brought it closer to her. "Rock monster! BIG rock monster! Coming this— Ah, I see you know already."

In retrospect, he was lucky Ashling didn't incinerate him the moment he spoke. As it was, he barely escaped losing his wings, but faerie luck was with him.

Ashling glowered. "What are you doing here, faerie?"

"I could ask you the same question," Endry said. "Last we saw you, you weren't there. Looked like you were taken for a ride."

"You could say that," Ashling agreed. "Now I'm carrying myself. I've got to get to that monastery up there," she added, pointing to the distant black spires of the Ember Fell monastery, which were glowing a dull red in the rays of the dim midnight sun.

"Why?"

"That's between me and the elemental."

"The other elemental, you mean," the faerie said.

"There's only one elemental that concerns me," Ashling said. "Everything else is an obstacle."

"That's a lousy answer," Endry said. "So what's next? Any news you want me to bring back to the sapling? Or do you aim to stand here until that obstacle comes up here and smashes your head?"

"The sapling?" Ashling asked, as guilt and suspicion wrestled for control of her emotions. "You're with the sapling? Why?"

"She . . . she wanted to help find you," the faerie dodged. "We all miss you back at the camp, you know. We were about to start singing campfire songs about . . . campfires."

Ashling examined the tiny creature. His flutter had taken on a nervous quality. "You're hiding something."

"I'm telling you everything, Matchstick!" Endry cried. "And you still haven't answered—"

Endry's words were drowned out in another cascade of tumbling rock as the stone giant pulled its massive bulk over the edge of the cliff below them and settled onto the wide path that had taken Ashling some time to reach.

"I think we're past that question now," Ashling said.

CHAPTER 13

The sun was high overhead when Maralen and her companions finally reached giant country. The Gilt Leaf elves' territory ended at a steep embankment that leveled out into a wide, spreading valley. A hundred yards of gentle, rolling hills covered the vast green basin between where Maralen stood and the rugged foothills to the northwest. Lorwyn's squat, blocky mountains sulked beyond these foothills, broad, square chunks of granite dotted with patches of shaggy green. Maralen closed one eye and extended her hand to the horizon. She could imagine those distant ridges of leaf-capped stone as moss-covered boulders an arm's length away.

The others had already moved down the embankment. These cheery open fields and hillocks were a marked change from the cloying shadows that blanketed the deep woods, and each member of the party was adjusting to the change. Rhys had no trouble, and the faerie sisters quickly took advantage of the wide-open sky to stretch their wings. Brion and Kiel were the slowest to acclimatize to the brightness, and both giants squinted as they wandered aimlessly among the low, rolling hills.

The sights of this new territory didn't affect Maralen so much as the sounds. She was once more struck by how far noise carried when it wasn't baffled by endless moss-covered trees, how clear and ringing an echo could be when it rebounded off sheer rocks instead of leafy boughs.

"Well," Maralen said. "We're here. Aren't we?"

"We are." Rhys crouched down on one knee and pressed his hand into the grass. "This is the edge of giant country. Now all we have to do is find Rosheen."

"We should have plenty of time," Maralen said, "after the fun the boys had with the Dauba bridge."

"That was not fun, Lady. It was an act of war."

"But it was necessary."

"I would not have done it otherwise. The Dauba span was a thing of beauty."

"That had long since served its purpose to the Nation. We had another, more urgent use for it. Cheer up, my friend. When this is all over, we can help them grow a new one, better and more magnificent than ever."

"When this is all over." Rhys nodded. "First things first."

"Find Rosheen," Maralen said. She pointed down the incline to Brion and Kiel. "Fortunately we don't have to rely on the giants exclusively for that. Wrecking the Dauba span was strenuous, even for them. Look at them—they weren't this woozy after we pulled the nettlevines off."

Rhys stood. "You'll send Iliona and Veesa to scout ahead?"

"As we agreed." She concentrated and thought, *Iliona, Veesa. Pay attention.*

Two simultaneous moans of childish disappointment floated down from above. The Vendilion sisters descended in an overlapping zigzag pattern that left a lattice of blue dust shimmering in their wake.

"What do you want now?" Iliona said.

"Time to go to work. Spread out and find Rosheen."

Veesa bristled. "We were already doing that, you stupid woman. We were busily taking the lay of the land when you interrupted us and called us down here to tell us to take the lay of the land."

"Well, now you can start again. Only this time it'll be because I told you to. Get busy."

Veesa folded her arms and tossed her head. "You're not my mother."

"No, but I'm the next best thing. I'm also standing right here, and if you keep being truculent you're going to displease me."

Veesa clapped her hands on her cheeks in mock horror. "Alas and alack," she said, "the weird, extra-bossy elf is displeased with me. How will I ever live with the shame?"

"It's not shame you have to worry about," Maralen said quietly. "Is it?"

Veesa stiffened slightly. Her hands dropped to her side, and she opened her mouth, but she wisely chose to keep silent.

"Is it?"

"No," Veesa said.

"Carry on then. Unless Iliona has any objections?"

Iliona locked her eyes on Maralen's. The largest Vendilion faerie shook her head. "None," she said.

"I thought not." Maralen tossed her head, and the faeries took the hint: Iliona and Veesa zipped off across the valley without another word.

"Someday soon," Rhys said, "I'll ask you to explain the particulars of your arrangement with those faeries."

Maralen smiled and cocked her head. "And on that day," she said, "I'll answer as best I can."

Rhys was neither charmed nor disarmed by her airy reply. "They've done us a lot of good, there's no denying. But I still don't see what they get out of it."

Maralen shrugged.

"It can wait, of course," Rhys said. "I'm going to see if the giants can get us started in the right direction." He gestured to Maralen. "Coming?"

"You go ahead," she said. "I'm going to sit for a moment and make sure the Vendilion sisters don't get distracted."

Maralen watched Rhys descend into the basin. She waited until he hailed the giants and they responded, then she sank cross-legged onto the grass.

Rhys's question had caught her off guard, and in that brief moment when her concentration lapsed, the buzzing nausea returned in full force. Maralen clenched her fists against the churning sickness in her stomach, and a single cold tear slid down her cheek.

If Rhys doubted her, she truly was nothing. Weeks ago, when she had suddenly found herself bereft and wandering aimless through the Gilt Leaf, she was terrified. She didn't know who she was or how she had come to be there. She didn't know her own name. Yet she did know Rhys. With no identity of her own or home to return to, she was impelled toward the only thing that seemed important. She had never known Rhys, never seen him before, yet Maralen felt him nearby. He was a priceless jewel lost in the tall grass, there but tantalizingly just out of reach, and in her panic Maralen groped blindly for it.

There. She had it. Maralen felt the cool, smooth surface of the gem against her fingertips. Her fist clenched around the stone, and she gasped. The back half of the gem was cracked and ragged. She had found her treasure and even claimed it for herself, only to find it broken and ruined.

Or, a hatefully familiar voice interjected, *perhaps it was the act of finding your treasure that ruined it.*

Maralen opened her eyes. The distant chorus of vague but insistent voices rose in her ears once more, and this time Maralen could clearly hear the words of their strident, soaring song.

I am the root. You are but the flower.
Yours is the will, but mine is the power.
I am the trunk and the enduring boughs,
Majesty no fleeting bloom can long house.
Grandeur beyond what one blossom contains.
While it fades and withers, Oona remains.

"No." Maralen clenched her teeth so hard her jaw popped. "Not now. Go away."

Who are you talking to? Iliona and Veesa spoke together, their voices momentarily rising above the noise in Maralen's head.

We can't go away, Iliona thought.

Because we're nowhere near you, Veesa added.

Just as you requested.

It's also our preference, Veesa added.

"Then get back to it," Maralen said aloud. "I will call if I need you, when I need you."

Hmph.

Sourpuss.

Maralen shook her head so hard her vision fogged. She endured another crippling wave of nausea and pain, then stood up, driving her hooves deep into the soft soil.

"I'm ignoring you, mighty Queen," she said. "And I will keep ignoring you." She waited, but the voices only repeated their song. Slowly, Maralen's mind cleared and the awful buzzing sickness retreated. The chorus faded, and Maralen allowed herself a long, sweet breath of fresh valley air.

She glanced around to make sure she was alone. She crept over a rise and squatted low while Rhys shepherded the giants across the basin, toward the rocky hills at the far side.

Between the faerie sisters and the giant brothers, they had an excellent chance of finding Rosheen. Maralen didn't know what to expect when they reached the oracular giantess, but she knew the faeries didn't know much about Rosheen, and that meant Oona didn't either. If Rosheen was worth anything as an augur, she might also have information that Oona didn't, and that was the kind of information Maralen wanted most of all.

At the very least Maralen hoped for something that would illuminate her own problems, something to help her address the increasingly intrusive presence of Oona. Even if Rosheen had nothing useful to say on the subject of Colfenor and Ashling and the sapling, the giantess might still have something to offer Maralen.

Maralen stared at the former Hemlock daen. Much of her memory returned to her shortly after she first met Rhys, but she still had no recollection of how she went from being a member of a Mornsong bridal party to wandering like a sleepwalker through the forest. Her past remained incomplete and her future—indeed, all of their futures together—were a confused, bubbling stew of earnest intentions and unpleasant realities. They had more difficult choices to make now, and still more would be forced on them before all was said and done.

Maralen tamped back the doubts and troubling half-memories. The only way any of them could shape their future into success or failure was to make these choices, and the only way to do that was to press on.

She wiped the tear trail from her cheek and called after Rhys and the giants as she headed down into the basin to join the search for Rosheen.

* * * * *

They found Rosheen Meanderer at midday, just after the sun peaked overhead.

It was Iliona and Veesa who first spotted the sleeping giantess. Rhys had expected Brion or Kiel to make the discovery, especially since Kiel was oracular himself, but the giants were oddly distracted and hesitant. They carried themselves as errant but chastened schoolboys anticipating a deserved punishment, rather than siblings on the verge of a family reunion.

"We found her! We found her!" Both faeries were more animated than Rhys had ever seen them, shimmering and scintillating even when they hovered in one place.

Iliona pointed repeatedly with alternating hands, her fingers stabbing toward the nearest large hill. "Past that rise, there's another hill that's even bigger. Past that there's a sharp, shallow valley."

"With the biggest woman anyone's ever seen sleeping length-wise across the bottom." Veesa flew down and latched on to the smallest finger on Rhys's left hand. "Come on! Come on! You've got to see this." Though she tugged mightily, she only managed to pull the elf's arm a few inches forward.

"Hang on," Rhys said. He gently pulled free of Veesa's sharp grip and waved to the giants nearby. "I think we've got something." He pointed. "The faeries say Rosheen is over there."

Brion blinked. He yawned and stretched, working the kinks out of his shoulders and neck. "You sure, Boss?"

"Of course we're sure, you great thumping oaf," Iliona said.

"Unless there are two mountain-sized ladies asleep in these parts."

Brion considered this. Kiel ambled over to his brother and stared at the faeries through half-lidded eyes.

"The one you saw." Brion rubbed his chin thoughtfully. "Was she talking?"

Veesa nodded as Iliona answered. "Babbling a blue streak. Though not a word of it made sense."

"Feet," Kiel said.

Rhys shared an amused glance with Maralen. "What did you say?"

"Feet," Brion answered. "It's a good question. What about her feet?"

Iliona scowled. "She had feet, if that's what you mean."

Veesa nodded. "Though to be fair, they were stuck into the mouth of a cave."

"That's Rosheen," Brion said with a smile. "She hates having cold feet while she sleeps."

"Well then." Rhys nodded to Maralen, and the dark-haired elf nodded back. "We should investigate."

"That's what we've been saying," Iliona said.

"Why don't any of you ever listen to us? We're always right."

The faeries' enthusiasm quickly infected Brion and Kiel, and so it didn't take long to get the entire group moving. The giants were sharper now than moments ago, more focused and less hesitant. Rhys and Maralen corralled the group over the first hill, then up the second. They stopped at the top of this larger hard-packed mound of soil and rocks. Below was the sharp crevice the faeries described, a jagged crease of stone dotted with scrub oak and covered by a thick carpet of sweetgrass.

Rosheen Meanderer lay flat on her back with her hands folded across her stomach. She was huge, remarkably huge for a female giant. Tall as Kiel and broad as Brion, Rosheen's body filled fully half the valley floor. Rhys's eyes followed the huge, slumbering form's outline from top to bottom, from her wild tangle of jet black hair down to the mouth of the cave at her ankles. Rosheen's feet were indeed wedged into the cave's interior and hidden from view.

"Look," Iliona pointed upward, her voice awed and delighted. Rhys and the others looked. High overhead, towering among the highest clouds, almost indistinguishable from them, was a gleaming, white-furred goat large enough for a giant Rosheen's size to ride—far larger, in fact. As Rhys took in the entirety of the vast, distant creature, he calculated it could easily seat the entire trio of giant siblings.

A constant, mumbling drone floated up from the crevice, tearing Rhys's attention away from Rosheen's loyal cloudgoat. Rosheen's voice was deep and booming, though she was only muttering in her sleep. The syllables she pronounced amounted to so much gibberish, a constantly evolving chant that had lost all meaning through countless repetitions. Except for the steady rise and fall of her chest and the constant fluttering of her lips, the giantess was completely motionless.

"That's her," Brion said happily.

"Rosheen," Kiel said.

"And Mr. Choppers." Brion nodded up at the huge white beast among the clouds. "That's her goat."

"At last," Maralen touched Rhys on the shoulder, and when he turned she said, "We made it, Daen. Congratulations . . . and thank you."

"Don't thank me yet. Apart from delivering Brion's message, there's no guarantee we'll accomplish anything here."

"You're too hard on yourself," Maralen said. "We escaped from the Gilt Leaf hunters, and we found the only being in Lorwyn who is older and might know more than Colfenor." Maralen folded her hand behind her back and studied Rosheen. "Look at her. Don't tell me you can't feel her presence. Forget sight, sound, and smell, you know she's right in front of you. Don't you feel the deep magic coming off her in waves? I do. There's power here, Rhys, and maybe answers too."

Rhys also turned his eyes toward the giantess. "I do feel it," he said. But he didn't like it. He had often seen thick clouds gather and form against the rocky barrier of Lorwyn's mountains. Rosheen was not a natural mountain, and the forces he sensed churning and pooling against her considerable surface were not natural but supernatural.

Rhys also had never fully considered what Maralen just said, that ancient beings like Colfenor amassed huge stores of knowledge and magic over the course of their long lives—and that Rosheen was even older than his mentor had been. The giantess might never tell them what they wanted to know, not even if they succeeded in waking her up. But Rosheen's very presence was affecting this whole area, concentrating the local arcane energy and perhaps even altering it. This was a rare opportunity for them all: What was impossible anywhere else in Lorwyn might well be achievable in the shadow of Rosheen.

"Let's get closer," Rhys said. "But we go slowly, carefully." He realized the words he was about to say were absolutely true, and that fact troubled him deeply. "None of us really knows what to expect."

"You go ahead, Boss." Brion waved amiably and sat down with a ground-rumbling thud. "We've woken up Rosheen before and trust me: She'll only forgive you the first time." He motioned for Kiel to join him on the ground, and after a moment's hesitation and a grunt of resignation Kiel did so.

"Message," Kiel said. "Tales."

Rhys reached into his pack and produced the noisome, tightly furled hide-scroll that the brothers had given him to deliver. "Right here."

"Good. You go. We'll wait."

"I think I need at least one of you to come with me," Rhys said. "Introductions are in order. And I was hoping you could translate that—what she's saying into something I can understand."

"You go on, Boss." Brion waved Rhys away. "Rosheen's always been friendly, so you don't need an introduction."

"But how am I going to understand her?"

"Listen," Kiel said.

"What?"

Brion scratched himself under the chin. "He means be patient.

If you sit and listen to Rosheen babble long enough, she does start to make sense."

Rhys eyed the brothers dubiously. "She does."

"Sure. And if you keep on listening, she goes back to nonsense, so you have to be there when it counts."

"I see. Is there anything we need to know before we meet her? Just in case she does wake up?"

Kiel turned at the waist so that he was facing Rhys and Maralen. The long-bearded giant sniffed loudly, twice, as if preparing to unleash the granddaddy of all giant sneezes. Then, to Rhys's astonishment, Kiel began to speak.

"Rosheen's story," the giant said. "One day Rosheen was born, and on that day everything changed." Kiel's eyes were clear, and his voice took on a strange, lilting cadence. "Rosheen says it's not her fault her birthday was special. It just happened that way. She said it right away too. Rosheen started talking with her first breath, though for a long time no one understood a word she said.

"After her first Name Sleep, she woke up and said her name, "Rosheen Meanderer." And people started listening to her because she started making sense. She was always Rosheen, though, always the Meanderer before and after the name found her. So she keeps talking. She's always talking, and if you're not patient, after a while you get tired of listening to it all just to hear the bits about you.

"She's always Rosheen no matter what. She's had two more Name Sleeps since the first, but she always wakes up Meanderer. Now her birthday is coming, and she decided to try for a new name one last time. Because things always change on her special birthday, and maybe this time it's her name's turn."

Kiel turned back to face them. His beard got stuck on a large berry bush.

Brion belched loudly. "All clear now? Good luck, Boss."

"Wait, wait. What was all that just now?"

"What?"

"Kiel hasn't said more than five words in a row since I met you. Where did that long speech come from?"

"Oh, that?" Brion made a rude noise. "We had that drummed into us since we were little giants. Rosheen used to make him say it every time she met him, just to make sure he had it down straight. He wasn't speeching, Boss. He was reciting." Brion turned and slapped the back of Kiel's head. "And you got it wrong again, dummy. You tell it different every time."

Rhys stammered as he searched for the right expression of outrage and confusion, but Maralen never gave him the chance.

"Let's go, just you and I," she whispered. "It's certainly easier and probably for the best. I'd like to have a closer look for myself, and we don't really need them until she wakes up."

"Leave a faerie to watch them," Rhys said. "I don't want any more surprises."

"Consider it done."

"All right. Let's go take that closer look."

The small squadrons of flies buzzing among the scrub trees drifted away when Rhys and Maralen edged by. They stopped on a mound of sod near Rosheen's midsection.

Judging from how far the grass had grown around Rosheen, the giantess had been sleeping here for quite some time. Like an ancient, hollow log, Rosheen's body had been partially claimed by moss and vegetation. Small, furry things scampered across her legs, dragonflies darted to and fro over her stomach, and there was a crow's nest in the buckle of her belt. Rosheen's voice was louder here, clearer, but the words still ran together in one thick, undecipherable stream.

Rhys stood listening for several moments.

"Giants must be patient folk, because I'm bored already," Maralen said. "How long do you think Brion meant for us to wait?"

"As long as it takes."

"I knew you were going to say that." Maralen sighed. She peered up toward the giantess's head and said, "What's moving up there?"

Rhys kept his eyes forward. "Probably another family of squirrels. There's a whole colony down by her knees."

"No, look. It's not . . . it's not anything normal."

Rhys looked. He blinked and looked again. There was something happening around Rosheen's chin and shoulders. There were vague, indistinct shapes that were . . . dancing?

"Well spotted," he said. He strode toward the top of Rosheen, careful to watch the oddly undulating figures as he approached. They seemed to flow together and then apart, never holding one shape for more than a few seconds.

"Is that real?" Maralen whispered. Rhys shared her confusion. The malleable scene was hypnotic, mesmerizing. Rosheen's voice was louder than ever. Rhys could feel it in his bones. Real or not, this hazy display was surely some sort of side effect of the magic that swirled and eddied against Rosheen's sleeping form.

As he and Maralen drew close, Rhys saw individuals among the throng half-covering Rosheen's chest and shoulders. The creatures were mostly a shimmering, opalescent blue, their bodies resembling rubbery, pot-bellied children with webbed feet. Their short, sharp tails curled behind them, and their wide, vacant eyes barely blinked. Their blank, blubbery features remained slack as they shifted and swayed.

"Changelings," Rhys said.

"I've never seen changelings do this," Maralen said.

"This place is special." Rhys relaxed briefly. He had never seen changelings do this either, but then again very few in Lorwyn ever saw changelings at all. Now dozens, maybe hundreds of the mindless, malleable things had settled on Rosheen, most likely drawn in along with the rest of the arcane energy that accumulated around the giantess. It made a certain kind of sense: The strange primordial creatures normally only mimicked whatever they were standing next to at the time, but they were easily influenced by powerful magic.

"Are they feeding, or . . ." Maralen's voice trailed off. "What are they doing?"

"I don't think it matters. They're no threat, but they're no help either."

"Oh." The dark-haired elf's face brightened. "Or they might be a huge help."

"How do you figure?"

"Brion said we had to be patient, right? To wait and listen. These gummy, little buggers have been here for who knows how long? If they've been listening for some time, maybe they've reached a point where Rosheen makes sense. All we have to do is figure out how to talk to them."

Rhys shook his head. "That just puts us right back where we started, in need of a translator."

Maralen cocked her head. "I can try, though, can't I? No harm in trying. With the faeries' help— They're experts at harvesting dreamstuff, after all. This should be a snap for them."

Rhys stared for a moment as the changelings mewled, nodded, and swooned. One of them stumbled off of Rosheen's left shoulder and rolled toward Rhys and Maralen. Veesa swooped down near the creature, but she was careful not to actually touch it. Nonetheless, Rhys watched as four reasonable (but rubbery) facsimiles of faerie wings sprouted from the top of the wayward changeling's back.

"Ew," Veesa said. She beat her wings and soared high over Rosheen again. The farther she went from the changeling, the faster its new wings dwindled.

"By all means," Rhys said, "please try. All I ask is that you not wake up Rosheen."

"Why not? It might be the best thing for us."

"Because it's considered bad luck to wake a sleeping giant for a reason," Rhys said. "It's suicidally stupid."

"We've done it before." Maralen beamed. "Twice."

Rhys shook his head. "The first time we woke Brion and Kiel up, they lashed out and nearly crushed us before they were fully awake. And the second time we had Ashling's help."

Maralen considered this. "Fair enough," she said. "I promise not to wake up the giantess."

Rhys watched the mass of changelings squirm across Rosheen. Maralen turned and concentrated, calling her faeries to her.

It couldn't hurt to try. They had time while Gryffid and the Hemlock made their way over the Dauba. He could afford to sit and listen to the changelings, to make an effort to understand what Rosheen had to say.

Then he would set out to find Ashling, and the sapling, and force the world to start making sense again.

CHAPTER 14

It wasn't long before the effects of the tainted arbomander's blood began to show on the two merrows. Sygg could feel his thoughts tending toward the bloody almost immediately, but with effort he was able to keep his wits.

Flyrne was going to be another matter. The big merrow had been lingering in Crannog Aughn since the malignants had gone on their rampage, and it was likely whatever had caused half the Paperfin school to go berserk had already touched Flyrne. The arbomander's blood only sped up the process.

The first sign that Flyrne was going to be trouble was one only Sygg noticed, and only because Sygg had known the big fish for many, many years. A dulling of the rainbow scales, a rapid flexing of the gills, the tail kicking out with just a touch more strain than needed. Sygg had to learn as much about what had happened as he could while Flyrne was still able to answer.

"Flyrne," he asked as casually as he was able, "When did this begin? Why hadn't I heard of any trouble in the crannog?"

"You've been gone," Flyrne said. "No one knew where. Most thought you were dead, Captain."

"I very nearly was," Sygg said, eyeing Brigid Baeli as she paddled hard to keep up with them. "More than once." The kithkin's swimming was improving exponentially with each minute she spent under the river's surface, but she would never be the equal of a Wanderwine native. "I had no idea anything like this was happening."

"None of us did until it was too late," Flyrne said sadly. "The watchmerrows were the first to fall. They attacked like . . . animals." The big merrow seemed to be having trouble forming his words. "Those they attacked became like them, or they died. The survivors fled for the redoubt."

"The redoubt?" Sygg said. "No one has used that for centuries. This isn't an enemy you can fend off. It's a disease." He blinked, cocking his head. "Isn't it?"

"They may have survived . . . they may be dead," Flyrne said. "I cannot say. Only . . . some of us . . . stayed behind. . . ."

The conversation came to an abrupt end as Brigid floated into view and Flyrne lashed out like a river adder and bit her on the leg.

Sygg shouted an alarm the kithkin clearly didn't need. Screaming in pain and surprise, Brigid drove the tip of her free boot into Flyrne's snout and shoved, which only served to force the big fish's jagged teeth deeper into her flesh. The archer was safe from drowning thanks to the new, more flexible shapewater membrane Sygg had placed over her face.

"Captain," she said as calmly as she could, "either pull his jaws apart or kill him. Please." Her pleading face was pink in the blood-clouded water, and the clouds swirled and roiled as Flyrne thrashed against the kithkin's limb.

Sygg nodded and did a backflip that put him to the side of the frenzied fish-man. The captain hooked one hand on Flyrne's upper lip, the other on the big merrow's chin, and pulled as hard as he could.

At first it appeared the big merrow wasn't going to budge, but Sygg knew he could wear Flyrne down. The malignancy had not yet taken over his senses completely, and the big fellow was fighting his primal urge to catch and eat meat. Perhaps a little encouragement would help his former crewman.

"Flyrne, I've told you a thousand times: No chewing on the passengers," Sygg said, pulling hard on the first syllable of the last word. A few inches. "You're going to get locked up in the tide-gaol for this. What do you have to say for yourself?" Another attempt to jerk apart Flyrne's jaws netted another inch of bloody teeth sliding out of the kithkin's leg, but there were still several inches of tooth to go. "Are you listening? I'm talking to you, you big clam-shucker."

"How many teeth does he have?" Brigid asked, panic showing through her shapewater mask. "And why won't he let go?"

On the word "go," Sygg's efforts finally bore fruit. Flyrne's jaw muscles gave out, and the ferryman hauled him the rest of the way off the kithkin. He gave the big merrow a shove and maneuvered himself between Flyrne and Brigid. The kithkin was clutching her leg to stanch the flow of blood. Sygg reached over his shoulder, made a shapewater bandage, and with his other hand he raised a simple shield of solid liquid before them.

Flyrne gnashed his teeth once, twice, then locked them together with a loud *clack*. His eyes lost their silvery sheen and became once again the milky white orbs of a bottom-dweller. "It's happened to me at last," the big merrow said. "I waited for you, or someone like you, Sygg, to come back to the crannog when the others left. I thought maybe if you lasted this long, the problem might not be upriver."

Sygg waved his hand again, and the shield dissipated.

"You could go on with us to the redoubt," Sygg said. "Maybe there's a way—"

"I am becoming malignant," Flyrne said, "and that is all there is to it, Sygg. You have to leave me behind. Soon you won't be able to trust me."

"I don't trust you now," Brigid interjected. "But then, no one really trusts me either, so I suppose that's only fair." When Sygg and Flyrne ignored her, Brigid muttered, "Don't mind me, I'll just be bleeding over here."

"You'll be fine," Sygg told the kithkin. "The infection hasn't ever spread to your kind."

"I don't want to know how you know that, do I?" Brigid snapped through clenched teeth.

"Flyrne, I need you to help," Sygg pleaded. "I'm but one tideshaper."

"No," the big merrow said. "The Paperfin—all the schools— must know what is coming. Perhaps if we scatter, hide . . ."

"I don't think hiding is going to help," Sygg said. "Nothing's going to help until we learn where this malignancy came from. It could be the source stone or something in the source itself. It might just be a bug in the water. But we've got to get to the redoubt and see how they've fared."

"Redoubt?" Brigid asked.

"The royal redoubt where Paupurfylln—that is, Paperfin— reejereys of old used to wall themselves in during the wars. The schools were always at war in the old days, before we all had our own territories mapped out. Merrow engineers carved the redoubt out of the deeps known as the Dark Meanders. That's got to be where the reejerey has gone."

"How is that going to help anything?" Brigid said. "This malignancy is in the water, isn't it?"

"Probably. But if we don't stop at the redoubt I can't be sure. And there's another reason . . ." Sygg's voice trailed off as he lost himself in memories long buried.

"When we're through here, Captain, I think you're going to owe me."

"I'm ready to settle up with you whenever you wish," Sygg said, snapping out of his reverie. "Listen here, kithkin: I'm going to the redoubt to see if I can fix this. If I have to swim all the way to the source to make it right, I will."

"We will," Brigid said. "But isn't the source at the top of—"

"Mount Tanufel," Sygg finished. "First, the redoubt. I've got to talk some sense into one of my wives, and I've got to do it quickly."

With a last sad wave to Flyrne, Sygg and Brigid set off up the mighty Wanderwine, leaving the big merrow to stand watch over the dead for as long as he could.

* * * * *

Brigid worried she might not fit through the narrowest bends in the pitch black tunnels of the Dark Meanders, but Sygg had planned ahead. The ferryman struck a sparkstick, a short-lived crystal flare that burned with a cold blue light, and he used it to point out the gaps through which Brigid could easily pass. The merrow held it over his head as he swam, using its light to keep the kithkin from colliding too painfully with the rocks—though Brigid did experience an occasional bump or scrape.

The kithkin archer felt her noble purpose slipping away again. She had forced her company upon Sygg to help atone for what she'd done, but atonement didn't seem necessary, in Sygg's opinion. And whether he intended it to or no, Sygg's ambivalence made Brigid's desire to find some real measure of redemption burn even brighter. Since leaving the others on her own personal quest, all she'd done was follow—follow Sygg's blue light through the tunnels, and before that follow Sygg's orders, and before that follow Rhys or Ashling or whomever needed following. It was time she changed that. She'd been living almost entirely underwater for days now, and swimming was at last becoming as natural as walking. With what she hoped was a powerful stroke, she edged around Sygg's scaly form and into the darkness ahead.

"This way," Sygg said. "I can sense we're close."

Brigid fancied she too could feel the deep-river redoubt, teeming with merrow chiefs, reejereys, wellgabbers and trout-herds. All of them, from the lordliest courtier to the lowest deeptreader, were filled with pride—pride and anger. It was palpable.

Brigid wasn't sure how she came by these impressions. Perhaps merrows had their own form of thoughtweft, or some-thing an expert weaver like herself could touch with just a little effort. That minor effort led her to crash headfirst into the rough surface of the tunnel wall, and as she cursed the darkness Sygg and his blue light arrived to reveal three potential routes forward.

Brigid had the misfortune of colliding with the leading edge of a relatively thin wall separating the two openings on their left. The one on the right was set farther apart from the others and appeared to drop downward after a few feet. Without pausing, Sygg sailed past Brigid and on into the solitary passage on the right. The archer swallowed what little pride she had left, kicked off the wall, and followed. She had managed to cover nearly three feet toward Sygg when a pair of pale, bloodless tentacles speared through the wall and wrapped themselves around the kithkin.

"What, again?" Brigid sneered, and reached to her belt for her short sword. A few swings of sturdy kithkin steel would take care of these grasping critters. This was their fourth such encounter by her count—these slimy creatures just didn't seem to learn.

Unfortunately, Brigid found her short sword gone. It must have slipped from her belt somewhere along the way through the darkness. The tentacles—or the thing attached to them—seemed to sense her disappointment, her sudden helplessness, because the rubbery white appendages wasted no time dragging her backward.

Brigid opened her mouth to call for the captain, but a third tentacle erupted from the tunnel wall and wrapped tightly around her head and face. Just before the tip of the tentacle closed over her eyes, Brigid saw Sygg and his blue light disappear around another bend some twenty-odd yards ahead. The kithkin managed a growl of frustration, but that didn't keep the tentacles from lashing around her wrists and ankles, digging in with thousands of tiny teeth into her skin. Her growl turned into a muffled roar when she felt two more tentacles latch on to her.

She'd been in worse situations. At least the shapewater mask hadn't slipped, and she could still draw thin breaths through her nose, even if she couldn't see. And so far her injuries were limited to shame and suction marks—Sygg had seen to the injuries Flyrne inflicted on her with a simple shapewater bandage that numbed the pain and encouraged the wounds to heal.

No, injuries were not the problem. Sygg's slipping away into the darkness ahead was the problem, and the frustration she felt was quickly giving way to fear and real panic. She was a long way from home and far out of her element. What happened when she got too far from Sygg for the shapewater to remain cohesive?

A quick death, at least, Brigid told herself grimly. If this thing tries to draw and quarter you, just drop the mask and it'll be over in no—

The tentacles attached to her limbs suddenly pulled her in four different directions while the one around her head held her in place. Despite her dark thoughts of heroic sacrifice, Brigid did not drop the mask. Instead, she struggled as best she could, trying to twist her body and find some kind of purchase, but there was nothing, and her thrashing had no effect. Still the tentacles pulled, and soon the pain of her joints being pulled apart overwhelmed thoughts of freedom or even suicide. Besides, suicide would hardly be necessary in a few seconds.

She had just begun to slip into unconsciousness when the pressure on her left arm went slack. Then her other arm was free.

She still couldn't see, but the tentacle around her head relaxed a moment later. Brigid pushed the dead thing off of her face in time to see Sygg, his trusty skinning knife in hand, trying to keep up with her as the last two tentacles hauled the kithkin away by her ankles.

Everything went topsy-turvy when the tentacles smacked her against the ceiling of the tunnel, and she saw blood in the water—the tentacles had not bled, but the milky, viscous substance they'd left in the water mixed with her blood to create a pink cloud that went purple as Sygg swam through it with his bright blue light.

The merrow was having trouble keeping up, however. Brigid had to do something to save herself or Sygg would never be able to reach her. Flailing with her stretched, aching arms, she caught a rough stone outcrop and managed to hang on for a few painful seconds. Then the pressure grew too great, and the stone was ripped from her hands. It was enough for Sygg to catch up. With his free hand, he took Brigid's arm and pulled himself past her body to reach her ankles. He drove the skinning knife into one of the two remaining tentacles again and again. By the time Brigid was free of the last tentacle, the water was almost completely opaque with milky gore and kithkin blood.

Sygg raised a hand to indicate they could rest here for a moment, but Brigid shook her head. "Can't stay. Can't stay here."

"Don't worry," Sygg told her. "Those things only have five tentacles."

"But who says there's only— there's only one of them?" Brigid said.

Sygg peered through the murk and nodded. "That's a good point. Do you think you can keep up?"

"You saved my life, again," Brigid said. "I'll keep up."

"For a murderous backstabber, you've got a self-sacrificing streak a mile wide," Sygg said with a smile. "I'll help you keep up, all right? This isn't the time for pride."

"That's also a good point," she agreed. "But I'd appreciate it if you could avoid smacking me into any more rocks. I'm really, really tired of that." She pressed her palm to the back of her head and was relieved to find the wound was not severe—though like any head wound, it bled like crazy.

"I'll do my best," Sygg said, his hands already weaving a net of shapewater with which he could pull the kithkin along. With her gill mask still in place, there was no need for another ride in "the bubble," which was a relief.

The rest of the journey was relatively uneventful, and for Brigid, far more relaxing. She allowed herself to be carried, only kicking this way and that to avoid collisions in the narrow tunnel confines. The kithkin no longer had even the faintest clue where they might be relative to Kinsbaile, Mount Tanufel, or any other distinctive landmarks. She relied entirely on Sygg to know where he was going. Fortunately, the ferryman did.

Where they were going, however, was a place Brigid had never imagined this far beneath the ground. One minute they were within the cramped tunnel, the next they were floating free some two hundred feet above the rocky floor of a mammoth underwater cavern. In the center of the cavern was a fortress built in what Brigid had to assume was traditional merrow style, and for the first time the kithkin could see how much the merrows had compromised in the structure of their crannogs to accommodate landwalkers. There was no wood used in the construction of the royal redoubt, only stone, bone, and gleaming shapewater walls. The magic that made those walls had about as much relation to the mask Brigid wore as she had to an elf—this shapewater glistened like crystal, forming spires, gates, and columns, and through it all she could see dozens, no, hundreds of merrow swimming to and fro. Most appeared to be preparing defenses.

"Sygg," she whispered through her mask, "why are we being

so secretive? I thought you wanted to come here. That your wife was here."

"I did," the captain said. "I do." He sighed a bubbling sigh. "And she is."

"Then why—"

"I just told you. Now hush and try to keep up."

* * * * *

"You should not be here," the merrow honor guard told Brigid as they entered the bizarre underwater fortress. "This is a place for the children of the river."

"She is with me," Sygg interjected, "and after the last few days, Brigid Baeli is as much a child of the Father-Lane as any landwalker could ever hope to be. Don't you worry about the kithkin. Just take us to the reejerey."

"Who are you to order me?" the guard demanded.

Sygg reached into a pouch on his belt and produced a small crescent of polished bone adorned with silver inscriptions Brigid didn't recognize. The crescent hung on a thread of thick, woven gold, which Sygg slipped over his head with calm importance.

"I am Sygg Gauhren Gyllalla Syllvar, mate of Reejerey Kasella and Heir to the Crescent of Morningtide. You will address me with the respect that's due."

As soon as he saw the jewelry Sygg wore the guard's demeanor and expression became subservient, and the armored merrow let himself float downward half a foot as a token of the respect Sygg insisted was owed. Brigid could not have been more surprised if the ferryman had sprouted legs and danced a kithkin jig.

Perhaps sensing what Brigid was about to ask, Sygg raised a clawed finger to silence her.

The other merrow nodded beneath his silver battle helmet and touched the end of his spear to his forehead in a sharp salute.

"Welcome to the redoubt," the guard said. "I shall notify my superiors of your coming."

"Notify whomever you like, so long as you tell the reejerey," he said. After a moment of awkward silence, Sygg added, "You are dismissed."

The guard nodded again and swam off toward the most impressive of the shapewater structures that made up this underwater fortress. The palace-in-exile for the Paperfin leader, she supposed.

Now that the guard was gone, however, Brigid could no longer contain herself. "Heir to the Crescent of Morningtide? What in the world is that? Why do they take orders from you?"

"Just because all any of you kithkin ever see me do is ferry landwalkers across the river doesn't mean that's my entire life," Sygg said. "I am secretly an important merrow."

"So it would appear," Brigid said wryly. "Why didn't you pull that on Flyrne?"

"It wasn't necessary," Sygg replied. "Flyrne is an old friend. I haven't spoken to my— to the reejerey for some time. Years. I wanted nothing of that world. But by the Lanes, I am going to use my title for as much as I can get. No point in hiding it now."

"Indeed, there is little point in concealing your arrival," said a new merrow voice from up ahead, "just as there is little point in coming here. We hold our dear cousin Sygg in the highest regard, landwalker, but he has chosen the wrong time to reassert his inheritance." The voice belonged to a female of the species adorned in a much more elaborate version of the same armor the honor guard wore, clearly a superior of some kind, if not the—

"Reejerey Kasella," Sygg said, raising a hand to bring Brigid to a halt. "It is good to see you again, though I admit I am at a loss as to why you have retired to this . . ." he paused for a moment, searching for the right word, "this hideaway," he finished.

"Cousin?" Brigid blurted. "You said she was—"

"It's complicated," Sygg said.

The reejerey did resemble Sygg in many general ways—the sheen of their scales in the dim blue light of a phosphorescent coral was nearly identical, as was the deep black of their intelligent, unblinking eyes. The female had fewer barbels than Sygg, and they were smaller, but her tailfin and dorsals were longer, more elegant. Her teeth were more visible. And sharper.

The net cradling Brigid disappeared, leaving her to float freely. The effect was invisible, but she could feel the shapewater lose cohesion—if this kept up she'd be a tideshaper herself before all was said and done. She suspected the other merrow did not realize Sygg had released her, however, so she resolved to be ready to move quickly if necessary.

"I owe you an explanation, is that what you are saying?" the reejerey asked with a peculiar lilt that made Brigid nervous—but not as nervous as the silver shadows she saw emerging one by one from the arched portcullises at the base of the redoubt. The silhouette of each merrow bore the profile of the same armor the honor guard wore, and they appeared to be clutching the same silver spears. Whatever the female's explanation, she meant to back it up with a few dozen—maybe hundreds—of very sharp points. "I intend to give you one, once we have secured our perimeter. We are at war, you know."

"I did not," Sygg said, and Brigid saw his tail twitch when he, too, noticed the reejerey's guards hovering in the depths. "So it appears I arrived just in time," he added smoothly. "I bring with me the Hero of Kinsbaile, the one called Brigid Baeli. She and I have faced many dangers together to bring you news of— news from beyond the perimeter. So that you may remain informed of—"

"Do not lie to me, Sygglet," Kasella said with a wicked, toothy smile. "And do not fear. We know you have been among the land-walkers for a long time. You cannot help what you have become, but we can. This mammal, however— I'm afraid we'll have to tuck her safely away for the duration."

"What?" Brigid exclaimed, and the honor guard turned on her with alarm.

"You do not speak to her most eminent—"

"Holgen!" the reejerey snapped. "Not now." She turned and examined Brigid closely for the first time—unsettling, since the kithkin got the feeling Kasella was looking at her as she would a familiar, battered toy.

"Landwalkers have long sullied our homes, kithkin," she said, "fouling our rivers and lakes and every lane running under or over the surface of Lorwyn."

"It's not as if we didn't invite them in," Sygg interjected. "Why are you doing this, Kasella?"

"I do not care what you wear around your neck, Sygg. Mate or not, I will have your silence or your tongue. The choice is yours." The reejerey turned back to Brigid, and her black eyes narrowed. "Now the landwalkers have gone too far. There is a malignancy in the Wanderwine. Already hundreds of merrow from every school that touches the Father-Lane have given in to its savage embrace. And so they had to die. I will not tolerate a landwalker within my last place of refuge while I am readying for the destruction of her kind."

"That is— Kasella, that is madness," Sygg said with as much respect as he could muster. "The landwalkers didn't cause this."

"Didn't they?"

"Do you have proof?" Sygg said. "Why would you undo generations of peace based solely on suspicions?"

"My consort—yes, I took a consort, Sygg, as you well know— was a victim of this landwalker plague," Kasella said with venom. "He led a party of our most talented tideshapers to the source stone, for they could sense it was . . . changing. We did not know it was the landwalkers' doing, we thought it was something that might be healed. We'd heard from other schools that their own stones were changing as well, but there was nothing we could do for them. And as the stone changed, so did we all." She turned back to Sygg. "The malignancy awaits us, Sygg. We can flee the source stone and avoid my consort's bloody end, and we can avenge ourselves on the ones who caused our downfall while we are still merrow."

"But you are still merrow," Sygg protested. "You've survived the malignancy. Let me help. Let me cure this. If I go to the source . . ." He tapped the bone crescent on his chest. "I may have inherited this little token, but you know as well as I do that I earned the right to wear it fighting every one of my siblings. If you insist on this course, Kasella, I will use the crescent."

"You underestimate our people, Sygg," the reejerey replied with a sneer. "They have been through much and will not be pacified with pretty words and flashy jewelry. The time for such things is past. The court has agreed, and I have given the command."

"The command?" Brigid bubbled. "Sygg, I've got to warn—"

"We begin with the flamekin," the reejerey said, ignoring her. "It was one of their accursed ilk who burned the day our people went mad. The day source stone changed, the day we changed."

"Stop this at once!" Sygg commanded. "Yes, you're changed. You're paranoid, placing blame where it doesn't belong. We are the children of the river. The landwalkers have their domain, we have ours, and at certain places we intersect. If there's a problem, it must be with the source. Great Lanes, Kasella, the landwalkers don't even know the source stones exist! How could they—"

"You think the landwalkers innocent?" the reejerey asked. "As I said, you've been far too long among them."

"No," Sygg said, eyeing the guards, who had stopped hovering and now swam slowly toward them. "That's not going to happen. There are many kinds of malignancy. I came here to warn you,

Kasella. I see I'm too late to save you. And you may be right. Perhaps the Paperfin will not follow me, whatever I wear. But I'm not letting you take this kithkin."

"You cannot stop me," Kasella replied, waving her guards forward.

"I will go to the source," Sygg said. "I will fix this, somehow. Just don't hinder me, and don't threaten my friends."

"Guards," the reejerey said, her voice suddenly loud and clear, "I have been mistaken. The Heir of Morningtide cannot be saved. The malignancy already has him in its wicked grasp. Kill them both!"

Without waiting to see what Sygg intended, Brigid spun in midwater and came face-to-face with a wall of scales and armor. She hadn't even heard them approach—but it was clear there would be no going out the way they came in. The archer was about to tell Sygg as much when the ferryman took her by the arm and swam as fast and as hard as he could for the center of the glittering redoubt.

"They cannot flee!" Reejerey Kasella shouted after them. "Hunt them down and slice out their eyes. Then we forge onward to Mount Tanufel!"

CHAPTER 15

"Left! Go left!" Endry cried. "No, your other left. Other! Now right. Right! Right, right, right— No, left! Left!"

With each call the flamekin pilgrim leaped in the direction her faerie spotter indicated in time to avoid another crashing footstep. Ashling didn't waste time gawking, she'd seen that foot enough times now, and the novelty was definitely wearing off.

"I think I'm—"

"Right!"

A jog to the right, another earth-shaking footstep. "I think I'm figuring out the pattern, thanks."

Ashling's flames blazed brightly, but try as she might she could not get her feet to leave the ground. That ability was lost to her for the time being—there wasn't a chance she'd be able to concentrate hard enough to make contact with her own fiery elemental, especially if it didn't want to be contacted. She faced the very real possibility, in fact, that the elemental was no longer atop the mountain. Ashling had been running for so long she just didn't know. . . .

No. It was there. It waited, expectantly, jealously guarding its power. Clearly, it didn't fear her approach. Ashling hoped to change that opinion soon enough. Now that she'd found the creature, she could take what was owed her and—

Something slammed into her left shoulder and sent her

stumbling. She looked up to see the faerie frantically flapping his blackened but still intact wings and realized Endry had caused the impact himself. "I said 'left,' Matchstick. Now get up. Here he comes again."

Ashling rolled to the left in time to avoid yet another footstep and realized she was gazing directly up at the towering giant. It was not, now that she got a good look at it, completely intact any longer. Bits and pieces had been chipped away over the course of the long run up the side of Mount Tanufel.

"Chip away enough of the bits and pieces," she said, "and no more giant."

"What?" Endry said. "No, that won't work. You're crazy. Run!"

The stone giant must have heard them because it chose that moment to lower its gaze. When the column-face came 'round to find where the sound had come from, Ashling was no longer there.

"It will work," Ashling said. "We just need more power. The elemental's got to give me more power, and I can do this."

"No, you can't," Endry said. "But that yewling can stop it, if you give her a chance."

"You keep saying that," Ashling replied, "but I haven't seen any proof yet."

"You will," the faerie replied. "In fact, just keep running—I'll go see what's keeping her."

"Fine, you do that," Ashling said. "I've got to find a place to catch my breath."

"I'll be right back!" the faerie called. "Oh, and left!"

Ashling sidestepped to the left just before the foot came down. It was so close the displaced air made her flames flicker, and the shock of the nearby impact almost knocked her off her feet again. She cast a glance ahead, where the trail—or the nearest thing to it—led up the steepest part of the path since the stone cliff face.

It would be a struggle for Ashling, but if she could use the brush and rocks along the trail to speed her progress, she might be able to stop her pursuer, or at least delay the thing for a while longer.

" 'Use the terrain against your enemy,' " Ashling said. "Now why do I feel like an elf?" Yet what else could she do? The steep incline and her much smaller size were all she had left. But if she could lead the thing up the slope far enough and knock it off balance somehow, she'd reach the top before the stone giant finished tumbling to the bottom. It was worth the risk and worth spending a ball of flame that spattered against the giant's chest.

"If you're determined to keep this up," Ashling shouted at the rock monster, "I'll meet you at the top!"

* * * * *

Endry had meant to go directly to the sapling, who had promised to catch up—the faerie didn't know exactly what the yew had planned, but he had no doubt she'd manage to do something. But that was before he saw the faerie ring. He'd been looking for a faerie ring for hours. He had to get in touch with Oona—no, not Oona. Maralen. His new mistress.

Endry wasn't sure how he felt about having a new mistress. In fact, the last couple of days were making him wonder whether he really wanted sisters either. And then there were those groundlings, creatures to be despised by all rights. Yet they seemed to see him as something of a hero. The faerie had been of great help to the sapling, who would be of help to Rhys, and that would make Maralen happy.

"No, not Maralen," he said. "Me. Endry!"

Endry's newfound sense of individuality was exhilarating, and he decided he just had to head to that faerie ring and tell his sisters all about it. Maralen would certainly want to hear of it too.

"Out of the way, butterfly!" Endry shouted, kicking a passing insect simply because he could, careful not to injure the beautiful little creature. Endry didn't want to get bug guts on his leg, so the butterfly got off easy with a bent wing.

Yes, individuality was wonderful. So many things to kick. And—

The faerie ring! There it was now, just below him. Endry veered toward the ring of mushrooms. They were new growth— the entire ring was hardly three wingspans across—but they would do. He stopped gracefully above the center of the ring, cleared his throat, and thought very, very hard at Veesa and Iliona.

When he was finished, he had a new sense of purpose and direction to go with his sense of individuality. He caught a whiff of yew leaves on the air and buzzed off to his next adventure.

It felt good to be Endry, Endry decided.

* * * * *

Ashling did regret one thing about dismissing the irritating faerie—the extra set of eyes helped her avoid her pursuer a fair sight better than her own reflexes, which were frankly growing sluggish, her flames dimming with exertion. The pilgrim had reserves yet, but they would not last forever. And the farther up the steep mountain trail she ran, the more exposed she felt.

The cold had little effect on the stone giant, which crashed along at its steady, heart-stopping pace even up the sudden incline. The only thing keeping it behind her was the terrain— its heavy feet were digging large furrows in the rock and soil—yet the monster made no effort to truly climb, instead preferring to drive its own steps into the mountainside. Ashling wondered if the thing even had a mind, as such, or just rage. Perhaps when she reached her quarry, she might even learn why that rage seemed aimed squarely at her. But the incline would give her a fighting chance. If creatures like this were known to the Monks of the Ember Fellowship it might even explain why they'd built only a shrine on the mountain's flank and kept their monastery near the summit. Surely the Monks of Ember Fell wouldn't stand for a stone giant knocking over their stalagmite tower.

Though if it came right down to it—if this incline didn't keep the creature from catching up—Ashling intended to lead the creature straight to the monastery and keep on going.

Finally, the pilgrim heard the sound she was waiting for with dimming hope. One particularly egregious misstep knocked the steady stride off for a beat, and Ashling took advantage of that moment to dash into a stand of hearty, scrubby trees. The blazing elemental atop the mountain might not be willing to allow her to take any of its power, but she stood upon the mountain that gave her life. There was power enough to spare beneath her feet if she could just take a few moments of peace to reach out and take hold of it. She kneeled upon the stone, forcing herself not to look in the direction of the elemental but to instead dim her eyes and look within—within herself, within the mountain, within her purpose. Almost immediately Ashling felt a rush of rejuvenating power flood her body. It was warm and welcoming, but another crash and the earth shaking beneath her forced Ashling to lose focus before she could truly revel in the sensation. She did leave herself a thin strand of connection to the mountain's fires in case she needed it for the long haul. This little jaunt was turning into a long haul indeed.

Ashling burst from the stand of trees and was another twenty paces up the side of the mountain when she realized the crashing footstep that had snapped her out of contact with the living rock was the last one she'd heard since. The steady beat of the stone giant's feet, her constant companion for the last several hours, had stopped. Despite herself, curiosity overwhelmed the pilgrim, and she jogged to a halt, turned, and looked back down the slope.

Had she seen the entire mountain had been transformed into a kithberry pie, Ashling would have been less stunned at what she saw.

* * * * *

"What in the name of all that's Oona are you doing, yewling?" Endry demanded. "You're covered in— What are those doohickeys? They look . . . bleh. Kithkin."

"Takes a kithkin to know a kithkin," said someone who Endry was absolutely certain was not the sapling. Nora stood astride one of the sapling's thickest shoulder-branches, clutching two fistfuls of yew needles to steady herself as she directed her fellow groundlings from above. Her face, legs, and arms had been painted with stripes of blue and black, the battle colors of the Fae. Upon her shoulders rested a curious contraption twice as wide as the groundling leader was tall. The thing resembled faerie wings in its basic shape, though the "wings" were made of leaves attached to a frame made of twigs. Attached to each set of wings by simple golden filaments was a living, buzzing dragonfly.

"Nora! What are— That is to say, you're a long way from home, groundling," Endry said with ill-concealed excitement.

"The sapling asked us for help," the familiar male groundling said from down below, where he was fastening his own pair of dragonfly wings onto his shoulders, except he was using what appeared to be a pair of mayflies. Dragonflies, Endry guessed, must be reserved for the really important groundlings, though the very concept was still laughable to him.

Then again, the groundlings seemed to think he was important, so who was he to think otherwise?

"How's that, Nora?" Endry asked, making sure to mention the groundling he wanted to speak to by name.

"We're going to lay these vines across the mountainside, all at once," Nora said.

"In a careful, intricate, but clever pattern," the male added.

"And then I will bring these vines together to form a living net," the sapling said.

"You think a net is going to stop that?" Endry asked, pointing at the still-raging stone giant taking sapling-sized chunks of stone out of Mount Tanufel with every step of its massive feet and every blow of its mighty fists.

"I remembered the way our friends the groundlings meant to topple me," the yew explained. "I assumed that the same principles could be applied to a much larger problem."

"So that's a yes," Endry said.

"I certainly hope so," the sapling said, "but we shall see."

"How did you find . . . them?" Endry asked, jerking a thumb at Nora and the other groundlings.

"I'm standing right in front of you," Nora said. "So allow me. It was sheer luck."

"They found me, in fact. I intended to pull these vines into place myself," the sapling said, "until I spotted Nora on her maiden flight."

"Of course it was a maiden flight. She's a maiden faerie," Endry said impatiently, then caught himself. "Wait. Those wings are new. All of this is new. Since when do groundlings build kithkin flying machines?"

"It was you, actually," Nora said, her voice tinged with something that sounded extremely odd coming from a faerie, any faerie—even one with homemade, insect-powered wings. Was it . . . embarrassment? "Your stories of the mighty Colfenor and your own adventures—we just couldn't stop talking about it all. So we decided we were through letting Oona or anyone else tell us we couldn't be true Fae. I hit upon the idea of using leaves and a frame from what I'd seen of kithkin machines." She indicated the male faerie. "Once Mullenick suggested capturing insects, we were well on our way. Mind you," Nora added, "I'm as yet the only one of us to make a successful voyage, and that was interrupted. But we're all ready to do our part to help the savior of Groundling Town."

"Groundling Town," Endry said, stone-faced. "You call the log 'Groundling Town.' "

"We do now," Mullenick said. "We're taking pride in ourselves. We're exiles, not monsters. So we deserve a village with a name."

Nora opened her mouth to add something, but a particularly violent effort by the stone giant to gain purchase in the mountainside nearly shook her from her perch. Even the sapling had to brace her legs to make sure they wouldn't slide out from under her.

"The behemoth draws too close," the sapling warned. "It's time we laid this trap. Are you ready, groundlings?"

"Wait, wait, wait," Endry said. "That's no way to motivate faeries. Let me handle this." He rubbed his palms together and turned to Nora. "All right, groundlings, listen closely. Now none of you know the first thing about flying because you're groundlings. You're not even faeries."

"Are we going to go backward now?" Nora asked.

"Excellent question, Nora. Yes, we are," Endry said. "We're going back to the basics. Now flying is all about two things: balance, lift, and velocity."

"That's three things," Mullenick pointed out.

"Stop arguing," Endry said. "I'm trying to teach you ground rats something. Now, as I said, three things: balance, lift, velocity, and endurance."

A few minutes and one terribly confusing flying lesson later—confusing, at least, to everyone but Endry, who thought he sounded quite impressive and learned—the groundling flyers had taken their positions at the ends of the vines. The sapling was walking across each cablelike length, touching the intersections of vines and magically grafting them together at those points. She did this for almost ten minutes while the giant below them laborious dug away at the cliffside, gaining every minute, albeit very slowly.

Whether by luck or design, the stone giant's mitt came over the top of the ledge at almost the exact same moment the sapling stepped off of her creation and backed quickly away.

"Endry," the sapling said, "Nora. Are you ready?"

"We're ready," Endry and Nora said in unison. Each was positioned at either end of the sapling's huge vine net.

"Take it up," the sapling said. "Now, please."

"Ground rats, its time to make history!" Endry said. "In every faerie's life, there comes a time when he must choose between his love of—"

"Now!" the sapling said, moments before the second stone hand cleared the edge of their temporary shelter.

"You heard her," Nora shouted. "Everyone, slap those bugs and get ready to lift!"

"One, two, three," Endry said, "and heave!"

With a buzzing like a plague-swarm of angry wasps, two dozen faeries—including only one who flew under his own power—hauled the sapling's vine net into the air.

Endry had never felt more exhilarated, alive, or supremely powerful. This, he thought, must be an inkling of what it's like to be Oona. So many hanging on his every word, under his command and doing his bidding. True, it was more the sapling's bidding, and Nora was certainly helping, but Endry felt an inordinate amount of pride when the net finally and completely cleared the ground and continued to rise. Soon they were over the sapling's head, but they needed to be higher. Much higher.

"Higher!" Endry shouted. "It's getting too close! We've got to be above it when it comes through!"

"We know!" Nora cried back from across the net. "It's heavy!"

"Then put some muscle into it!" Endry called. "Threaten your dragonflies! Flap your phony wings! Just get some elevation!"

Below them Endry could see the sapling move to meet the stone giant before it ran headlong into the net and made everything for naught. This wasn't part of the plan, he knew, but someone had to do something if the net was still going to do the job.

"Down here!" the sapling called as she marched down the slope. "Hey! Hey, you! Look down here!"

The stone giant refused to comply. In fact, it didn't even seem to notice the sapling was there at all. Nine feet—no, at least ten, maybe twelve, she'd been growing like a weed—of talking tree hadn't even gotten the monster to turn its head.

"Faster!" Endry cried. "Nothing is going to stop this thing but us now. Fly, groundlings! Fly like you've never flown before! Which you haven't, actually, but that's not the point. Heave!"

In the end the stone giant cleared the outer edge of the sapling's vine net by mere inches, but inches was all this makeshift plan required. Endry raised one hand to Nora. "Wait. . . . Wait for it to get to the center."

"We're waiting," Nora said. "But it's heavy."

Endry would never have admitted it, but his own grip on the rough-barked vines was beginning to slip too. He checked on the stone giant's position. Not the exact center but close enough.

"Groundlings, on my mark, release!" Endry said. "One—"

At once the wingless faeries in their flying contraptions released the net, jerking Endry along with it for a moment until he thought to let go.

" 'One' is not a mark!" Endry shouted, but his words caught in his throat when the net dropped gently down to settle over the stone giant.

"Next phase!" Nora called out once the edges of the net had struck the mountainside. They had perhaps just a few seconds to drop in for a landing before the stone giant's feet became entangled in the net. It struggled mindlessly for a few moments, but soon gravity took over and refused to allow the entwined monster to stay on two feet. It toppled face-first onto the steep mountainside with a crash that sent the sapling flying back down the slope.

Endry didn't have time to follow the yew's tumble. The most crucial part of the plan was the responsibility of his groundling allies. One by one they dropped to the ground, each taking a position opposite one of their fellows until they formed a wide circle around the struggling stone giant. Then each grabbed the edge of the net and pulled it down until it made contact with the ground.

"Sapling!" Endry shouted. "Now! We need you now!" He shot a glance down the slope and saw nothing but a cloud of dust where the sapling had crashed down the mountainside. "Yewling! We can't hold him down much longer!"

"On my way!" the sapling shouted. She charged with a speed Endry wouldn't have imagined possible straight up the slope, and as soon as she reached the edge of the net she dropped hard onto one knee with a sound like cracking timber. She slammed her wooden hands onto the vines and poured as much poisonous yew magic into them as she possessed, as much as she could spare and remain conscious.

The yew magic flooded the vines with the raw stuff of death, and the vine net died all at once. But as it did the blackening, withering ropes fused with the stone itself, sizzling and crackling. Every knot became embedded deeply into the living rock, while the dying vine's exposed tendrils drew taut and tough as woven steel.

When the sapling finally stepped back to survey her work, Endry did the same. The stone giant was neatly pinned against the mountainside, its massive simian arms folded beneath its bulk in a way that gave the monster no leverage and bound to the stone on all sides with vines as thick as cables.

"Now that, my dear Endry," Nora said, "is how you pull down a giant."

* * * * *

"Ouch!" Endry said. "Doesn't that hurt, yewling?"

"I do not 'hurt' in the sense you mean," the sapling said.

"You mean trees don't feel pain?" Ashling asked skeptically. The flamekin had greeted the yew without her accustomed orange smile, and the sapling feared she might already have lost the opportunity to continue with Colfenor's plan. She wished she had as much faith in the plan as her seedfather had. By not giving the sapling the belief in the plan, only the exacting description of what it was to accomplish and how, Colfenor had probably made an error. She felt a tiny twinge of uncharacteristic disappointment in her parent.

"Trees feel pain as a signal of trouble," the yew finally said. "Then we shut it off, patch it up. There is never any prolonged 'hurt.'"

"You're lucky, then," Ashling said distantly, eyeing the pinned and trapped stone giant now several hundred feet behind them. The groundlings, whose insect companions needed time to recuperate from their exertions, had offered to stay behind and stand watch over the monster. They would send warning should it manage to break free.

Now that she had the flamekin's attention, the yew felt

compelled to make her pitch. "I have been seeking you, Ashling of Tanufel," the sapling said. "You have an important destiny."

"A lot of people seem to think so," Ashling said, taking a casual step back from the tree. "You're the second person to tell me that today. And you all seem to forget I've done that ritual. You, sapling, you should know better than anyone my part in that is over. I'm on a different path than you are now. Than Rhys is. You should not have tried to find me."

"Aw, come on now, Matchstick," Endry said. "That's no way to greet a friend."

"A friend?" Ashling said, her eyes flaring white with sudden fury. "This tree is not my friend any more than the other one was. If I didn't need to conserve my strength, I'd burn her to the ground right now. I appreciate the help with the big rock back there, but I'm done with other people's ideas of destiny. I know my path now, and neither of you is on it."

"You're wrong, Matchstick," Endry said. "You too, yewling. I don't think there's any grand destiny happening for anyone anytime soon."

"Why is that?" the sapling asked.

"Because I think there's going to be another fight. If anyone cares what I think, that is."

"How so?" the pilgrim said.

"You're telling me you're going to take on all of them yourself?"

The sapling followed the direction Endry's tiny hand pointed. As first she could see nothing but the sheer mountain slope glittering in the bright sun. Then she made them out, white and gold against the stout emerald trees and black volcanic rock. They were spinning furiously, tiny whirlwinds upon the mountainside.

"What are they?" the sapling asked.

"Wind devils. Little cyclones, and they hunt in packs,"

Ashling said, speaking more to herself than any of them. "I haven't seen any of them in years, but then I haven't been to Mount Tanufel in years either. I can get rid of them if I can get into the middle of them. Enough heat and they'll have to subside, reform."

"Won't they, you know, toss you off the mountain?" Endry asked nervously.

Ashling stared fiercely at the sapling, who involuntarily drew back at the glare. "Not if I have an anchor," the flamekin said. "You, though—you might need to find a rock to hide under. A faerie wouldn't last two seconds in the cone of a wind devil."

"Rock? I don't need any rocks, I— Rock! Ground!" Endry gasped. "Groundlings! I've got to warn Nora!" With that, he shot down the side of the mountain toward the captured giant and its groundling guards.

The flamekin turned to the yew. "I wasn't lying, sapling, when I said I'd like to just burn you down. But practicality demands I don't. I give you my word—"

The sapling was already extending her roots into the stone, sending filaments into every crevice and tiny crack that ran through the volcanic rock. "Please," she said, "you need not reassure me of anything, Ashling of Tanufel. You will 'burn me down,' as you say. Don't you see? That is part of Colfenor's plan." The sapling smiled. "But not yet."

"I don't see anything but a pack of wild wind devils about to knock us off the side of this mountain," Ashling said. "You should lift me up. By the legs. I'm going to be getting pretty hot, so the less of you is in contact with me the better."

"I understand," the sapling said.

"I'll try to wait until they have us surrounded to really burn."

"I appreciate that," the yew told her, "but why do you care? I don't understand. You appear to harbor a grudge against me for something that is truly wonderful. You and I will become a vessel that carries this world of eternal dawn—"

"What are you talking about?" Ashling asked. "We're not going to become anything. And if you try to perform any kind of rite, ritual, chant, or spell I'm going to break my word, wind devils be damned. Now hold on tight. They're almost here."

* * * * *

The sapling grabbed hold of Ashling by the arms and swung the flamekin onto her broad shoulder-branches. From there, Ashling took hold of the sturdiest looking bough atop the yew's head. The pilgrim held on tightly as furious gusts filled with pebbles, sticks, and other mountainside debris pelted them both. It took all the flame she could muster to keep from being blown out and smothered, especially since she was trying to keep cool enough not to ignite the sapling. It worked, for a time, but then the second wind devil was upon her, then another, and another.

"Lift me!" Ashling cried over the screaming wind. Without a word the yew complied, reaching over her head to take the flamekin by the lower legs and lift her overhead, like a kithkin raising a sacrifice to her ancestors.

One of the wind devils grew bold enough to try to take a bite of the flamekin pilgrim, whipping at her with flashes of static and lethally accelerated air. This was how they hunted, taking turns with their prey, nipping away bits of heat, life, and flesh until the body was stripped bare, be it elf, kithkin, faerie, or treefolk. Their preferred food was flamekin fire, but already a great deal of yew needles spun madly within the cyclones. Ashling thought she could hear a breezy laugh from above and something like a hungry growl to her left.

"Brace yourself!" Ashling shouted, hoping the sapling had heard the intent if not the exact words. Not out of any real wish not to harm Colfenor's spawn but to prevent the yew from dropping Ashling when the flamekin's legs went white-hot. She poured far more of her jealously guarded scraps of elemental fire into the wind devils. The cyclones gorged themselves on it.

The ones nearest to her were the first to collapse in upon themselves, imploding with a blistering release of uneaten fire. Naturally the wind devils behind them tried to consume that too, only to find themselves similarly overwhelmed. This triggered an exhausting chain reaction that forced Ashling to burn away almost everything she had. When at last the final wind devil popped with a smoky yellow bang, she was dangerously close to putting herself into a guttering spiral that would have put her out for days.

"I think you might be useful after all, sapling," the flamekin rasped as the yew gingerly lifted her from overhead and set her down upon the mountain trail.

The sapling didn't answer. Most of her face was blackened and charred, though no longer ablaze. The only needles she had left were on the bough upon her back. The others were little more than blackened sticks. Her hands, though cracked and brittle, appeared more or less intact, but they were dripping with blackened sap as the tortured sapling struggled to heal the worst of her burns.

That same blackened sap lined her mouth when the sapling finally spoke. "I have rare, possibly unique, knowledge, Ashling of Tanufel. I know exactly the purpose for which I was created. I know how I was born, how I will die. Usefulness is my reason for being." The yew spat pitch. "Colfenor did not give me foreknowledge of the parts in between everything else. Of events and experiences such as this. I hurt. I hurt."

"I shouldn't wonder that you do," Ashling said.

"You misunderstand. It is not a plea for sympathy. I simply have not been truly hurt until this moment. You've granted me an experience that was unexpected. I just wished to thank you."

"Thank me?" the flamekin said. "I nearly killed you."

"But not yet," the sapling said.

CHAPTER 16

Iliona and Veesa flew long, slow loops around the top half of Rosheen Meanderer. Very little had changed: The giantess was still mumbling, the changelings continued their aimless, undulating dance, and Rhys and Maralen still waited for any of it to make sense—which was where the faeries and their dream magic came in.

Maralen, Rhys, and the giant brothers were all sitting in a line near Rosheen's left shoulder. To a casual observer it might have appeared that an unlikely gathering of three giants and two elves had chosen the same quiet spot to sit and rest for a bit, but their effortless tranquility was only possible after hours of taxing labor from the Vendilion sisters. Overhead, Rosheen's immense goat steed continued to ignore the proceedings with an aloofness that only a stubborn, horn-headed herbivore could muster.

Maralen had stuck Iliona and Veesa with the drudgework, as usual. She didn't care how difficult it was for Iliona and Veesa to prepare for the collection of dreamstuff without Endry, nor did she acknowledge the challenges of combining the dreams of elves with those of slow-witted giants and no-witted changelings. She didn't even praise the sisters after they had done the hard work and set the complicated spells in motion. Iliona fumed. It was one thing to be the foul elf maiden's servant, but it was quite another to be treated like, well, like a servant.

"It's getting light," Veesa said.

"That happens when the sun comes up," Iliona snapped.

"Yes, but all I mean is—"

"And I still don't like the looks of that goat." Iliona nodded up at the sky, where Rosheen's huge white cloudgoat kept its standoffish vigil.

"I don't like the looks of any goat," Veesa said tersely. "But do I burden you with that information? No, I do not."

"Forgive my sharpness, sister dear, but we've been at this for hours. When is something going to happen?"

"That's what I'm saying, you goon." Veesa broke their looping flight pattern and intercepted her sister. "Look." She pointed toward Rosheen. "It's like dawn."

Iliona looked. The changelings on Rosheen were losing all those characteristics they had mimicked from the giant, shrinking, deflating, and ultimately reverting to their natural, rubbery blue bodies. Their woozy dance slowed until they were all swaying in place. Iliona and Veesa both felt their magic take hold of the entire valley as the last aspects of this unique dream-stuff harvest fell into place.

Rosheen and the changelings slowly disappeared under a spreading cloud of bluish green haze. The mist hissed and seethed as if boiling, then a galvanic crackle danced across its outer surface. Rosheen and the changelings were all swallowed up by the fog, and within that fog appeared an entirely different but no less familiar landscape. Rhys and Maralen and the giant brothers still sat sleeping at the edge of the tableau, only now they sat facing a wide stretch of trees and moss instead of Rosheen and grass.

The strange, abstract picture was clearly that of a forest, most likely the Gilt Leaf. As the Vendilion sisters watched carefully, a vast stretch of woods quickly spread to cover the entire surface of the cloud. Once the vision was complete, the cloud's shape changed so that it took on the solid shape and dimensions of the picture it contained.

The eastern edge of the forest scene turned brighter, more vivid green. This haler shade slowly spread across the miniature landscape, putting Iliona in mind of sunlight moving across a darkened expanse of trees.

The sisters swooped down and slowly circled the spectacle. They hovered over the crawl of lighter color as they followed it all the way across the image. Moments later a darker stain of green rose at the far edge. This too spread across the phantom forest until it reached the Vendilion sisters.

"I get it, I get it!" Veesa clapped her hands happily. "Dawn, daylight, dusk," she said. "That makes sense, right?"

"It certainly does. But I still don't hear any actual words." Iliona peered down. "You think there are still words coming out of that windy cavern Rosheen snores through?"

"It doesn't matter. Miss Maralen said to wait until things made sense. I say they're making sense now. If she doesn't get it, well, it's not our fault she's not as clever as we are."

Iliona hesitated, then smiled wickedly at her sister. "You know," she said, "when you put it that way, any other point of view seems crazy."

Veesa drew her tiny dagger. "So we can get started?"

"Let's."

"It's about time. One more hour of watching these brainless blue bogeys and I would have eaten my own head."

"I quite agree," Iliona said. "My own head, of course." She drew her own blade. "You start with Mister Bossy Elf. I'll handle the oddball."

Veesa's brow creased. "Careful," she said. "Endry had trouble with her last time, and you know how that turned out."

"I could fill a week listing all the ways in which I am superior to Endry." Iliona batted her eyes. "But thanks for the warning."

Veesa snickered and zipped down beside Rhys. She lit on the elf's forehead between his ruined horns, then casually cleaned the tips of her fingernails with the dagger. "Whenever you're ready, sister dear."

Iliona floated down and landed lightly on Maralen's shoulder. "Remember," she said, as much to herself as to Veesa, "don't worry about sharing just yet. Concentrate on finding. We can decide what to do with it once we've got it in hand."

"Gotcha." Veesa stepped off of Rhys's head and hovered down beside his neck. She leaned in and gently pressed the razor edge of her dagger against his throat. Iliona did the same to Maralen, though the largest Vendilion was painfully precise in positioning the blade.

Iliona made eye contact with Veesa. The two faeries nodded. Eldritch energy crackled in the air between them and danced along the edges of their blades.

Like guiding a ribbon of smoke into a wide-mouthed jar, the Vendilion sisters teased equal portions of dreamstuff from Rhys and Maralen. Iliona's waking view of the vision-forest shimmered, and when it cleared she saw instead a vast stretch of Lorwyn's entire countryside, not just the heavily forested part. Iliona had not visited all of Lorwyn, but the Fae as a whole had, so she recognized everything she saw below. There were great swaths of green forest; wide, verdant plains; and jagged, sturdy mountains. There was even a smaller version of the Wanderwine River running lengthwise down the center of the scene.

The panoramic view of Lorwyn was in constant flux, much the same as the forest-in-a-cloud had been. As it had before, light gathered at the panorama's eastern edge. The soft glow spread across the whole of the terrain and was then replaced by a rolling wave of darkness.

The cycle of dawn-daylight-dusk repeated three times before the shifting imagery grew far more complex. The trees and plant life experienced an entire year's worth of seasons in the space of a few seconds. Vegetation bloomed and sprouted amid alternating periods of sunlight and spring rain. Summer's uninterrupted heat caused the landscape to flourish and thicken until the trees were wreathed in fat, healthy leaves and their boughs hung low with fruit and flowers. Then the live greenery shrank and withered as a cold breeze swept across it. Moments later every tree and bush was denuded and bare, their stark, woody skeletons clicking and shivering in the cold.

This will work, Iliona thought. Maralen's big idea was actually bearing fruit. The spell was in place, and the flow of faerie was magic strong and responsive. Everyone was sleeping, dreaming, sharing, and though Rosheen's words were still indecipherable, the giantess still spoke.

Let's see what she's saying, Iliona thought. She pressed the edge of her dagger against Maralen's throat. Or even better, let's see what this one is hearing.

* * * * *

Maralen concentrated as her dreaming mind gazed down on all Lorwyn. Supervising the Vendilion while balancing the necessarily calm aimlessness of her resting state was a challenge, but she had no choice but to rise to it. Maralen was determined to learn something useful from Rosheen, if possible, without revealing it to the others, especially not Iliona and Veesa.

She felt Rhys nearby, though she could not see or hear him. Would he see and hear exactly what she did? Maralen forced herself not to reach out to him. Whatever Rosheen revealed, Maralen preferred to receive and examine it on her own and at her leisure. Show me, she thought, and her yearning was so deep and instinctual it transcended words.

Several distinct features emerged from the sprawling

landscape. In the south a great red tree rose above its neighbors. Instead of spreading its upper branches wide, as was natural, this tree clenched its boughs tight around its crown until it resembled a many-fingered fist.

A wide, flat thorn thicket spread out at the center of the scene. Spike-studded canes stretched up and curled around each other until they took on the appearance of a woman's upper body. Wide, flat petals encircled her head like a flowery crown. Flickering flies blinked their light around the thorn queen's regalia, creating a glittering shower of blue, green, and yellow light.

A long, equine shape appeared over the mountains at the northern edge of the living map. As the ghostly white form cohered, Maralen saw its hooves and mane were both aflame. The majestic equine figure floated back and forth across the top half of the scenery, prowling and testing the limits of its range like an anxious, caged beast.

A host of flaming figures ignited below the equine spirit, their fire striking jagged shadows from the rocky peaks and crags. This blazing host followed the horse's every motion with their eyes of flame.

Maralen recognized the red tree as Colfenor, Rhys's yew sage and mentor. She also knew the great horse as the elemental spirit Ashling sought, and the fire folk as members of Ashling's tribe. The elf maiden was quietly thrilled to see such things, for in recognizing them she knew they signified her plan was working, that all their thoughts were aligning with Rosheen's.

The dark-haired elf was most interested in the regal figure who continued to expand and fill center of the tableau. Maralen recognized this player as well, and, just as Colfenor was the author of their current troubles, the hedge-woman posed and would continue to pose the greatest threat to Maralen herself.

Maralen watched as the thorn queen extended toward her a

single curling tendril. The vine crawled forward, then folded back on itself. It continued to wind and curl until it had created another woman's body beside the thorn queen's, though this new one came with fully formed legs.

The smaller, bipedal figure snapped off from the main thicket. The hedge-queen bowed, bringing her head down to touch the new figure's. Half of the fireflies split off from the main swarm and drifted toward the newly sprouted creature, with half the thorn queen's crown floating with them. The colorful sprites settled around the shoulders of the smaller figure and set the half-crown on the front of her head.

Something to the north of this caught Maralen's eye. She watched a blister of sickly yellow light form, growing larger as the smaller crowned figure stepped away from its source. The bubble swelled fat and then popped, coating the surrounding vegetation with an oily yellow film. Acrid smoke wafted up as the film quickly dissolved everything it touched, melting the surrounding forest into a noisome black wasteland.

The subordinate royal figure stood motionless for a moment, her featureless face turned toward the blackened circle left behind by the bubble's eruption. She began to walk, and, after several unsteady steps, the newly crowned thorn princess's gait grew stronger, more confident, and she set out toward the red yew in the south.

Maralen knew the figure had far to go. More, she knew the princess would never reach her destination in time, for even as the thorn princess crossed into the southern half of the landscape, the red yew there was already reaching in the opposite direction.

For a moment Maralen could not determine what its purpose was, but then the ghostly horse veered directly at the great red tree. The yew snapped its branches out straight and lunged up, violently snatching the equine from the air. The horse snorted and kicked, but the yew branches held tight and dragged it down.

The yew pulled the horse in and embraced it. Back among the mountains, the fire folk huddled together and formed one single massive flame. A high-pitched sound rose over the scene, somewhere between a whinny and a scream, and the collective flame doubled in size and intensity.

Maralen felt a thump and heard a boom. Fire and explosive force blew the yew's branches apart, and the towering red tree toppled. Its freedom regained, the horse surged upward, its flames flaring so brightly that the southern half of the landscape became bathed in painful yellowish white glare. Maralen saw the thorn queen's body flinch when the yew exploded and saw the figure shudder and dig her roots deep into the soil.

Strange lights in the skies over the scene flickered and danced in a perfect re-creation of Lorwyn's annual Aurora event. Each year the great tribes observed the Aurora in some fashion—the kithkin with their storytelling festival, the elves with a solemn ritual followed by a huge banquet—but this light show either caused or coincided with something far greater and more profound. As the Aurora danced, the horse raced in circles over the northern half of the scene. In the center, the thorn queen recovered her balance and her poise. To the south, the great red yew stood once more.

Or rather, a smaller, decidedly more feminine version of the yew stood. Leaner, more flexible, and not at all wizened, the new yew curled its branches into a fist once again, then spread those branches wide as her roots also sank into the soil of Lorwyn.

Maralen suddenly laughed, and tears of relief splashed from her eyes. The answer . . . The answer had been in front of her the whole time. The great yew's capture of the elemental horse had been self-destructive but also self-renewing. More, it had affected everything in Lorwyn, somehow delivering a brutal shock to the entire world that the world could endure but not deny.

Maralen's joy cooled. She considered the impact of this revelation, of the dangers that would come from acting on it. Colfenor's ritual was the key to her future as well as their shared past. Her course was clear. It would be costly. It would jeopardize everything she cared about, everything of value she had worked to attain, but without it she would have nothing anyway.

It could be done. All she needed was a little time, a little luck, and the help of the Vendilion clique.

"Well, well now." Iliona's mocking voice was clear and distressingly close. "That changes everything, doesn't it?"

"If we do this for you," Veesa said, "what do we get out of it?"

Panic rose in Maralen, but she smothered it with a thought. "If I get what I want," she said, "you'll get what you want." As she had hoped, this bold statement silenced the Vendilion sisters for a moment.

"We should talk," Maralen said. "About our future. And our mutual benefit."

There was a pause. Then Iliona and Veesa both said, "We're listening."

"But I'm not speaking. Not yet." Maralen smiled. "Not here and not now."

"Where then? When?"

The dark-haired woman quietly searched for any sign of Rhys and found none. "Soon," she said. "Very soon."

* * * * *

Though Rhys had dedicated himself to the practical and pragmatic magic of the Gilt Leaf tribe, he was also versed in the ways of vision and insight. Though he had been equally attentive and dismissive of his mentor during his tenure as Colfenor's apprentice, communing with the old log had prepared him to receive just this sort of revelation—as well as the attendant strangeness that came from sharing others' points of view.

So he was quick to take in and digest the sights and sounds of Rosheen's augury, filtered as they were through the Vendilion's dream spell. The scene before him was Lorwyn, a representation of the entire world. He followed the Wanderwine from its source in the mountains, where scores of tiny flamekin flickered like candles, all the way down to its mouth on the southeast shore. He watched the ghostly white horse with hooves of flame circle the mountains. He saw the red yew's growth surge until it surpassed all other trees in size and importance.

Rhys fixed his eyes on the representation of Colfenor. The tree-folk sage remained at the center of their shared mystery as surely as he dominated the southern half of the phantasmal landscape, and Rhys knew the answers he sought lay with the great red yew.

He ground his teeth when the miniature Colfenor seized the fiery horse elemental. Re-created in miniature, this unaccountably cruel and barbaric act was as painful and as mystifying as it had been in the real world.

His mentor fell, but a smaller version of Colfenor stood up in place of the original. The yew sage had used Ashling to catch the horse, but he also used Rhys to bring about the rise of the sapling. Though this event was also embodied in the vision-Lorwyn, seeing it anew added nothing to Rhys's understanding of it.

Distracted, Rhys let his attention drift until it naturally settled on the Gilt Leaf Wood. The Blessed Nation's territory blanketed over half of the living map, an unbroken fortress of green and brown trunks. A wave of bitterness rolled through Rhys's gullet. Fitting that even this re-creation of the Nation had no doorway, nor windows, nor any point of access from the outside.

A flash of motion drew his attention back to the sapling. Featureless, she stood tall and straight with her leafy arms extended upward. The largest of these creaked and shifted, reorienting to the north. Rhys stared as the wooden limb unfolded, inexplicably transfixed by its glacial motion.

Hissing came to his ears from the top of the map, the sound of a kettle boiling over onto the campfire. Rhys stared until he was certain the sapling's limb would move no more, then dragged his gaze north to investigate the sound.

There, underneath the lights of the annual Aurora, an ink black and shimmering darkness had gathered. The thick, oily cloud roiled and bubbled across the outer perimeter of Lorwyn's northern half. It rose high along the outer edges of the tableau, a cresting wave that threatened to engulf the entire world.

The dire wave broke, but, instead of flooding the world, its substance dispersed and drifted away. Lorwyn did not disappear under a deluge of silky black. And so Rhys was able to see clearly its effect on his home.

Change crawled south across the landscape like some terrible wind, slow but inexorable, entirely irresistible. Sunlight-dappled meadows and lush green forests of oak gave way to stale, murky bogs and gaunt, haunted willows. Wildflowers curled and sharpened into brambles that were tipped with glistening red. The pure, clean flow of the Wanderwine slowed to a dank, muddy crawl in the south, while up north it raged and frothed through a new series of white-water rapids. The flamekin candles gathered above in the mountains all burned out, and in place of their living fire arose countless streams of ashes and smoke.

Rhys followed the wave down the length and breadth of Lorwyn. When it was through, the terrain was still recognizable, but it was inescapably different.

The former daen reeled as the disturbing vision gave way to a memory: the forest elemental that confronted him in the wake of the disaster that cost him his horns. As it had then, the grand, winged elk stared coldly at Rhys for a dreadful moment. Then it was eclipsed by the familiar figure of Colfenor as Rhys remembered him, alive, inscrutable, stern, but with a secretive twinkle in his eye.

Rhys's mind cleared in the shock of sudden revelation. The changed Lorwyn shimmered back into view, but Rhys's thoughts were not of the present or the potential future but the past. Both his yew mentor and the elk spirit had warned of a coming change, a fundamental shift in the nature of things that would shake Lorwyn to its foundations. Now Rosheen, through the magic of the Vendilion, had confirmed this warning. Was the change inevitable, as the ancients believed? Was it to be as dark and terrible as he saw here?

His eyes sought out the sapling, but finding her on the map only created new questions. She still stood as before, exactly as before, the only living thing unaffected by the spreading gloom. Rhys grimly realized this made perfect sense. Colfenor's self-immolation, his cruel use of Ashling, and his blasphemous abuse of her elemental had achieved their intended effect—the knowledge of the yew had endured and was safely encapsulated within the sapling.

Rhys turned once more toward the Gilt Leaf. The green fortress stood vastly diminished, shrunk to less than one-half its original size, its formerly solid and unbroken perimeter now riddled with spaces and wide gaps.

The surrounding territories also squeezed against the Blessed Nation on all sides. The boggarts and kithkin and giants had always been manageable neighbors, well under the dominating, civilizing influence of the elves. But in this new Lorwyn, these minor tribes were aggressors, invaders. They encroached on elf territory, actively eating away at the Gilt Leaf's already diminished borders.

"No," Rhys whispered. Mere anticipation of this dire change had brought out the worst in Colfenor, somehow driving him to sacrifice his own life as well as Ashling's life as a pilgrim and Rhys's as an elf. Now the terrible change itself threatened to cast the rest of Lorwyn into similar darkness and despair.

"Maralen," he said, "I've seen enough."

The elf maiden answered crisply, though she did sound slightly dazed. "What just happened, Rhys? Did you see? Everything became different."

"I saw," Rhys said. "And it was not everything. The sapling was unchanged."

"No, you're right. The thorn queen . . ."

Rhys did not understand Maralen's additional observation, nor did he care to investigate it now. "End this," he said. "Tell your faeries to make it stop."

"But I—"

"We have our answers," Rhys said, "such as they are, such as we understand them. We got what we came for. Now we must decide what to do with it."

CHAPTER 17

"Quiet," Sygg reminded Brigid, who hadn't said a word for ten minutes. She simply nodded, and he returned the nod before peeking back over the top of the wooden wreckage they'd used to conceal themselves. It wasn't easy for her to keep her mouth shut for so long.

Despite Sygg's hopes of drumming up support among the population of the redoubt, his pleas had fallen on deaf ears. It wasn't long before potential allies raised the alarm, Crescent of Morningtide or no Crescent of Morningtide. Sygg's wife—and cousin, apparently—had refused to listen, and Sygg feared it would be their death. Maybe the death of all merrows. He wasn't looking for power. Not Sygg, even though it could have been his for the taking. He said he preferred the life of a ferryman by far. Problem presented, problem worked on, problem solved. Such a life almost never left a merrow floating, hungry and cold, waiting for a pair of malignants to pass by in the darkness.

The malignants had nearly caught the two of them unawares. Sygg had been studying the currents, trying to find one he could augment with tideshaping magic to accelerate their journey through these deep passages beneath the redoubt, never suspecting the passages harbored the crazed and savage merrow. It had been easy enough to give the reejerey's guards the slip, even for a clumsy swimmer like Brigid. They were far too used to facing aggressors since the malignancy broke out, it seemed, and now the Paperfin had lost the talent for pursuit. Either that, the kithkin thought, or they already knew these tunnels were rife with malignants and chose instead to seal them off.

The archer had taken advantage of an underwater air pocket—what was left of an ancient dungeon built to house landwalker prisoners, Sygg had guessed—letting the gill mask slip from her face to take cold, clean breaths of real, albeit stale air for the first time in what felt like days. Ye gods, Brigid thought, had it been days? Or weeks? Months? She didn't know anymore.

It was then Brigid let her guard down. She should have seen the silver shapes beneath the water, but the gill mask Sygg had doubly enchanted to grant her vision in darkness as well as air underwater was pulled away from her eyes. The archer should have heard the light splashes they left on the surface in their wake, but she'd taken the opportunity for real breathing to hum a few rounds to lift her spirits. It took a sharp poke from a nearly invisible shapewater tendril—Sygg's private alarm—to alert her to the danger. She'd slipped into the water as quietly as possible, pulling her gill mask back into place as she went. Brigid saw Sygg immediately, waving her to his hiding place, and then she saw them, the malignant hunters. She joined Sygg with a few kicks of her short legs.

The malignants reminded Brigid of the woodcuts she'd seen in books of bizarre river reptiles that lived in the distant southern climes, purely predatory creatures with long faces, scaly hides, and jagged teeth—and these two had teeth that would have made Flyrne jealous. Their eyes were black and cold with animal intelligence. The ribs of their fins had grown long and sharp as kithkin knitting needles. Their scales had taken on a thick reptilian look, and the webbed fingers of their hands were tipped with long, hooked claws. Each of them clutched a sharp, jagged spear made from the jawbone of a fish whose head had been half again as long as Brigid was tall. The weapon the one on the left carried still bore pale hunks of torn flesh stuck to its serrated edge.

A kithkin archer, underwater and without a bow. Brigid couldn't figure out how she could possibly be more useless. And she just knew these two malignants were going to attack them, and Sygg would once again have to save her life. Some hero.

The captain shook her from her short bout of self-pity with a nudge. He held his skinning knife by the blade, offering her the handle, and nodded for her to take it. Brigid shook her head, but the look on Sygg's face said he would not take no for an answer. He indicated with hand signs she would need it in a moment, and she finally acquiesced. The knife felt strangely balanced. The handle was far too long for her, but she knew firsthand that the blade was razor-sharp and sturdier than it looked. She smiled grimly and nodded. Sygg winked and indicated she should keep an eye on the malignants. He reached down into the detritus on the floor of the tunnel and wrenched free a length of rusted steel that looked to be the equal of the malignants' improvised spears.

Now what? Brigid mouthed to him.

Now, Sygg silently replied, we ambush.

Moments later, the first of the altered merrows emerged from around the bend ahead. Without a word of warning, Sygg hurled his rusty spear, catching the malignant in the neck. Unfortunately, the makeshift harpoon was no honor-guard pike, and instead of transfixing the creature's throat it merely entered its armored skin, made it an inch or so, and stopped. The malignant roared, a sound immediately picked up by its partner. Far away, upriver, to Brigid's dismay, she heard distant answering cries. The alarms were not even words, but there could be no mistaking that sound—Brigid had never heard anything like it above or below the water. It was clear, however, that they would soon have company.

"Don't just float there," Sygg cried. "Get 'em!"

He gave Brigid a shove, and she managed to bring up the long knife before she reached the first malignant. It was still struggling with Sygg's spear and didn't see Brigid draw back her arm until it was too late. She drove her blade into the monstrous merrow's neck, just below the gills, and used the oversized handle as a lever to twist the blade upward, which must have severed the malignant's spinal cord. The black, cold eyes went milky-white, its powerful tail went limp a half second later, and when the kithkin wrenched her hand free of the bleeding creature it sank into the deep water without a sound.

Keep your head, Brigid, she told herself. That's just one of them. She spun in place and searched the murky, blood-clouded water for the dead malignant's companion and saw only thin beams of morning light doing their best to slice into the water and encountering heavy resistance. She turned back to Sygg in time to see that missing malignant arc over the wreckage and thrust his spear directly at the ferryman's head. Fortunately Sygg had been keeping his eyes open and wasn't taken unawares. He bobbed out of the way of the spear and, to Brigid's surprise, grabbed hold of its jagged edge with both hands. His palms leaked clouds of blood, and the pain in his eyes was palpable, but Sygg was giving her the opening he needed—if he could keep his grip.

The malignant might have survived if it had simply let go of the spear, but it refused, like a dog with a bone, to release the weapon. Brigid knew where to aim now and this time was able to sever the merrow's spine with less effort—it was all in the aim.

She turned to Sygg and allowed herself a small whoop of victory. Instead of joining her in their shared, albeit small, victory, the captain widened his lanternlike eyes at something over the kithkin's shoulder.

"Aw, no," Brigid said, raising the knife and turning in the same direction.

It was another malignant, one they both recognized.

"Hello, Flyrne," Sygg said. "I have to say this is a surprise. How are you feeling?"

* * * * *

Ashling held on tight to the wiry twine the sapling had twisted from its own roots, roots that had been treated with the same yew magic as that which pinned down the stone giant. It was enough to keep her from burning the vines away, and the vines were the only way for Endry to carry her up the outer wall of Ember Fell. The faerie yelped and squealed as he bobbed and weaved to avoid the flaming missiles that had begun raining down upon them once they'd been spotted. That made Ashling even angrier than being punched off the side of the mountain—they were targeting Endry; there was no way the monks thought this little hail of fire would be of any impediment to her.

"You're doing fine, Endry," she said encouragingly. "Just get me to the top of the wall and you can get back to the sapling."

"No way!" Endry said, dodging a small fireball that caught Ashling in the shoulder. She easily absorbed the flame and made it her own. "This is the most fun I've had in hours! Days, maybe!"

"Really?"

"I have a lot of—" Ashling felt her makeshift carriage dip suddenly as the faerie maneuvered away from another missile. "I have a lot of fun," he finished.

"That's not what I meant," the pilgrim said. "But I'm glad you're enjoying yourself. Just be careful. Without you the rest of this won't work either."

"Don't I know it," Endry agreed. "But I don't mind you

two coming along on my adventure. I just wish—wish the groundlings could have sent some help."

"The sapling needs their help more than we do," Ashling said. "Besides, those little toys of theirs—I don't think it's really a substitute for real wings, do you? Raw lift isn't the same as truly elegant flight."

Endry grinned wide. "No, it's not. My ground rats would have been punctured in a hundred places by the time they reached the top!" And as if to impress upon her exactly why, he dropped suddenly to dodge another blazing missile.

"All right. We're almost there. Just get me close enough to the edge."

"Coming right up," the faerie said, and a few seconds later Ashling was able to reach out and hook her fingers into a handhold only a foot or two below the top of the wall. "I'll wait until you're ready. It'll be more dramatic."

"Just don't get hit," Ashling said, "and good luck." With that, she hauled herself over the wall.

Her feet came to rest upon a guard path at the top of the wall that was currently occupied by only two people—a pair of familiar monks. "Hello," the pilgrim said. "It's been what, days? Knocked anyone off a mountain lately?"

The blue monk turned calmly and strode to Ashling, who raised a blazing hand to stop him. "Wait," she said. "Just tell me, are you really going to try to keep me from passing through here? You insisted I take this route, and I'm not seeking a fight with you. But I will give you one that you will not likely walk away from. Is that what you choose, Brother Blue?"

"It does not matter what I choose," the blue monk replied. "Or what any of the Ember Fellowship choose. The only choice that matters here is yours: Will you enter the monastery? If so, you will face what the monastery holds. If not, your Ritual of the White Flame will be incomplete. You will bear the power but not the right. You will be an abomination."

"Really," Ashling said, glancing up to make sure Endry was in position. "An abomination? I tell you, Brother Blue, you sure know how to pay a compliment. No wonder you live on the side of a mountain."

"Either enter or stop wasting our time."

"Now you sound like a real flamekin," Ashling said. "Getting a little angry, are you? I'm angry too. I've been angry for a while now. And so help me, it will not go well for you if you don't just let me pass."

"I do not think so," the blue monk said and raised a hand to fire a golden flare into the sky. Seconds later, at least two hundred monks in two hundred different individual monk's robes stepped from the inner gate and filled the courtyard below. "Yes, you might have merely had to fight my apprentice and me," the blue monk said, "but I think you have not quite learned enough on your walk up this mountain. You need to be—how do the kithkin put it—'taken down a step.' "

"Funny," Ashling said, "I was just thinking the same about you." She turned her face skyward and shouted, "Endry, go!"

The monks looked up to find the faerie but could not draw a bead on him in time. Endry outmaneuvered every blast of flame and every missile of fire the monks could throw at him, and he was out of their range within seconds.

"I do not know what you think you have accomplished, Ashling of Tanufel," the blue monk said.

"You will," Ashling said. In the distance she heard a familiar drumbeat, and it grew louder by the second. Moments later the stone giant's head appeared over the crest of the mountainside. Endry must have flown his wings off to reach the sapling that quickly, but Ashling couldn't complain.

"Master?" the younger monk asked, his crown flickering nervously.

"Remember," Ashling said, "I tried to do this peacefully."

Ashling took a running start and bolted past the stunned gate-keepers and into the crowd of flamekin below.

The bodies of the novices and apprentices—not one of them shone with the blue of an Ember Fell master—cushioned her fall, and she rolled to her feet without losing much of her balance or her senses. The stunned monks around her could not seem to decide what to do. They were to fight this one, they'd been told, but their master had not yet ordered the attack.

Ashling didn't intend to give them a chance to decide and instead plowed directly through them to reach the inner gate. Once she was within a stone's throw of her destination, she turned back to the assembled fellows and pointed through the gates.

"You all may want to get out of the way. Either that or you can ask your boss to shut that thing down. It seems rather set on following me, and I don't think it intends to bother with gates, or rules, or watching where it steps. Thank Brother Blue for that."

* * * * *

"How are you feeling?" Brigid snarled. "That was the best you could do?"

"What did you expect me to say?" Sygg objected, shouting to be heard over the rumble of the downriver current rushing past their ears. "I thought he might be . . . I thought he might have made it."

"Well, he didn't," Brigid said. Then, after considering this might not be the time for her kithkin sensibilities, she added, "For what it's worth, I'm sorry, Captain."

"Me too," Sygg said. "For one thing, he wouldn't be trying to kill us right now."

"That is true," Brigid agreed.

It hadn't taken Flyrne long to drive them from the passages and back into the Wanderwine proper, racing upriver as fast as Sygg's tideshaping magic could carry them. Neither the ferryman nor Brigid even had to swim, not when the shapewater carried them along so quickly that they left a respectable rooster-tail wake behind them. In the hope that Flyrne, a bottom-dweller, might resist getting too close to the river's surface, they were sailing along just beneath it. So far Sygg's former crewman did not seem fazed in the slightest. He followed along behind them, not losing any distance but not yet closing on them either.

"How is he even keeping up with us?" Brigid asked. "You're using all you've got—not even a merrow can swim that fast . . . can he?"

"He can," Sygg said. "He's a tideshaper too."

"But he's all, you know, deformed. Monstrous."

"Why ever would that keep him from using his magic?"

"I just assumed— Well," Brigid said, "I should stop assuming." Another silver streak shot past them traveling in the opposite direction, and she remarked, "At least he seems to be the only one so far. If the rest of them could keep up, I might really be worried."

"It does take concentration to maintain this speed," Sygg said.

"Ah, right," Brigid said. "Sorry. Just one more question."

"Aye?"

"Which one of you is going to run out of strength first?"

"That's not something I want to find out," Sygg replied, "but keep that knife handy just in case."

It was fortunate she did. Despite his bravado, Sygg had not rested at all—and even merrows needed rest, Brigid knew, even if they didn't "sleep" in the usual sense. Brigid herself had only gotten a few catnaps, but Brigid wasn't trying to move both a kithkin and four hundred pounds of fish-man against the currents of the Lorwyn's greatest river. Brigid didn't even notice the slowing at first—what she first noticed was that Flyrne, terrifying and bite-happy Flyrne, was gaining on them.

"Captain," she said, "Sygg, are you all right?"

"Don't know," he said. "Hands are tingling. I think . . . I think there might have been poison on that . . . the spear. Slow poison."

"Perfect," Brigid muttered as their speed started to slow drastically. Flyrne would be upon them in moments, and Sygg looked as if he might just sink to the bottom if she didn't keep a grip on his shoulder. The kithkin awkwardly twisted around to face her doom at the hands and teeth of the malignant Flyrne.

"Come on, Ugly," Brigid snarled, raising the knife in what she hoped was a menacing fashion. She doubted that hope would do much good.

Flyrne came on like an underwater arrow, and the kithkin tried to turn the blade toward his throat. Before she had time the malignant snatched the blade from her hand, then smiled.

"You won't need that," Flyrne said. "Sygg. Sygg! I've got a cure for the malignancy!" Flyrne frowned at Brigid in what she recognized as merrow concern. "What's wrong with him? Did the malignancy catch up to him?"

"No," Brigid said, "the malignants did. Poisoned spear. You said you can cure the malignancy, but can you help him?"

"With poison?" Flyrne said. "I doubt it. But I've learned how to strain the malignant particles from the bloodstream—it's simple, really, for a capable tideshaper. You have to—"

"Flyrne!" Brigid shouted, "I'm glad you're cured. You cannot believe how glad I am you're cured. But I'm not a tideshaper so you're wasting your words and the time Sygg's got left. If we don't do something for him, he's going to die." The kithkin turned to her unconscious friend, who was growing pale as his eyes grew dimmer. "Just look at him."

"I do not know what I can do," the hulking merrow replied.

"I do," Brigid said. "If you'll wait here with him . . . I think we're in the right neck of the woods. . . ." She made a game effort to see past the river's surface and was surprised to see she did know this stretch.

"Right neck of the woods? For what?" Flyrne asked. "I do not spend much time in 'woods,' you understand."

"The right neck of the woods for some ancient kithkin remedies," Brigid said. "If I can find them, and find them fast."

* * * * *

Brigid left Flyrne and Sygg near the riverbank—when the kithkin found her remedies, assuming she did, Sygg would need to be hauled up onto the beach to administer them. Brigid had no idea what would happen to them in the water, or whether they would even work. She had been on her hunt without encountering anything more hostile than a nettle-bee when she saw the children: a band of four young kithlings playing in the forest.

Kithlings never played in the forest unless that forest was very close to a kithkin village where their parents could keep an eye on them. That meant a kithkin settlement was not far. But which one? This river was lined with many kithkin villages, and Brigid had lost track of the distances she'd traveled underwater days ago. If only there was some familiar marker, something to give her a clue as to where—

"Hey, look!" one of the kithlings, a little girl in a pink checked dress cried. "It's Brigid Baeli!"

"My mummy says she's not a hero anymore."

"We should go tell them."

"But what if she runs away?"

"Then the grown-ups will catch her," the girl in the pink

checked dress replied. "She's a wanted criminal. Look, she's even wearing a mask."

"Ah," Brigid said. "So this would be Kinsbaile."

The children screamed when she spoke, and it sunk in that she must look like a monster, with her river-soaked clothes, torn by rocks, weapons, and worse. Probably even more frightening to the children was the gill mask that she'd forgotten to remove in her haste to help Sygg. Before she could stop them, however, the children were gone.

She had a minute or two before the archers were alerted, maybe longer if they didn't immediately believe the children. But from listening to the kithlings Brigid guessed they would. Word of her "criminal exploits" seemed to have gotten around. No one had ever broken free of the thoughtweft. Who would want to?

Fortunately, the archer now knew exactly where she was, and while she was no elf hunter, she knew enough about herbs and remedies to find what she was looking for in less than a minute.

And a good thing too. No sooner had she gathered what she needed than the band of archers she'd been expecting emerged from the forest. What she hadn't expected to see was the man at the head of the small group—her former superior Paertagh Marphi.

"Hello, Taer," she said with a short bow of her head. "I don't mean to cause any trouble. My friend is sick. I just need to bring him some medicine, and this was the nearest place."

Marphi nodded. "I don't care. You are no longer welcome in this village, Brigid Baeli. The only reason you are not already full of arrows is my standing order that you are to be brought in alive, in order that your fellow conspirators may be exposed."

"Conspirators?" Brigid said. "I have no fellow conspirators. You're looking at a conspiracy of one, my friend." She forced herself not to look in the direction of the river. If she had to flee suddenly she didn't want Marphi to know her destination—it might still be possible to lose him if he wasn't expecting it. And Sygg needed these herbs.

"The elves," Marphi demanded, "where are they? Why are you trying to keep them alive? They have crimes to answer for. They stole—"

"They stole nothing," Brigid said darkly. "We rewarded their friendship with betrayal, and, worse, I was the one who did it. I intend to make up for that to the people that matter to me. I know who I am and what I've done, and if you didn't have doubts about what they're saying about me you would have shot me already. So why don't we just say good-bye, and I can help my friend, and you can return home." The kithkin swallowed hard. "Do that, and I swear I will— I will never come back."

Marphi turned to his archers and ordered them back to town, then returned to Brigid. "And if I make this deal with you, how will I know you intend to keep up your end of the bargain?"

"Why wouldn't I?" Brigid said. "I don't want to die, and I don't want to— I don't want to be humiliated. If you take me back alive, I'll be pilloried. If I die when and where I choose, for reasons that I believe in, so be it. But not that, Taer. Don't do that to me."

"Why?" her former superior asked. "Just tell me that. We are your home, your village. The heart of your hearth, Brigid Baeli. You have offered me a deal, and so I will offer one to you. You're the best damned archer I've ever trained, and I need you—Kinsbaile needs you. There are strange things happening out there, and from the look of you you've seen most of them. When those strange things try to come after us, we need to be ready. And to be ready, I need you, archer."

The powerful Kinsbaile thoughtweft touched her then, and for a moment she had never heard of an elf named Rhys, the strange flamekin pilgrim, a fish-man named Sygg, or the most irritating trio of faeries this side of a children's play. She was the Hero of

Kinsbaile once more, and Kinsbaile needed Brigid Baeli.

But the people of Kinsbaile were strong, she told herself. Together, they were much greater than the sum of their parts, and Brigid knew that better than anyone.

Sygg needed her too. And the others. If she didn't return to the river, Sygg was dead. If she brought a pack of archers hot on her heels, Sygg probably wouldn't be much better off. She had no choice but to trust in the basic decency of the man she'd followed for most of her life.

"Taer," she said with as much formality as she could muster, "I must refuse. There are others who need my help, and I cannot overlook my responsibility to them. I hope you can understand and believe me when I say I have done nothing that was not ultimately for the good of Kinsbaile and Lorwyn." She felt clammy sweat forming on her forehead but plowed ahead anyway. "I will offer you a warning though. Merrows are restless. There's a plague among them they call 'the malignancy,' and it's making them violent. Dangerous, and savage. Stay away from the rivers."

"I have not said you may go," Marphi said.

"You have to let me go," Brigid replied. "Kinsbaile needs you, Taer, not me. There are heroes everywhere. I am just a lucky archer. Now please let me go, Taer. Let me help someone who actually wants my help."

Maybe it was a group decision of the Kinsbaile thoughtweft, but Brigid didn't think so. She chose to believe Marphi allowed her to slip back into the forest because it was simply the right thing to do.

* * * * *

"Sygg," Brigid said, "you'll never believe where we are."

The merrow ferryman blinked, blinked again, and finally

shook his head, but nothing seemed to shatter what had to be a hallucination. He was dead, that had to be it. He was dead, and he now swam the Eternal Lanes. It was a bit odd that a kithkin would be in the Eternal Lanes, let alone a kithkin he knew, but then Brigid had spent a great deal of time underwater lately. Perhaps the keepers of the holy locks had allowed her special dispensation.

Flyrne's presence made more sense. The hulking shape of his former crewman filled most of his vision, but he'd not yet spoken. Clearly he'd died after the malignancy had devoured his mind and was now merely a silent, brooding spirit in the great waters of the afterlife.

"Sygg," Flyrne said, puncturing another wall in the captain's carefully considered hypothesis. "Sygg, are you all right?"

"Flyrne?" Sygg said dreamily. "I'm sorry you're here, old friend. How long has it been?"

"Since when?" Flyrne asked.

"Since you died."

"Oh, for— Sygg!" Brigid barked. "Wake up! Snap out of it! You're not dead, I'm not dead, and Flyrne—" she jerked a thumb over her shoulder at the big merrow who, now that Sygg took a closer look, was carrying them all along with his own shape-water magic, "Flyrne is going to get us to the source. You've been— Well, we thought maybe you were dead there for a few minutes. But a little bit—all right, a lot of bit—of Doctor Baeli's homemade herbal remedy seems to have done the trick."

"Wait, where— You said I'd never guess where we are."

"That's right," Brigid said.

Sygg cast his eyes around the rushing water and the shallow upward curve of the riverbed before him. "We're at the base of Mount Tanufel!" he whispered. "I haven't been this far upriver in years. We're not far from the source!"

"I'm glad you're figuring all this out on your own," Brigid

said, clearly miffed. "Wouldn't want to surprise you or anything, like, say, with an old friend who we both thought was dead."

"Flyrne!" Sygg said again, and this time his former crewman's presence really sunk in. "You're not—"

"I'm no longer infected," Flyrne said. "I can show you how to do it, but I'm afraid it's a trick that only works with tideshapers. There's little we can do for the others, but it should keep you safe."

"Then we'll make it work," Sygg said. "Once we talk to the source."

" 'Talk' to the source?" Brigid asked. "How do you talk to the source of a river?"

"Well," Sygg said with a grin, "I usually find it's a good idea to start with 'Hello.' "

The greatest of the merrow Lanes narrowed considerably as it moved from the familiar and comfortably wide lowland Wanderwine to where it became a fierce mountain channel, relentlessly carving its way down the side of the largest mountain in Lorwyn. Mercifully, however, Sygg, Brigid, and Flyrne didn't run into any more malignants, not this far upriver. Probably because almost no merrows ever came up here, Sygg had opined, reminding Brigid and Flyrne—who both knew it quite well, having heard it many times before—that Sygg was one of the few merrows ever to travel to the source more than once.

What Brigid didn't understand was how they were supposed to speak to a stream, or at best a small lake. The kithkin assumed it must be a figure of speech, that Sygg would "speak" to the source by studying it, or perhaps even using some kind of tideshaper magic to look into the water's component parts. To the kithkin's surprise, she turned out to be completely wrong.

But that would be later. First, her merrow companions had to grapple with an increasingly shallow, fast-moving river that was now more waterfall than stream. They'd seen nothing but white water for miles. Thanks to Flyrne's and Sygg's combined efforts they'd made it this far, but Brigid hadn't a clue how much further they had to go or whether the merrow's magic could move them up a river too shallow to hold them.

As it turned out, she needn't have been concerned. The merrow simply gave up on complete immersion, and the trio broke the surface, skipping along like stones thrown by bored kithlings—but much faster.

Two-thirds of the way up the mountain Brigid could have sworn she heard a crash from the rough and craggy cliffs on the far side of Tanufel.

CHAPTER 18

The stone giant struck the gate with both fists and shattered the ancient edifice to its foundations. The pilgrim had to admit she had underestimated the blue monk's determination, however. When the stone giant had come barreling up the mountainside, Ashling had been certain that alone would be enough for him to call off his creature. As the stone archway rained down upon the bent and twisted gate and hundreds of novices panicked and fled in every direction, Ashling began to wonder if the giant really was the blue monk's creature anymore.

But such was the danger of bluffing, Ashling told herself. When you're called on the bluff, the bluff becomes a promise, or there was no point in bluffing at all. An old kithkin cardsharp in Dundoolin had told her that many years ago, but she'd never quite understood it until now.

The giant shoved its way through the wreckage of monastery and monks to spot Ashling at last. As it raised its fists with a roar, she answered with a roar of her own and charged toward the giant, running between its feet and over the pile of jagged rubble standing where the gate had been. It wasn't until the giant, once again lumbering around to face her, froze in midstep that Ashling saw the blue monk again, hovering where he had stood atop the wall, the orange apprentice at his side. Unlike the roaring jet of flame Ashling had required to rocket up the side of Mount Tanufel, the two of them appeared to float with little effort, their feet glowing brightly with diffuse jets of light that matched their flames. "I suppose I might have a little something to learn about control after all," she called up with a hoarse laugh. "What do you think?"

"I think," the blue monk said, slowly descending upon waves of nearly invisible heat, "that you have walked through the gate. You were not traveling in the direction I expected, but you walked through all the same." The monk's descent ended a few feet overhead, and he looked down at her from his perch as she struggled back to her exhausted feet.

"But your monastery," Ashling said. "You don't mind . . . ?"

The blue monk waved a hand at the frozen stone giant, sending a wave of almost invisible heat into its center of gravity. A few seconds later, that center exploded in a hail of stone. Moments after that the entire thing collapsed. Improbably, no one was hurt, though Ashling was beginning to suspect the blue monk had seen to that as well.

"Those youths you met inside the gate will learn much by rebuilding it from the rubble," the blue monk said. "It will not be the first time I've seen such a thing ordered—I placed the old keystone myself, once upon a time." His face remained impassive, but the harsh blue light in his face warmed a degree or two. "It will also teach them the value of standing their ground. It is a thing of stone and earth. The outer gate means nothing. The inner gate leads to the true monastery . . . and beyond that, you walk alone."

"Why?" Ashling asked.

"Yeah, why?" Endry repeated.

Ashling froze. "Endry, not now."

"The sapling sent me," the faerie continued, oblivious. "Wanted to see if you're all right. You look all right. So I asked why." He fluttered boldly up to the blue monk's face and peered into the flamekin sage's blazing eyes. "Why does she have to go alone? Why couldn't she take, say, a handsome, little faerie hero?"

The blue monk surprised both Ashling and Endry when he tipped back his head and laughed. "A faerie hero," the monk said. "Now I have seen everything. And I mean that. You are indeed brave, tiny child of Oona, but this is not for you. Nor for your treefolk friend, wherever she has gotten off to."

"That's a big load of babble," Endry challenged.

"If you take the tiny one with you," the monk said, "its fate is on your conscience."

Ashling gazed at the inner gate. Unlike the rubble behind her, these doors were of much sturdier construction. The pilgrim doubted even the late, unlamented stone giant could have harmed this metallic edifice. The gate itself was set into a mammoth cave that had been left undisturbed by the denizens of the monastery, and its twin doors were solid iron a foot thick, polished to a mirror surface that swirled with the reddish plasma of aggressive enchantments. Runes and decorative, perhaps arcane carvings adorned the metal, but Ashling could not read any of it. The only thing that made sense was a relatively small pictograph cut into both doors and split at the seam. It depicted a flamekin covered in curling tongues of fire below a forced perspective of the gate—an almost perfect miniature of the one before her—that floated above the figure's head. Joining the figure and the gate were two straight lines that met in the exact center of both the drawing of the gate and the gate itself.

The end of the path.

"I'll go," she said. "Endry, get the sapling. She'll be . . ." the pilgrim cast a look at the monk, "she'll be safe here." And almost silently, just loud enough to be picked up by tiny faerie ears, she added, "And invite your little friends, if you're able."

"Sure thing," Endry said loudly and with a broad, utterly false smile. "Endry away!"

Ashling watched the faerie go with a sad smile. Something had changed in her upon seeing the figure carved upon that gate. Maybe it was the sapling's talk about destiny or the fact that so much about her terrifying first encounter with the elemental was utterly unique in the experience of any flamekin. Perhaps she was being manipulated by powers she couldn't see or understand. Whatever the reason, Ashling knew—knew—that she was the figure depicted in the engraving, which didn't make any sense. She was after the elemental, fully intending to bend it to her will. How could the engraver have known that?

She turned slowly on the blue monk, flames rippling skeptically. "Anything else I should know?" she asked the monk. "Anything else you want to tell me?"

"Know that few have seen what you will see," the monk said. "Your discoveries will be your own. But when you emerge, you will not be the same."

"I've seen plenty not many have seen, Brother Blue," Ashling said. "I imagine I've seen a lot that you haven't seen either. A simple 'yes' or 'no' will go a long way next time." She took the final few steps and pressed both her hands against the doors and pushed.

Nothing happened.

"All right, I give up," Ashling began. "How do I—"

With a low, angry groan, the doors to the heart of Ember Fell were thrown open.

"Ah," the pilgrim said. "Just like that." She took a moment to peer through the widening gap, took a deep breath, and strode into the monastery.

Ashling felt a brief moment of panic when she heard the doors of the inner gate slide back into place. She had no idea whether she could open them from within the monastery—if this cavern was actually within the monastery. It had an otherworldly air that made her doubt that reality. The only light in the place came from Ashling's flames until the door shut completely with a resounding clank. At the sound the cavern's interior flooded with rich, reddish light. The cavern was not at all empty—at the very least. And it was not an empty city either. The reddish light emanated from its many spires, from the top of every structure, from home to hovel to amphitheater, from the fortress towers to the glittering crystalline rooftops of a fantastic palace complete with a quartet of crystal banners that flew despite the complete lack of breeze. A golden path lay before Ashling, its trail so convoluted yet appealingly serpentine it was clear to the pilgrim the path had been built, not trod. And within the lights, the shapes of flamekin shadows played on the walls and windows. They were distorted a bit, probably the deep color of the light.

All of it fit within a monastery? "If I end up tied to another damned tree . . ." Ashling swore.

After a few minutes, Ashling noticed she was being followed. A dark, floating shape, like a bat but with a long, pointed beak, flew along after her with quiet menace. Ashling readied herself for a fight against the shadowy thing, and white fire crackled up her arms.

The bat-thing veered off and disappeared into the depths. Ashling wondered if the crevasse reached all the way to the living rock. A sudden wave of vertigo made her steer herself away from the ledge to focus on her goal—the shining city ahead. After a few minutes without further incident, she neared the town gate.

Another gate. Ashling was growing tired of gates. Tired of tearing them down, tired of opening them, tired of entering them. Fortunately, these swung open of their own accord, welcome and inviting. Through the gate she could see more of those curiously distorted flamekin silhouettes, and Ashling found it odd they still appeared so strange to her this close.

The first one she saw up close was an elder, stooped and dim. At least that's what she thought at first, but closer examination revealed this flamekin was in far worse shape than mere age could have caused. His torso and limbs appeared to have shrunk and withered, burned out from the inside. His head was cracked and brittle, and he had hardly any crown left at all. His fingers were long and misshapen, ending in claws.

She jumped back a second too late. The old flamekin snarled like an animal and lashed out with its long, simian arm. Yet although she should have lost at least a forearm from that blow, she felt nothing. Again the beastly flamekin tried to strike her, tried to rend her in half from the look of it, to be precise. This time she watched as its hand entered her chest and emerged from the other side without so much as a twinge.

"Ghosts," she whispered. "You're some kind of ghosts?"

A low murmur of scrapes, clicks, and whistles citywide was his only reply. The murmur had been there since she entered the city, but she only noticed it when she said the word "ghost."

Another of the freakishly misshapen flamekin emerged from around the corner, moving with predatory grace, long claws almost dragging as they ran, hunched, directly at her. She steeled herself for the impact but didn't really expect one. As she thought, the two wolflike flamekin bounded right through her. She whirled and saw them do the same, confused and snarling.

"Who are you?" Ashling asked. "Why are you—What happened to you?"

A sickly flare more like black smoke than burning flame, the gnashing of ethereal teeth, and the murmur of the city was the only answer she received.

The whole city was exactly the same. No matter where Ashling went, what secret quarter she searched, these savage, ghostly flamekin saw her and gave pursuit. By the time she reached the point where she was almost certain she'd scoured the entire place, she rounded a corner and saw something that made her flaming jaw drop.

She saw a statue carved from black, pitted igneous rock. The sculpture depicted a blazing flamekin—a normal one, not one of these sickened creatures. The figure held aloft a blazing sword with a blade made of flame, and her foot rested upon a stylized depiction of Mount Tanufel. Despite the difficulty of doing so in this rocky medium, the statue was engraved with symbols Ashling recognized. One was the symbol for her name. The other was "Avatar."

Ashling walked up the steps leading to the statue's pedestal and placed a hand upon the hilt of the sculpted sword. Then the world exploded.

Flames, living flames, the flames of the purest elements, the fires of the gods—the flame was centered on Ashling, but it rolled over the city like a shock wave, burning everything in its path. Flamekin architecture was designed to withstand great temperatures and remained unharmed, while the people, the simian flamekin monsters . . .

Monsters that appeared now to be flamekin once again, burning with healthy fires and walking proud and tall. Ashling relished the experience, granting life, burning life to an entire city of the dead.

For the first time in a long time Ashling heard the distant sound of hoof beats.

Now you see.

"Wait!" Ashling cried. "What does this mean? How am I supposed to save these people. I don't even know who they are!"

Yes, you do.

"I do?" She looked again at the thriving, blazing ghosts, looking for something familiar. When she saw it, she could not fathom what it meant.

All of the flamekin in the city were Ashling. Some were male, or youths, or older flamekin looking forward to the day they'd die in a glorious blaze. But their faces were hers. Their walks, hers.

Their voices—definitely hers, even the males.

The fire cannot be extinguished, the elemental said. *It must carry on. Change is coming, and too soon. The world is not ready. A vessel must carry the flame into the darkness and out the other side.*

"I don't care," Ashling said, although the words felt hollow. And well they should have, for they were a lie. She had sought to tame this creature, this untamable force of nature, a fool's errand if ever there was one.

Yes, the elemental said. *You did not hunt me. I called to you. Stoked the fires of revenge within you. Made you seek me out, for the time is short.*

"The monks," Ashling said. "How much do they know?"

The master of Ember Fell knows nothing but what I have shared. A child of the flame who seeks to reach the next level of the Path—he believes that is all you are. He cannot know the truth, for he would not believe. But you, the last child of Tanufel, know what you must do.

And she did. Ashling strode through the city of ghosts until she reached the far gate. Without a word, the pilgrim pushed the golden doors aside to clatter resoundingly against the stone.

* * * * *

"It's coming," Sygg said. Flyrne murmured in agreement.

"What's coming?" Brigid demanded.

"Something," the captain said. "I can't say . . . what. I just know. Don't you? Can't you sense it?"

"I can sense it," Flyrne said. "I fear I may have cured myself in vain. Whatever is coming is going to change everything."

"I'm not going to change," Brigid said. "And neither are you two. Now come on, you lazy fish-bones. We've got to be getting close to the source."

Indeed, the source was less than a mile away when Brigid spoke, and with the powers of two tideshapers combined to speed them on their way it seemed to pass in no time. At first the kithkin archer thought she was looking at exactly what she'd expected: a small lake, suspended in a fishbowl-shaped indentation only a few hundred feet from the summit of Mount Tanufel. With a great sigh of relief, she paddled to the rocky shore and slipped the gill mask from her face. Moments later she put it back on—the air was thin up here for some reason. The gill mask let her breathe easy as Sygg and Flyrne swam up over the white falls, diving like spawning salmon, until they made it to the lake. Brigid jogged along the bank to meet them.

"Well?" she asked. "Does it look like you thought it would look? Is there something wrong with the source?"

Sygg ignored her. He clutched the bone crescent around his neck and held it aloft. "I am Sygg Gauhren Gyllalla Syllvar, Heir to the Crescent of Morningtide. I seek an audience on a matter of great urgency. I appeal to your mercy, wisdom, and power, Source of Lanes."

On the last word, the water in the lake began to roil and bubble. A lump beneath the surface pushed upward, and as it lifted itself out of the river Brigid could see it wasn't something beneath the surface—the lump was part of the surface. The column of water rose until its gleaming top blocked out the sun. Then its shape changed, rolling and flexing until it took on the rough form of a gigantic merrow—or more accurately, a giant merrow from the waist up. A female.

"Yeag fryn yggli, Sygg Gauhren Gyllalla Syllvar," the source said.

"Source of the Wanderwine," Sygg said, keeping his eyes trained on the smooth water before him and not on the towering impossibility. "My people, the Paupurfylln, and many others who dwell in the river have been—they are ill. They blame the source stones you gave us, your children, in the days before there was time. My people think the stones have changed, and the stones have changed them. And I cannot deny it. They have changed, and not for the better. Something is wrong in the river. Are you . . . are you all right?"

"You speak to me in the tongue of landwalkers, Sygg," the source said with a voice like a rushing waterfall. "I will respond in kind but only because you wish it."

"You honor me, Source of the Father-Lane," Sygg said with a curt bow. "It is said, Source of All Life, that the Father-Lane shall never abandon her children in time of need. I tell you, I plead with you, the Father-Lane's children need help."

"Why is the Father-Lane female?" Brigid asked.

"The Father-Lane is neither male nor female," Flyrne said, "for the Father-Lane is above such considerations. It's a problem with the common landwalker tongue."

"You ask of change, Sygg Gauhren Gyllalla Syllvar. A change in your people. The answer is yes," the incarnation of the Wanderwine said. "I am changing. The merrow-children change with me. But too soon, too soon."

"What's too soon, Great Lady?" Sygg asked.

"The Heir of the Crescent does not know," the source laughed. "What has become of the merrow-children?"

"We are sick," Sygg said. "Or rather, many of the merrow-children are. We have been healed, but we are but two. There are thousands in need of your aid and guidance."

"The merrow-children are not ready. I am not ready. The change that is coming . . . it is not natural. Orderly. Something has happened far beyond my influence. Very far. But it is no matter. Change cannot be stopped but need not be feared."

"How could I fear it?" Sygg asked. "I don't—"

"We don't even know what it is," Brigid added, stepping

forward and reaching out with a nimble hand before Sygg could launch into another formal request. "Pardon me, Captain. I don't have my own crescent. May I?" She plucked the bone talisman from Sygg's hands. "Brigid Baeli, Hero of Kinsbaile. You'll have to be more specific," Brigid went on. "From our perspective, the change you speak of has already happened. Your . . . your merrow-children are destroying each other. Devouring each other," she added, still feeling sharp twinges of pain now and again in the leg Flyrne had tried to bite off. "If you could help them . . . change the water back somehow, or—"

"You do not understand, child of Kinsbaile," the source said. "The Great Aurora will come to all of Lorwyn. All of this summer world will die, leaving a world of winter and death. The malignancy is just the beginning. The merrow-children are most susceptible to its effects."

"Great Aurora?" Brigid asked.

"Great Lady," Sygg said in a bid to reassert control over the questioning, "Forgive the directness of the child of Kinsbaile. We simply do not understand. What is this Great Aurora?"

"The normal Aurora is the natural cycle of things. The time between day and night. Summer and winter. Dawn and dusk. But darkness comes too soon, too soon."

"You did say that," Brigid said. "Already. Twice. When? When is it happening? And what will it do to us?"

"No one knows," the source said. "But there are those who have prepared for the worst."

CHAPTER 19

The valley around Rosheen Meanderer was peaceful once more. The sun was bright and warm, a gentle breeze rustled the grass, and birdcalls echoed through the air. The giantess still slept, mumbling and snoring, and the changelings had long since resumed their aimless, undulating dance. Brion, Kiel, and the faeries had withdrawn after the dream ritual so that Rosheen, Rhys, and Maralen were left alone with the changelings and the valley's more usual wildlife. High overhead, the great cloudgoat still perched on the horizon, so high it could barely be seen.

"I have to go," Rhys said. He turned to Maralen, who had been sitting on the ground with her elbows on her knees and her head in her hands.

"Go where?" she said.

"Somewhere else." Rhys stood up. "Somewhere that isn't here. I need to clear my head, but all I see are pieces of the vision."

Maralen scanned the valley through half-focused eyes. The faeries' spell took a toll on Rhys, but Maralen was visibly weakened by it. The dark-haired elf was so drained and sick she could barely stand, and the simple act of turning her head sent twinges of pain cascading across her body. For a moment Rhys thought she might vomit.

But Maralen steadied herself and rode out the wave of nausea. She wiped cold sweat from her forehead and exhaled deeply. "It's a good idea. You should go," she said. "A clear head is what we need right now. Take as much time as you need. I doubt anything crucial is going to happen for the next few hours." She smiled, but her pallid complexion made the expression false, even unsettling. "Not if it requires any effort from me."

Rhys stepped forward and crouched beside Maralen. Stiffly, he laid a hand on her shoulder. "Are you all right?"

Maralen's color improved at Rhys's touch, but she remained listless, distracted. "I'm . . . overwhelmed. I only understood part of what we saw, and that part frightens me. Everything's going bad, and I— I'm afraid anything I do will just make it worse. Then again, I can't resign myself to doing nothing."

"I understand," Rhys said. He squeezed Maralen's shoulder and stood once more. "I'll be back directly. If you don't start feeling better soon, I suggest you get away from here yourself."

"Thank you," Maralen said. "If a change of scenery helps you, I may well give it a try." She lowered her head back into her hands. "Go on, Daen. I'll take care of things here."

Rhys bowed curtly, but Maralen had already sunk back into her contemplative torpor. He paused, then decided there was nothing more to say. Rhys turned and strode up the incline.

His mood improved once he turned his back on Rosheen and again as he reached the top of the incline and stepped out of the giantess's valley. He doubted there was any practical benefit to increasing the distance between himself and the site of the vision ritual, and so he ascribed the lift he was feeling to his own weakness. Walking away from his problems was far easier than confronting them, and he cursed that part of him that wanted to just keep walking.

There was no escaping what he must face, and this stubborn fact gnawed at him even as he moved away from Rosheen. The Blessed Nation would be diminished and suffer the indignity of hostile invasion. The flamekin tribe would burn out and expire.

The great change Colfenor had spoken of and Rhys had seen in the ritual through his mind's eye was all encompassing, all consuming, and inevitable.

Inevitable. Rhys hated that word, for his every instinct was screaming for him to act. Something terrible threatened the Nation and his companions alike, and it was the elf way to answer threats before they arose. The path to perfection was littered with dangers, and so danger was a thing to be anticipated, minimized before its impact could be fully felt. Rhys shared Maralen's frustration—any action he might take was either pointless or would exacerbate the situation. He only had to think of the sapling, who endured the great change intact only after a concerted effort was made on her behalf, one that came at a terrible cost.

Ashling must be told, Rhys thought. The pilgrim had a right to know what Colfenor had done to her, why he had done it, and of the awful fate that awaited her tribe if Rosheen's prediction came true.

Rhys's surge of conviction shriveled when he remembered how helpless he truly was. He did not have the wisdom of an ancient yew sage or the power of a primal elemental spirit. He could not atone for the ordeal Colfenor inflicted on Ashling in advance of the coming change, nor could he blunt the suffering all flamekin would experience once the change occurred.

Worst of all, Ashling's path had taken her far from Rhys, and if he called her there was no guarantee she would answer. Even if he told her what he'd seen, if Rosheen's augury was entirely accurate and Ashling heard his confession, there was no way to make her understand, believe, or prepare. There was no way to make her forgive.

Rhys descended down to the tree line and walked among the scrub trees. The scattered collection of scrawny timber was completely unlike the vibrant abundance of the Gilt Leaf Wood, but it was still familiar to him, still part of the Lorwyn he knew.

He wondered if he would still feel that comforting affinity when the Blessed Nation itself was as threadbare and wasted as this scrubland.

He began to run. His legs felt loose and strong, and in moments he had achieved the perfect hunter's pace—fast, steady, and almost completely silent. His hooves dug into the dry soil, his arms pumped back and forth. Rhys lowered his head, and he ran, losing himself in the simple demands and rewards of physical exertion.

Soon the motion of his mind aligned with that of his body. They could not stay in Rosheen's valley much longer, not with the Hemlock Pack on their heels. He would have Maralen locate Endry and the sapling first. Colfenor's offspring still had vital information, and Rhys would tolerate no more of the sapling's hazy, unfocused detachment. Once she shared more of the knowledge she inherited from her sire, Rhys would take their pooled information to Ashling so they could all decide on their next step.

Rhys also resolved to cut loose Brion and Kiel with whatever payment they required. They had earned a reward, or at least fair compensation for the trouble they'd been through. The brothers would be free of elf pursuit once they were no longer traveling with Rhys and could fend for themselves.

Rhys weaved between a long line of trees, alternating from left to right and kicking up small puffs of dirt with each pivoting step. The scrub forest thinned at the end of the line, and the terrain opened up into a wide, rocky basin.

A bowstring twanged, and a thin, sharp shock exploded through Rhys's shoulder. He stumbled, and as he fell he saw the tip of an arrowgrass shaft protruding through his collarbone. His knee slammed into the turf, and he rolled through a series of awkward somersaults until his momentum was spent. Crouching, breathing heavily, Rhys held perfectly still and strained his ears.

More elf bows let fly, and a half-dozen arrowgrass shafts sang high over Rhys's head. He spotted all six in a single glance, calculated their speed and trajectory, then twisted his body into a painful, irregular curl. Six bolts rained down around him, each narrowly missing his arm, torso, and legs.

Rhys rolled away and quickly sprang to his feet. He lunged forward, planted both feet deep in the soil, and leaped twenty feet into the air. Rhys soared gracefully toward the highest bough of the nearest tree, but he never reached his destination.

The long body of a vinebred elf hit Rhys in the midsection halfway to his intended perch. The enhanced warrior wrapped his arms tight around Rhys's waist as the weight and speed of the tackle carried them both to the far edge of the basin. The vinebred's tough, woody armor tore through Rhys's layered tunic as hunter and prey slammed hard into the rocky ground.

Rhys strained to break his enemy's grip, but he had no leverage and no purchase. He felt as if he were pinned under a statue of heavy stone. Five more vinebred appeared in a tight circle around him, though they made no effort to help their comrade. The magnificent silent warriors simply stood and stared as Rhys's struggles grew fainter, then ceased entirely.

Snarling, Rhys willed his unresponsive body to continue. He had no illusions about breaking free, or even of surviving this encounter, but he was determined to fight on. Though he was in the hands of his enemies and his failure was now complete, he could not allow himself to quietly accept a death without honor.

Rhys continued to struggle until one of the vinebred stepped forward and lashed him across the face with a sharp-hoofed foot. Rhys tasted blood and felt a tooth floating freely in his mouth. His vision went red. His head sagged. He was beaten.

Sensing his surrender, the vinebred that held Rhys relaxed his grip. The other nettle-encrusted hunters quickly seized his arms and legs. They stretched his limbs out straight, almost snapping them from their joints. Then they raised him overhead and ran forward, slamming Rhys's spine against a sturdy oak. The vine-bred folded Rhys's arms and legs around the tree behind him and held him fast, agonizingly pinned several feet above the forest floor.

Rhys's head lolled, but he refused to pass out. He meant to die with his eyes open, and so with a titanic effort he lifted his face.

Gryffid stood facing him, his eyes blazing with hate. Rhys's former comrade drew a long, silver sword and held the weapon point-down by his side.

"You delivered yourself to us, Rhys." Gryffid said. "Ran right into our arms. Have you finally gone truly and utterly mad? Or do you just want to die as much as I want to kill you?" His lip curled into a contemptuous sneer. "No matter. For the memory of Taercenn Nath and the good of the Nation, it shall be done."

A clipped, precise voice interrupted before Gryffid could raise his sword. "For those very same reasons, Daen, I must insist you stay your hand."

Rhys peered past Gryffid. A glorious elf stood behind his former comrade, dressed not as a hunter but in the finery of a noble dignitary. The newcomer clearly held high status. Perhaps he was a member of the Sublime Council. Now Rhys knew the face of the elf who was backing Gryffid's vengeful hunt, but even this was meaningless—he had no idea who the lofty nobleman was.

"Taer?" Gryffid's face was a study in confusion and frustration.

"Stand down, Daen Gryffid. I would speak with the prisoner."

"Taer, I—"

"You are dismissed, Gryffid." The elf's patrician bearing hardened, and his words were sharp. "Remove yourself until I call for you."

Gryffid fired one last acid glare at Rhys. "Yes, Taercenn." The Hemlock daen seethed as he sheathed his weapon. Gryffid then spun in place, showed Rhys his back, and stormed from the basin.

The high-ranking elf waited until Gryffid was out of sight. He turned and appraised Rhys with a cold, calculating eye. "Let the prisoner down," he said. The vinebred relaxed their grip slightly, and Rhys slid down the tree trunk until his feet touched the forest floor.

"My name is Eidren," the newcomer said, "Gilt Leaf Perfect and acting taercenn of the Hemlock Pack. Is my name familiar to you?"

Rhys managed to twitch his head from side to side. "No."

"Strange," Eidren said. He came forward a few paces and then gathered his capelike wrap around his right forearm. "I am a man of some reputation and no small standing. Odd that so many should know me, yet you do not. Especially considering the company you keep. Surely you've heard the name Peradala?"

The name struck a memory from Rhys's foggy brain. He fumbled with it before answering. Maralen had spoken of such an elf but only in passing. "A Mornsong Perfect," Rhys said, "possessed of a beautiful singing voice."

"An unparalleled singing voice," Eidren corrected, "the finest in her tribe and so the finest in all Lorwyn. She was to be my bride, you know. She was murdered along with the rest of her entourage in the wilds between Mornsong and Gilt Leaf. There was only one survivor, an Exquisite lady-in-waiting."

"I mourn your loss." Rhys felt his strength returning, "And I share your grief, Taer." The blighted elf knew he'd never break free of the grip that held him, not even at his best, but at least now he felt able to seize an opportunity for escape if one presented itself.

"You've been engaged to be married then?" Eidren asked. "And lost your prospective bride?"

"No. No, of course not."

"Then you *cannot* understand the depths of my grief. Still, it was very kind of you to say otherwise. Where was I? . . . Ah, yes, the survivor. I believe you know the lady. Dark hair, sharp eyes, pale complexion? I look forward to getting to know her better once I'm finished with you."

"You mean Maralen." Rhys chuckled harshly. "You've a difficult task ahead, Taer, if you want to get anything out of that one."

"I do mean Maralen," Eidren said. "But I do not know the person to whom you now refer. But let us come to the point. You are accursed, outlaw. Traitor, eyeblight, kin-slayer, and worse. The Nation demands your death."

"I am all of those things." Rhys straightened as much as his restrained position allowed. "I deserve the Nation's judgment. But I will not recant, and I will not beg."

"Bravely put. Though I must say you are in no position to rule out what you will and will not do in the near future." Eidren nodded warmly. "I'm going to release you now. You are not free, of course. You are a prisoner of the Blessed Nation, and for all intents and purposes I am the Blessed Nation. You will answer for your crimes. If you attempt to flee or to attack me," the elegant nobleman smiled confidently, "which I fully expect, given your habit of killing superior officers, I promise you will not succeed. And more, that you will be gravely injured by my honor guard." Eidren folded his arms and said, "Down."

The vinebred released Rhys entirely. His legs wobbled, and his joints were riddled with pins and needles, but he managed to keep to his feet.

"Walk with me," Eidren said. He turned away from Rhys and strolled casually toward the edge of the basin.

Rhys glanced at the stoic faces of the vinebred half-surrounding him. He stretched his neck and shook the kinks out of his shoulders, then moved up behind Eidren. The new taercenn seemed to float through the trees, effortlessly elegant. Rhys heard the squadron of vinebred falling to step behind him.

"I was frankly impressed by that business with the poisoned grass," Eidren said. "And the fog. And the Dauba bridge. You have a terribly practical approach to things. Very effective. You are a formidable opponent."

"The facts say otherwise, Taercenn. You are here now, and I am your prisoner."

"Don't let that trouble you. Gryffid is an effective and dedicated daen. He drove the pack through the Dauba Ravine at a blazing pace. I merely provided advice and assistance."

Rhys took several extra long strides until he was only a half step behind Eidren. "And what is your advice now that you have me?"

"Oh," Eidren said breezily. "Your life is over, of course. Forfeit in exchange for the great debt you owe our people. The others in your party shall die, only much, much sooner than you. I have forty Hemlock archers positioned around the rim of the valley that sheltered you. When I give the word, the giants and the faeries will fall. Those that do not bleed out in the first exchange will be inducted to the ranks of my lesser vinebred."

They took a few more steps in silence. Rhys said, "And Maralen?"

Eidren stopped. His face was open and guileless. "Who?"

"Peradala's attendant. The Mornsong with whom I have been traveling."

"Hmm? Oh, I see. You are referring to your elf companion."

"Maralen," Rhys said.

Eidren shook his head. "The woman you travel with is not Maralen of the Mornsong. As part of my wedding preparations, one of my servants met and dined with Peradala's retinue twice over the past six months. Exquisite Maralen was present both times. I of course made sure my servant went on ahead to get a good look at her in your valley. By his description—and what was the colorful phrase he used—ah, yes, I remember: 'That isn't Maralen,' he said. 'More like someone wearing a defective Maralen glamer.' "

"She wears no glamer," Rhys said. "That is her natural appearance."

"I am a grower and tender of living things," Eidren said seriously. "And I sincerely doubt there's anything natural about her." Eidren smiled a thin smile. "But I look forward to verifying that for myself." He resumed his soft, nimble stride. "So it's your contention that you'd recognize a glamer if this . . . person was employing it?"

"I believe I would."

"Because you are so familiar with glamers. And what they can conceal."

Rhys stopped. The vinebred behind him also halted, but Eidren continued to walk. "What do you want from me, Taercenn Eidren?"

"Only what's best for the Nation." Eidren called back over his shoulder. He reached a stand of trees and stopped. He ran his palm gently over the bark on the thickest trunk, tracing its contours. "Like Nath, I am dedicated to that higher ideal, even at the expense of my own position or even my life. In killing Nath, you robbed the Nation of a valuable asset, not to mention one of its staunchest defenders. The Gilt Leaf feels that absence most keenly, former Daen Rhys. Especially during these confused and troubled times. I now extend my hand to you for payment."

Rhys shook his head. "I have no payment to offer, Taercenn."

"You are quite wrong. Before you turned against your own kind, you were a hunter and a leader of hunters. So long as you live, you have a potential value to the tribe."

"I am of the tribe no longer, Taer." Rhys bowed his head and touched his jagged, broken horns with the tips of his fingers. "I am eyeblight, outcast, just as you said. The Nation has no place for me."

"But I do. Under the aegis of myself and . . . other like-minded nobles, Nath and even Gryffid came to understand that disfigurement doesn't necessarily mean ouster from polite society. It only precludes one from holding status in it. Here in the wilds, among the boggarts and giants and other enemies of progress, warriors are a necessity. And in truth it does not matter what hunters look like under their glamer, so long as they advance our cause."

"That's impossible," Rhys stammered. "The proscriptions against eyeblights were handed down by the Sublime Council decades ago. The law was signed by the high king and queen themselves."

"And those proscriptions are sacrosanct throughout the bulk of the Nation. But things are rarely so pristine and orderly out here on the edges of our territory. When it comes to pacifying the lower denizens of Lorwyn, I and those of my faction have accepted the necessity of certain . . . deviations from the norm." Eidren turned away from the stand of trees and swept over to Rhys. "Shepherding kithkin and merrows and false elves is a waste of your talents, hunter. You belong with us. I offer you a new place in the Blessed Nation, a provisional one, to be sure, and a dangerous one. You will never again be accepted in the company of righteous, upstanding elves, but you will serve the Nation more fully than any of them could ever dream. Be my agent. Become a Hemlock hunter once more, and lead hunters under my direction. Do so loyally and with all due vigor and you may yet be buried with honor among the secret heroes of the Gilt Leaf."

Eidren's words hit Rhys like a hammer blow in the stomach. "I . . . I . . ."

"The alternative," Eidren said, "is to die a messy, painful, and ignoble death on the point of Gryffid's vengeful sword." Eidren extended his hand. "And before you question Gryffid's acceptance of your restored status, know this: The current daen had entered into a similar agreement with Nath not long ago. He became Nath's creature in the wake of the Porringer Valley massacre, but with Nath gone, Gryffid is now mine. It is for me to say what Gryffid will allow or deny. It is for me to say if he lives or dies, and how."

Rhys stared into Eidren's handsome, confident features. A thousand thoughts collided in his head, thoughts of Maralen and the giants in a hail of arrowgrass, of Ashling and the sapling and their shared trauma that would never heal, of Sygg and Brigid and the Vendilion clique. He had failed them all once more, failed himself and his own people. He would have settled for doing no more harm with what remained of this life. But would Eidren's way allow him to do more than that, to make a positive difference in the world to come?

Rhys glanced back at the vinebred honor guard. Stiffly, he bowed his head once more and said to Eidren, "What would you have of me?"

A loud crashing sound blasted through the trees before the noble elf could respond. The vinebred bristled and swelled, instantly ready for action. Eidren calmly stepped past Rhys, away from the sound, so that his honor guard stood between him and the huge creature tromping toward them.

Brion broke through a massive deadfall to the west. He lurched into view and shook his head, sending a shower of sticks and debris cascading down his shoulders.

"Hello, Boss," the bald giant said. He waved happily. "I saw you runnin', and I thought I should see that you were all right.

And when I got closer, I smelled—" Brion's eyes widened as he noticed the vinebred and Eidren. A hungry smile split his burly features.

"It's those elves," he whispered. He licked his lips. "I hate those elves."

"Brion, wait—" Rhys said, but he was far too late. With a piercing, joyful roar, Brion threw his arms wide and rushed at the Hemlock hunters and their new taercenn, shattering the trees as he came.

CHAPTER 20

The Gilt Leaf elves scattered as Brion thundered through their ranks. Rhys took advantage of the confusion to sprint clear of his captors, then promptly dived for cover when the top half of a tree came crashing down almost on top of him.

Pinned under the broken timber, Rhys struggled through the dense foliage. He couldn't get free, but he did have a clear view into the mounting chaos.

Two vinebred had latched onto Brion's right wrist, and another hung from his shoulder blade, clinging to the sword he had lodged there. The giant was unfazed by this injury. Indeed, Brion was bellowing with savage joy. He lifted his right arm and hauled the clinging elves over his head, then snapped the arm down sharply. The vinebred were torn loose and sent plowing face-first into the ground. Rhys winced at the horrid, crumpled state of the vinebred's bodies.

Still hooting, Brion hopped up and threw himself onto his back. The ground shook, and Brion yelped as the elf's blade drove deeper into his back. The owner of the blade made no sound, however, and when Brion rolled back to his feet the vinebred was completely gone but for a viscous smear across the back of his tunic.

Rhys weighed collecting Kiel and escaping with Maralen against leaving Brion to the mercy of the elves—and the elves to his. Since the remaining half-dozen vinebred were having no luck changing Brion's mind about the fight, Rhys did not put much faith in his chances to do the same. Could he collect Kiel and return in time for it to do Brion any good?

Brion hammered both fists into the ground and sent a shock wave rolling across the forest floor. Vinebred and trees alike were tossed aside. The giant was having his way now, but Rhys knew there were more than enough elves nearby to bring him down.

A flash of flowing silver drew his eye. Rhys spotted Eidren, who had just vaulted from the ground to the crotch of a tall tree. The taercenn was both fast and strong, his face a study in effortless calm.

Brion grabbed a vinebred in each hand and brought them together with a loud clap. He brought his hands up near his face, peeked inside, and said, "Bleah."

"Enough." Eidren did not raise his voice, yet his words cut clear through the noise and clamor. The remaining vinebred all froze in place, ready to spring or strike if Brion lunged toward them. Confused by his foes' sudden paralysis, Brion wiped his hands on his belly.

"Give up?" he said.

Eidren sprang from his tree and soared high over Brion's head. The taercenn bent at the waist when he reached the apex of his leap. He turned an elegant, unhurried somersault and came down hard, driving his straight legs into the top of Brion's skull.

Brion blinked. "Ow," he said. He swatted at the taercenn, but Eidren leaped clear so that Brion battered his own head. As Eidren sailed past Brion's open mouth, the taercenn cast his arm and tossed something to the back of Brion's throat. The giant gagged and hacked. He pressed both hands against his own windpipe and staggered back as he tried to squeeze and cough his throat clear.

Eidren landed at Brion's feet and gracefully tumbled away.

The nimble elf stopped at the broken base of Rhys's tree. As Rhys finally hauled himself clear of the branches, Eidren carefully straightened his clothing, threw his cape back over his shoulders, and only then turned to face Brion.

Rhys hesitated, frozen by the horrific sight. Brion's bald head and fleshy face were flushed deep crimson. The giant's eyes rolled back, and he dropped heavily to his knees, sending a fresh tremor across the forest floor. Brion coughed up flecks of purplish black foam, and Rhys smelled the unmistakably bitter, caustic smell of moonglove.

"For your gross insults to the Hemlock hunters and the entire Blessed Nation," Eidren declared, "die."

Brion gurgled once more. The giant let out a small, soft sigh that became a wheeze, then a rattle. With all ten fingers still dug into his own neck, Brion pitched forward and landed facedown on the ground. Eidren beamed triumphantly.

Rhys pounced. Brion was dead, and he would be mourned, but only if Rhys made it out of here alive. The taercenn was fast, but Rhys was desperate. The outlaw was on Eidren before the Perfect finished basking in his victory, bearing Eidren to the ground. The elegant elf let out a most inelegant grunt on impact, and Rhys clamped on to one of Eidren's thick, sturdy horns. He twisted the taercenn's head to the side, wrapped his other arm around the Perfect's windpipe, and squeezed.

"Steady, Taercenn," Rhys hissed. He bore down on Eidren's throat. "I'm in the habit of killing superior officers, remember?"

The taercenn's body relaxed, and Rhys eased up on the pressure to allow Eidren to speak, The noble elf said, "Stand back." His vinebred honor guard complied instantly, edging away from Rhys and their master until they were all lined up beside Brion's body.

Rhys maneuvered Eidren to his feet, careful to maintain his death grip on the taercenn's throat and horn. He forced Eidren back until Rhys felt the sturdy trunk of the broken tree behind them.

"Well," Eidren said. "You have me. What are you going to do with me?"

Rhys did not reply. It was yet another question to which he had no good answer.

* * * * *

Maralen sat sifting through the information the Vendilion clique provided. Her thoughts were urgent, but she knew this was too important to rush, even if Rhys was due back at any moment. If the world was going to change, she would change too—and not back into what she was but into something entirely new and different. Something free.

Everything was almost in place, everyone was almost ready. Iliona and Veesa were proving reliable so far, or, at least, they were characteristically focused on the short-term benefits Maralen promised them. Endry was another matter. The Vendilion's only brother was stubbornly resisting his part of the plan, and his was the most crucial.

"Just do as I say," Maralen whispered.

Endry's voice was plaintive in her ears. "I don't want to."

"We've explained this to you. Do this for me and you need never listen to me again."

"Sure, you say that. But where's the proof?"

"Iliona and Veesa have already agreed."

"Then let them handle it."

"You are the Vendilion clique. You act together. It's all arranged."

"But she's my friend . . . now. Sort of."

"And she will continue to be. Everything is about to change. Everything except her and us if you just do as I ask."

Endry was silent for a moment, then said, "Does this have to happen? I have a lot of friends, you know. I'm considered a very popular and heroic faerie in certain circles."

"It does have to happen. Nothing can stop it. But we can make sure it happens the way we all want." Maralen sensed his resistance faltering. She concentrated to carefully apply the influence she wielded without sparking another tantrum. "I speak with Oona's voice, Endry, the Queen of the Fae and mother to you all. Remember that. She decreed you must do what I want, not what you want. I want you to do this, and so it must be done."

"Fine," Endry spat. "I'll tell you when I'm ready."

Endry broke off their connection and Maralen exhaled. Each small step was painful, but it brought her closer to her goal. She opened her eyes and leaned forward to rise and made it halfway to her feet before a blinding jolt of agony ran through her entire body and dropped her gasping to the ground.

You've made a mistake at last, my dear. The Fae Queen's presence ripped through Maralen's mind, and the dark-haired elf shivered. Oona's voice was alone, no distant chorus to accompany her. *And a clumsy one.*

Maralen forced herself to breathe. Her face was so near the ground she sucked in tiny particles of dirt. "You're too late," she rasped. "Far too late. In a few moments I will go someplace you cannot follow."

There is nowhere I cannot follow you, my errant child. I made you what you are.

Maralen showed her sharp teeth. "Then you have truly failed, my Queen, because I am not what you made."

No? What are you then, if not my creation? A slightly over-sized elf? A willowy kithkin? Or just an unwitting catalyst to disaster?

Maralen's vision rolled. Once more she was in the woods near Porringer Valley, dazed, directionless but for a half-formed yearning to be near the elf named Rhys, whose yew magic she sensed nearby.

Rhys, Maralen thought. Where was he? Had he returned?

I have been more than generous, Oona said. *But my patience is not infinite. Return what you took from me now, willingly, or I shall pluck it from your corpse.*

"That won't happen," Maralen said. She fought her way up to her knees. "The Vendilion are mine. Mine, until I release them.

But it will happen. Oona replied. *You said so yourself. It is happening now.*

A wide ring of fat white toadstools sprouted in the soil, surrounding Maralen in a twenty-foot circle. *I am coming, thief. Prepare yourself.*

"I defy you, Oona." Maralen bared her sharp, white teeth in feral joy. "Now you have made a clumsy mistake. I didn't dare hope you'd be fool enough to leave Glen Elendra. But you have— and you are not welcome here."

Oh? And what makes you say that? My roots extend across all Lorwyn, child. I can manifest anywhere.

The grass inside the white ring stretched tall. The blades wound around each other and huddled together, forming a wide mound of green.

"No. Not here." Maralen felt real panic gouging at her insides. Oona's distant voice had brought the elf maiden to her knees. What would the actual presence of the Fae Queen do to Maralen?

She leaped to her feet and hurdled the growing mound. Maralen hit the ground running, driving for the woods where Rhys had gone. She did not dare make a stand against Oona by herself, but with Rhys beside her . . .

Once before, the combination of Oona, Maralen, and Rhys had set off an explosive surge of toxic force. If a second such alignment produced a similar result, that would be enough to drive Oona away, or perhaps even harm the Fae Queen. Maralen didn't need to conquer her nemesis. She just needed to fend her off for a while.

Maralen reached deep into the reservoir of arcane power Oona had given her—its might was still hers to command—and felt her muscles grow stronger. Her pace increased, her eyesight and hearing grew keener. The plants and bushes in her path hissed and rustled, instinctively bending and pulling themselves aside so that she passed by them untouched, then settled back once she was gone.

A chorus of ethereal voices and rustling leaves swelled up from the valley behind Maralen. The elf maiden continued to run.

She would find Rhys. She would make her stand. Oona would be beaten back. And Maralen would be free.

* * * * *

The vinebred honor guard made no aggressive moves, but the combined weight of their dire attention made Rhys nervous. He tightened his grip on Eidren. "I will kill you if I have to," he said.

"I've no doubt. I'd prefer to avoid that outcome, of course. What are your terms?"

Rhys's mind raced. "Order a retreat," he said. "Send the entire pack all the way back to the Dauba Ravine. Once they're gone, I'll release you."

"Hm. No, that doesn't suit my needs at all." Eidren straightened his head, forcing his horns upright in Rhys's grip with just the muscles in his neck. The Perfect's strength was unexpected and remarkable—Rhys had to give way or risk breaking his own arm. The blighted elf redoubled his efforts, but Eidren casually reached up and peeled Rhys's arm from his throat. Rhys resisted, but it was all he could do to hold his ground.

Still holding Rhys's wrist in his hand, Eidren spun out from under his foe's grip and threw the former daen to the ground. Rhys bounced back up and threw a clenched fist at Eidren's smiling face. The taercenn easily sidestepped, but as Rhys lunged past he rammed his broken horns into Eidren's chest.

Rhys's head stopped short as if he'd butted a stone wall. Eidren stared down with a look that showed more inconvenience than pain. He swung his arm up and backhanded Rhys into the trunk of a gnarled tree.

Rhys fell to the ground, stunned almost as much by Eidren's surprising strength as he was by the impact. There was no accounting for the taercenn's power, unless . . .

Rhys raised his head. Blurred, doubled images of Eidren approached him. Rhys's jagged horn stumps had torn through the taercenn's robe, and Eidren's chest showed through.

Vinebred, Rhys realized sickly. A breastplate of thick, tough nettlevines covered Eidren's torso. The Hemlock vinebred's master was himself enchanted with the same magic.

"This has become a farce," Eidren said. "And not at all how I wanted our first meeting to go. Let me make this simple for you, eyeblight." He took Rhys by the throat and held him out at arm's length with no sign of exertion. Rhys choked and gagged, unable to do anything but fumble with his flailing hands and stare at the woven, wooden braids on Eidren's chest.

Eidren pointed past Rhys to Brion. "That creature," he said, "insulted the Hemlock Pack and the pride of the Blessed Nation. He has paid the price. Now you must decide if you will allow your own insults and blasphemies to stand and so follow him into an ugly death, or if you will honor the Nation and yourself. You will serve me, Rhys, as my agent or as the example I make of you. One way or the other, the Blessed Nation will benefit."

Rhys felt blood trickling down his face. His legs were numb, and his spine ached. He could barely muster the breath to respond, much less defend himself or escape. His vision fogged to gray, then crimson black.

Eidren's iron grip eased slightly, just for a second, and Rhys heard the taercenn speak softly, almost to himself.

"Maralen?" Eidren said, and his tone was confused, hesitant.

"Get away from him. All of you. Now." The voice was Maralen's, but it was tempered and sharp as steel.

Someone shouted, and Rhys felt himself moving. Still blind, to him it seemed the world itself rose up and slammed into the side of his head. The noise alone temporarily deafened him as Eidren's fingers slipped off his throat. Rhys floated aimlessly, faceup, in a bottomless pool of black. Then he felt hard, unyielding soil under his back.

Rhys's dazed and foggy brain barely registered the horrific sounds around him, but his sharp ears drank in every one: the screams, the awful wet ripping of flesh, the piercing crack of splintering wood and bone. The screams and shouts soon stopped, but the rest continued for many long, dreadful seconds. When those too at last died down, Eidren's smooth, powerful voice rolled out over the forest.

"Greetings, Maralen of Mornsong. If indeed that is who you are."

Maralen's voice was just as strong, just as sure. "Leave this place, Taer. Now. Or there will be more Gilt Leaf blood on my hands and your conscience."

Rhys struggled to raise his head. He felt his eyelids part, but he saw nothing but dizzying flashes of purple and white light.

"I cannot agree to that, Lady. I have business with you as surely as I do with this eyeblight."

Rhys's vision slowly cleared. The forest around him took shape, first as vague, shadowy outlines of trees. He blinked and concentrated until he could see Maralen and Eidren facing each other across the glen. No other elves or eyeblights were standing, though there were at least a dozen crushed and broken bodies scattered around the forest.

Inexplicably, Maralen turned her back on Eidren and faced the woods behind her. "Where are you now, Fae Queen?" Her tone was savage, triumphant. "Gone so soon? I thought you had come for me!

"Is that which you feared coming for you, then? Are you too late after all?" Maralen turned back to Eidren and cocked her head. "Or are you simply afraid of me?"

Eidren simply stood amazed at Maralen's ravings. Rhys knew how he felt.

"It's happening." Maralen mockingly bowed to Eidren. "And I've no more time for you. You must leave here, Taercenn. I insist." The elf maiden threw her arms out, and a strong black wind rushed from her body to Eidren's. The stream of dark air plucked Eidren up and carried him high over the tree line. To his credit, the nobleman did not utter a single sound as he arced out of sight.

Rhys felt Maralen's small, strong hands cradling his head. He stared up into her eyes as she stroked his forehead.

"Rest now, Daen," she said. "I can fix this, I can fix it all. Rest here and I will return as soon . . . as soon as I have done what needs to be done." Maralen gently lowered Rhys's head to the forest floor and stood up. She smiled down at him, her eyes sad, then she turned and stepped out of sight.

Unable to speak or even move his head, Rhys let his eyes drift shut and tried to muster his body into obedience.

Rhys. Can you hear me? Rhys recognized the sapling's voice instantly. It was not like Colfenor's, but it rang in his head with the same strength and clarity that the old log's had.

"I can," Rhys said. Even at a whisper, the words sent ripples of pain across his skull.

I wanted to say good-bye. I wish we'd had more time to talk. Perhaps in the next world, we will.

Rhys hesitated. How should he answer? How could he answer?

Then the sapling screamed a terrifying wail of anguish that drowned out everyone and everything around him.

CHAPTER 21

Ashling spotted the sapling when she stepped from the top of the long, stone stairway leading out of the Ember Fell monastery, just as she had known she would. The yew raised a blackened, but healing, wooden arm in greeting and stood patiently waiting for Ashling to reach her. Patiently, Ashling saw, and probably quite painfully. At a distance it wasn't as easy to spot, but the sapling still bore many injuries and scars from the ordeal with the wind devils. The flamekin felt a twinge of regret, but considering what she intended, it was only a twinge.

Accepting one's destiny is one thing, Ashling mused, but what if your destiny is as a tool? A weapon? A vessel? What then? Why should she accept a role foisted upon her when she could forge her own?

She voiced none of these questions upon greeting the sapling, causing a more palpable guilt that joined the regret in a part of Ashling's fiery heart she shut off from her conscience as best she could.

"Sapling," she said, "it's time."

"Yes, Ashling of Tanufel," the sapling agreed. "Colfenor's wishes will be fulfilled, and our destinies will carry us into another age. I am glad you have decided to accept your role."

"And I, you," Ashling replied. She turned her face to the mountaintop and the sky beyond. The elemental had reappeared, more glorious than ever before against the darkening storm clouds. They were the first thunderheads seen by inhabitants of Lorwyn in living memory, but the flamekin pilgrim recognized them immediately. Beyond these clouds, high above them, Ashling saw the first flickers of the Aurora's lightshow. "Those clouds," she said. "Water is going to fall from the sky soon. How odd."

"It's waiting for us," the sapling said. "Can you see it?"

"I can."

"It's beautiful."

"It is at that," Ashling agreed. And cruel, she added silently. The elemental appeared to have been feeding off of the power within Mount Tanufel just as the pilgrim had. Compared to its condition when she had first seen the bedraggled thing being led from its Kinsbaile prison, the elemental had nearly doubled in apparent physical size and now resembled a winged horse some twenty feet tall—though Ashling knew looks, especially with elementals, could deceive a great deal. Its glorious golden wings remained aloft and alight with bluish white flames that shone like a beacon against the heavy rain clouds.

She turned to the sapling and beckoned her onward. "Come. We must not be late."

Beyond the monastery, a well-preserved and apparently little-used road led them straight to the summit. To Ashling's relief, they didn't run into a single wind devil, rock giant, or avalanche along the way. With every step she could feel the connection to the elemental growing stronger and stronger. But this time, she knew what to expect. She was prepared.

With the elemental to guide their way and speed them on with gifts of power and strength, it did not take long for the strange pair to reach the mountaintop.

"Purest of flames, blazing monarch, Lord of Cleansing, we are honored beyond—" Ashling said just as a bolt of lightning ripped into the north face of the mountain and sent a deafening peal of thunder rolling across the summit. Overhead, the Aurora's lights were all but swallowed up by the purplish black clouds and the dazzling white lightning.

The pilgrim cleared her throat to start over and thought better of it when another multiforked bolt struck nearby. "We are ready."

"Yes," the sapling said, taking her place at Ashling's side. "We are ready."

Then let us begin, the elemental said.

* * * * *

What are you up to, little man? Maralen's voice whispered inside Endry's tiny head. *All of the puzzle pieces are not yet in place. Where is your sapling?*

On the way, Endry replied. *We had a minor setback. Had trouble getting your mushrooms growing. She's awfully green.*

Do not fail me, Endry. I am not the only one counting on you. Your sisters will be terribly disappointed if you do not come through. Have you been apart from the clique for too long? Must I dispatch Veesa or Iliona to complete your work?

No! Endry replied. *Just one minute. Now leave me alone or you'll have yourself to blame!*

The faerie then did something he had not even thought possible—he forced Maralen out of his mind. Since the last faerie-ring contact she had kept a tendril of thought in his skull, chiding him now and again to hurry but mostly to let him know he was not off of his leash. That was how Endry chose to take it, at least.

"Well, now I am off the leash," Endry said. "Take that, you fat-headed tree-cow!"

"What did you say?" Nora asked. She was fastening the

second of her two dragonflies to her wing apparatus after allowing the trained insects to feed and water themselves.

"I said," Endry told her as he whirled in midair to face his groundling friend, "a lie! To her! How about that?" He could hardly believe it himself.

"Then we're going to do it?" Mullenick asked, slinging his mayfly contraption over his shoulders.

"We are," Endry said. Fighting back the nausea that felt like it was going to wrench his torso in two, he floated about two parallel lines of Groundling Town faeries, all of them slipping into or already wearing their own bug-powered wings. Endry imagined this was how the famous generals of old felt upon the eve of a great battle, whoever they were and whatever an "eve" was.

"Faeries of Groundling Town!" he began. "You know why we're assembled here and what's on the line. This isn't going to be easy—there isn't one of you dirt rats that can lift a quarter of what I can carry with two broken legs. But together, you lifted the net that brought down a giant. A real giant! And you almost pulled down the sapling too! That was one of the funniest things I've ever seen, really. You all should be proud of that one."

"Endry," Nora said, "focus."

"So what I'm saying is that you all can do anything, so long as you've got me. And each other. Now I've got our flight plan all worked out, but if you get lost just follow your wingmate. Nora and Mullenick also know the route."

"But Endry," said a young groundling female named ... something that started with a "Z" sound. Or maybe a "B" sound. Endry wasn't good with names. But he'd definitely seen her before, and he knew she had a name. "Shouldn't we just do what your mistress says? If Oona hears of this—"

"Oona hates her as much as we Vendilion do," Endry assured young B-or-Z. "When we are victorious, the Great Mother will hear of your ingenuity, courage, and resourcefulness in the face of insurmountable odds, and I swear to you on my honor as a Vendilion faerie, I will tell her you all exist!" A few scattered shouts of encouragement left Endry feeling something was missing. "I will tell her . . . twice!"

The cheers of the groundlings drowned out the buzzing of wings as the tiny airborne flotilla took to the skies in a burst of color and light.

* * * * *

Agony pierced Rhys's mind like an arrow, knocking him to his knees. It took every last bit of Colfenor's training—almost forgotten of late—to push the dagger from his thoughts, quiet the pain. It was not his. It was hers. The sapling's. She was Colfenor's creature, his offspring. All that he was, but with none of the wisdom or experience. She had her own experiences now—searing pain, for one.

It was dawning at last on Rhys that he, despite everything, could not and would not be Colfenor's creature ever again. He was lost. He'd gotten many elves killed, some of them his own friends. He'd made anyone who had contact with him a target for execution, and he'd betrayed his oath to Colfenor by allowing the sapling to wander freely to her doom like a child in a slaughterhouse.

What had he truly accomplished by turning against the Nation? And to what purpose? The people to whom he had dedicated himself were all gone. Maralen, whoever and whatever she was, could not be trusted. Sygg and Brigid had vanished from the face of Lorwyn, and the sapling was in what felt like agonizing death throes atop cloud-enveloped Mount Tanufel, where the flashes and sparks did not come from lightning but a raging inferno named Ashling.

"Taercenn Eidren," Rhys said, "I accept your offer. I will serve the Nation, and only the Nation, until the day I die."

Somewhere far away, the sapling's agony continued unabated, but Rhys could hardly feel her cry at all.

"Let us hope that day is none too soon," Eidren said. "You will not regret your decision."

A bolt of flashing white energy lanced through the sky, which was filling with dark, misshapen clouds that had as much in common with Lorwyn's usual weather as a springjack did with a common hare. These were fearsome clouds, fierce with the color of the river depths, the untrammeled cave, and the violated tomb. They swirled with turbulent, crackling energy, sending another arc of lightning—something Rhys had heard of but never seen in his lifetime—crashing into the ground, and much closer this time.

"No," Rhys said. "Not now. Not yet, I haven't—"

"What you haven't is immaterial. What you have is a new pack. You have carved your own place in the history of the Blessed Nation, even if only for a select few with the right to read your name. And you have," Eidren said, "already agreed. Any regrets you are feeling would exist with or without this confounding weather. Do not back out on me, my blighted friend. The consequences would be most unfortunate for both of us, but for you they would be instantly fatal." The flawless Perfect's visage was cracked with a deep frown. "Am I understood?"

Rhys considered a suicidal lunge. The world itself appeared to be coming to an end. What did it matter whether he choked the life out of this arrogant, calculating Perfect? Eidren glanced at Rhys for only a moment, but in that moment the former daen saw not fear or concern but the same challenge and implied threat that had been in his voice.

Here was a chance to serve the ideals he believed in again. No boggart slaughter or merrow hunting but work that would help preserve his people. The people he thought had abandoned him. But in the end, only the Blessed wanted anything to do with him.

"You are understood, Taer," Rhys said, kneeling and bowing his head. "My life is yours to spend as you choose."

* * * * *

Night embraces the world, the elemental intoned. *The fires of life and the roots of knowledge persevere, feed, grow, and endure.*

"Night embraces the world," Ashling and the sapling said in unison. "The fires of life and the roots of knowledge persevere, feed, grow, and endure."

As dawn passes into day, day into dusk, so shall night pass into dawn. The fires of life and the roots of knowledge persevere, feed, grow, and endure.

"As dawn passes into day, day into dusk, so shall night pass into dawn. . . ." And so it went as precious minutes ticked off, drawing ever closer to the full-fledged Aurora lightshow that marked the tipping point, the day's retreat and the onset of night.

Ashling and the young yew still stood side by side before the towering elemental like penitent kithkin schoolchildren. Several minutes and the onset of a full-blown thunderstorm later, the pilgrim started to wonder if she would ever get her chance, if the Aurora would ever come.

And you shall be the light that guides us through the darkness and out the other side.

"And you—" Ashling began, but noticed the sapling was not joining her.

There was no need to repeat that, the elemental said.

"I understand," Ashling said. She scanned the skies, now impossibly red and tormented. "I didn't expect it to be so sudden."

"If it was not sudden and over in the blink of an eye," the sapling said, "then more would remember it. That was Colfenor's belief. I look forward to the opportunity to learn whether he was right."

As if to set an example, the rains that had so suddenly begun ended without warning with an explosion of thunder that sounded as if Lorwyn itself had been cracked in two. The lights and colors within the clouds seemed to burn through the water vapor, until the clouds were hardly visible anymore and the entire sky was a black canvas adorned with colorful, shifting tapestries suitable for gods.

Now, the elemental said.

Without a word, Ashling and the sapling turned toward the elemental. It bowed its muscular neck solemnly and enveloped them within its fiery wings.

Within, the flamekin pilgrim could sense the zenith of the Aurora drawing nearer. She had to time this perfectly, before either the elemental or the sapling could react.

The sapling, miraculously, was still more or less intact—not even a dropped needle or a smoldering branch—inside the domelike cathedral of the elemental's wings. The walls of the cathedral crackled and sparked with all colors of fire, mana, thought, and power. Every one that whipped across Ashling or her treefolk counterpart sent a surge of knowledge and energy into each of them, and together they grew strong.

At the same time, the elemental was drawing subtler forms of power from its fellow participants in this strange, blazing ritual. Ashling could feel the elemental teasing out details of her own history, as well as the sapling's, but that was just the start. The elemental wanted to go wherever it pleased. The sapling, on the other hand, was simply careless and inexperienced. Which was too bad, but Ashling had made her decision.

At the twenty-eighth heartbeat mark Ashling spoke. "You

should be careful, inviting yourself in," she told the elemental. "What if someone locks the door behind you and you never get out?"

Twenty-nine.

Ashling stretched one long, blazing arm and wrapped a strong hand tightly around the yew's arm. "I'm sorry," she said.

"Ashling of Tanufel?" the sapling managed before Ashling thrust her free hand into the fiery dome. She was now a conduit between the two, but the pilgrim also intended to be a siphon. She would take all of the elemental's power, not just a loan or a conduit's worth. The elemental would merge with her living flames. The sapling, too, would be consumed. Elemental fire would run through Ashling's arms and back again for as long as she could hold on . . . or as long as the Aurora lasted.

Thirty. The sapling's remaining boughs burst into flames.

"Look alive, yewling!" a ridiculously tiny voice wailed at the moment the Aurora reached its apex. Endry burst through the fiery wings with a flash, frantically patting himself out as he whirled in midair, just out of reach, and called back, "Groundlings! Attack!"

Thirty-one.

The interior of the elemental's "dome," already beginning to flicker and sputter due to Ashling's efforts, now erupted with the strangest rescue squad the flamekin had ever seen: twenty faeries, none of them with true wings but all wearing insect-powered, homemade gliding contraptions. The brief contact with the guttering wings of fire caused the groundlings no trouble at all, but finding places to grab hold of the burning sapling without putting themselves in the path of powerful fire magic proved tricky. Had Ashling not still been focusing on taking all the elemental had, she might easily have stopped Endry's groundling gang from accomplishing anything.

Thirty-two.

But by now the power tasted sweet. When Endry's makeshift team began to tug on the screaming tree, Ashling offered almost no resistance. The sapling's purpose had been fulfilled, though not as Colfenor's offspring expected, and was of no further importance.

* * * * *

Maralen watched the sky with a smile. Endry's independent streak would have to be dealt with, assuming he survived the Aurora, but he had done the job. The tiny cluster of white-capped mushrooms he'd silently affixed to the sapling's neck was as close as a thought for her, and as the elemental took flamekin and treefolk into its blazing embrace, Maralen struck a similarly dramatic stance, hands splayed against the chaotic skies, awaiting the arrival of power. Power on a scale that would release her from her debt to the so-called Great Mother, Oona.

And if Maralen could brush aside the longest-lived being in the world, she doubted there was anyone she couldn't defeat.

Lightning struck less than a hundred feet away, and Maralen heard a tree die in slow pain—one that had nearly been ready to walk, making the final transformation from tree to treefolk. "You're better off," she muttered wryly.

All around her, in the land, the trees, every living thing, the sky itself, raw power crackled and flared as two realities found each other. They collided, embraced, merged.

For sixty heartbeats they would overlap, these two worlds, and when they separated again those who survived would face the winds of infinite possibility. The Aurora had reached its peak.

The flood of unfocused energy threatened to overwhelm Ashling, but even so she reveled in the power. It lifted her physically from the ground, carrying her into the sky with blazing urgency, and she completely gave herself to the rush of knowledge. Colfenor's secrets filled her mind too fast to count. The simple secret of creating fire from thin air. Why faeries came in threes. The curious relationship between boggarts and elves. The oldest living thing in Lorwyn. The prophecies of giants. A forgotten war between treefolk and kithkin. Even the reasons the source of the Wanderwine had chosen to poison and infect her own children rather than allow them to enter the dark, new world too soon.

Maralen readied herself to receive even more power as the colors in the sky reached a feverish intensity. They were at the thirty-heartbeat mark, the split-second in which day and night occupied the exact same space and time. The moment came. Two worlds froze in perfect balance between what is and what will be.

At that precise moment, the flood of energy vanished, leaving nothing for Maralen to grasp. She choked back a wail of fury and anguish as the keys to the new world slipped away.

After a few stunned moments, the elf maiden's eyes narrowed. Seconds later those eyes burned with blood red flame.

Endry, she thought, *I hope for your sake I never see you again.*

Not as much as I do, Endry sent back. *My friend the sapling sends her regards.*

And with that, Endry gave Maralen's mind an aggressive shove that nearly knocked her off of her feet. She stood there, fuming and watching the mad nightmare of colors and disturbances in the sky, all signs of the great Aurora's arrival.

Though galling, the Vendilion brother's betrayal was but a minor irritation. She had won, and not even an insubordinate slap from her servant could sour the victory. Now that Maralen had obtained the power to survive and to choose her own way, she could afford to be magnanimous. She would overlook Endry's treachery for now. But soon, very soon, she would catch up with him, and there would be a terrible reckoning.

Maralen smiled and cocked her head to one side. She stood and watched as the Aurora's dazzling lights blanketed the sky.

* * * * *

"Are those clouds?" Brigid asked, staring awestruck at the darkening sky. "Why are they so . . . black?" She stood ankle-deep on the banks of the source's lake, where she stepped to get a closer look at the sounds of fiery explosions coming from atop Mount Tanufel, and was stunned to see the entire sky seemed to have gone mad while she had looked away for just a few minutes.

"Those are clouds," Flyrne said. "But something's wrong with them."

The usual wispy and fluffy white clouds that hung over Lorwyn had disappeared, along with any trace of blue in the sky, to be replaced with towering thunderheads that glowed and flashed with raging power. A jagged bolt of lightning struck on the horizon, and several seconds later the peal of thunder nearly made Brigid's heart stop. She'd never heard anything like it before.

"What was that?" Brigid shouted, her ears still ringing.

"That's what I'd like to know!" Sygg replied in a similar fashion.

"It's the end of the world!" Flyrne shouted. "We're all going to die!"

"Flyrne! We don't know that," Sygg said, trying to keep his voice more level in the apparent hope it would soothe Flyrne. The big merrow was clearly panicking, and Sygg had his hands full. Brigid took advantage of the opening to further question the source herself.

"Source," Brigid said, "what's happening? Is the world coming to an end?"

"No more so than the shore ends when the tide rushes in," the source declared. A second lightning flash licked the ground just a few miles closer, followed even more quickly this time by a thunderclap. This bolt illuminated the source's feminine form from behind, and she looked for a moment like a glass sculpture Brigid's grandmother had kept on her mantle. "The morning songbird gives way to the evening raptor."

Brigid did not like the sound of that, or the look of the sky. The blackened, rain-heavy clouds were flashing with mad swirls of delirious color. The kithkin found them utterly hypnotic and completely terrifying. "What does all that mean?" the archer demanded. "As plainly as you can, please. I'm a simple kithkin." Brigid felt inordinately proud that she did not jump when another bolt of lightning descended from the heavens in the middle of "simple."

"Simple," the source repeated, taking on a tone that reminded Brigid of her mother. "Very well. The Aurora is coming."

"The what?" Brigid asked.

"The Aurora marks the change from lasting daylight to perpetual dusk. Under its far-reaching glow, the Lorwyn you know and have dwelled in all your life changes into the Lorwyn that will be."

"The whole world changes?" Brigid considered for a moment. "Even me?"

"There is no point in telling you that, for you will not remember. What is important is that you know this: This is no ordinary Aurora. There should have been several more decades of the daylight, but now the darkness has come early, out of sequence." The source's face turned toward the top of Mount Tanufel. "Something is wrong, fundamentally wrong."

"I don't follow you," Brigid said. "The sky's going crazy, but I don't feel any different. Sygg, have you ever heard of this Aurora?" There was no reply. "I said, Sygg, have you ever . . . heard . . ."

The merrow turned toward her, the hellish sky reflected in his black eyes. His brow creased, and his gills flapped slowly. Those eyes held not a glimmer of recognition, nor did Flyrne's. Both merrow hissed with guttural ferocity. Flyrne snapped his teeth. Neither spoke a word.

"Ye gods," Brigid whispered and cautiously moved to back away as the sky grew redder and lightning crashed all along the horizon. "Source, why has Sygg changed already? I feel exactly the same."

"An artifact steeped in my own unyielding elemental power," the source bubbled to her, "the Crescent of Morningtide, could have allowed Sygg Gauhren Gyllalla Syllvar to strike a light within the darkened Lanes until the long night was over. Now he joins the rest of my children in the shadows."

Brigid looked down at the Crescent of Morningtide, still clutched tightly in her palm, as she took another step back from the suddenly predatory merrow she'd recently counted as allies.

"Uh-oh," Brigid said.

ravenLoft™
the covenant

ravenLoft's Lords of darkness have always waited for the unwary to find them.

From the autocratic vampire who wrote the memoirs found in *I, Strahd* to the demon lord and his son whose story is told in *Tapestry of Dark Souls*, some of the finest horror characters created by some of the most influential authors of horror and dark fantasy have found their way to RAVENLOFT, to be trapped there forever.

LaureLL k. hamiLton
Death of a Darklord

christie goLden
Vampire of the Mists

p.n. eLrod
I, Strahd: The Memoirs of a Vampire

andria cardareLLe
To Sleep With Evil

eLaine bergstrom
Tapestry of Dark Souls

tanya huff
Scholar of Decay

JEAN RABE

THE STONETELLERS

"Jean Rabe is adept at weaving a web of deceit and lies, mixed with adventure, magic, and mystery."
—sffworld.com on *Betrayal*

Jean Rabe returns to the DRAGONLANCE® world with a tale of slavery, rebellion, and the struggle for freedom.

VOLUME ONE
THE REBELLION

After decades of service, nature has dealt the goblins a stroke of luck. Earthquakes strike the Dark Knights' camp and mines, crippling the Knights and giving the goblins their best chance to escape. But their freedom will not be easy to win.

VOLUME TWO
DEATH MARCH

The escaped slaves—led by the hobgoblin Direfang—embark on a journey fraught with danger as they leave Neraka to cross the ocean and enter the Qualinesti Forest, where they believe themselves free. . . .

August 2008

VOLUME THREE
GOBLIN NATION

A goblin nation rises in the old forest, building fortresses and fighting to hold onto their new homeland, while the sorcerers among them search for powerful magic cradled far beneath the trees.

August 2009

Land of intrigue.
Towering cities where murder is business.
Dark forests where hunters are hunted.
Ground where the dead never rest.

To find the truth takes a special breed of hero.

THE INQUISITIVES

BOUND BY IRON
Edward Bolme
Torn by oaths to king and country, one man must
unravel a tapestry of murder and slavery.

NIGHT OF THE LONG SHADOWS
Paul Crilley
During the longest nights of the year, worshipers of the
dark rise from the depths of the City of Towers
to murder . . . and worse.

LEGACY OF WOLVES
Marsheila Rockwell
In the streets of Aruldusk, a series of grisly murders has rocked
the small city. The gruesome nature of the murders spawns
rumors of a lycanthrope in a land where the shapeshifters were
thought to have been hunted to extinction.

THE DARKWOOD MASK
Jeff LaSala
A beautiful Inquisitive teams up with a wanted vigilante to take
down a crimelord who hides behind a mask of deceit, savage
cunning, and sorcery.
November 2008